Eloisa James

Born *to be* WILDE

piatkus

PIATKUS

First published in the US in 2018 by Avon Books,
an imprint of HarperCollins Publishers, New York
First published in Great Britain in 2018 by Piatkus
by arrangement with Avon

1 3 5 7 9 10 8 6 4 2

A CIP catalogue record for this book
is available from the British Library.

ISBN 978-0-349-41772-1

Printed and bound in Great Britain by
Clays Ltd, Elcograf S.p.A.

Papers used by Piatkus are from well-managed forests
and other responsible sources.

MIX
Paper from
responsible sources
FSC® C104740

Piatkus
An imprint of
Little, Brown Book Group
Carmelite House
50 Victoria Embankment
London EC4Y 0DZ

An Hachette UK Company
www.hachette.co.uk

www.littlebrown.co.uk

*The book is dedicated to my brother-in-law Sunil,
whose courage in the face of cancer is truly heroic.*

Acknowledgments

My books are like small children; they take a whole village to get them to a literate state. I want to offer my deep gratitude to my village: my editor, Carrie Feron; my agent, Kim Witherspoon; my Website designers, Wax Creative; and my personal team: Kim Castillo, Franzeca Drouin, Leslie Ferdinand, Sharlene Martin Moore, and Anne Connell. My husband, daughter Anna, and (occasionally) my son Luca cheerfully debated plot points with me, for which I'm endlessly grateful. In addition, people in many departments of HarperCollins, from Art to Marketing to PR, have done a wonderful job of getting this book into readers' hands: my heartfelt thanks go to each of you.

Born *to be*
WILDE

Chapter One

Lindow Castle, Cheshire
Country seat of the Duke of Lindow
June 4, 1780

*M*iss Lavinia Gray considered herself reasonably brave. In her twenty-one years, she had been presented to both an English and a French queen without losing her composure. She had squeaked, but not screamed, after a close encounter with an exceedingly large bear. Perhaps "bear" was an exaggeration. One could call it a dog, but only if a dog had huge bearlike fangs and lunged from the shadows.

Screaming would not have been uncalled for.

There was also the time she had waded into a lake rumored to be inhabited by leeches. She had shuddered but soldiered on every time something soft bumped her legs.

But this?

Hovering in the corridor outside a gentleman's bedchamber?

This was a whole new level of uneasiness. She'd prefer to swim in a leechy lake up to her neck than knock on the door before her.

The ironic thing was that she'd soothed many a young gentleman who had fallen to his knees to offer marriage, although now she realized she should have been even kinder. Drumming up one's nerve to propose was terrifying.

That's what she was about to do.

Propose.

A silent shriek went through her head. *How in heaven's name have I come to this?*

She shook off the unhelpful thought and tried to muster her courage. Generally speaking, she found dresses to be a formidable suit of armor, useful in marshaling courage, but even one of her best Parisian gowns wasn't helping. Champagne-tinted silk clung to her figure and then opened into frothy ruffles at the hem; modest padding at the hips emphasized the swell of her breasts and made her waist look smaller.

Ordinarily, she would have felt invulnerable in it, but at the moment, she felt only self-conscious dread.

The problem was that Parth Sterling had never shown any sign of being attracted to her figure—or any other part of her, for that matter. Just last night he had entered the drawing room, nodded to her, and promptly moved to the other side of the room.

After not seeing her for *two years*.

Bring on the leechy lake.

"You have no choice," her cousin Diana had fiercely insisted, not ten minutes ago. "You *must* marry Parth. He's the only one who can save your mother."

Lavinia took a deep breath, forcing herself to stand

still and not dash down the corridor. Hands fisted at her sides, she firmed her lips and took a step closer to the door. Her mother, Lady Gray, needed to be saved, and an ordinary, garden-variety gentleman wasn't going to do it.

She needed Parth, not only because he was the richest bachelor in the kingdom, but because he—well, he *got things done.*

He fixed things.

Problems of all sorts.

The thought stiffened her backbone, and before she could stop herself again, she knocked. And waited.

A swooning sense of relief came over her when no one opened the door.

She would return to Diana and report that Parth Sterling unaccountably hadn't been in his chamber waiting for a marriage proposal.

He was—

He was standing in the open doorway, staring at her there in the dark corridor.

"*Lavinia?*"

She managed a wavering smile. "Hello!"

"Jesus," he barked, and then looked both ways. "What in the hell are you doing out here?"

Before she could answer, he grabbed her by the elbow, pulled her inside, and slammed the door.

Earlier, talking to Diana, it had all made sense, in a cracked sort of way: Parth was rich, Parth was unmarried, and Parth was a problem solver.

But faced *with* Parth? Who was taller than most men, broader in his chest, with thick hair, skin like warm bronze, dark eyes . . . and that beard! Unlike the other gentlemen of her acquaintance, he wore a close-trimmed beard that made him look as if he belonged in a Shakespeare play, or the court of Henry VIII.

He looked like a king.

"I find myself in a predicament," Lavinia said, the words tripping over each other. "Well, more than a predicament, a problem. Yes, 'problem' is the right word for it." Usually she had no trouble speaking, but now it felt as if sentences were knocking about in her head.

"It must be an appalling sort of problem, to bring you to my door." His voice wasn't chilly, precisely, but she caught a distinct ironic edge.

Oh, God, her sins were coming home to roost.

"I used to call you 'Appalling Parth,'" she said, clearing her throat. "It was merely in jest, and I apologize."

"To be sure, a jest," he agreed, his voice indifferent. "Whatever the case, why are you here, Miss Gray?"

"You used to call me Lavinia. In fact, you did seconds ago."

"Seconds ago I was shocked to find a lady standing at my bedchamber door. It seems we were both guilty of a lapse in decorum."

Well, that was blunt. Lavinia twisted her fingers together, trying to work out how to broach the subject of marriage. This was a disaster. She ought to leave. She told herself to leave, quite firmly. Her feet remained rooted to the carpet.

Parth raised a brow. "Well?" he said, when she had apparently stood in silence too long. "What can I do for you, Miss Gray?"

Before she thought twice, her eyes flew to his. Yes, she had teased him. But she didn't believe he *hated* her.

"Lavinia," he corrected, his eyes softening. "That was graceless of me, because you are clearly in extremis. What can I do to help?"

The humiliating thing was that the mere sight of him made her heart pound. Never mind that he was monstrously arrogant and would make a terrible husband. From the moment she'd first seen him, two summers before, he'd done something to her. He aggravated her. He infuriated her. He intrigued her. She hated that the most because he had made it clear from the first time he saw *her* that he considered her trivial, silly, and intellectually inferior.

Why in God's name had she allowed Diana to talk her into this?

She cleared her throat. "I was wondering if you had made any plans for marriage."

He froze.

"Because," Lavinia said, propelled forward by the terrible narrative that she and Diana had devised. "I am . . . I am . . ."

She couldn't do it.

She tried again. "It's just that I thought—"

"Are you offering to marry me?" His voice rasped. "Bloody hell, Lavinia—are you proposing marriage?"

"Something like that," she admitted.

She had imagined surprise, or blunt rejection. She had not imagined . . . pity.

But she saw pity in his dark eyes, and a wave of humiliation made her stomach cramp. Instinctively she swung her gaze away and caught sight of the two of them in a looking glass hanging on the wall.

Lavinia looked the same as she had two hours ago, before her mother revealed the truth about their finances. Her thick hair was the color of new guineas; her blue eyes were framed by lavish eyelashes that she darkened religiously. A buxom figure and lips that she didn't bother to color because her looks already skirted the edge of respectability.

That showed just how deceiving an appearance could be.

She was no longer the Lavinia of two hours ago. For one thing, she was no longer respectable. A hysterical giggle rose in her chest at the thought. Miss Lavinia Gray, daughter of Lady Gray, an heiress who had been wooed on both sides of the Channel, was no longer—

Respectable.

Or an heiress.

Still desirable, perhaps, but poor. *Worse* than poor.

Her eyes moved to Parth again, and it struck her that he wasn't wearing a coat, just a white linen shirt, and he'd rolled up his sleeves, revealing powerful arms. No wig, no coat. She looked down. No boots.

"We aren't from the same world," he said, catching her thought but not understanding it. "You don't want to marry me, Lavinia. I can't imagine why you got that in your head."

Out of nowhere, a streak of blind stubbornness appeared. "Would you . . . may I know your reasons for refusing me?"

He looked at her, incredulous. "Lavinia, are you feeling well?"

"Not particularly," she said in a burst of honesty. "Perhaps because I've never done anything like this before." She was confident around the men who'd courted her; their attentions confirmed her desirability. But something about Parth made her feel uncertain and defensive. At the same time, everything in her prickled into life.

"I gather you are saying no," she added.

"I am indeed saying no," Parth replied. His tone wasn't unkind, but it was unambiguous. He moved to stand behind a chair, as if to put an obstacle between them, as if she were a feral dog who might lunge at him.

This wasn't the way this was supposed to go.

Diana had been confident that Parth would agree, and she had talked at length about how he would fall in love with Lavinia after they had wed. With a sickening jolt, Lavinia realized that she had gone along with the plan because it involved *Parth*.

Who was precisely the sort of man who would never accept a bride he hadn't chosen himself. Let alone one he disliked. Parth, of all men, wouldn't want to be married for his money. He didn't wear flashy jewels as buttons, or ride in a carriage trimmed in gilt.

She was such a fool.

"Lavinia, is there anything I can—"

"No, nothing at all," she said brightly, turning toward the door. "I can't imagine why I ever had such an idiotic notion."

He stepped in front of her. "Why did you?"

She couldn't tell him about the money and the emeralds, and how Lady Gray would end up in Newgate Prison if Lavinia couldn't solve the mess her mother had gotten them into.

"I have had a lingering infatuation," she said, the words pouring out before she caught them. "You don't believe I give every man pet names, do you?"

"*What?*"

She saw the muscles tense through the sheer linen of his shirt. It was . . .

"I'm joking!" she cried. "It's time I return to my own chamber. You certainly don't want me to be caught here. I can assure you, Parth, that I may ask a gentleman to marry me, but I would never compromise one."

His hand whipped out and caught her arm. "I'm not the first you've proposed to?" It was a growl.

"As a matter of fact, you are." Then she added, with reckless bravado, "But now I've broken the ice, so to speak, who knows where I'll stop?"

Parth shook his head. "When you left England, you were the most desirable lady on the marriage market. You have no need to woo a man, Lavinia."

"Times change," she said lightly.

His gaze moved from her toes to her head. "No, they don't. You look—" Then his eyes sharpened. "Wait. I see."

"You do?" She pulled her arm free and began to back toward the door. Why had she listened to Diana? Everyone knew that her cousin was prone to wild ideas. Just look at the way Diana had run away from her own betrothal party with no more than a hatbox, and after that, had become a governess in the home of her jilted fiancé.

He took a step toward her, eyes intent. "It's not a disgrace, Lavinia."

Her heart sank. He must know. He owned a *bank*, for goodness' sake. Resentment prickled down her spine. If he'd realized that her dowry was lost, couldn't he have said something?

"You *know*?" There was gravel in her voice.

"I can guess."

"Oh." The word was small and ashamed.

"I'll find him," Parth said, low and ferocious. "And I'll *kill* him."

"What?"

"The father of your child." Parth's large hands closed around her shoulders. "Tell me his name." His eyes fell to her bosom, assessed the size of her breasts, descended to her hips. "Three or four months on the way, I would guess?"

Lavinia's mouth fell open, and then she snapped it shut. She'd been humiliated before, but now . . .

"You believe I'd deceive you so?" The words came out broken and aching. "I know you don't like me, Parth, but you think me capable of that? That I'd— that I'd ask you to marry me in order to disguise the fact I was carrying another man's child?"

His eyes went blank and his hands fell away.

"You feel that I'm—that I had—that I would—" Her throat ached so much she couldn't speak. She had known he disliked her. But she hadn't imagined he thought she was loose. Or worse, conniving.

That was the moment when, looking back, Lavinia decided that she could consider herself brave. Because she didn't cry or scream. She summoned the last dregs of her courage and drew herself upright.

She might have even given him a polite smile. "I apologize, Parth. Excuse me, I meant to say Mr. Sterling. I intruded into your chamber and embarrassed both of us, for no good reason."

She skirted him and fled, somehow finding the discipline to close the door quietly behind herself.

Chapter Two

Elisa is a contessa," Parth called over to North—
that is, Lord Roland Northbridge Wilde, heir to the
Lindow dukedom, and his closest friend since childhood. Parth was seated on Blue, a sixteen-hands
chestnut gelding whose cantankerous attitude had
been giving North problems.

North leaned against the post-and-rail fence sur-
rounding one of the exercise rings dotting the stables,
and gave a bark of laughter. "You've told me a hundred
times that you have no plans to marry, and in particular,
that you will never marry a lady. You told me after
my disastrous betrothal party that you'd never give a
woman the chance to jilt you. And yet here you are,
intending to marry a noblewoman?"

Parth turned his mount in yet another tight circle.
"Elisa is different. For one thing, she's Italian."

Keeping a firm seat, and with the reins steady, Parth

deftly moved the big horse through his paces, around and around the enclosure.

It was this activity that had built up the muscles in his arms, driving his tailor and valet to despair. Parth didn't care. There was nothing better than the joy of pitting his strength against that of a magnificent animal like Blue.

"How did you meet her?" North asked.

Blue's ears were twitching, suggesting rebellion, but Parth hadn't lost his seat since he was a boy, and he wasn't going to now.

"Her late husband and I were good friends in Florence. He was a conte, but he wasn't as useless as most noblemen. He died more than a year ago now."

Blue tried to toss his head, and moved his rear sideways, a sign of the temper that had him throwing a dozen riders since North had purchased him.

"I wasn't aware you were looking for a wife," North exclaimed. "You always refuse to attend balls with me."

"I'm neither titled, nor pretty, as you are. Or as you used to be." Parth tossed it over his shoulder, because Blue was rebelling in earnest now, prancing to show off his displeasure, lunging around the ring as if he could intimidate his rider into giving over control.

"Going to war changes a man," North said, shrugging.

Before Diana, his bride-to-be, had fled their betrothal party two years ago, North had been one of the most fashionable gentlemen in all England, rarely seen without a pristine wig and an embroidered coat. His clothing had been superlative, the heels of his shoes red, his stockings silk.

Now he was wearing a plain white shirt, frayed at the wrists where lace cuffs had presumably been ripped away. No wig was in evidence, and his skin was browned by the sun. He'd spent the morning working with his horses, and had a smudge of dirt on the cheekbone that used to be dotted with a beauty patch.

The sight of him now gave Parth a feeling of deep satisfaction. North hadn't been foppish when they were growing up together; rather, it was Horatius, North's late older brother, who had reveled in ducal attire. Who had been faultless in appearance and manner most of the time—unless he was drunk, as he had been the night he died.

"I take it, then, that the contessa is not interested in your fortune," North said. "That's important."

Parth nodded. The success of Sterling Bank had propelled him into the view of polite society. Young ladies of high birth had proved to be feverishly eager to marry a man whose private fortune ranked among the top in the country.

He frowned. Having ruled out pregnancy, he couldn't think of a problem that would have driven Lavinia into his arms. Financial difficulties? That didn't make sense. Any number of gentlemen would be happy to take her on, dowry or no.

He had no intention of telling North about Lavinia's visit to his bedchamber that morning, let alone her absurd proposal. He could make no sense of her peculiar visit—but he damned well meant to find out before night fell what had driven her to such an extreme.

That feckless girl with her lavish bonnets and disrespectful manners had always perturbed him, but now he felt a prickle of guilt. She'd shocked the hell out of him with that proposal, and he hadn't responded as well as he might have.

"Watch out!" North barked.

Parth didn't bother to answer. He had already sensed the change in his mount: a tensing of powerful haunches, a shudder running over the glossy coat.

Abruptly, the gelding arched his back and jumped straight into the air, four hooves off the ground, landing only to do it again, trying his best to dislodge his rider. Parth clung to him like a burr, relishing the battle of man against beast, respecting the tremendous power that Blue put into his fight to rid himself of the nuisance of a man in the saddle.

When the horse finally settled, blowing hard, hair darkened by sweat, Parth leaned forward and said, "That was an excellent effort, Blue. I wish you'd put all that energy to better use."

Blue pulled his lips back and trumpeted his aversion to that idea. Parth braced himself, his knees pinning him to the saddle as Blue threw his front half up into the air, trying with every acrobatic twist to free himself.

When they were both on the ground again, Parth ran a soothing hand down Blue's powerful neck.

North was still leaning back against the fence, arms draped over the top rail. "I paid over eighty pounds for him, but it was worth it. He'll make a fine hunter."

While Blue began another bid for liberty, Parth made up his mind. He shouted over his mount's enraged trumpeting, "I'll pay you double."

North waited until Blue settled back on all four hooves. "If you want him, he's yours. I only had the money to buy him because you made it for me."

"I'll pay a fair price."

"No, you won't. Family doesn't make family pay."

Parth's last name might be Sterling, but he was a Wilde in all the ways that counted. His parents had sent him from India to England, a ward of the Duke of Lindow, at age five, and the duke was the closest thing he had to a father. Horatius, North, and Alaric—the duke's first family—were his brothers. Hell, the duke's younger children were his siblings as well, right down to little two-year-old Artemisia.

"I'll put the purchase price in your account," Parth said, because he'd be damned if he took Blue for free.

"We never should have let you open a bank," North said, jumping over the rail of the training ring and heading toward the open stable door, pausing to shout, "The power has gone to your head."

Parth ignored that. A couple of years ago, his companies began returning such high profits that he had trouble reinvesting them in solid ventures. A bank's security was reliant on its management, and Parth didn't care to depend on other people's ability to judge investments.

What could be safer than a bank of his own? The Wilde fortunes—all of which he had managed since he turned twenty—were promptly moved to his bank.

After that, the nobility lined up to beg him to shelter their money. Sterling Bank was no competition to the Bank of England, but it was—to Parth's mind—much more solid and a better risk.

Blue was blowing air, his sides pumping in and out. His head slipped downward. Parth immediately leapt off. Incongruously long lashes blinked as the gelding raised his head to examine the man whom he hadn't managed to throw off his back.

"Damn, you're good," North said. He had returned with a horse blanket over his shoulder, and was leaning against the fence again.

"He's an excellent fellow," Parth said, giving Blue a rub between his ears. "You'll add him to my group?"

Parth owned a manor house a few miles down the road from the castle, but his outbuildings were devoted to experiments, not horseflesh. He maintained only a few carriage horses on his premises. His other horseflesh—hunters, a racehorse or two, a foal that had caught his fancy—were stabled here.

North nodded, tossing the blanket to him. Parth caught it with one hand and wrapped it around Blue's neck. Then he met the horse's eyes with all the respect that he gave a ferocious competitor in the banking world. "Blue."

The horse snorted, but with an uncertain undertone.

"You're mine, Blue," Parth said. He ran a hand down the gelding's nose, and Blue breathed warm air into his palm. "No more antics like that. You could hurt someone."

Hell, he'd already broken a groom's arm.

Blue made a snuffling noise. Parth stroked him under the chin. After another few minutes Blue sighed and put his head on Parth's shoulder. It wasn't surrender.

It was compromise, and they both knew it.

Chapter Three

Back at Lindow
Miss Diana Belgrave's bedchamber

I'm terribly sorry!" Diana cried, sitting down next to Lavinia, who was huddled on the settee. "I would never have imagined Parth could be so rude."

"He wasn't," Lavinia said dully. "He simply refused, that's all. He was appalled at the idea."

"Was that a joke on 'Appalling Parth'?" her cousin said, dropping a kiss on her cheek.

"No, a factual description of his expression." Lavinia's voice caught. "I've never been so humiliated in my life."

"It's all my fault," Diana said. "I promised North that I would consider carefully before acting on rash ideas. I should have held my tongue."

"You didn't force me to his chamber, Diana," Lavinia said. "I believed it was a good idea too. I was such a fool." She pressed her lips together, trying to hold back tears.

Diana wrapped her arms around her. "I don't like Parth any longer. Perhaps I'll cut him over tea."

"It's not his fault that he doesn't want to marry me."

"Why not? You would be a perfect wife for him. And frankly," she admitted, "I thought he'd be too much of a gentleman to refuse."

"People are seldom who they appear to be," Lavinia said, hiccupping with sobs. "Who could have believed that my mother would steal your emeralds? No one imagines Lady Gray a thief, but she is."

"Might you conceive of your mother as a Robin Hood in skirts?" Perhaps because she was well on the way to marrying a future duke, Diana seemed gleeful unmoved by the revelation that her aunt had stolen her emerald parure, sold the necklace and diadem in Paris, and lived on the ill-gotten proceeds thereafter.

"You should be angry," Lavinia said wearily. "*Your* mother blamed you for the loss of those jewels, if you remember—and yet you compare *my* mother to Robin Hood, who stole from the rich and gave to the poor?"

Diana laughed. "You *are* poor. I'm not angry; I love you, and it's not your fault. Lady Gray, and not you, resorted to theft. How could I blame you for her missteps?"

"Mother blames me. She says the theft of your emeralds is my fault because I've refused so many marriage proposals and I don't deserve to have a dowry." Despite herself, a sob escaped. "She isn't repentant in the least."

Diana produced a handkerchief and blotted Lavinia's tears. "Parth is scarcely the only wealthy man in the kingdom. Proposing to him was a foolish idea, but frankly, there are many men who would help you, and you won't need to embarrass yourself, because they will throw themselves at your feet."

Lavinia shaped her lips into a smile. "I'm sorry for being such a wet blanket. It was just—you should have seen Parth's face."

"Put it out of your head," Diana ordered. She rose and pulled Lavinia up. "We have an hour before tea. I want you to wash your face and then lie down with a cool compress on your eyes."

"I can't join you," Lavinia said with a shudder. "I can't face him."

"Yes, you can. You will act as if *nothing* has happened between you." Diana's tone would allow no further protest.

"I told Mother that we must return to London tomorrow morning. I shall be married when I see Parth again," Lavinia whispered, her voice rasping. "Happily married."

"To a duke," Diana said, nodding. "A very *rich* duke. If only I weren't marrying North, he would be a perfect tool for revenge."

Lavinia gave a watery chuckle. "I don't suppose you'd be willing to give him up."

Diana's mouth curled. "It might be hard to convince him."

"Let's go in. I have to bathe before tea," North said, as a stable boy took Blue away for a good currying and some warm mash. "You must tell me more about your contessa."

Parth laughed. "You don't give a damn about my contessa. You mean to find your fiancée."

"True," North admitted, grinning.

Parth slung an arm around his friend's shoulder. "The woman is in love with you. She will never run away again."

"Does the contessa feel the same about you?"

"Not yet, but she will. I'm thinking of inviting Elisa to the ball planned for your wedding. She would enjoy a masquerade ball."

North stopped. "Make certain of her feelings first. It's no pleasure to chase your fiancée down the road to London after being jilted."

"Considering Elisa's extensive collection of Wilde prints, *she* may chase you down the road," Parth joked.

North guffawed. "Even if I hadn't managed to woo Diana, I was never in the market for an Italian noblewoman."

"Until Diana has your wedding ring on her finger, unwed ladies will throw themselves at you. Witness the unexpected arrival of Lavinia Gray and her mother, under the pretext of rescuing Diana from the drudgery of being a governess."

Lavinia must have been devastated to find North affianced to Diana once again. After all, why would she have blurted out that proposal? Parth had to be the fall-back when North turned out to be engaged.

There was only one answer to that.

Hell, no.

Irritation swept through Parth when he realized he was thinking about Lavinia again. Damn it, her problem must have to do with money. She would never have approached him otherwise.

She wanted his money, just like the other ladies who'd thrown themselves in his way. He meant to solve her financial problems. But not by marrying her. Why didn't she just ask him for a loan, rather than propose to him?

Despite himself, his mind went back to that sentence she'd blurted out, about having a "lingering infatuation" for him. She couldn't have meant it. And yet she'd looked as if she'd shocked herself . . .

No.

"I will bring Elisa," Parth said, making up his mind. "Do you expect Lavinia and her mother to attend the wedding?"

"Absolutely. Lavinia may be a distant cousin, but the Grays are the only family Diana has, since her confounded mother has disowned her. Why do you ask?"

"That woman does not like me," Parth replied, almost certain that it was true. "The feeling is mutual."

"Why don't you? Lavinia is amusing, intelligent, and remarkably beautiful."

"She is as shallow as a puddle," Parth said, guilt pushing him to be harsher than he might have been. "She cares only for frivolities. Remember when she returned from Manchester with a carriage full of bonnets? Just one of those headdresses costs more than a housemaid makes in a year. I'm sure that wasn't the first time."

"Lavinia is an extremely kind young lady," North protested. "She traveled all the way from Paris to save Diana from the grip of the villain—*me*—who had compelled her into servitude."

"That was just an excuse. She came here to seduce you." His voice grated.

"No, she didn't," North said firmly, adding: "Lavinia will be Diana's witness, and I'd like you to be mine."

"I don't understand why you haven't eloped. Hell,

considering that Diana's mother disowned her, you wouldn't even have to contend with irate relatives. You could set out for Gretna Green tomorrow."

North shook his head. "I shall marry Diana with pomp and circumstance. My father intends to invite half of polite society to Lindow for the wedding, and I want every one of them to know that I love and honor my wife—even more so for the time she spent as a governess."

It was romantic; Parth had to give him that.

"We'll keep it a secret until the invitations must be delivered," North continued. "After the stationers get wind of our reconciliation, Diana will be plagued to death."

For years, the Duke of Lindow and his large and lively family had been a source of endless fascination not only to much of Great Britain, but also to a sizable cohort on the continent: Popular prints depicting scenes—ranging from reasonably true to entirely fanciful—from their lives circulated throughout the kingdom and abroad, and were avidly collected by duchesses and dairymaids alike.

The duke's three marriageable daughters, Betsy, Viola, and Joan, were constantly reported to be desperately in love with men whom they'd never met. Leonidas and Spartacus were depicted strolling into brothels. But as heir to the dukedom, it was North's love life that received the most attention.

Diana's flight from her betrothal party two years before had been exciting material for printmakers; when it turned out that she was serving as a governess in the castle, they rejoiced. Their depictions of Diana as a downtrodden servant to an evil lord sold like hotcakes. The news that North and Diana were betrothed again would cause a frenzy that was sure to dwarf the previous scandal.

"Your contessa must come for the wedding," North added. "It's the chase, isn't it? You want her precisely because she hasn't succumbed to your charms."

"I'm used to acquiring the best." Parth grinned. "And I do like a challenge. The fact that Elisa does not consider me a possible spouse makes the chase more pleasurable."

North burst into laughter. "How *does* she consider you, if not as a marriage prospect?"

"I believe she groups me with her husband's friends—who are in their fifties. The conte was a good twenty-five years older than his wife."

"How astonishing: a woman who has overlooked your obvious assets. We'll play charades one evening and I'll contrive it so you have to act out King Henry VIII, just to make certain that the contessa recognizes what a noble catch you are." He reached over and gave Parth's bearded chin a rub. "*And* since Henry supposedly viewed his beard as a symbol of his throne."

The four of them—Horatius, Alaric, North, and Parth—had grown up mocking each other, and North's belly laugh felt deeply satisfying. With Horatius gone, Alaric and North were the dearest people in the world to Parth.

They walked through the last row of trees that circled the stables, and rounded the bend to find Lindow Castle sprawled before them. Unlike the elegant palaces that Parth had seen on his visits to the Loire Valley, Lindow was a chaotic stone pile, built and rebuilt over many centuries, with newer turrets heaped on older towers. Wings, buttresses, and terraces protruded without any regard for rhyme or reason.

Spreading away from its east flank was the Lindow Moss, the vast and treacherous peat bog in which Horatius had lost his life.

The manor house Parth had built on neighboring land was, in many ways, everything Lindow was not. It was designed to present not strength and impenetrability, but openness and beauty. The ceilings were high, and the rooms graciously sized. He'd acquired the finest furnishings, and covered the walls with a priceless assortment of Italian paintings.

Wind didn't whistle down the corridors, and ill-tempered peacocks didn't scream challenges at each other in the night. The kitchens were modern, and the gardens perfumed by flowers rather than peat. His bedchamber boasted both a dressing chamber and a bathing chamber, with an attached water closet.

And yet, he preferred his London townhouse or, when he was in Cheshire, his boyhood bedchamber.

But time moved on, and he had to move with it. Horatius was dead. Alaric was married, and North soon would be. Elisa was warm, exuberant, and beautiful. She would transform his country house into a home. Fill it with children and laughter, so that it resembled Lindow Castle in the most important ways.

"I'll see you at tea," North said over his shoulder, as he hastened through the courtyard.

Parth didn't bother to answer; North was off in search of his beloved. Having already witnessed several such reunions since his arrival the day before, Parth knew that North would pull Diana into his arms and kiss her senseless, regardless of who might be observing them.

He tried to imagine feeling so passionately about a woman—and failed. Elisa was delightful in every way. He would welcome a chance to kiss her. But he would never succumb to desire the way North had. It wasn't in his nature.

An errant memory imposed itself: Lavinia Gray's big blue eyes looking up at him in his bedchamber. He'd moved behind a chair because a blazing—and wholly inconvenient—surge of lust had overtaken him.

The man who succumbed to a woman like that would find himself with a wife who had no thought in her mind other than her reckless expenditures on ribbons and lace. He'd have to face her over the supper table for the rest of his life, with nothing to talk about.

Desire would inevitably wane, and Lavinia's husband would find himself listening to disquisitions about bonnets.

Lectures about petticoats.

Nothing that happened in the marital bed could make up for that. The images his mind presented him—of a happy, flushed, *satisfied* Lavinia—were quickly banished.

Marriage was just another transaction.

Chapter Four

*T*ea was served *al fresco* on the Peacock Terrace. As Lavinia walked with Diana through the library toward the terrace, the clamor of voices told her that the entire family had already assembled.

They paused in the doorway for a moment. Parth was seated to one side, playing chess with Spartacus, the duke's eighteen-year-old son. Lavinia instantly turned away, ignoring the way her stomach tightened at the sight.

All the names she'd called Parth a couple of years ago—Fiendish Sterling, Proper Parth—sounded in her ears. The world had been golden back when she made up those silly names. She had been confident that she'd make an excellent marriage. Miss Lavinia Gray would be an asset to any man, bringing her beauty and a fortune to the union. Parth Sterling was virtually the only bachelor who'd regarded her with indifference, and it had driven her to tease him.

For the first time in her life, she felt completely adrift. Who was she, if not an heiress with a penchant for dressing in beautiful clothing? Her fortune lost, all she had left was her beauty. On the heels of that came another painful realization: How shallow was she that she had given such importance to ephemeral things?

The duke and duchess, their family, and a handful of other guests were seated around a large table cluttered with cakes and delicacies. Her mother, Lady Gray, was nowhere to be seen.

Diana tugged her gently toward the table, but Lavinia stood rooted in the doorway, another awful realization crashing over her head.

Any of the proposals she'd received would have dissolved like smoke the moment her proposed husband's solicitor learned the truth about her dowry. How had her mother imagined marriage negotiations? Did she presume that any man would be sufficiently smitten with her daughter to overlook it?

Lavinia had already been ruined, even when she teased Parth two years ago. Even when she'd bought all the bonnets that aroused his disdain. Even more so because those cursed bonnets had been paid for because her mother purloined Diana's jewels and exchanged them for glass counterfeits, as worthless as Lavinia now was.

The irony was sickening. Lavinia had always believed her fortune made her a diamond, but she was really no more than polished glass.

Parth saw through her, obviously. No wonder he looked at her as if she were not a diamond, but a *toad*. A toad that invaded his garden and sat on his lily pad and couldn't be thrown out, but couldn't be touched either.

That was the sort of flight of fancy that would have made her friend Willa burst out laughing. Especially if Lavinia pointed out that if *he* were the toad, then *she* could kiss him and . . .

She lost the thread of the thought. She had an odd feeling, as if she were supposed to do a French *récitation* in school but had forgotten her lines. There was a rushing sound in her ears, and a dizzying throbbing in her belly.

"You need a cup of tea," Diana said, giving her another tug. "Your cheeks have no color."

Lavinia drifted at her cousin's side. She took an empty seat beside Lady Knowe, the duke's twin sister. She felt like an automaton, a mechanical figure. One that could raise a cup of tea to her lips, turn her head, even flutter her fan. She drank tea. She ate too many muffins. She laughed and conversed with Lady Knowe, Diana, and assorted Wilde offspring.

Lavinia was particularly fond of the youngest Wilde, Artemisia. Artie was tough and sweet at the same time, and Lavinia had the vague idea that she might have a daughter just like her someday.

After three cups of tea, she rose and walked over to the balustrade, hand-in-hand with Artie. They tried to coax Fitzy, the elderly peacock who ruled the south lawn, to take bits of muffin from Artie's hand.

But Fitzy ignored them. He was irate, stalking back and forth and rattling his train in warning. Floyd, his arch rival, had encroached upon his territory again. Floyd had arrived at Lindow only recently, and had not yet learned to respect Fitzy's temper.

Right now the younger bird was lurking a few feet away. He fanned his tail with an air of bravado that quickly deflated when Fitzy scratched a claw in his direction.

Rather like me, scuttling away from Parth's bedchamber, Lavinia thought.

Artie wanted to give the rejected muffin to Floyd, who had retreated to a spot well away from his aggressor, but instead Lavinia promised they'd visit Floyd later. She felt too tired to pursue a skittish peacock across the lawn.

Her earlier weeping fit had left her leaden with exhaustion. Normally she didn't allow herself to cry—but she'd like to meet the woman who wouldn't have wept after being so humiliated.

Diana's little nephew Godfrey was sitting on the duke's lap, and Artie ran over to sit on His Grace's other knee. Lavinia returned to her seat and ate another muffin that she didn't want, her mind racing in circles, fearful rabbiting circles.

Her mother had stolen not only from Diana, but from her own ward, Willa. Over the years, Lady Gray had billed Willa's estate for all their household expenses, rather than just Willa's.

Another terrible thought: What if Lady Gray had purloined other valuables that Lavinia didn't know about?

Her hand shook, causing her teacup to clink against its saucer. Parth and Spartacus had finished their match and joined the group. The family was laughing . . .

North was teasing Parth.

The subject of the teasing finally sank in.

Parth was in love. He would be departing Lindow the following morning, determined to win the lady's hand. He meant to bring her to Diana's wedding, his ring gracing her finger.

The information burned into Lavinia's mind. In love. Parth was in love. A ring. Betrothal. Marriage.

"Otherwise," she heard Parth saying to Spartacus, "she might take one look at Sparky and throw my ring at my feet."

Despite herself, a choked sound escaped Lavinia's lips.

Parth was seated near the end of the table, laughing at North, parrying Spartacus's contention that only a madwoman would accept Parth's proposal. Only after Lavinia's inadvertent gasp did his eyes settle on her.

She cleared her throat. "Who is the lucky woman?" she asked, aiming at a casual tone. "I missed the beginning of the conversation."

Rather than reply, Parth frowned and said, "Aunt Knowe, Miss Gray looks unwell."

Really? He not only ignored her question, but pointed out that she wasn't looking her best? Her back stiffened in indignation.

Lady Knowe was a strapping, tall woman, easily the height of her brother. She peered at Lavinia through a jeweled lorgnette, then dropped it, likely because—as she had once confided—she saw better without it. "Lavinia, my dear, Parth is right; you look like the underbelly of a fish." She rose. "Up you go. We'd better get you to your room."

Lavinia stood obediently. Her napkin fell from her lap, spilling crumbs over the flagstones.

Parth's brows knit. "Are you ill?" he asked her, the question dropping into a pause in the general conversation. Every head on the terrace turned to look at Lavinia.

"There is nothing the matter with me." She tore her eyes away. "Except I do not feel well." She dashed to the edge of the terrace just in time before the muffins made their way back into the world.

"Bloody hell," Lady Knowe said from just behind her shoulder. And then, bellowing at the family butler, "Prism!"

"Ugh!" Artie yelped, before her mother hushed her.

Stomach empty, Lavinia clutched herself around the waist. "Please forgive me," she whispered, her throat raw.

Lady Knowe thrust a napkin into her hand and Lavinia wiped her mouth, willing herself to turn and give the others a rueful smile and apology.

But before she could make herself do so, someone reached around her from behind, picked her up, turned, and marched straight through the library and toward the stairs.

She knew instantly who it was. Parth smelled better than any man she knew. It must be a soap imported from China, or somewhere equally exotic.

She would know his scent anywhere. He smelled like fresh apples, wind, and rain.

One of the reasons she always tried to be witty around him was that foolish observations like that kept popping into her brain. She could just imagine his scornful glance if she praised his soap.

She remained silent, closed her eyes, and leaned her head against his broad chest as he mounted the stairs. She was not going to cry. Nor was she going to throw up again.

When he reached her room, he set her on her feet. She went straight to the washbasin to brush her teeth. She had to lean heavily on her dressing table because she felt so weak, and she was just straightening when Parth scooped her up again.

"You shouldn't still be here!" she protested.

Without responding, he carried her to her bed and placed her on it. Her head swam so much that she clutched his sleeve, an anchor in an unsteady world. At that moment, it occurred to her that she wasn't merely upset about the criminal tendencies of her nearest and dearest, or that dreadful scene in Parth's room. Nor was it a matter of a surfeit of muffins.

She was sick, well and truly ill.

She probably wouldn't see Parth at breakfast to say goodbye. She blinked up at him and rasped, "Good luck with your lady. If I'd known, I never would have—have done that."

He stared down at her, his mouth grim. "I'll dispatch a doctor from Stoke on my way to London."

"I merely have a stomach ailment."

"She ate too many muffins," Lady Knowe said, coming into the room. "Gluttony is my favorite of the deadly sins. Prism has sent a footman to fetch your maid, Lavinia."

Diana entered as well; she put a hand on Lavinia's forehead. "This has nothing to do with muffins; Lavinia has a fever."

"Oh, my," Lady Knowe said, feeling Lavinia's forehead for herself. "You'd better leave, Diana. We don't want the children taking ill."

Over her protests, Diana was sent from the room. Lady Knowe returned. "Your mother is resting, dear, but would you like me to wake her?"

Lavinia shook her head and then winced. Even that small movement made her head feel as if it might fall off. After the revelation and subsequent hysteria of the morning, Lady Gray had almost certainly taken a big dose of Dr. Robert's Robust Formula. Sometimes no one could wake her for hours.

Despite herself, a tear slid down Lavinia's cheek. Parth reached out and brushed it away, but before he said anything, Lady Knowe bustled him out of the room as well.

"I'll get some comfrey down her throat, and she'll be right as a trivet," Lavinia heard Lady Knowe say, out in the corridor.

Sure enough, once Lavinia's maid, Annie, had bathed Lavinia's face with a cool cloth, bundled a nightgown over her head, and poured a gallon of comfrey tea down her throat, the feeling that her head was about to explode faded, leaving room for fear to return.

Annie turned the lamp low and tiptoed away. Lavinia watched her go, but then the door opened and a group of constables marched in and thronged around her bed demanding money. "Miss Gray," one of them barked at her, "did you know that there is a crowd of creditors down in the kitchen? The housekeeper is unable to bake; His Grace will have no dinner. The babies have no warm milk!"

In her dream, Lavinia started trying to find her reticule so she could pay back the creditors. It was nowhere to be found, but ropes of pearls and strands of emeralds glinted at her from corners of the bedchamber. Whenever she reached out to gather them up, they winked into airy nothing.

With a hoarse gasp, she thought she woke up, but a moment later she was feverishly chasing Parth up and down the corridors, demanding that he marry her. Parth was holding hands with a woman in a nightdress and they were laughing, and then he started kissing the woman while Lavinia was watching.

She stood in the shadow of the corridor and watched as Parth wound his fingers into the dream woman's hair, kissing her so sweetly that tears ran down Lavinia's face at the sight.

That dream was so hideous that she did actually wake, pushing herself up on a pile of pillows and using her sheet to shakily wipe sweat from her forehead.

She was staring numbly at the dimly lit furniture on the other side of the room when her door opened.

"You can't enter my room," she whispered in a hoarse voice.

Parth closed the door behind him, the cast of his mouth as obstinate as ever. "You needn't be afraid that I'll compromise you."

If her head hadn't hurt so much she would have laughed. "We both know you don't want to marry me," she said, with a weak chuckle.

"I'm sorry, Lavinia." His voice was awkward, the first time she'd heard it so.

She couldn't think of anything to say so they just stared at each other for a moment.

"Is your fever down?" he asked.

"I'm fine. Please do leave." She looked away, because the truth was . . . well, the truth was that something about Parth made her feel weak. It wasn't the breadth of his shoulders, or the sturdy force of his presence.

It was *Parth*. The man who took care of everyone. The Wildes freely said that he'd taken the family fortune and more than doubled it.

The man with dark brown eyes who looked at her silently, no matter how she teased him, no matter what names she made up for him.

He ignored her command, and instead of leaving, he poured cold comfrey tea into a glass and made her drink it. Then he sat down in the half darkness. After a while, he reached out and took her hand. "Will you tell me the problem now?"

Lavinia managed a smile. "I lost my muffins."

His direct gaze met hers. "Lavinia."

Another tear rolled down her cheek, willy-nilly.

"Tell me."

As any number of his clerks could have told her, it took a stout heart to refuse Parth Sterling's direct command. Lavinia, her fingers swallowed in Parth's strong, warm hand, found herself blurting out the truth, or at least part of it.

"I lost my dowry," she said, her voice cracking. "It's gone."

"I suppose your father's estate was not sufficient to support you and your mother."

"I know what you have concluded." Lavinia rolled her head on the pillow, wishing that it didn't ache so much. "My father didn't leave enough money to pay for all my bonnets."

His expression didn't change. "Lady Gray does not strike me as financially prudent."

That was a wild understatement, but Lavinia held her tongue.

"More importantly," Parth continued, "your dowry is not the reason so many gentlemen wish to marry you, Lavinia."

"My mother moved us to Paris two years ago, because it's cheaper to live on the continent." She took in an unsteady breath. A burning hot tear rolled down her cheek. "She never told me, and I didn't—I didn't know."

Parth's fingers tightened around hers. "Please don't cry, Lavinia. You know that you will always have a home with North and Diana."

"I have to marry," she said, her voice wobbling. "I don't want . . ." But the rest of the sentence was lost in a sob.

He pulled her against his shoulder and she cried into his coat, until he moved to the side of the bed and lifted her into his lap.

"I'm sorry," she whispered a few minutes later, when she finally stopped shuddering with tears.

"You mustn't worry," he said, his low, deep voice soothing her tattered nerves. One large hand slowly rubbed her back. "You will have as many suitors without a dowry as you had with a purported fortune."

Lavinia forced herself to thank him. Lack of dowry might be accepted by some, but a criminal mother? No. She kept her eyes screwed shut, head against his shoulder.

Parth Sterling was reassuring her that she was desirable? Was it possible to feel more humiliated?

"Once you come to London, I shall select a couple of the best candidates and introduce you," he added.

Yes, it *was* possible. Mortification burned through her body.

"I know the men who have courted you to this point, and you were right to turn them down."

She raised her head and blinked at him. "You do?"

"None of those men would keep you in the manner to which you are accustomed." He gave her a wry smile. "Eight bonnets at a time."

Lavinia winced. "That's not entirely fair." Her voice sounded very small in the still night air.

His dark gaze met hers and his mouth softened. "I

didn't mean it as an insult, Lavinia. I'm not very good at jests, but I thought that was one."

She deserved to be teased about bonnets, especially after the way she used to tease him. "Well," she said, realizing that her throat hurt, and the achy feeling behind her eyes was back, "that would be kind of you."

He nodded curtly. "I will find you an excellent husband, one who is neither reckless nor impulsive."

Her throat had tightened again, and she could scarcely summon up a smile.

She went back to hating him a bit, because he was so matter-of-fact about her deficits. A thin veneer of kindness covered his contempt. He might as well have said that the man she married would need his own bank in order to pay for her reckless purchases.

And now *he* was going to find her a husband? It was one thing to refuse her proposal, but this was like a slap in the face: *I won't marry you, but I'll do my best to foist you off on another man who can afford you.* Kindness and an insult wrapped together.

Yet how could she refuse? The man Parth found would presumably have the equivalent of his own bank, and a man that rich would be able to bury the truth about her mother's crimes.

The stab of fury that went through her just made her feel more ill. The truth was that she needed the husband he was offering as a substitute for himself. She was lucky to have Parth's help.

No matter whether she felt cursed or not.

"I'm sure you wish to be asleep," she whispered, her voice shaky.

Parth's eyes narrowed and his arms tightened, not

allowing her to move from his lap. "I said something wrong again, didn't I?"

"I do need a husband. A rich one. Very rich, so he can buy bonnets and emeralds." Oh, dear. The fever must have come back, because she felt as if words were darting out of her mouth like little sparrows. "He has to like me, not dislike me. Money is important, but that's important, too. I tried to tell Diana how you felt about me, but she wouldn't listen."

His body stilled under hers. "Was it Diana who sent you—"

She waved her free hand. "It's no matter." She watched him from under her lashes. He was studying her as if she were a set of numbers he had to calculate. "I'm not a lace factory."

A smile lifted one side of his mouth. "I know."

"Not many men can do that," she observed.

"Do what?"

"Smile on one side. If you find me a husband, then you and I needn't argue any longer. I'll argue with my husband instead, the one who likes me."

His brows drew together.

"I suppose you never argue with Eliza," she said, and then, hearing wistfulness in her voice, "which is marvelous. And you like her!"

"Her name is Elisa," Parth said evenly. "I also like you, Lavinia. Would it be all right if I felt your forehead?"

"Why not? You're here in the middle of the night. I am sitting on your lap—in my nightdress." A giggle flew into the night air. "I'm pretty sure that Diana would believe that was good enough, but she'd be wrong, wouldn't she?"

Parth's hand wrapped around her forehead.

"Your hand feels so good," she said with a sigh.

"More comfrey," Parth stated, picking up her mug. "This is cold. Would you like me to have the house-keeper make you a fresh pot?"

She rolled her head back, feeling as if it might drop from her neck. "Cold is better."

After making her drink two cups of comfrey, Parth settled her back on the pillows, pulled up the covers, and sat back down in the chair beside her bed.

"You should not be here," Lavinia said sleepily. "You might find yourself obliged to marry me if we were found out, and then what would you do?"

He smiled wryly. "I'd marry you."

"You're in love with Elisa," she reminded him. "Diana thought you'd fall in love with me, but we both know that wouldn't have happened. You mustn't worry, though. I'll be very, very nice to the man you . . . you find for me."

He didn't say anything to that, just reached out and took her hand again. For the first time since Lady Gray broke the news of their impoverishment, Lavinia felt safe.

She fell asleep like that, her fingers tight around his.

But she woke alone.

Chapter Five

5 Cavendish Square, London
Leased to Elisa Tornabuoni Guicciardini,
    the Contessa di Casone
Six days later
A morning call, paid in the afternoon

*E*lisa was having a wonderful afternoon. If her father had any idea of what she was doing, he would have an apoplectic fit. But luckily he was in Italy and she was in England.

Babbo would turn red and start huffing like a prize bull. He would howl, blaming her mamma for the part of Elisa that never succeeded in becoming a good Florentine *signora*. Mamma was from Rome, and every Florentine knew that Romans were decadent, if not downright debauched.

When Elisa's husband, Donatello, had been alive, she had tried very hard to be a proper Florentine *signora*: chaste (which she was), silent (which she wasn't), and obedient (most of the time).

Donatello was gone, and with him the requirement

that she comport herself like a Florentine rather than a Roman. Not that she meant to be immoral . . . but unladylike? Definitely!

Just at the moment, Elisa's Roman blood had definitely risen to the surface.

She gave Mr. Sterling her widest, most sparkling smile, hugging the feeling of rebellion to her bosom. During the past year of mourning, Elisa had discovered that there was nothing she liked better than breaking the rules drilled into her head as a child.

For example, here she was, alone in her very own parlor, serving coffee to a *man*.

And not just any man!

Mr. Sterling was a man of the people. A man who owned a bank. A man who worked for a living. A man who wore a beard. This was the most exciting thing she'd ever done, other than bringing herself to London. And just now he had asked her a personal question, the sort that no proper Florentine gentleman would ask a lady!

"I met Donatello shortly before we wed," she explained. "My father is most strict and I seldom left the *palazzo* as a young woman." In case Mr. Sterling disapproved, she added, "That is quite normal for an Italian lady, even a widow."

"Certainly," he said, as courteously as if she'd offered an observation on the weather.

That was part of Mr. Sterling's intriguing aspect. He behaved precisely like a gentleman, and he was wickedly handsome to boot. No woman could overlook that strong jaw or that finely shaped nose.

Yet it was all superficial. He might have resembled a gentleman, but he was in trade. Her father—if he knew—would be most displeased that she was serving him coffee, even if it had been under the vigilant eye of a chaperone. The thought sent a happy little thrill of freedom through her.

"For this reason," she went on, embellishing on their inappropriate conversation, "I decided to travel to England—against my father's strict orders." She beamed at him and said it aloud for the very first time: "I intend to choose my own spouse."

Mr. Sterling was not the sort of man whose face revealed his emotions, but she fancied that she saw approval deep in his eyes.

Her father had wanted her to stay in Italy. He had even promised that he would permit her to choose her next husband, but she knew he didn't mean it. For one thing, he would introduce her only to eligible men.

Elisa was sick of honorable, respectable, stolid men. Her husband, Donatello, had been obliging to a fault. Her father and brother were both dutiful and loving— and excessively protective. They would never pair her with someone who wasn't of their caliber.

Another sedate Florentine willing to marry her. She could have groaned aloud at the thought.

No.

She wanted a *sinful* husband. She wanted a devil, a man whose nature was black as night, a man she could tame. Nothing and no one in her life so far had presented a challenge, and she was desperate for one.

According to all the gossip columns, the most wicked man in all England was Lord Roland Northbridge Wilde, the future Duke of Lindow. He had broken off a betrothal after seducing the lady, and then made her work as a nursemaid for their bastard! Elisa had never heard of anything so terrible.

He was perfect.

She intended to marry him and have him at her knees, and she didn't care which came first. A few years of marriage would turn him into a reasonably good man, if one with a decadent edge. She would break down the arrogance in his gaze. Make him look at her with desperation.

Beg her.

And if it didn't work?

That possibility didn't worry her. She would set up her own establishment and make friends with other English ladies living in solitary splendor. She would be as wild and wicked as her husband.

The marvelous thing was that Mr. Sterling—the sole person she knew in the British Isles—had grown up with Lord Roland. Such an astonishing coincidence was obviously a sign from Saint Adelaide, the patron saint of brides.

Elisa intended to charm Mr. Sterling into introducing her to the devilish Wilde.

"I wish you to call me Elisa," she said now, reaching out and patting Mr. Sterling's arm. "You see how English I already am? As a widowed lady, I am free to address you as I wish. We may become friends." She paused expectantly.

Mr. Sterling had been raised in the family of the Duke of Lindow, so quite likely he was aware that familiarity of this sort was allowable only within a family. Certainly not between a widow and a man who scarcely knew her—a man who was not a member of the peerage.

But, on the other hand, no gentleman could refuse a lady's direct request.

His gentlemanly training prevailed and he nodded.

"I would be most honored if you addressed me as Parth."

"Parth? What an interesting name!" Elisa exclaimed. "But then, English names *are* interesting, are they not? I have a footman whose name is Bumpsley."

Oh, no!

She shouldn't have compared him to a footman; perhaps he was sensitive about his rank.

With a glance under her lashes, she allowed his expression to calm her. There was nothing sensitive about Parth Sterling.

"Parth is not uncommon in India, where I was born," he told her. He put down his coffee cup. "I'm very afraid that I must leave, Elisa."

He had stayed precisely the recommended twenty minutes. He really did have lovely manners.

"This has been a pleasure," Elisa said, rising. "Perhaps you could show me your favorite places in London next week. Unless you will be busy?"

She happened to know that Parth Sterling ran an empire that spanned three continents. He had ships, mines, mills, and now a bank.

But she had the sense he was lonely. And—how could he refuse her direct request?

Sure enough, he bowed. "It would be my pleasure, Contessa."

"Elisa," she reminded him. "I understand that the royal princesses address each other by their given names. But even if they didn't, I am determined to make my own rules. You and I shall be the best of friends."

She smiled at him and—triumph!—he smiled back.

Chapter Six

Lindow Castle
June 12, 1780

$\mathscr{L}$avinia stretched cautiously. When her stomach didn't immediately protest, a smile spread across her face. Thank heavens! After what had seemed like endless days of fever and vomiting, she believed she might be able to leave her bed at last.

The doctor sent by Parth had visited her a few times, and her maid, Annie, had cared for her tirelessly. Diana had stopped by several times a day, as had the duchess, Ophelia, and Lady Knowe. She had a vague memory of her mother drifting in and then back out of the room.

She also remembered that Parth had come by her bedchamber in the middle of the night, most improperly. But had he really promised to find her a husband? Or was that a product of her fever?

Hopefully, it was only a figment of her imagination. She could find a groom without Parth's help. All she had to do was identify a bachelor as rich as Parth. *Richer* than Parth, if possible.

Lavinia was contemplating the pursuit of wealthy men when Lady Knowe bustled into the room and stopped short. "Look at you, my dear!" she exclaimed. "There's a sparkle in your eye. I'm reasonably certain you're not going to lose your breakfast today."

Lavinia pushed herself upright. "I'm very grateful," she began, feeling an unusual flash of shyness.

"Annie has done everything necessary for you," Lady Knowe said, sitting down beside her. "You didn't imagine that I'd bathe you myself, did you?"

Lavinia shook her head, smiling. "Certainly not, Lady Knowe. But I do remember you coming at all hours of the night and making me drink a loathsome brew that cleared my head, so I have much to thank you for."

Lady Knowe's eyebrow flew up. "You remember that, do you? I'm always fascinated by what people recall after a fever. You babbled so much that I'm surprised you knew I was in the room."

Lavinia felt heat creeping up her neck. Surely she hadn't . . . "What did I babble about?" she asked cautiously.

"Parth, for one thing."

Lavinia's heart sank, but Lady Knowe burst into laughter. "'Appalling Parth'! 'Spoiled Sterling'! I thought I should take notes. When I next see Parth, I shall try out a few choice phrases."

Well, that was better than it might have been. "Those are merely play names I used to call him," she said awkwardly.

"I know the two of you don't get along," Lady Knowe

said. "Parth isn't for all appetites. He's ours, and we love him, but the man doesn't know how to dance a pretty measure."

"Yes, he does," Lavinia said, surprising herself. Her flush grew even hotter at Lady Knowe's newly raised eyebrow. "We danced together at midsummer two years ago . . . He couldn't avoid it. That is to say, he would have avoided it, if he could have."

"Interesting," Lady Knowe said, looking delighted. "I meant it metaphorically, but during the ball Ophelia is planning for the wedding, I shall demand a dance from Appalling Parth, and I won't take no for an answer. We did have a dance master living here when the boys were young, so they have no excuse for ignorance."

"Mr. Sterling doesn't seem to be inept at anything," Lavinia ventured.

What was the matter with her? It must be weakness left over from her illness. She felt as feeble as a kitten, as if she'd like to pour out all her troubles to Lady Knowe. The duke's sister was so large and comforting, with her brusque demeanor and expression that did nothing to hide her kindness.

She couldn't do that. Her mother would never forgive her if she knew that Lavinia had told Lady Knowe everything.

"Now, we need to get you fattened up again before I allow you out of this chamber. You are shockingly emaciated."

Lavinia glanced down at herself, but buried under a mound of blankets, she looked as round as ever. Now that she was well again, she had to go to London, and open the townhouse. She had to speak to her mother's solicitors.

Perhaps her mother had exaggerated the situation. Hopefully.

"I'm sure my mother is longing to return to London," she said, wiggling upright again, as she had somehow slipped down in bed.

Lady Knowe sighed at this, and put a hand over Lavinia's.

Lavinia froze, then looked up slowly, her heart thumping. Lady Knowe's eyes were filled with sympathy.

"She's not dead, is she?" Lavinia asked with a gasp. Her mother was . . . She wasn't very maternal, but Lavinia loved her.

"No, certainly not! I'm dreadfully sorry to have given you that idea for even one moment," the lady cried. "But she is ill."

"Did she catch the influenza?"

"No, thank goodness! In all, four members of the household caught it, and for someone as delicate as Lady Gray, the consequences could have been devastating. Just look how ill you were, and you are young and strong."

"She has a different illness?" Lavinia asked.

"Your mother is not herself." Lady Knowe's hand tightened. "Lavinia, I will be direct. Lady Gray has developed an addiction to laudanum."

"An addiction to what?"

"Laudanum."

"Do you mean her cordial? The drops the doctor prescribes for her nervous condition?"

"Exactly. How long has she been taking those drops?"

Lady Knowe's voice didn't suggest even a hint of condemnation, but Lavinia felt defensive of her mother just the same. She didn't respond immediately, mostly because she was trying to remember a time when her mother hadn't carried those drops with her everywhere. Could it have started with her father's death?

"The addiction is not your mother's fault," Lady Knowe said, when Lavinia didn't respond. "Laudanum can all too easily result in an addiction, and, regrettably, doctors rashly prescribe it without concern for the consequences. That said, we must wean your mother from the drug; it can lead to irrational behavior and, at the worst, death."

Oh.

They had that first symptom covered.

"Your mother has been taking enough laudanum to knock out a horse," Lady Knowe added.

"What?"

"The longer one takes the drug, the less effective it is," Lady Knowe explained. "Apparently, it is agonizing to stop, so people take larger and larger doses."

"I see," Lavinia whispered. And she did. A number of hitherto confusing things clarified themselves, including her mother's precious valise full of clinking bottles.

"The night you fell ill, Lady Gray did not wake for almost forty-eight hours. The doctor whom Parth sent to attend to you spent most of his time trying to rouse her, and mercifully, he finally succeeded. But he felt strongly that if she were left to her own devices, she would not survive another such dose."

"Oh, no," Lavinia cried, slipping her hand away from Lady Knowe's, pushing the covers down, and swinging her legs over the side of the bed. "I had no idea. I will speak to her. I'll take her drops away and I'm sure that she will—"

"Lavinia, my dear, she would *not* understand. At the moment she needs the drug more than she needs her daughter."

In truth, her mother spent most of her time reclining, drops in hand, and had done so even during Lavinia's debut. Willa had been a more effective chaperone than her mother; Willa didn't allow Lady Gray to accept any of the fortune hunters who had asked for Lavinia's hand.

Her mother would have agreed to the first man who offered.

There were whole weeks in Paris when her mother's weak nerves had kept her in a darkened room while Lavinia rode around the city in the company of whichever gentleman first appeared at their door.

"I didn't know," she whispered, looking up at Lady Knowe. "I thought . . . the doctors always said that her nerves were fragile. Even when my father was alive."

"In my opinion, a great many doctors in this kingdom should be hanged, drawn, and quartered. They are all too likely to hand out dangerous medicines—to women, in particular—without a thought for what it does to the body and spirit."

They sat in silence as Lavinia tried to focus. When he'd known he was dying, her father had told her that she would have to take care of her mother. She hadn't done a very good job.

"Don't blame yourself; there's nothing you could have done to fight it," Lady Knowe said gently, as if she'd read Lavinia's mind.

"At least it explains some of her actions," Lavinia said. It was a feeble attempt to look on the bright side, but it was all she could come up with. "What did the doctor advise?"

Lady Knowe answered in a roundabout way. "You were very ill," she began. "My brother and I felt that a decision had to be made, and you could not be burdened with it, given your fever. Once the doctor managed to wake your mother, the duke asked him to escort her to a restful sanitarium nearby. Mrs. Aline, who runs the establishment, is a good friend of mine, and your mother will receive the care and attention she needs."

"You sent her away?" Lavinia gasped. "Without even telling me?"

"You were very ill and your fever might well have worsened if we told you of such a distressing problem. I assure you, my dear, that Lady Gray will recover, given time. They know of such cases, and everyone who works in the sanitarium is kind."

Lavinia felt a wave of confused panic. "Is that the place where you sent the mad playwright, two years ago? My mother could never defend herself against someone like that." Her voice rose despite herself. "She's a gentlewoman, and she's never had to even *think* for herself."

"Absolutely not. Lady Gray is staying at a place where ladies temporarily retire from society to rest," Lady Knowe said quickly. "Prudence lives in a different sort of establishment. Your mother desperately needed help, Lavinia, and while I know that you would do anything for her, from what I've seen among our friends and neighbors, the love of family members is not enough to overcome the lure of laudanum."

Lavinia took a deep breath. "I see."

And she *did*. Lady Knowe was the sort of person whom one instinctively knew would always tell the truth, for good or ill. "But she will get better?"

"God willing," Lady Knowe said. "At the very least, they will prevent her from taking too many drops and sleeping her way into the grave."

Lavinia swallowed at that blunt statement. "Mother may have taken an excessive number of drops, but it was an error."

"I've no doubt of that," Lady Knowe said, patting her hand. "I wouldn't advise visiting her for some time, but if you wish to write her a letter, I'll have it delivered this afternoon."

Her father would have expected Lavinia to solve their financial problems before her mother returned from the sanitarium. She forced herself to stand up. "I must return to London immediately. I have a great many things to do to prepare for my mother's return. Did you say she'd be released in a month?"

"No, dear, I didn't say it. It might be as long as six months, or even a year."

Lavinia reached out for the bedpost as her head swam. Yes, she felt awful, but she had to leave. She would go to London, talk to the family solicitor, and arrive at a plan.

Or a man.

The words tangled in her mind. Plan, man. Man, plan. Whichever came first.

If she didn't assert herself, Lady Knowe would ride roughshod over her. She had wondered why Diana had accepted a governess position in the ancestral home of her former fiancé—which was bound to cause a terrible scandal—and now she understood. Lady Knowe had made her do it.

She firmed her chin and turned to give the lady a grateful smile. "I am so appreciative of the kind care you gave myself and my mother."

"My dear, I cannot allow you—"

Lavinia had turned too quickly.

It was a good thing that Lady Knowe was as broad-shouldered as her twin, because when Lavinia's knees buckled, the lady caught her up and put her back into bed, tucked in so tightly that she couldn't move a limb.

Chapter Seven

June 25, 1780

*O*nce Lavinia felt well enough to get out of bed again, a different problem presented itself. "This will hang on you like a sack," her maid, Annie, said with dismay, holding up a gown with skirts like pale mist. Its bodice had been fitted to Lavinia's precise measurements.

Those measurements, alas, had changed considerably since she'd fallen ill. Even now, she had almost no appetite, and scarcely sipped half a mug of broth before putting it to the side and falling asleep again.

All her Parisian gowns were too large, so she spent another few days in her chamber, helping Annie and the household seamstress alter a day dress and an evening gown to fit her newly slim figure.

"I'm surprised you know how to sew, miss," the seamstress observed.

"I was lucky enough to have a governess who believed in practical skills," Lavinia said. Mrs. Granville had for all intents and purposes reared her; she couldn't remember seeing much of her mother even before her father died, which made Lavinia wonder just how long Dr. Robert's Robust Formula had been her mother's dearest companion.

Luckily, her inner fortitude was returning with her physical strength. Lady Gray would stay in the sanitarium for at least six months, perhaps more, according to Lady Knowe. Her mother hadn't responded to any of Lavinia's letters, but the important thing was that she was safe for the moment.

It gave Lavinia time to snatch up the first rich man who crossed her path. She shuddered at the thought. It wasn't . . . it wasn't who she wanted to be.

Or the way she had dreamed of finding a husband. She pushed that thought away. Saving her mother from a prison sentence was more important than Lavinia's fanciful wish to marry for love.

That evening she made her way downstairs to the drawing room. After exchanging greetings with a roomful of Wildes, Lavinia slipped into a chair beside Diana, and told her quietly that she would return to London on the morrow.

"How will I ever order a wedding dress without you?" Diana wailed.

The whole room overheard, leading to a general clamor of objections. Diana, in particular, wanted Lavinia to stay at Lindow until her wedding.

"Diana, your wedding is on All Hallows' Eve—and that's more than four months away! You shall visit me in London, and we will order a wedding gown together," Lavinia said, squeezing Diana's hand.

"Go to London?" Diana gasped. "I can't go to London! What about Godfrey and Artie? We haven't found a governess, remember?"

"I have an agency looking for just the right person for us," the duchess said. "Even if we don't find someone immediately, Godfrey is very happy in the nursery with Artie. He feels safe and loved."

"It's not as if Mrs. Butterworth in Mobberley could make your wedding gown," Lavinia pointed out. "What about your *trousseau*?"

"What is a *trousseau*?" Lady Knowe inquired. "My French is rubbish."

"Living in Paris for two years was remarkably useful in that respect," Lavinia said. She laughed aloud, her eyes meeting the duke's. "I used to be paralyzed by Madame LaFleur, our French teacher. I only survived thanks to a secret weapon. A talisman that I would kiss for good luck."

His Grace shook his head, a slow smile spreading over his face. "I have a suspicion . . ."

"I can guess," Spartacus crowed. "It was a Lord Wilde print!" The fame of Lord Alaric, the duke's third son, had led to a proliferation of heroic images of the explorer, engaged in daring exploits of all sorts, from climbing mountains to wrestling wild animals.

None of which Alaric had ever done.

As a girl, Lavinia had nurtured an infatuation for "Lord Wilde," but it had withered on meeting him—luckily, because it was the same moment her friend Willa discovered how much *she* fancied His Lordship.

"I had a great many Wilde prints," Lavinia admitted. "Which one do you think helped with my pathetic French?"

Lady Knowe let out a bellow of hilarity, and Lavinia joined her. Laughing made her feel better than she had in weeks.

"The one in which Alaric is wrestling the kraken," Spartacus guessed. "Because French is worse than a sea monster."

Lavinia shook her head. "Good try, though."

"I have it!" the duchess exclaimed. "The one in which—ahem—Lord Wilde is entertaining Empress Catherine, because the language of the Russian court is French."

"Another excellent guess," Lavinia told Her Grace, "but my mother wouldn't allow me to see *Wilde in Love*, fearing the play too disreputable. A print depicting a lady's bedchamber—whether a monarch or not—would not have been allowed in the house."

"It has to be one of the heroic ones," Diana mused.

"It was Lord Wilde wrestling a polar bear," Lavinia confessed.

"I know that one!" Spartacus cried. "There's a funny title at the bottom . . . what is it?"

"Amorous, Glamorous, Uproarious, and Glorious," Lavinia said.

Spartacus howled with laughter, and everyone joined in.

"'Uproarious' pretty much summed up my relationship with Madame LaFleur," Lavinia continued, once the room had settled down. "To return to our previous topic, Madame LaFleur would be dazzled by my current vocabulary, which includes the word '*trousseau*' . . . the wardrobe that a bride brings with her to her husband's house."

North instantly said, "My bride must have the most magnificent *trousseau* ever seen in London."

"No," Diana said, shaking her head. "I haven't—"

The duke intervened, his calm voice cutting through a babble of voices. "My dear Diana, I consider you my daughter already. It would give me great pleasure to provide you with a *trousseau* fit for a future duchess."

"Artie is a happy child, partly because of your care," Ophelia put in, nodding. "We owe you so much, Diana. You were the best governess any family could have had."

"That's so kind," Diana said, and burst into tears.

Instantly North pulled her onto his lap and began whispering in her ear. Lavinia stared down at her hands. It had been bad enough when Willa fell in love. Being around North and Diana made her feel terribly lonely, as if the ache in her heart would never heal.

"Diana and I will travel with you to London," Lady Knowe announced, acting as if Diana wasn't most improperly wrapped in her fiancé's arms. "If you will wait a day or two for us, perhaps a week?"

What could Lavinia do? She smiled and assured the lady that she would be happy to have their company on the trip.

"I'd love to join you," the duchess said, smiling at Lady Knowe. "I shall, if I have found a new governess to replace Diana by then. If not, you three can order a gown for me and I'll arrive in time for fittings."

In the midst of the frenzy of planning that ensued, Lavinia rose and smiled at the Wildes. They were so eccentric, so loving, and just so *dear*. She couldn't take any more of their company without growing maudlin. "If you will all forgive me, I will take supper in my bedchamber again tonight, as I am still regaining my strength."

Lady Knowe looked at her with a slight frown, so Lavinia widened her smile until it fairly sparkled with confidence. It was the smile of an heiress without a care in the world.

"I'm so grateful for your kindness to my mother." She caught the duke's eyes. "I shall expect a full accounting of the cost of Lady Gray's care, Your Grace. My mother would be comfortable with nothing else."

Another lie. Amazingly, considering that Lavinia used to pride herself on her honesty, she was growing expert at delivering falsehoods without so much as a guilty look.

She went back to her room and started fretting again. Her mother had not only stolen Diana's emeralds, but had taken all of Lavinia's jewelry—gifts from her father and aunt—and had the pieces counterfeited in paste.

What if she had done the same with other people's jewels? During Lavinia's debut ball, a countess had lost a diamond brooch. Now it occurred to Lavinia that her mother might have purloined the brooch to pay for the event. Last year, in Paris, one of Marie Antoinette's ladies-in-waiting had complained bitterly when she couldn't find a string of pearls. What if that loss was due to Lady Gray as well?

Lavinia's mouth firmed. As soon as her mother left the sanitarium, she would insist on a full accounting of all the thefts. Once she was married, her husband could discreetly make restitution, as well as help Lavinia put a stop to her mother's larcenous inclinations.

One striking aspect of that terrible conversation with her mother was Lady Gray's utter lack of guilt or remorse. She had veered between blaming Lord Gray, for dying; Willa, for marrying; and Lavinia, for *not* marrying. The memory sent Lavinia back to bed with a wretched headache and no wish to eat supper.

Rather more than a week had passed before Lady Knowe was prepared to have her trunks loaded onto the duke's traveling coach. Lavinia spent the time writing letters to her mother that disclosed no signs of alarm, and letters to the family solicitor that verged on panic.

Thankfully, just before they left, she received a reassuring letter from London. Their financial situation was dire, but if Lady Gray would agree to sell the country estate, she would have enough to pay her debts and allow her—if she practiced economies—to keep her townhouse.

Lady Knowe was an excellent travel companion, quick to point out interesting sights and skilled in card games that could be played in a moving vehicle. But none of it stopped Lavinia from bouts of worry about her mother's possible future in Newgate Prison.

On a happier note, she also had spent time mulling over Diana's *trousseau*. At the time of her debut, her cousin had been the most fashionable young lady of the Season—because Diana's mother paid outrageous sums to every *modiste* with a reputation for extravagance.

The result?

Diana had debuted with the widest skirts, and the showiest plumes, and the most outlandish wigs. In Lavinia's opinion, she had worn absurdly exaggerated versions of current styles, but never introduced a fashion of her own.

Lavinia meant to change that. Lady Roland Wilde's wedding gown would set fashion, as would every other garment in her *trousseau*.

Chapter Eight

$\mathscr{L}$ady Knowe, Diana, and Lavinia arrived at the Lindow townhouse in Mayfair on a bright morning in July. After taking a few days to recover from the long journey, they climbed into the duke's town coach.

"Where will you take us first?" Lady Knowe asked.

"We will begin at Nichole's in the Strand," Lavinia said. She had already informed the coachman of the direction.

"Excellent," Lady Knowe cried. "I hope Nichole has many pattern books. I want to order three or four new gowns, as well as something for the wedding. And I mean to order a few gowns for Ophelia as well." The duchess had decided not to accompany them to London.

"Nichole is a stay maker," Lavinia said.

Lady Knowe's face fell.

"Underpinnings are the most important part of a woman's appearance. I learned that in Paris, and it is true."

"That was one thing I adored about being a governess," Diana said gloomily. "I stopped wearing uncomfortable corsets, which are forever pinching one's waist, or flattening one's breasts."

Diana and Lavinia had been endowed with matching, and generous, bosoms—or, at least, Lavinia's *had* been generous, before her illness. Like the rest of her, it was now sadly shrunk.

"Nichole's corsets will surprise you," Lavinia promised. "He begins with seventeen or more pieces, instead of the usual eight. Rather than employing boning to produce a desired shape, he shapes each pair of stays to the individual client's figure."

"No boning?" Diana asked, astonished.

"I will not be ordering one," Lady Knowe announced. "I will allow alterations only by my own seamstress, my dear maid, Berthe. I brought her back from Paris years ago, when I was a mere child, and she's been with me ever since."

Lavinia's eyes widened. How on earth did Lady Knowe expect a London *modiste* to agree to that unheard-of demand?

"They don't mind a bit," Lady Knowe advised, guessing her thought. "It saves them work. They take a look at me and make the gown most of the way, leaving extra length because I'm so deuced tall. I've brought Ophelia's measurements with me, and they'll do the same with the gowns I order for her."

"You refuse to be fitted?" Diana asked, her eyes lighting up. "I had no idea one could! It took days and days when my mother was preparing for my debut, and I counted each hour a lost one."

Lavinia intervened quickly. "Diana, you simply *must* be fitted for your wedding dress. There's no escaping it."

"True," Lady Knowe said. "I'm merely saying that *modistes* will happily hand over half-finished work, and Berthe will complete their gowns to my measure. I pay full price, after all."

"A wedding dress must be fitted a minimum of four times," Lavinia said. And then, over Diana's groan, "After Nichole's, we'll go to G. Sutton, in Leicester Square."

"Is G. Sutton a *modiste*?" Lady Knowe asked hopefully. "With books full of delicious ladies, looking perfect in every way?"

"No, he is a silkman, a mercer."

"A mercer?" Diana asked, confused. "Couldn't we simply ask the *modiste* we choose to make a gown in whatever fabric we prefer?"

"In the two days it will take to make your stays, we shall visit all the best mercers in London," Lavinia said. "When we do visit a *modiste*—or rather, several *modistes* in order to choose the right one—we shall know precisely what are the finest fabrics available, and how much they cost. Then you will be measured for your wedding gown while wearing a proper corset."

"My mother never bothered to visit a silk merchant," Diana observed. "Her *modistes* showed us little scraps of fabric."

"You might well have been shown—and paid for—a fine watered silk," Lavinia pointed out, "but who knows what silk was used in the end? Especially given the abundance of ruffles sewn onto every garment you owned, not to mention the spangles and lace."

Lady Knowe huffed, a smile in her eyes. "I didn't realize that I was creating a monster when I asked you to help with Diana's *trousseau*."

Lavinia grinned at her. "I know it's shallow and

not at all noble, and doubtless worthy of disdain by people with better things to do, but I adore the art of dressing."

"I see nothing shallow about it," Diana said. "Remember when I wore that polonaise so padded around the hips that it made me feel like the largest marrow at the village fair? I was miserable."

"You were unable to sit down," Lavinia said, nodding. "Most of your gowns were unfortunate in one respect or another, but that one was particularly criminal."

They laughed all the way to the stay maker's shop, debating the varieties of boning, kidskin edging, silk embroidery, and lacing.

Lavinia enjoyed herself every bit as much the next day, as they visited two more mercers and a linen draper, right up to the moment, that is, that Lady Knowe asked, "We will be visiting Parth's lace factory, won't we?"

Lavinia's heart dipped. She had been successful—more or less—in pretending that Parth didn't exist. Parth *and* that woman he was in love with . . . the one he was courting.

No, neither of them existed.

Her heart squeezed again, because a stubborn part of her was having trouble with the idea that Parth was in London, no matter how often she reminded herself that he had no interest in seeing her. Or speaking to her. Or . . .

Or marrying her, obviously.

"I'm afraid not," she managed, arranging her features into a sweetly apologetic expression. "The very best lace comes from Brussels, Lady Knowe. Not from a factory in London. Parth's lace is all very well, but

English lace simply can't compare, and a duchess-to-be must wear the very best."

"Fiddle-faddle!" Lady Knowe barked. "Diana would never wear anything but Parth's lace. He's *ours*: our nephew, our lace."

Diana, that traitor, was nodding enthusiastically. "I don't care if my gown hasn't any Brussels lace, Lavinia."

I do, Lavinia wanted to cry.

I want lace that has nothing to do with Parth.

Common sense prevailed. Parth merely owned the factory; he didn't *work* there. He probably hadn't darkened its door since he'd bought it.

"He visits the factory every Thursday, in the late afternoon," Lady Knowe said with satisfaction. "If we leave now, we will almost certainly find him there, and he can show us his lace."

"Doesn't he spend most of his time at his bank?" Diana asked.

"I suppose," Lady Knowe said, shrugging. "But Sterling Lace was his first factory, you know. There was all that unpleasantness about the children working there."

"He sent them to the country the moment he bought the factory and saw what was happening," Lavinia said. She turned pink, meeting Lady Knowe's eyes.

"So he did," the lady agreed jovially. "My Parth is a man of honor, through and through." No blood relative would have spoken more lovingly, but then Lady Knowe *was* Parth's aunt, in all the ways that mattered.

"I had a note from him this morning," Lady Knowe said. "I mean to write back and ask him to escort us to Vauxhall sometime soon. I haven't been there in years."

"I have never been," Diana said. "My mother didn't approve of the tightrope walkers."

Lavinia and Lady Knowe both looked at her in surprise.

"We are all aware that your mother is remarkably old-fashioned," Lady Knowe said, "but what on earth is there to dislike in a man who walks along a rope? It's not a skill that I have any desire to emulate, but it strikes me as unobjectionable."

"Apparently they wear very tight breeches," Diana explained. She brightened. "I should probably visit the gardens, if only because my mother no longer dictates my actions."

"That decides it," Lady Knowe said. "We shall all go see the tightrope walkers. I'll ask Parth to bring along his contessa; I'm most curious to learn how his courtship is going."

Parth's beloved was a noblewoman. Lavinia had forgotten that detail in the aftermath of her illness. The lady probably had a fortune too, a real one, not just the rumor of one.

"Well," Lavinia said briskly, "I have an idea. Since we haven't yet gone to Felton's in Oxford Street—and John Felton is one of the very best purveyors of silk worsteds in London—I shall continue to his establishment, and the two of you will go to Sterling Lace."

"Certainly not," Lady Knowe squawked. "How would you go there, or return home? You can't take a hackney by yourself!"

But Lavinia had Lady Knowe's measure. If a person didn't look out, she would find herself dancing to a tune piped by Her Ladyship, and Lavinia would not allow herself to become that person, no matter how well-meaning the lady might be.

It was bad enough that Parth might escort them to Vauxhall, with or without his contessa; visiting him in his factory was too much.

Calmly, but with an intensity that came from her conviction that she'd prefer never to see Parth Sterling again, she managed to convince Diana and Lady Knowe that she was entirely serious.

FELTON'S EMPORIUM WAS a well-lit place, with a high ceiling and walls lined with pigeonholes housing rolls of various fabrics. Groups of ladies bent over counters examining silks and satins, or peered up at bolts of fabric, searching for the color they had in mind.

Mr. Felton himself was a jovial man with a large mustache and twinkling brown eyes. Taking Lavinia into his private office, he showed her samples of paduasoy silk and told her all about the new, more efficient loom invented in France, which he had shipped in pieces to his factory in Northumberland.

After he called for a pot of tea, Lavinia told him of Diana's *trousseau*, of Lady Knowe's wish for new gowns, of the duchess's request of a gown for the wedding as well as a costume for the All Hallows' Eve masquerade ball that would follow the wedding.

"What will *you* wear to the wedding?" Mr. Felton asked. "I have a damask satin in front that would make you look like an angel. Pale blue, shot with violet."

She fiddled with a biscuit that he'd brought out with tea. "May I tell you something in confidence, Mr. Felton?"

He nodded. "Most certainly, Miss Gray."

"I haven't the money to buy your damask," she said, all in a rush. "Everyone believes I'm an heiress, although I'm not. But I have gowns, many gowns, that my mother and I had made in Paris last year. I intend to remake them, so I have no need to buy new fabric."

Mr. Felton showed no particular shock. "You'd be surprised how many ladies can't afford the clothing on their backs."

"Really?" Putting this revelation together with images of ladies sipping laudanum, Lavinia felt as if she had had no understanding of the workings of polite society. "I can assure you that the Duke of Lindow and his son, Lord Roland, can afford Diana's *trousseau*."

"Oh, I know that. Wilde money is held in Sterling Bank," Mr. Felton said.

Lavinia flinched. "I see."

"Indeed, I moved all my money there. Now, I have a proposal for you, young lady."

"If you are offering to give me that damask at a discount, Mr. Felton, I still can't afford it. But I am deeply grateful."

"You don't need my damask," he said. "Remake your French dresses. Do you know that there are thousands of silk looms in Lyon? I imagine you have some splendid fabrics there. No, Miss Gray, I am offering you a commission."

"A what?" she asked, startled.

"You are clearly a young lady who possesses a true *sens de la mode*." His piercing brown eyes fixed on her. "The *modistes* condescend to me because I don't speak French. They go to other establishments, although I offer the best silks and the best wools. I and I alone have the best lace!"

"Better than Sterling lace?" she asked, unable to stop herself.

He snorted. "My lace comes from Holland." He turned around and caught up a length of lace as light as gossamer, knotted into a beautiful floral design. "People talk about lace from France, but in my opinion, Holland lace is more artistic."

Lavinia instantly imagined the lace edging a nightdress that Diana could wear on her wedding night. Sterling lace would embellish Diana's wedding dress, but there was a great deal more to a *trousseau* than just the wedding dress.

She reached out and touched the lace with the reverence it deserved. "I could imagine this in a champagne color."

Mr. Felton pursed his lips. "A bold idea. Most people feel that fine lace is too dear to risk dyeing."

"I don't see how a gentle dye, in tea for example, would be harmful. Beetroot might lend this a rosy glow without being harmful to the threads."

"If the future duchess acquires this lace for her *trousseau*, I myself will dye it with tea to a pale gold," Mr. Felton said. "*And* I will pay you twenty percent of the cost, Miss Gray. The same will be true of any of my fabric that is purchased through a *modiste*, any *modiste*, by your direction."

Lavinia gasped. "Is that what you mean by a commission?"

He nodded. "You and I, young lady, understand how luxurious clothing is meant to be worn. I have had no success making these infernal *modistes* pay attention to me and my fabrics. They prefer to charge their clients a fortune and save money on inferior materials."

"I don't want to take money from my friends," Lavinia began.

But he cut her off. "I'd be giving you twenty percent from my cost. It's worth it to lower my profit per bolt, because you and your friends will bring other people to me. A future duchess who marries in my silk? That is invaluable."

A pragmatic side of Lavinia was calculating percentages. Mr. Felton had the best fabrics she'd seen in the city. If they used his silks for Diana's gown and *trousseau*, she could begin to repay her mother's debts.

Then there were Lady Knowe's gowns, and the duchess's. What if another lady asked for Lavinia's help creating a *trousseau* after seeing Diana's wedding gown?

In time, perhaps she could pay off her mother's debts—the stolen jewels, and the merchants' bills charged to Willa's estate—by herself.

Not by marriage . . . by *herself.*

It was an intoxicating thought.

Chapter Nine

The Duke of Lindow's townhouse
Mayfair
Later that evening

The ground floor of the ducal townhouse comprised, among other chambers, two adjoining drawing rooms. Tonight the doors between two chambers had been closed, creating a more intimate space. Lady Knowe and Diana were nestled on a ruby-colored sofa, and as Lavinia entered the room, they burst into laughter.

"You are as amusing as a litter of baby pigs," Lady Knowe told Diana, as Lavinia walked up to them.

"I'm not certain that's a compliment," Diana replied, as they came to their feet and bade Lavinia good evening.

"Adorable, chubby, pink . . . Your hair *is* looking very red this evening," Lavinia said, sitting down.

"I am not chubby," Diana said. She glanced down at herself. "Well, if I am, North likes me just so."

"I had a splendid time at Mr. Felton's emporium this afternoon," Lavinia said.

"I've forgiven you for your beastly independent streak," Lady Knowe cried, waving her glass so vigorously that she almost spilled its contents. "For your information, we too had a fine time with Parth, whom we did indeed find at his factory."

Lavinia took a deep breath and gathered her courage. While returning to Belgravia from Mr. Felton's, she had decided that if she accepted commissions from him, she had to reveal the truth about her mother's thefts to Lady Knowe, and then explain her plan to repay them.

Lady Knowe proved as kind as she was unsurprised. "Erratic behavior caused by laudanum can certainly include theft. I've heard worse stories. Accepting commissions is a brilliant solution."

"I don't agree," Diana objected. "Look how much trouble I got into by taking a position in the nursery. Just imagine if the news were to come to light that Lavinia is earning money."

Lady Knowe's eyebrows waggled. "You are beginning to plan ahead, aren't you?"

"I'm trying to be less impulsive," Diana admitted.

"I fully understand that my reputation will be lost," Lavinia said. She reached out and took Diana's hand in hers. "As long as you will remain my friend, I don't care. My mother is a *thief*. My reputation is already shattered, no matter how one looks at it."

"A lost reputation has never stopped a determined man," Lady Knowe said. "Just look at Diana. She and I managed to ruin North's reputation—and her own, in the bargain—and still he fought to win her hand."

"Gentlemen will always fall in love with you, Lavinia," Diana said encouragingly.

"I shall make a point of inviting any number of eligible men to the wedding festivities," Lady Knowe chimed in. "One look at you, Lavinia, and they'll forget the whole question of reputation. *After* you've regained some weight."

Lavinia managed a smile. "I am trying."

"Now, to return to the important subject," Lady Knowe said. "My brother has more money than he knows what to do with, and he will be paying for Diana's clothing. May I suggest, Diana, that you order the most luxurious *trousseau* that London has ever seen? Naturally, you shall insist that Mr. Felton supply the fabrics. Moreover, I have many friends who would be *much* better dressed if they took advice from Lavinia, and I shall make certain that they do so."

"I shall buy so much fabric from Mr. Felton that you will be able to afford several emerald necklaces," Diana announced.

"Emeralds are essentially green glass," Lady Knowe said dismissively, waving her hand. "Diana must look like a future duchess walking down that aisle, and never mind whether North renounces the title in the future, or not."

"We'll inform every single person in London that Miss Lavinia Gray arranged for my *trousseau*," Diana added.

"But your wedding is a secret!" Lavinia pointed out.

Diana leaned forward, her eyes fierce. "No longer. I shall allow the stationers to publish as many prints of me as they wish, under the condition that the prints note that you are helping with my *trousseau*."

"Are you certain?" Lavinia asked. Hope was swirling in her heart. "That would be wonderful, but for you—"

"Pooh," Diana said. "I've already been portrayed as Cinderella, and North has been depicted as a Shakespearean villain . . . what more can the printers do? Other than make my beloved cousin justly renowned for her excellent taste?"

Lady Knowe was tapping her chin with her fan. "I agree that it would be better to announce Lavinia's role in the *trousseau* ourselves, rather than allow it to be discovered by a reporter."

At that moment the door opened and Simpson, the duke's London butler, entered. "Mr. Sterling."

"Oh, good!" Lady Knowe cried. "I asked Parth to join us for dinner, but he wasn't certain he would be free."

Lavinia sucked in her breath. She fixed her eyes on Lady Knowe with a look that she'd perfected over the years, one that stopped even lascivious Frenchmen from pressing their advances. "You may not tell him about my mother. I don't mind if you share the truth with His Grace, but not with Parth."

"She won't say a word about Lady Gray and my emeralds," Diana murmured, springing up as Parth entered the room. "Will you, Aunt Knowe?"

"Parth could be so *useful*, my dears. He—"

"*No*," Lavinia stated, her voice low but insistent.

The lady groaned.

"Parth!" Diana cried, stepping forward and kissing the gentleman on the cheek.

Lavinia didn't take her eyes from Lady Knowe, until the lady reluctantly nodded.

"Good evening," Parth said, stepping forward and bowing. "Aunt—"

"Oh, tush, these young ladies are driving me mad," she said, cutting him off. "Give me a hug."

Lavinia blinked as Parth's serious demeanor eased and he wrapped his arms around his aunt.

"You give the best hugs in the world," Lady Knowe said, kissing his cheek and stepping back. She looked at Diana and Lavinia. "He entered the family at the age of five, the sweetest boy you ever did see. Never too busy to hug me."

"Miss Gray," Parth said, bowing.

"Mr. Sterling," she replied, dropping a curtsy. It was too late to escape dinner. She'd have to listen to all the details about his beloved contessa.

"You don't appear well," he said flatly.

Lavinia felt her eyes widen, and her hands went to her hips without conscious volition. "I beg your pardon. Did you really say what I just heard you say?"

"Yes, I did," he stated. Irritatingly, she could feel the weight of his gaze, faintly disapproving and surprised, as if *she* had been rude rather than he.

"Dearest, you know better than to mention a lady's appearance if you haven't anything flattering to say," Lady Knowe advised him.

"I am merely pointing out that Miss Gray appears to be wasting away," he said, voice even, as if he were discussing the weather. He turned to Lady Knowe. "I presume you have noticed this?"

"I assure you that I am *not* wasting away," Lavinia retorted, heat flooding her cheeks. She was so infuriated that her mind went white-hot along with her cheeks. No one—*no one*—put her in a rage the way he did. "I would prefer that you did not make remarks of a personal nature, Mr. Sterling." She dragged her eyes down his body. "I'm sure we would all be more comfortable if I didn't embark on a description of your figure."

"Go right ahead," Lady Knowe invited. "I've always maintained that what's sauce for the goose is sauce for the gander."

Diana dissolved into giggles at this, which was hardly sympathetic.

"I merely observed, Miss Gray, that you appear to have lost a significant proportion of your body weight," Parth said, his voice dry. "I fail to see why your response need be so emotional, but if it would make you feel better to describe me, by all means, do so."

Lavinia could feel exasperation getting the better of her. She was, by nature, a sunny person. A cheerful person. Not one who ground her teeth and stared with open hostility at an acquaintance.

"How would you feel if I told you that you looked ill?" she asked from between clenched teeth.

"I daresay it would depend on whether I was ill or not." He looked at Diana. "Don't you agree with me that Miss Gray has shriveled, for want of a better word?"

"So now I'm not an autumn leaf but a raisin?" Lavinia inquired.

"Your beauty won't protect you from consumption," Parth said flatly.

She instantly went from feeling insulted to feeling nonplussed. Her "beauty"?

He considered her beautiful?

Before Diana could answer, Lady Knowe intervened. "Lavinia hasn't got consumption, Parth. Far from it. A young lady who has so many suitors necessarily finds herself going about London at all hours."

"How foolish of me to insufficiently appreciate the exertion required to be so adored." A muscle leapt in his jaw.

"Lady Knowe is jesting," Diana said. "We have spent the entire day working on my *trousseau*. In truth, I am longing for any activity that doesn't involve clothing. Bring on your suitors, Lavinia!"

"On that subject, I would be most happy to escort all three of you to Astley's Amphitheatre tomorrow night," Parth said. "I took the liberty of inviting an old school friend of mine, Oskar Beck, an excellent fellow."

"I know who that is!" Lady Knowe exclaimed. "He's that prince who owns a sizable chunk of Norway, isn't he?"

"An exaggeration, although his proper name is Holstein-Sonderburg-Gottorp-Beck, and he is third or fourth in succession to the throne of Norway. Relations are so entangled over there that he's in the succession for Denmark as well. North and I were good friends with him at Eton."

"Excellent!" Diana said enthusiastically. "He sounds like someone we shall like immediately."

It was transparently obvious that Oskar Beck was being brought along in order that Lavinia could entrance him into marriage. Parth had not only found her a husband; he'd come through with royalty, no less.

Lavinia was trembling with the impulse to scream, but instead she snatched up her drink, tipped back her head, and drank it down. It burned her throat just as she realized that she'd picked up Lady Knowe's glass instead of her own.

She convulsed into a breathless coughing fit, recovering herself to find that Parth was pounding her back and nearly shouting at his aunt. "Did you ask the doctor to check her lungs?" he demanded.

"Glory be," Lavinia cried, stumbling away from him.

"Brandy sometimes goes down the wrong way," Lady Knowe said, ignoring Parth. "Sit down before you fall over, my dear."

"How can you drink that stuff?" Lavinia croaked, sinking into a seat. "I thought it was my sherry."

"Oh, no," Lady Knowe said, going over to the sideboard and pouring herself another glass. "Brandy is quite a different beast from sherry."

"I'll try a glass of that," Diana said, following her.

"Simpson must fetch a doctor," Parth said, looking as stern as a Puritan preacher at the pulpit.

"I don't need a doctor," Lavinia said, her throat still raw. "I was merely caught unawares by that lethal drink."

"It's quite nice if you sip it," Lady Knowe observed. She had seated herself on the ruby sofa again, hands around her newly poured glass. She looked mightily amused, Lavinia noticed with annoyance.

Parth strode from the room, and Lavinia could hear him barking at Simpson out in the corridor. "Wonderful," she groaned. "Now he'll have some infernal doctor poking at me all night. Oh! He drives me mad!"

"That sounds like an accusation," Diana said, smiling broadly. She had seated herself beside Lady Knowe and was sipping her brandy in a ladylike fashion.

"It's a statement of fact," Lavinia said. "Parth Sterling cannot seem to be courteous to me."

"Parth doesn't like to worry," Lady Knowe said. "I don't know many men who do. His parents died of a fever within days of each other when he was very young, and that changed him. How could it not?"

Parth came back into the room as if nothing had happened, picked up his glass, and remarked, "Dr. Lancer should be here within the hour."

Lavinia stood. "Did you not hear me earlier, when I informed you that I was perfectly well?"

His eyes met hers, and she was startled to see that instead of his usual chilly indifference, he looked . . .

Something.

Angry. He was probably angry.

"He will listen to your lungs and heart and examine you," Parth said, as if he were speaking to a small child who had come out in red spots all over her face.

No, because one would try to *soothe* a child, and no matter what was in his eyes, she heard only indifference in his voice.

Behind her, she heard Lady Knowe muttering something *sotto voce* to Diana.

"What?" Lavinia snapped, swinging about.

"The two of you are as entertaining as a Punch and Judy puppet show," Lady Knowe clarified.

Parth threw a long-suffering glance at his aunt, then turned back to Lavinia. "Miss Gray, forgive me for expressing concern. Would you feel better if I insisted the doctor see you in order to ensure that you do not give an illness to my elderly aunt?"

"Elderly!" Lady Knowe barked. "Gone too far this time, my boy!"

"I don't know what regrettable set of circumstances allowed you to grow up imagining yourself the cock of the walk, but you are *not*," Lavinia said, forcing herself to speak evenly. "You are a rude, condescending man, with appalling manners and worse taste."

"Don't stop now," Lady Knowe cried encouragingly. "'Appalling Parth' was my favorite!"

"North will be so sorry to have missed this evening," Diana put in.

"I apologize," Lavinia said, seating herself. "My response was quite uncouth."

"I needn't anticipate further insults?" Parth asked, his tone lazy. Lazily dangerous. Dangerously lazy?

Primitive instincts prickled all over Lavinia, but she didn't allow her gaze to waver. "No, I shall not call you jesting names, because that's all they were," she said. "A way to try to divert everyone's attention from the scorn you have always shown me."

His brows drew together.

"You have." Her voice was frosty . . . firm.

He just stared at her. Fine. He needn't admit it, but they both knew she was right.

Just now he was regarding her with all the haughty arrogance of Henry VIII, before the man grew so rotund. Back when the king's royal countenance threatened to behead a woman if she didn't bow to every one of his wishes.

Lavinia straightened her spine and summoned the politeness drilled into her at the elite seminary she had attended. "Mr. Sterling," she said, pitching her voice to an exquisite condescension, "I am grateful to you for your concern. If I feel unwell, I shall summon Dr. Bosworth, our family physician. Perhaps you have heard of him, since he treats the queen."

Parth's lips eased into a smile . . . a genuine smile. "Well played."

Was that a concession?

"An excellent retort!" Lady Knowe agreed.

Lavinia spun on her heel, and with one look at her face, Diana leapt up. "My cousin and I will dine in my chamber," she said, swooping over and grabbing Lavinia's arm.

"Miss Gray is welcome to retire after my doctor has listened to her lungs," Parth said cordially.

Not a concession, then.

Lavinia decided it was better not to answer that statement. Instead, she marched away, Diana at her side.

At the door, she paused and looked back. Parth was raking one hand through his tumbled curls and speaking emphatically to his aunt.

Diana muttered something.

"What was it you said?" Lavinia asked.

Parth wasn't looking at her, so it didn't matter that she was staring.

"I said, 'He really is beautiful.'"

Lavinia gaped at her. "Parth?" Then, before she thought better, an objection tumbled out. "You're betrothed to North. You're not allowed to look at Parth!"

Diana giggled and put an arm through her elbow. "Come along, or he'll turn around and catch us ogling him."

If Lavinia had whipped around any faster, she would have woken up the next morning with a stiff neck. Without another backward glance, the two of them made their way upstairs to Diana's chamber.

"You can hide here," Diana said. "Come on, sit down. I'll ring for our supper to be brought up." She reached over and pulled the bell cord. "No one can compel you to be examined by a doctor."

Their retreat was disrupted by Lady Knowe, who barged in without even a token tap on the door. "Oh, good," she cried, "no one is unclothed. My dear Lavinia, Parth is being a protective ass, but you must forgive him."

"It wasn't his insistence on my seeing the doctor as much as his utter lack of civility," Lavinia flashed back.

"Yes, he *was* disagreeable, wasn't he?" Diana agreed from her bed, where she was propped up against the pillows. "Quite surprising, really. He's always been lovely to me, even when I was a mere governess and beneath his notice."

Lavinia wrinkled her nose. "He's not that sort."

"What sort is that?" Lady Knowe asked.

"A man who would look down on Diana for working as a governess."

"Certainly not," Lady Knowe said, making herself comfortable in a chair by the fireplace. "He's not exactly a member of polite society himself."

"Why isn't he?" Diana asked. "He was the duke's ward, wasn't he? Who were his parents?"

"His father was an excellent fellow," Lady Knowe said, a nostalgic look crossing her eyes. "Good old Oswald; we grew up with him. He was the only surviving son of a squire, but there was nothing for him to inherit, so he left for India. We never saw him again."

"If Parth's grandfather was a squire, then Parth has a greater claim to polite society than I have," Diana pointed out. "*My* grandfather was a grocer."

"Parth has every right to dance the night away at balls," Lady Knowe agreed. "If only he didn't find them so confoundedly boring. He's always refused to attend events outside the family, and then of course he began making money hand over fist, which was considered somewhat disreputable—though that opinion has changed now that he opened his own bank. I expect it would have been different if his father and mother had returned to England."

"So Mr. Sterling planned to return?" Lavinia asked, fascinated despite herself.

"Oh, yes," Lady Knowe said. "After Oswald fell in love and married Uma, Parth's mother, he sent Parth to be educated here, and planned to bring his family home in a few years. He and Uma ran out of time."

"That's *so* sad," Diana said, sighing.

There was something dreamy about her tone that surprised Lavinia. She glanced over and saw that her cousin had brought her glass with her. "What are you drinking?" she asked.

"This lovely brandy," Diana said. "So Parth's father fell in love, and sent their son back to England to live with the duke, and then he and his wife both died. *Sad. So sad.*"

"Have you eaten much today?" Lady Knowe inquired.

Diana shook her head. "I see why you like brandy. It feels powerfully . . . powerful. I like it more than sherry." She finished her glass.

"Drunk as a fizzle," Lady Knowe concluded.

Diana giggled. "Did I ever tell you how much I like North? Because I do. And he's such a wonderful father to Godfrey." She began humming a little tune.

"How are you feeling?" Lady Knowe asked Lavinia. "I doubt you've eaten much today either."

"I hadn't time after breakfast," Lavinia said. Then, to change the subject, because she did not wish to invite further remarks about her figure: "Diana always used to get tipsy on one glass of Rhenish wine, and it seems she hasn't changed."

"Light-headed," Lady Knowe said. "Whereas it seems you are like me, my dear. We can drink like sailors. Have you rung the bell for supper? I told Parth that I'd join him after the doctor's visit."

"Yes, I did," Diana said. She had put away the glass, slid down in the bed, and folded her hands above her waist. "When I am dead, I shall lie just like this, with North at my side, and we'll be together for all eternity, like Romeo and Juliet."

"Good Lord," Lady Knowe said, giving the bell a firm tug. "I'm ordering you some tea, Diana, and you'll drink every drop of it. I'll have some toast brought up as well. And I have an idea: When the doctor appears, we'll point him to Diana."

"Brilliant idea!" Lavinia exclaimed.

The lady twinkled at her across the bed. "It's not as if the doctor will know which of you is which. I don't approve of Parth's behavior this evening, and so I told him. He shouldn't have described you as wasting away, nor me as elderly. I prefer to consider myself around thirty-seven. At most, thirty-eight."

"That's a good age," Diana said. "When I am thirty-seven, I will have been married to North for many years." She sighed happily.

When Simpson knocked on the door and announced the doctor's arrival, Lady Knowe ushered him in and gestured toward the bed. "Your patient, Doctor."

"There's a strange man in the room," Diana observed, unnecessarily.

The doctor glanced at her and set his traveling case down within easy reach.

"My dear Lavinia, you must stay away from all hard drink in the future," Lady Knowe informed Diana. She turned to the physician. "Miss Gray had quite a violent fit of coughing, and Mr. Sterling is worried that she has an infection of the lungs. Or consumption. Or something else."

Diana managed to push herself up on her elbows.

"You may listen to my lungs, Doctor. My name is . . . my name is . . . Lavinia Gray!" she finished triumphantly.

"I fear I gave her too much buttercup syrup," Lady Knowe told the doctor. "Excellent for a cough, as I'm sure you know, but somewhat befuddling."

"That woman is intoxicated," the doctor stated. "She also has red hair and a pointed nose."

Diana sat all the way up. "I do not have a pointed nose! That's an insult. No duchess has a pointed nose."

Lavinia had been gazing out the window into the back gardens, but at this exchange she turned about.

"Miss Gray was described to me as a young woman with golden hair and the smile of an angel," the doctor added, a distinctly sardonic note in his voice.

Lady Knowe laughed into the silence that followed his statement. "Darling Parth. One does continue to underestimate the man. No," she told the doctor. "That is your patient on the bed—although you ought to apologize for the insult to her nose. The lady in question has a lovely nose."

Dr. Lancer obediently leaned over Diana, who smiled up at him drowsily.

"It doesn't matter about my nose. He's already agreed to marry me, and he can't back out now, even if he wanted a duchess with a better nose."

"I am glad to hear it." The doctor bent and listened to her lungs, but found nothing wrong with them, to no one's surprise. Then he asked, "May I palpate your chest, Miss Gray?"

Diana glanced over at Lavinia. "Never say I don't love you." She turned back. "Please be gentle; my breasts are quite tender these days."

"Are your menses regular?" the doctor asked, straightening up.

"I don't remember," she answered, closing her eyes.

As the doctor prepared to leave, he took one more look at Diana, now peacefully slumbering, and stated, "Recent speculation suggests that imbibing spirits may inhibit an unborn child's growth."

Lady Knowe took a step forward. "Miss Gray is not carrying a child, and I'll thank you to hold your tongue around an innocent, Doctor!"

"Just so," he said, his face impervious.

"Thank you for coming to our house at this unappealing hour," Lady Knowe said, in a kinder tone. "I am sorry you were summoned here on a fool's errand."

"The health of a future duchess is always important."

Lavinia sighed. "You recognized Diana."

"The popular prints of Miss Belgrave appear to be fairly accurate," the doctor said. "My wife is fancifully inclined, and she collects images of the Wilde family. I believe she feels that Miss Belgrave's life has been a tragic one; she is of the impression that the lady is engaged in menial labor as a governess. I shall be happy to inform her that Miss Belgrave is in *good spirits*, shall we say?"

"Nice pun!" Lavinia said, deciding she liked the doctor.

The doctor looked at Diana, who had rolled on her side and was now fast asleep. "May I suggest that this wedding take place with some celerity?" With that he bowed, bid them good night, and took his leave.

"'Celerity'?" Lady Knowe demanded, once he was gone. "What on earth is that man talking about?"

"It means speed," Lavinia said. She sat down beside her cousin and gave her a gentle nudge. "Diana, wake up."

"No," Diana groaned.

Lady Knowe plumped down opposite Lavinia. "No rest for the wicked!" she said cheerfully.

"That doctor believes you're carrying a *child*," Lavinia said, nudging Diana harder this time.

"There's no chance of that." Diana's voice was calmly certain.

"Oh, thank goodness!" Lavinia exclaimed.

Lady Knowe looked across the bed at her. "Many a child's been born six months after a wedding, my dear. Please don't show me a prudish side. I like you so much."

"I'm not prudish, but I am *very* interested in Diana's wedding gown. Babies change one's figure quite dramatically."

"I hadn't thought of that!" Lady Knowe leaned over and gave Diana a poke. "Wake up, Diana. Most gently bred young ladies have no understanding of their own bodies, and nothing I know about your mother leads me to believe you might be any better informed than the rest."

"Must you both jab me awake? Going about London is more exhausting than being a governess," Diana complained, finally opening her eyes. "My mother was *very* informative. She told my sister and me everything about bedding men."

"Oh, she did, did she?" Lady Knowe said. "Well, let me ask you this, Diana. Did my nephew give you any opportunities to employ the knowledge your mother taught you?"

Silence.

Lavinia rolled her eyes. "I can't believe North! He took advantage of the governess. It's such a hackneyed story."

"I'll tell him you said so," Lady Knowe said, a huge smile spreading over her face. "A *baby*! Well, here's a wonderful thing, and no mistaking it."

"I'm not carrying a child," Diana said, sitting up, alarmed. "It's impossible."

"Then it's a virgin birth," Lady Knowe crowed, clapping her hands. "I have always wanted to witness one of those! Such a confusing part of the Bible and leads to so many questions."

Lavinia laughed. "Much though I love you, Diana, I doubt you are a likely candidate for such an honor."

Diana humphed and pushed herself up against the bedboard. "I may not be a likely candidate, but I'll have you know I went to church twice a week for my entire childhood. Lady Knowe, what on earth is there to question about the conception and birth of Jesus Christ?"

"What about that angel?" Lady Knowe asked, eyebrows waggling. "Gabriel, wasn't it? The one who announced Christ's birth. If I had been Joseph, I would've had a question or two about a shining fellow who miraculously appeared in my lady's boudoir, wings or no."

"You're a heathen," Diana said affectionately.

"I agree, I agree," Lady Knowe said, unrepentant. "Perhaps it's because I would be quite happy to see such a being materialize in *my* boudoir. I can't help having a skeptical mind. It's been a curse, I assure you."

"I do agree that there are holes in the story," Lavinia said, getting into the spirit of the conversation. "Can you imagine how difficult it was for Mary to tell her parents, let alone Joseph, about what was to come?"

"I don't imagine North will be quite as shocked as Joseph must have been," Diana said slowly. "That is, if the doctor is correct. Which he's not."

"Not a virgin birth, then," Lady Knowe said, chuckling. "Just as well, my dear. You are notorious enough, what with appearing in all those prints depicting you as a poor downtrodden servant, seduced by a cruel lord."

"A child will affect your measurements," Lavinia said, her mind racing. "As soon as we've chosen a *modiste* to design your wedding gown and *trousseau*, we'll have a discreet word about the situation. And your corset! Oh, Diana, you should have told me!"

"Told you what?" her cousin exclaimed. "That doctor was mad. Who does he think he is? How could he possibly know such a thing?" She swung her legs over the side of the bed. "Are we having dinner? I'm starving."

"You might be a trifle more generous in the front than you were last week," Lady Knowe said, eyeing Diana's chest.

"More to the point, when's the last time you had your courses?" Lavinia asked bluntly.

Diana's brows furrowed.

"A baby!" Lady Knowe crowed. "Glory be, we're having another little Wilde!"

Chapter Ten

The following day

$\mathcal{L}$avinia, Diana, and Lady Knowe spent the next day visiting *modistes*, and thanks to a snarl of traffic around the Strand, they returned home with scarcely an hour remaining before Parth and the prince were due to escort them to Astley's Amphitheatre.

"It doesn't matter what I look like," Lady Knowe said as the carriage drew up. "I'll throw something on, and go down to the drawing room to receive Parth and the Norwegian. I realized last night that I've met the fellow."

"What is he like?" Diana asked. She was a bit green and had pressed a hand to her middle every time the carriage rounded a corner.

"Wealthy. *Very* wealthy." Lady Knowe gave Lavinia a significant look. "The prince could take a string of emeralds and throw on a few diamonds without a second thought."

"Excellent," Lavinia said.

"Now, you must wear a gown that shows off your apple dumplings," Lady Knowe ordered. "I know you don't want to tell Parth about the stolen jewels, Lavinia, but I would guess that he's caught wind of your lost dowry, probably because he knows everything about finances and fortunes in this country. He's bringing Beck as a present to you, mark my words."

"It's very gallant of him to bring you a present," Diana said, grinning mischievously.

Lavinia was failing miserably to stop feeling humiliated about the fact that Parth—the man she'd asked to marry her—was throwing her a consolation prize, but she put on a huge smile. "Perhaps I will wear a dress from Paris that my mother decreed to be too immodest to be worn in London."

"Perfect!" Lady Knowe cried. "Prince Oskar Beck will be on his knees by the end of the evening, if not the end of the first hour!"

Lavinia would be *damned* if Parth would witness a friend of his reject her the way he—

Well.

Consequently, when Diana knocked on Lavinia's door an hour or so later, her cousin fell back, eyes wide. "You are ravishing!"

Lavinia smiled and turned in a circle. "The Princess of Guémené ordered a gown identical to this one for the opening of her salon."

"After she saw you wearing it, obviously," Diana breathed.

"The style has not yet crossed the Channel." The gown was soft slate-blue silk, wrapped closely around her. Swaths of creamy lace were interwoven in front, barely covering her chest; a keen observer could peek at the curve of her breasts. Lavinia's favorite effect was the lace around her neck, which stiffened into an upright collar.

That style had made Queen Elizabeth look majestic, but on Lavinia it functioned like a signpost, drawing all eyes straight down to her breasts. Subtlety had not been the designer's aim.

"Do you see all the false pearls I'm wearing?" she asked, an ironic note in her voice. She had ropes of them around her neck and woven through her hair. "My mother likely sold the real ones years ago."

"Irrelevant," Diana breathed, shaking her head. "Prince Oskar won't be able to look away from your dumplings."

"*Apple* dumplings," Lavinia said, smiling.

"Even mentioning food makes me feel ill," Diana confessed. "Will you forgive me, Lavinia, if I don't accompany you tonight? As much as I'd like to meet the prince, I am longing to go to bed."

"Of course," Lavinia cried, giving her a swift hug.

She made her way downstairs, and entered the drawing room feeling as if she were wearing a particularly splendid suit of armor. Not that she wanted to attract Parth's attention, but . . . she *did*.

She told herself that she meant to lure the prince, but inside, she knew the truth. More than anything, she wanted to make Parth feel desire for her, along with regret that he had refused her hand in marriage. And she wanted him to take back his remark that she was "wasting away."

She didn't merely walk into the drawing room. She sauntered, steady on her high-heeled slippers, the roll of her hips telling any red-blooded man in the vicinity that a woman was coming.

Not a lady: a *woman*.

Parth was standing beside Lady Knowe, and on the other side of him was a tall fellow in a cream silk suit with pale blue trim and a blue cape attached to one shoulder.

The prince turned as she entered, causing the cape to swirl around his legs. His eyes lit up with gratifying swiftness.

Excellent.

As Lady Knowe introduced her, His Highness bent himself in half in a deep bow. "Miss Gray, this is indeed a pleasure." The prince's voice was deep and smooth as a Norwegian fjord.

What's more, the man was truly striking, with piercing eyes the color of dawn. Parth had found her a legitimate candidate for marriage. It was absurd to feel a trickle of resentment.

"There ought to be a law against women as beautiful as yourself," he said, almost under his breath, as Lavinia held out her hand to be kissed.

"I believe," Lady Knowe said with a naughty laugh, "there may be one outlawing Lavinia's gown."

Naturally, this quip drew all eyes to her gown—or rather, her breasts. No, "all eyes" wasn't quite true. Parth's stayed on her face.

"You know how it is," Lavinia said lightly. "Laws of that sort are merely suggestions, meant to be ignored."

"The law would be in place to protect gentlemen from making fools of themselves," Prince Oskar said. His smile crinkled the corners of his eyes in a charming manner.

"Since the law doesn't exist, you can make a fool of yourself at will," Parth said.

Lady Knowe elbowed him. "Don't be a grumpy fellow, Parth." She turned to Prince Oskar. "If we happen to come across a puddle tonight, you will have to sweep off your cloak and throw it on the ground, because Parth will allow our toes to get wet."

"I don't know how you imagine I could toss down a cloak I don't own," Parth said. *And will never own* hung, unspoken, in the air.

The comment was near to an insult, but Prince Oskar just grinned at him. He had nice white teeth, Lavinia registered.

"Believe me, Lady Knowe, Parth is an old friend, and my memories of him from school concur with your assumption." He glanced sideways at Lavinia, an engaging twinkle in his eye. "All puddles are mine, Miss Gray. Although I may choose to carry you across rather than sacrifice my cloak."

She had to smile at that.

"We must leave or we'll miss the entertainment," Parth said sharply.

Lady Knowe took his elbow and escorted him toward the door, saying something *sotto voce* that Lavinia guessed was a reminder that the prince was his guest.

"I've never seen an equestrian act before; have you?" she asked Prince Oskar.

"We are mad for horses in Norway," he said, smiling down at her and holding out his arm. "As a young boy, I waited excitedly for my older brothers and cousins to compete against each other, even if informally."

"Did you also compete when you came of age?"

He nodded. "Norwegian children are put on horse-back as youngsters. I participated in my first event at eight years old."

"Was it a race?" Lavinia asked, fascinated to imagine this large man as a boy, galloping around a ring.

"No, it involved taking my pony over a series of obstacles," he said. "I was most proud of the final moment, in which I circled the ring standing on my pony's back. My mother was furious."

"I can imagine she was! It sounds terribly dangerous."

"The exercise was part of the training of candidates for knighthood—devised back when knights really did whip off their cloaks to protect a lady's slippers."

"Naturally," Lavinia said, grinning. "A knight in full armor must be able to clamber up on his saddle and go round a ring."

He laughed, a sound as pleasant as his voice. "As a rule, Miss Gray, men are inclined toward showing off before ladies, whether in armor or mere cloaks."

ASTLEY'S AMPHITHEATRE WAS a large, graceful building fashioned with rows of seats enclosing an arena. On arrival they were escorted directly to a box draped in blue velvet, next to the ring.

"The royal box!" Lady Knowe exclaimed. "May I take it this is your doing, Your Highness, or has my darling Parth leapt into the nobility while I turned my attention?"

"I happen to know that your darling Parth refused a title a month or so ago," Prince Oskar said, smirking at Parth's irritated look. "The Prince of Wales told me himself. The king is apparently still disgruntled."

Lady Knowe swatted Parth with her fan. "Naughty boy! I suppose you didn't think twice."

"No," Parth stated.

"Despite His Majesty's vexation, he very kindly invited us to use his box," Prince Oskar said, leading Lavinia to the front.

She seated herself beside Prince Oskar, with Parth on the far side of Lady Knowe. She certainly didn't want him to watch as she wooed Prince Oskar.

Wooed?

Beguiled?

Whatever she was doing, it proved effective. Between thrilling acts of equestrian daring, acrobatic feats, and even a dog who braved a flaming hoop, Lavinia learned a great deal about Norse mythology.

It was genuinely interesting and she enjoyed herself enormously, other than the moment when she happened to glance to the side, only to catch Parth staring at her.

He had no right to look so sardonic. She turned back to the prince and treated him to her best laugh, the low and throaty one that made men melt into a puddle.

She could feel Parth's disdain, even with her back turned, but the look in Prince Oskar's eyes was wholly admiring. "Do you by any chance speak French?" he asked. He not only respected her; he thought she was intelligent.

"Yes, I speak French fluently," she replied. The prince was thrilled to hear it. French, it seemed, was the second language in the courts occupied by his family: Norway, Sweden, Denmark . . .

By evening's end, Lavinia had Prince Oskar right where she wanted him—*if* she wanted him. And she did, more or less.

As a prince, he could definitely sweep her mother's crimes under the rug. He was friends with the king of

England, for goodness' sake! No mother-in-law of his would ever be sent to prison.

Unfortunately, he was returning to Norway the following day. But she had the feeling that his insistence that he planned to travel back to England without delay was sincere.

Parth and Prince Oskar escorted Lavinia and Lady Knowe into the townhouse, and the prince lingered, displaying an altogether flattering reluctance to leave. It should have been a triumphant moment when he bent over her hand to bid her good night, the slightly dazed look in his eyes confirming her opinion. Prince Oskar had just met the woman he'd been waiting for.

She summoned just the right smile in response: friendly, charming, modest, engaging, seductive . . . all of it at once. She was *everything* he wanted, in one pretty, French-speaking package.

The door had no sooner closed behind Prince Oskar than Lady Knowe thumped Parth on the back and trumpeted, "This is exactly why I tell everyone who will listen that my darling Parth can solve any problem!"

He scowled at her. "If you are suggesting that Lavinia should marry Beck, I disagree. He's grown into a conceited ass."

"So now I'm 'Lavinia'? Surely you mean 'Miss Gray'?" Lavinia asked.

"Conceited?" Lady Knowe snorted at the same moment. "What man *isn't* conceited? Did you imagine that he would ask Lavinia for her opinions?"

"He babbled about inconsequential nonsense," Parth said. "Thor and Freya—and a cart drawn by goats? Lavinia isn't interested in foolish stories from Norse mythology."

"True, it's my friend Willa who is interested in ancient manuscripts," Lavinia said. "All the same, I found the stories about gods and goddesses very entertaining."

Her voice must have been a bit more revealing than was prudent, because Lady Knowe announced that it was time to retire to bed. "We have finally chosen a *modiste*, Madame Prague," she told Parth. "Tomorrow we are returning to her atelier to choose a design for the wedding gown."

"Shall we make an arrangement to visit Vauxhall?" Parth asked. "I thought I might invite Lord Jeremy Roden to accompany us."

Lady Knowe raised an eyebrow. "Lavinia, my dear, have you met Lord Jeremy?"

She shook her head.

"He's an old friend of the family. The boys have always been close, and he went to war with North. A good man, one of the best."

"Rich as Croesus," Parth added. His voice was absolutely flat.

Lavinia winced. *He* was the one who'd offered to introduce her to gentlemen, who promised to help her marry. And now Parth was acting as if the whole endeavor were beneath his contempt.

As if *she* were beneath his contempt.

Words hovered on the tip of her tongue: Had she any other choice? Could *she* begin a bank, or voyage to China and bring back tea, or do any of the other things his sex allowed him to do?

Would she be a better woman if she wasn't so interested in corsets?

Lady Knowe's arm tightened on hers, and she steered her from the room before Lavinia could open her mouth. Lady Knowe called over her shoulder as they went. "Vauxhall, yes; Jeremy, yes; and don't forget, you *must* bring along the contessa."

She propelled the two of them directly up the stairs, chattering so incessantly that Lavinia couldn't hear herself think. Not until she was alone in her bedchamber did she realize that Lady Knowe had gleaned her secret, the way she felt about Parth.

The lady hadn't allowed Lavinia to embarrass herself.

This time, at least.

Chapter Eleven

July 13, 1780

S ince the doctor's visit, Lady Knowe had spent a good deal of her free time considering possible names for the baby.

"Amos. Amos Wilde," she said at breakfast, carefully tapping her soft-boiled egg so that the shell cracked in a perfect circle. "No, he sounds like a farmer. Athenio, Atreus, Atticus, Attila—"

"Wasn't Attila a warrior of some sort?" Lavinia asked, seating herself.

"Asmoroth," Lady Knowe said. "Asmody, Askew, Arthiopa."

"Where are you getting these bizarre names?" Diana asked. "And why do they all begin with A?"

"You told us you want many babies," Lady Knowe reminded her.

"Not twenty-six, and certainly not burdened with such outlandish names! Do you know what happened to me at dawn?"

"No," Lavinia answered. "Dare I ask?"

"I threw up," Diana said. She put down her spoon. "I am too queasy to eat this egg. I'm going back to bed, Lavinia. I'm sorry. Perhaps I can try again later."

"All right," Lavinia said. "I planned to visit a tailor in an hour or two and choose patterns for riding habits for you and the duchess. Do you think you will be able to join me?"

"If I am not still hanging over a chamber pot," Diana said gloomily. "I wrote to North and asked him to come to London. He should have to suffer along with me."

"No gentlemen in your bedchamber until you are married," Lady Knowe said.

"Too late for that rule," Diana said, pushing away her egg and picking up a piece of dry toast. "I didn't mention the baby in my letter to North." She frowned at both of them. "I will tell him in person."

Lady Knowe nodded. "I shall send a note to Parth and put off our visit to Vauxhall until North arrives. I'm sure North will want to meet Parth's contessa, and Lord Jeremy is one of his closest friends."

She nodded at a footman, who poured Diana some fresh tea. "You must drink sufficiently to make up for all those liquids you're losing."

"I don't know if tea will agree with my stomach," Diana said dubiously, eyeing the steaming cup.

"Why don't I visit the tailor by myself?" Lavinia suggested. "This afternoon, we could meet at Felton's Emporium and select fabric for both habits."

Lady Knowe waved a toast finger at her. "Is that a Parisian morning gown you have on today?"

Lavinia smiled. "It began that way." She looked down at her morning gown, a garment fashioned from silk the color of spring leaves. "It was serviceable but rather staid. Annie and I added these pink ribbons to the skirt."

"Green and pink together." Lady Knowe shook her head. "I'd never have considered it, but you look marvelous."

"*Au courant*," Diana agreed, then clapped a hand over her mouth and dashed for the door.

Lady Knowe picked up another toast finger. "There are times when I wish I'd had offspring, but I invariably come to my senses. Do you plan to wear that fabulous walking costume with the large buttons today, my dear? I saw a glimpse of it yesterday when Annie was taking it for pressing."

Lavinia nodded. "It had a blue under-bodice, but we refashioned it in cream, which offers a more flattering contrast to the apricot skirts."

"The buttons are very dashing."

"They are covered in the apricot silk, edged with silver filigree."

"I need a new walking gown, and I'd like the same design, though in a different color. Could you perhaps order me one from the tailor, and choose the fabric?"

"Of course!" Lavinia beamed. "Would you consider forest green?"

"Green?" Lady Knowe wrinkled her nose.

"Yes," Lavinia said decisively, "to be worn with aubergine boots that lace in front."

"Did you know that aubergines are called eggplants in other parts of the world?" Lady Knowe asked. "Purple and green? I already look like a string bean, Lavinia."

"You will be the most fashionable bean in high society," Lavinia teased, and then ran away before she was pelted with toast fingers.

By the time Lavinia left the tailor's, the clear July sky had been replaced by a pelting rain that showed no sign of easing. Much as she would have loved to curl up at home with a good book, she had a job to do, and commissions to earn.

She was glowing with happiness: the tailor had heard from Mr. Felton about Diana's *trousseau* and he promptly offered her a commission on every garment she ordered from him. Gathering her umbrella, she dashed across the muddy sidewalk into the hackney waiting to take her to Felton's, where Diana was due to meet her.

The bell over the door rang as she entered, and Mr. Felton hastened to her side. "Miss Gray, what a pleasure to see you!"

Lavinia smiled at him. Odd though it might be, Mr. Felton was fast becoming one of her closest friends.

"You must have some tea immediately," he said. "It's not cold outside, but it is wretchedly wet."

"That would be lovely," she replied. "The weather is beastly, is it not?"

As Mr. Felton turned to order tea from an assistant, the bell over the door rang again. A lady ran into the shop squealing with laughter, the gentleman at her shoulder holding a large umbrella over her head.

The umbrella, Lavinia recognized immediately, was from Maison Antoine on rue Saint-Denis in Paris. No other umbrella makers made such clever use of striped fabrics, and the small bobbles hanging around the edge were delightful.

The gentleman turned away to shake the water from the umbrella, and said something over his shoulder as he did so.

Lavinia stiffened all over. She would know that voice anywhere.

The lady answered in an Italian accent—at least, Lavinia assumed it must be an Italian accent.

The contessa.

And Parth.

Lavinia gripped the edge of the counter so tightly her gloves were in danger of ripping. Mr. Felton had returned, and was talking about painted cottons. She watched as Parth helped his lady remove her pelisse. He took the garment from her, rather than allow the attendant to touch her.

Lavinia was appalled to find that she was baring her teeth, for all the world like a rabid cur. It reminded her of the time when Willa had almost poured a cup of tea over Alaric's head. But Alaric had been wooing Willa at the time; Lavinia had no right to feel possessive of Parth.

Parth handed the contessa's pelisse to Mr. Felton's assistant, and surveyed the room as he removed his hat.

He looked straight at Lavinia—and his eyes skated past her, oblivious.

It was true that she had spent a good deal more time ogling Parth than he had her. *If* he'd ever ogled her.

But he hadn't even recognized her! And he'd just seen her a few days ago with Prince Oskar.

She might have stopped breathing, just for a moment or two. What would she say to a friend who found herself in this situation? "Cheer up, buttercup?" No, because that would be unfeeling, and her hypothetical friend might be truly sad, as if she had lost something dear.

A stupid dream that she had treasured without ever letting herself believe it, because it was too impossible.

Feeling unsteady, Lavinia leaned against the long wooden counter and watched as Mr. Felton bustled over to greet his new customers.

Parth's eyes snapped back to her face.

Ah. So he'd finally recognized the woman he'd met . . . oh . . . a hundred times. His brows drew together, and he started toward her, remembering that a lady had her hand in the crook of his elbow only when she protested.

They began walking in her direction, but Mr. Felton diverted them with an offer of tea. Lavinia resisted the impulse to check the tilt of her bonnet. A fluffy plume bobbed at the corner of her vision, quite as dashing as the one the contessa wore.

Parth nodded abruptly to Mr. Felton, then turned and strode toward her, leaving his lady talking to the shopkeeper. There was only one word for his expression.

Apoplectic.

In the time it would have taken to say the word softly, all those lovely syllables drawn out, Parth arrived in front of her.

"What the hell has happened to you?" he demanded in a low, furious voice. "You look even worse than last week."

Marvelous.

She opened her mouth to defend herself, but Parth hadn't finished. "It wasn't a mere bout of influenza, was it? Damn it, Aunt Knowe lied to me."

"How are you, Mr. Sterling?" she asked. "As a matter of fact, I am fully recovered from my illness, as you'll remember inasmuch as you summoned a doctor to my side."

"You didn't allow him to listen to your lungs," Parth said, his expression darkening still more.

Lavinia saw the contessa making her way toward them. Her conte must have left her a fortune. Her skirts glittered with gold thread, and five ropes of pearls graced her neck. She was outrageously beautiful, like a maiden in a painting waiting to be ravished by Jupiter, all luxuriant curves and skin like a flower petal.

No wonder Parth was in love with her.

There was nothing English about her whatsoever.

"Good afternoon!" the lady said, in the most delightful accent Lavinia had ever heard. "Parth!" she prompted. "Will you introduce me to your friend, *caro*?"

The woman addressed him as "Parth." And *"caro,"* whatever that meant. Lavinia could guess.

A million years ago, in a fit of longing for a reaction from an uninterested gentleman, *Lavinia* had begun addressing Parth by his first name. It had exasperated him to no end.

Clearly, he and the contessa had a different understanding.

"By all means," Parth said. "Contessa, may I introduce Miss Lavinia Gray? Miss Gray is a very good friend of Lady Alaric Wilde, whom you've met. Miss Gray, this is Elisa Tornabuoni Guicciardini, the Contessa di Casone, an acquaintance of mine from Florence, Italy."

Lavinia dropped into a deep curtsy. When she straightened, the contessa was beaming. "Your bonnet is lovely, Miss Gray. That plume is *incantevole, bellissima*!"

"Your hat is also ravishing, and I couldn't help noticing that your umbrella came from my favorite Parisian shop."

They smiled at each other with the mutual pleasure of women recognizing a kindred spirit, at least as regards umbrellas—and umbrellas, to Lavinia's mind, revealed a great deal about their owners.

"Are you unaccompanied?" Parth demanded, seemingly trying to find something wrong with Lavinia's presence, as well as her health.

"I am waiting for Miss Diana Belgrave," Lavinia said, including the contessa in her smile. "Diana is in the process of assembling her *trousseau*."

"I have been visiting mantua-makers," the contessa confided. "But this city is much larger than Firenze. There, everyone comes to me. Here, I am going in circles, very confused."

"I told her that they would happily visit her, if she wished," Parth growled.

"Parth, *caro*, you might return to the carriage and work on the notes you are making for that bank meeting," the contessa said, giving him a sweet smile.

Many years ago, Lavinia had a nanny who sent her to the "naughty corner" when she misbehaved. Her lips twitched with amusement at the memory. Or, to be more precise, the similarity to the contessa's suggestion.

Parth seemed indifferent to his dismissal, his face as imperturbable as ever. He bowed, took his hat from the attendant who magically appeared at his shoulder, and walked out. The contessa didn't watch him go.

"Won't you call me Elisa?" she asked. "I am to live in England, you see, so I am—how do you say?—

embracing the ways of you *Inglesi*. So much less formal than we *Fiorentini*."

Elisa was not just beautiful and elegant. She was clearly kind, probably a better person than Lavinia in every way.

"English is so difficult," the contessa continued. "I have few people to talk to, except for Parth. I am starving for conversation!"

Lavinia could see that.

Elisa kept going without pausing for breath. "My husband was very old and quiet. I was in mourning for a year. Then I leaved."

"Left," Lavinia amended.

"*Left*. Thank you. These irregular conjugations are difficult." Elisa's face shone with delight. "Does your friend Miss Belgravè bring her fiancé with her?"

Lavinia couldn't help from laughing. "North would flatly refuse."

Elisa frowned. "Her fiancé is called North?"

"It is a shortened form of one of his given names," Lavinia explained.

"North, as in, 'north and south'?"

"It's what he prefers to be called."

"It would seem very peculiar to address one's husband by a direction. Though"—Elisa giggled suddenly—"it might change one's opinion of the North Pole!"

Lavinia felt a slow smile spreading across her face. "Contessa! You are wicked!"

"It is true," Elisa said complacently. "It is for this that I come to England. Because I am not one of the Florentine matrons who are happy knotting lace and gossiping. I am too wicked. Is 'wicked' a very bad thing?"

"'Naughty' is more exact," Lavinia amended.

"'*Cattiva*' in Italian." And then, when Lavinia tried out the word, "You don't speak Italian. French instead?"

"*Oui*," Lavinia said. "I lived in Paris for two years."

Mr. Felton joined them, and Elisa treated him to her blinding smile. His step hitched, but he managed to stay upright. "I should like to see material for a riding habit," Elisa told him. "I saw a design that I liked, but the fabric samples offered by the *modiste* were of low quality. I decided to purchase my own fabric and have it sent to her."

"I have a woolen superfine, from Norwich," Mr. Felton said. "It is not for all tastes, as it is a cobalt blue with a large, pale yellow floral pattern."

Elisa's eyebrows flew up. "I should like to see that."

Half an hour later, five more bolts of fabric had been laid over the counter to be fingered and assessed, and Diana had still not arrived. Lavinia paused in the middle of a spirited discussion of whether the cuffs of the contessa's riding costume should be a dull gold or blue with gold braid, realizing that she liked Parth's intended wife.

Truly liked her.

Elisa and Parth would be a wonderful couple. Their children would have loopy curls and giddy smiles. They would be able to babble in Italian and English.

"If you'll excuse me," she said, breaking into Elisa's interrogation of Mr. Felton, "I'll just pop out of doors for a breath of fresh air."

"The rear door opens onto a portico that will shelter you from the rain, Miss Gray," Mr. Felton said. "It faces a quiet street, whereas you might be splashed if you leave by the main door." He signaled to an assistant.

Elisa's mouth drooped slightly.

"I shall return directly," Lavinia assured the contessa. She knew what loneliness looked like; she had felt it often after moving to Paris.

The rain had not diminished, and she hesitated in the doorway for a moment. Even a small amount of moisture could ruin her elegant hat. At length, she pulled out her hatpins, handed the hat to the assistant, and walked out under the portico. She motioned to the man to close the door behind her, and then she was alone.

Whereupon she gave herself a stern, albeit silent, lecture. She *would* be happy for Elisa and Parth, as she was for Diana and North—and had been for Willa and Alaric, for that matter. It was merely the shock. And, if she was completely honest, the disappointment.

Her old life seemed to lie in shards around her feet. Among other things . . . she had to make new friends.

She needed at least one friend who wasn't buying a *trousseau*.

At the thought, she stepped out from under the shelter of the portico, closed her eyes, and tipped back her head, letting the warm rain fall on her face. Mr. Felton would be shocked when she returned inside, but she didn't care.

She felt peaceful for the first time in weeks—at least, until large hands caught around her shoulders, gently shaking her back into the world.

"Lavinia, what in God's name are you doing?"

She blinked open wet lashes. The cocked hat Parth had worn into Felton's must have been left in his carriage along with his coat. Rain was splashing down on his thick hair and white linen shirt.

"I'm standing in the rain, just as you see."

Parth was regarding her with familiar, simmering fury. She glowered back at him. "Remove your hands from my person, if you please."

"You have been unwell," he barked, as if she hadn't said a word. "You should be in bed eating a warm chicken soup. Instead, you're standing in a dirty London rain, which might make you even more ill."

During those weeks together at Lindow, Lavinia had tried her best to provoke him, but she saw now that she'd missed a foolproof tactic: Get sick, get wet.

"I'm perfectly fine," she told him, blinking more raindrops from her eyelashes.

A sound perilously close to a growl came out of him.

Lavinia's gaze had drifted to his chest, because his wet shirt was clinging to every muscle, but she returned it to his face. He was scowling. Again.

She sighed. "I'm fine, Parth. It's been a long day, and I needed a bit of fresh air. I shall return to Elisa, and ask Mr. Felton for a towel. She's lovely, by the way."

"You are *tired*? It's only three in the afternoon."

She'd been up at dawn making lists, but that was neither here nor there. "I've missed my nap," she said instead. "There's nothing better than cuddling up, falling asleep, losing the afternoon."

Something flickered in his eyes and then died. "The anatomy of a lady's day," he said flatly. "When did you last eat?"

"Luncheon." It was a lie, but lying was becoming easier by the day.

His mouth twitched.

"Very well, you caught me out," she admitted. "I came straight from a tailor and had no time to eat a meal. But please don't be preachy about it. I'll go inside and say farewell to Elisa—did I tell you that I like her very much?—and return home."

His jaw was clenched.

"Please, just return to your carriage and Elisa will join you presently."

He ignored this. "Where is your carriage?"

"I took a hackney."

"You took a hackney. You took a public carriage for hire, one that could be driven by *anyone*. Your driver could look at you and know that he had a gold mine. He could demand more than shillings." His voice had gone quiet and even, and it turned out that Parth's "quiet" voice was more fearsome than his bellow.

His fingers bit into her shoulders. She'd forgotten he was still holding her, evidence of how flustered she was.

She wriggled, trying to free herself. "Let go."

He ignored this as well; his hands tightened even more. "Lavinia, something is wrong with you. You are gaunt. You must see a doctor."

"For goodness' sake," she bit out. "We both know you don't find me attractive, Parth, but you needn't harp on the subject. Many, many people have told me that I look more beautiful than I did when I debuted!"

"They are wrong," he said flatly.

Her stomach knotted. "Just what a woman wants to hear," she managed.

"What do you mean I don't find you attractive?" he roared.

Rain ran down her forehead as she looked up at him. "I don't believe we need to itemize the evidence, do you? Look, I lost some weight after falling ill. I'll be fine in a few months."

His eyes burned down into hers. The problem with the way he was gripping her—well, there was more than just one—was that even here, in the rain, she felt safe because he was nearby. She twisted away again, turning toward Felton's rear door.

He pulled her back, too sharply. "The hell I don't find you attractive."

Lavinia froze.

"There's not a man in this city who isn't ravenous for you, Lavinia." His face was hard, his eyes burning with desire.

Yes: *desire.*

And then his lips were on hers, his tongue deep in her mouth before her mind caught up to his words. Their bodies came together with a slap of wet cloth, and one of his hands slid down her back and trapped her against him, pulling her against the lower part of his body.

What she felt was unmistakable. A hard . . . *cock,* to use the word that ladies weren't supposed to know.

Lavinia had never felt such a thing before—her previous fourteen kisses had been wan, polite encounters in comparison. She should have been shocked. Slapped him, perhaps. Instead, her treacherous body melted even closer. Without meaning to, she whimpered.

At that small sound, he kissed her harder, deeper. It wasn't a gentleman's kiss; it was a raw, sensual exploration.

He tasted like rain. But she could also taste frustration and lust, the same lust that was burning through her, making her tremble from head to foot and wind her arms around his neck as if their bodies weren't already as close as they could be.

She had never yielded to her other suitors. They had kissed her, and she had observed how it felt even as it was happening. But this time, she succumbed. She yielded. In a greedy panic, she surrendered to him, as if opposition might make him stop kissing her. As if that would starve her in truth.

Which is when he made a harsh sound and pulled his head away.

Lavinia opened her eyes.

Too stunned to grapple with her pride, she searched his face. His skin was a warmer brown than that of most gentlemen; she'd never seen him blush with anger or shame. But now his color had deepened.

"You shouldn't have done that," she said faintly, stepping back. Her heart was thudding in the base of her throat.

His eyes remained dispassionate, whereas she felt shaken to her core. "You said that I didn't find you attractive." He sounded rational, as if she'd asked him to prove a theorem, and in response he had scratched a proof on paper.

Reaching out, he pushed a heavy lock of wet hair behind her ear. His fingers, rough and callused, brushed her temple.

"So this was a . . . what was it?"

"It was nothing. I merely wanted you to understand that you are desirable, even now, thin and wringing wet." His mouth eased. "Perhaps even more so."

In the silence between them, she heard rain pattering on Felton's slate roof. She was trying to sort through her feelings. Was it stupid to feel hurt? She was tired of being confronted with his indifference, not to mention his brutal honesty about her shortcomings, physical and otherwise.

Apparently, he had been trying to be kind. She shouldn't take that amiss and be insulted. It would be childish.

"Kiss number fifteen," she said, trying for a cheery tone.

His eyes glittered, and she had the sudden feeling that mentioning her previous kisses might not have been a good idea.

"Before he sailed, Prince Oskar thanked me for introducing him to his future wife," Parth said, out of the blue.

Lavinia was staring at him, surprised into silence, when the back door opened and Elisa's head emerged. Her mouth widened into a beaming smile.

"Hello!" she cried. "Here you are! Is this an English game you are playing? In Italy we try to stay away from bad weather for fear of a *frescata*, but this is fun!" She bounded out into the rain, turning in a circle, her palms up. *"Molto divertente!"*

"I am grateful to have met the prince," Lavinia said to Parth at last, shaking off the shameful, sweet ache that lingered in her body.

He nodded and then turned to the contessa, and smiled at her the way he hadn't smiled at Lavinia— ever. "Shall we escort Miss Gray to tea, Elisa? She hasn't eaten."

Now she was 'Miss Gray' again. Of course.

"You will remember that I am awaiting Miss Belgrave," Lavinia said, maintaining a smile as she led the way back into the shop. She took her pelisse from an assistant and wrapped herself in it, covering the wet silk clinging to her figure.

Through the plate-glass windows looking out onto Oxford Street, Lavinia glimpsed the Duke of Lindow's carriage pulling up in front of Felton's. Diana's timing, however unwitting, was perfect. Lavinia dropped a curtsy like a manic butterfly.

"I must say goodbye. Elisa, this has been a pleasure. I hope we will meet again soon."

"We will!" Elisa cried. "We are going to Vauxhall together." Never mind that they'd just met; Elisa swooped in and kissed her cheek.

"I'm not sure if I will join you," Lavinia said. "I have many engagements."

"We will choose an evening when you are free," Elisa insisted.

Parth was staring at Lavinia with his usual somber look.

An assistant opened the front door, so Lavinia escaped without bidding farewell to Mr. Felton. She would apologize some other time.

"I'm so sorry to be late," Diana said from the door of the carriage. Lavinia almost bowled her over on her way into the vehicle.

"Please let's go," she gasped, throwing herself onto a seat. She jerked her chin at the duke's groom and he closed the door.

"Aren't we going inside?" Diana asked, toppling into the opposite seat.

"No," Lavinia managed, trying to stop panting. "I told the coachman to take us home."

"Home? But why? It took me two hours to get here from the townhouse," Diana cried.

The carriage jerked into motion, and Lavinia welcomed it with such relief that she felt dizzy.

"Parth is in there," she said, her voice coming out queer and husky, cutting off Diana's explanation about the traffic near Oxford Street.

"Ah," Diana said. "With his contessa?"

Lavinia nodded. "Do you know if they are betrothed? I believe she is acquiring a *trousseau*."

"I don't know for certain," Diana said. "What is she like?"

"She's perfect for him," Lavinia said, leaning back and feeling inexpressibly exhausted. "Her name is Elisa, and she's utterly charming."

"That's what North said."

"Perfect for Parth."

"Suitable for Sterling?" Diana countered, with a giggle.

Lavinia felt as if her heart was trying to beat through a flood of treacle. "I'm not funning," she said, waving her hand. "You'll love her; I did." She closed her eyes. "I'm so tired."

"Why are we running away, Lavinia?"

Lavinia opened one eye. Diana looked worried. They might not have been very close during their debut, but now they had become something like sisters. Not that Lavinia could truly say that, since Diana had lost her little sister, and Lavinia had never had a sister or a brother.

But she imagined a sister would be like Diana.

"I already selected the fabric for your outerwear," Lavinia said. "Mr. Felton will send the fabrics on to the mantua-maker."

Thankfully, Diana dropped the question of Lavinia's escape from Felton's. "Will you receive a commission? Oh, and I've been meaning to ask: Has your solicitor produced a figure as regards the money your mother took from Willa's estate?"

"Yes," Lavinia said. She bit her lip. "I shall be able to repay it and the emeralds from the clothing the

Wilde family is ordering, because the tailor offered me a commission as well. Oh, Diana, am I taking advantage of friends?"

"Certainly not, because we are paying precisely what we would otherwise," Diana said. "I need a gown and a *trousseau* fit for a duchess, and there is no one else who could provide it for me."

"Lady Knowe has ordered so much, and the duchess keeps writing and asking for more garments. She has decided that she and His Grace will be dressed as sea gods for the masquerade party."

"What on earth does a sea god wear?" Diana asked.

"Blue-green costumes," Lavinia said. "I came up with an idea last night for using tulle so that it would look like sea foam. I have to speak to Madame Prague about it. At any rate, Ophelia also wants me to order clothing for the children."

Diana leaned forward and took Lavinia's hand. "The Wildes are *wildly* wealthy, if you'll forgive me all the alliteration. They would buy clothes for the wedding and the ball, no matter whether you were involved or not. Your commission is subtracted from the merchants' fees."

"Yes, but . . ."

"Imagine how frequently they must have been defrauded by unscrupulous tradesmen," Diana said. "Her Grace often sends off to London for a new gown, with no regard for the cost of the fabric or trimmings. I would expect you are going to provide them clothing that will cost less than they are used to paying."

Lavinia brightened. "That may be true. I am certain that your mother paid double the worth of your gowns during our debut."

"Without question," Diana said. Then, "Lavinia, you'll have to see the contessa when we go to Vauxhall."

Apparently her cousin grasped exactly why Lavinia had dashed out of Felton's in the rain.

"Lord Jeremy Roden will be there," Lavinia said, not bothering to pretend. "With luck he will be wildly infatuated with me."

Diana shook her head. "Why didn't you tell me that you were in love with Parth when we came up with the plan to ask for his hand, Lavinia? I never would have sent you to his bedchamber."

Lavinia dropped her gaze to her fingers, which were busy pleating and repleating her damp pelisse. "He's never thought me interesting. If there was any chance, I had to take it." She raised her eyes and gave Diana an unsteady smile. "The fact is, you offered an excuse, and I took it. I wouldn't have had the courage without your prompting."

Diana moved to the seat beside her and put her arms around Lavinia. "I want you to be as happy as I am."

"I will be," Lavinia promised, hugging her back. "Parth would make a wretched husband. In fact, I *pity* Elisa."

Diana held her tongue, and Lavinia knew why.

Sisters don't point out obvious lies.

Chapter Twelve

July 27, 1780

The next fortnight passed in a flurry of visits to cobblers and milliners, but day by day, Lavinia was happily aware that they were making progress. By the day that North was due to arrive, her notes regarding the *trousseau* had swollen to haystack proportions, so she remained home to catalogue every item, while the bride-to-be bounced from window to window, peering from the morning room out at Mayfair.

"What can possibly be taking North so long?" Diana moaned. "The groom he sent ahead said we could expect the carriage by ten in the morning!"

"You know what the press of carriages is like in London," Lavinia said, not looking up.

"I hate London," Diana said. She hiccupped inelegantly, and wrapped her arms around her waist. "No, no, no! I've thrown up three times today."

Lavinia winced with sympathy. "Perhaps if you sit down?"

"The only thing that helps is Lady Knowe's peppermint tea," Diana said, ringing the bell as she plumped down on the settee beside Lavinia. "I can't wait to tell him. Do you think he'll guess?"

"Absolutely not," Lavinia said, glancing at Diana's still-slender waist.

"I mean when he opens his present." Carriage wheels rattled in the street and Diana jumped up and ran to the window. "He's here!"

Lavinia went to the same window and watched as her cousin flew out the front door and hurled herself at her fiancé. North's arms closed around her, and Lavinia caught just a glimpse of his face as he bent his head to kiss his fiancée.

Right there in broad daylight, in the middle of Mayfair, where any number of people from polite society might see them.

Obviously, he didn't care.

Lord Roland Northbridge Wilde, future Duke of Lindow, didn't give a damn.

It gave Lavinia a queer feeling. North was embracing Diana so tenderly—and it wasn't because of the baby; he had no idea about that.

It was because Diana was precious to him. In herself. In everything about her.

Lavinia discovered she was pressing her forehead to the cool glass, and made herself turn away and cross the room. She had never before understood that loneliness doesn't come from nowhere.

It follows moments in which one's own poverty was exposed. Not lack of money, but lack of love. She'd written another letter to her mother that morning, although Lady Gray hadn't yet responded to a single missive.

Diana and North entered the room, saving Lavinia from a bout of withering self-pity. "North is here!"

Diana cried happily. "And just look: He brought me paintings made by Godfrey and Artie! This is clearly Fitzy." She held up a bluish blob that was graced with a spreading tail.

"That one is Artie's," North said, moving toward Lavinia. "Godfrey told me his is a portrait of one of the ducal pigs."

"Hmm. It is pink," Diana said, looking at the other. "I miss them both so much!" She put down the paintings and picked up a silk-wrapped parcel.

Lavinia curtsied before North, who bent and kissed her cheek, because she was "part of the Wilde family now."

If only.

"This is for you," Diana said to North. She held the parcel out with a huge smile.

"It's not my birthday," he observed, taking it. "Hmm, it's soft." He squeezed it, giving Lavinia a squinty look as he did so. "This isn't a garment designed to replace those fancy embroidered vests that my valet stole, is it?"

"Lavinia had something to do with it, but no," Diana cried. "Please open it, North!"

"You might wait until Lady Knowe joins us," Lavinia interjected.

He looked up, surprised. "Is this a family occasion?"

At that, Diana broke into a stream of giggles. Lavinia reached for the bell, intending to ask Simpson to call for Lady Knowe, but the door swung open.

"Nephew!" the lady shouted. "You wicked boy, why didn't you come to greet me directly?"

"Forgive me, Aunt; I was ambushed by my fiancée," North said, setting the parcel aside in order to bow and kiss Lady Knowe's hand. He hugged her for good measure. "How is my favorite aunt?"

"Your *only* aunt is doing very well," she said tartly. She sat down beside Lavinia and gestured at the parcel. "Open it!"

"I don't remember this much excitement over a gift even when I came of age," North said. He sat down beside Diana, who retrieved the parcel and placed it in his lap.

The three conspirators watched intently as he untied the braided ribbons and then slowly unfolded the silk wrapping. Lavinia could feel her heart speeding up, and a smile curling her lips.

North slowly raised his present into the air. It was a tiny gown, made yet tinier by his large hands. Light blue silk was covered with a delicate azure gauze, caught up by embroidered roses flirting with lace.

It was exquisite—as well it should be, since Lavinia had ordered it based on her memory of a gown worn by Marie-Thérèse, Queen Marie Antoinette's infant daughter.

North turned to look at Diana, and the laugh died in Lavinia's throat. If she'd thought he looked tender before? The fierce glow in North's eyes was too private to be shared.

Lady Knowe apparently agreed, because she hopped to her feet and pulled Lavinia up with her. "Time for a visit to the ladies' retiring room," she trumpeted, steering Lavinia straight out of the room.

In the corridor, Lady Knowe pushed the door closed behind them and then shook her head. "I need a brandy. Too much sweetness in the air makes my teeth hurt. Don't you agree?"

"Absolutely," Lavinia said.

Though she wasn't certain it was her teeth that hurt.

Chapter Thirteen

The Duke of Lindow's residence
A gathering before a visit to Vauxhall Gardens
July 29, 1780

*P*arth arrived at the ducal townhouse in an irritable mood. He hated being in the grip of complicated emotions, and no one could say his life at the moment wasn't complicated—not with Elisa on his arm, and the memory of that kiss with Lavinia in his mind.

His *mind*?

That kiss had sunk into his bloody bones. He could almost taste her wild sweetness just by picturing her lips.

Pushing the thought away, he escorted Elisa into the drawing room, which was uninhabited save for North, seated at the far end of the long room. North immediately rose.

"This is Lord Northbridge Wilde," Parth said *sotto voce*, as North crossed the room toward them. "Is he as splendid as your prints led you to believe?"

"Alas, I have read in the paper that he is betrothed,"

Elisa said, twinkling up at him. Then, in a whisper, "Not my only disappointment, as His Lordship is less elegantly attired than one might expect from those prints. *È deludente!*"

North was wearing a perfectly respectable bronze-colored costume, but his wig was modest, his stockings white, and his shoes black. He bore no resemblance to the peacock he had once been.

They met in the center of the room. "Contessa, may I present Lord Roland Wilde?" Parth said. "North, I am honored to introduce Elisa Tornabuoni Guicciardini, Contessa di Casone."

North bowed and kissed the slender fingers that were held out to him. "It is a pleasure, Contessa."

"I am happy to meet you, Lord Roland," Elisa said, sinking into a graceful curtsy.

"My aunt, Lady Knowe, sent a message that she will join us shortly," North said, smiling. "The ladies are still readying themselves. In the meantime, may I offer you a glass of ratafia?"

"No, thank you," Elisa said. "Will Miss Gray join us? I understand that she is staying with you. I met her recently."

"She will indeed," North said, leading Elisa to a sofa. "My aunt, Miss Gray, and Miss Diana Belgrave, my fiancée, will join us."

"Won't you please address me as Elisa?" she said to North. "I am embracing English informality."

"I should be honored," he replied, seating himself next to her, "and you must address me as North."

Parth threw himself into a chair and watched moodily as North put on the show one might call "perfect aristocrat." All that was missing was a snuff-box and a feathery fan.

"Lavinia mentioned that you prefer to be called North!" Elisa exclaimed. "If you would forgive the impertinent question, why do you not use your given name? Roland is so romantic."

"I made the decision as a boy, when romance was something I had not yet come to appreciate," North explained.

He obviously liked Elisa. Hell, everyone to whom Parth had introduced Elisa liked her instantly. Parth liked her himself. She would be a perfect addition to the Wilde family. She would be a perfect spouse for him. She was . . . she was perfect.

He would marry her. It would be a sensible transaction.

"But you are named after the marvelous Italian poem, the best of its kind," Elisa cried indignantly. "*Orlando furioso!*"

Parth translated. "Roland the Mad?"

"Well, yes," she said, "but—"

Parth started laughing despite himself, and once Elisa recounted the sad story of Roland—or Orlando, in Italian—who went mad for love, North joined in.

"I've had mad moments in pursuit of Diana," he admitted.

"I read about your betrothal," Elisa said, giggling.

"The first or the second?"

"Both," she said, dimpling at him. "I read about the demise of your first betrothal in the Italian papers, and last week I read in the paper that Miss Gray is helping your betrothed with her *trousseau*—although this I already knew. Your fiancée has excellent taste in accepting Miss Gray's help!"

Parth barely kept a scowl from his face. When Elisa had dragged him into Felton's Emporium, he hadn't even recognized Lavinia, merely registered a lady who, from her plume to her boots, seemed to be a fashion plate come to life. She had reminded him of a dainty china statue: a pleasure to look at and display, but not something for everyday use, as it were.

But an hour later? Her hair darkening to old gold and her wet cheekbones shimmering in the rain? There, in the alley, Lavinia had looked like a siren who could lure every man into her snare.

Simpson appeared at the door. "If you will excuse me, Lady Knowe wonders whether the contessa would wish to join her and Miss Belgrave upstairs. They are in Miss Belgrave's chamber."

"*Volentieri!*" Elisa cried. "How delightful!"

The men rose automatically and remained standing until Elisa had followed Simpson from the room.

"That summons suggests that Diana will require at least another half hour for her *toilette*," North said, after the door closed behind Simpson. He retrieved a deck of cards from the gaming table at the other end of the room and sat down at it. "How about piquet? We might as well use the time. I say, weren't you bringing Jeremy Roden with you this evening?"

"He will meet us at Vauxhall," Parth said, taking the chair across from North.

Another throb of irritation went through him. He had promised to find a husband for Lavinia, and Prince Oskar fit the bill, except he had grown into a dunderhead.

Jeremy was a better candidate: wealthy, titled, and a true gentleman. At least the fellow used to be, back when they'd been at school together.

But going to war seemed to have darkened his outlook. Parth would have to keep an eye on him. He didn't want Lavinia matched with someone damaged by battle, even if Jeremy had returned a hero.

She deserved better.

Perhaps he should send word to Jeremy and call the whole thing off. Or go to Vauxhall now, in advance of the others, and intercept the man before Lavinia arrived.

WHEN LAVINIA CAME downstairs, having finished readying herself before the others, she found neither Simpson nor a footman waiting in the entry, so she let herself into the drawing room.

Across the room, Parth and North were playing cards at the gaming table. Neither looked up when she entered and silently closed the door behind her.

Both men were handsome, but to her mind, Parth's male beauty was honed to a point, like a sword that flashed gold in the lamplight. She only had to look at him to feel awkward, shy, stupid . . . all the things she never felt in the company of other men.

That afternoon at Felton's, Elisa hadn't flirted with him. No, she had briskly sent him back to the carriage. No wonder Parth was in love with Elisa. She wasn't giddy or foolish around him; she was *herself.*

It stood to reason that he would want to marry a woman who was independent and resourceful. A widow with experience and confidence. Who never found herself playing silly games, flirting to cover up her embarrassment.

Lavinia leaned back against the door, thinking about it. When was she most herself?

The answer came readily: when she was discussing

fabric. Paduasoys and damasks, bonnets and petticoats, and all the other superficialities Parth despised about her.

And in that moment Lavinia realized that the odd, tangled-up desire she had felt for Parth Sterling was gone.

He wasn't right for her, and he never would be.

She wanted a husband who, although he might not share her interest in bonnets, would nevertheless respect her fascination with the artistry of fashion, in the ways clothing could transform a person. *That* man would allow her to be herself around him, without feeling as if she had to flirt, or stumble into jokes that made no sense.

Her heart stirred at the sight of Parth, but now she understood why. Parth possessed distinct qualities in common with her beloved father: Both were calm, loyal, and assertive. After her father's death, her mother had become fretful and often ill, which, now that she knew about the laudanum addiction, Lavinia could at last explain. Even a grievous explanation was better than none at all.

She had never really desired *Parth*. Rather, she had longed for the security that she'd known in her childhood. With that thought, she began walking toward the men, promising herself that from this moment she would look forward, not back.

"If Diana needs another half hour, Lavinia probably needs double," she heard Parth say as she came nearer. "Perhaps I should leave for Vauxhall to meet my guest. The rest of you could join us."

Lavinia froze.

"That's because you . . . what was it that you said

about her?" North was dealing cards so quickly that his hands were almost a blur.

Lavinia didn't want to hear the answer. Before she could clear her throat, North answered his own question.

"'Shallow as a birdbath,' wasn't it?" he asked. "No, 'shallow as a puddle.' I strongly disagree, but as Diana's cousin, Lavinia is about to be part of the family. You have to stop this nonsense of not wanting to be around her."

Lavinia was flooded with a fiery wave of humiliation that made even her ears feel warm. She sucked in a soundless gulp of air. She'd already known how Parth saw her. Learning now that he'd denigrated her to the Wildes? That changed nothing.

"Aunt Knowe says that you're intrinsically incapable of lying," North continued, blithely ignoring Parth's scowl. "She's wrong, though. When it comes to Lavinia, we both—"

Enough. She couldn't bear to hear another word about what people she counted as her friends thought of her.

"Good evening!" Lavinia cried, starting forward.

Parth's head snapped up from his cards, and he stood so quickly that his chair went over with a clatter.

North rose more deliberately. "Lavinia! I didn't hear you enter." There was an unmistakable ring of trepidation in his voice.

She stopped a few feet from them and dropped a curtsy. "How pleasant to see you both."

Lavinia didn't look at Parth. It would take a while to convince herself that she didn't care for him. Starting this evening, she would be herself around him: not flirtatious, not foolish, not insulting.

Herself. No more and no less than her true self.

A bonnet lover—an unabashed, unrepentant bonnet lover.

"Elisa tells me that the gossip columns are full of the news that you are putting together Diana's *trousseau*," Parth said.

Before she could answer, Elisa entered the room, Diana at her heels. "Lavinia!" she cried, clearly bursting with excitement. "How lovely to see you! I cannot wait to see Vauxhall. My husband was ill for a long time, and then I was in mourning for a year . . . I am just so happy to be among friends and to be going to such a celebrated place as Vauxhall." She beamed and kissed Lavinia on either cheek, as if they were in Paris.

"That must have been difficult," Lavinia said, kissing her back. "Did you and Mr. Sterling meet in Florence?"

"You are using 'Mr. Sterling' tonight?" Parth said, on her other side.

Elisa had turned to North and didn't seem to be listening.

"I should never have called you 'Appalling Parth,' or any other disparaging name," Lavinia said. "I hope you'll forgive me."

She had no right to feel wounded by his opinion of her; after all, she had begun the round of insults. All else being equal, was it worse to be called "shallow" than to be called "appalling"?

In her own defense, her insults had been a foolish, foolish attempt to get his attention. Childish, indeed.

A muscle in Parth's jaw ticked. "I was not insulted."

"Assuredly not," Elisa put in, turning back to join them. "It's quite clever because the two words sound the same, do they not? Although you must explain to me what 'appalling' means."

"'*Terribile,*'" Parth said flatly.

His translation sounded too much like "terrible" to possibly be anything else. The best Lavinia could do was to behave with punctilious politeness toward Parth in the future.

Lady Knowe poked her head into the room. "Who is ready for an exhibition of tightrope walking?"

Parth frowned. "Tightrope walking?"

"Handsome men walking overhead," Lavinia said. She smiled at Elisa. "I went to a similar exhibition, and those who don't resemble Adonis resemble Apollo."

"What does a mythological male look like, Miss Gray?" Parth asked.

Like you, she thought. *Big and tawny and muscled.* Thank God, she was so much more mature than she used to be. "Slender and strong, with the ability to put one foot in front of another," she told him.

"Well-endowed," Elisa put in rather unexpectedly, a naughty grin on her face.

"Not that ladies are interested except for comparison purposes," Lady Knowe put in, adding, "I'm not even interested in that, having no grounds for comparison. So for me, this will just be an informative visit."

Parth looked as if his face had turned to granite.

"That is true for me as well," Lavinia said, feeling more cheerful.

"Diana has no need for comparisons," North said. Not only was his tone smug, but he crossed his arms over his chest. "Perhaps she and I should stay home."

"As one with experience of marriage," Elisa said, "I must tell you, Diana, that you must never allow your husband to control whether or not you attend a pleasurable event."

"Although I can't claim the contessa's experience, I agree," Lady Knowe said. "I would never allow a husband to influence my choice of entertainment."

"It is your marital duty to demonstrate to your husband the errors of his ways!" Elisa added.

"I can scarcely imagine a situation in which I would allow any man to make decisions for me," Lady Knowe announced. "My brother has occasionally made feeble attempts, but I set the duke straight every time."

"Aunt Knowe, you are not helpful," North growled.

"I am grateful for the advice," Diana announced. "Naturally we are going to Vauxhall, so I can appreciate all the wonders on display there."

"We'll bring our own version of Adonis with us," Lady Knowe said, tucking her hand into Parth's arm.

Parth couldn't help smiling at his aunt's roar of laughter. That was one of his earliest memories, after his arrival at the castle, five years old and terrified. Aunt Knowe had crouched down before him, eye to eye, and he had inadvertently said something that made her laugh . . . and after that, it was fine.

"You might as well give up," he said to North. He glanced at Lavinia and saw that she was giving Elisa a mischievous smile. Desire washed over him like firelight.

"North can escort us if you have no interest in tightrope walkers, Mr. Sterling," Lavinia said to him, her expression cooling. "According to the *Morning Post*, you have an important meeting at the Bank of Scotland tomorrow morning."

"You read the newspapers!" Elisa cried in delight. "None of my friends at home read more than the gossip column in the *Gazzetta Toscana*."

Parth registered further evidence that Lavinia was far from shallow, but he was focused on Vauxhall. The hell he would permit Lavinia and Elisa to wander down dim garden paths gazing at men in tight breeches prancing about overhead.

It wasn't safe for the performers: He could easily imagine one of them glancing down at Lavinia's big blue eyes and plummeting to the ground.

"My meeting is not important," he stated.

"Yes, it is," Lavinia countered, frowning. "Sterling Bank may well be given responsibility for setting the banking guidelines that will be used throughout the kingdom."

He shrugged uncomfortably. "I'll present the standards we established; it's up to other bankers to employ them or not."

"Unfortunately, the room will be full of numbskulls," North said. "It seems that I *will* be accompanying my fiancée, so you might as well go home and get some rest."

"I shall come with you, because I invited Lord Jeremy to join our party at the gardens," Parth said, glancing at Lavinia to make sure she understood why he had invited the man.

He hadn't realized until he watched Oskar make a cake of himself that the prince would take Lavinia to another country. To a royal court somewhere else. The very idea was . . . unacceptable.

But if Lavinia married Jeremy, she would stay here in England, where she belonged. As Diana's cousin, she would be at Lindow on occasion. For holidays, for example.

He pushed away another image of that rain-soaked kiss because it was obviously an aberration. As Aunt Knowe was so fond of saying, he was damned protective. Seeing a woman he—he cared about, standing in the rain, paying no attention to her health, made him lose his head.

"*Andiamo, caro*," Elisa called, turning and holding out her hand.

When had he become her "dear"? One moment he'd agreed to use first names, and then suddenly he was her "dear."

"No more scowling," Elisa continued. "I can sense you are grumpy, *caro*, but you must place a smirk on your lips, no?"

"A smile, not a smirk," he said, taking her hand.

The pleasure gardens of Vauxhall were arranged into a mile or more of curving, tree-lined paths, lit by dim lanterns. Ladies and gentlemen—and anyone else with a shilling for admittance—wandered about, randomly encountering the garden's diversions.

As soon as they arrived, Parth paid for a box on the edge of the dance floor. No sooner were the ladies seated in the three-walled enclosure than they jumped up and demanded to stroll about.

He looked around for Jeremy. Seeing no sign of him, he left word with the waiter that they were wandering the grounds. It was a warm evening, and Lavinia, Elisa, and Diana shed their pelisses. The three of them were so beautiful that every man in the place turned to stare.

North drew Diana's arm through his. "This place isn't entirely safe."

"True," Aunt Knowe said. "Vauxhall is a pleasure garden, but it has a darker side."

"We are aware," Lavinia said. "We won't be foolish."

Strangely enough—given that he had concluded two years ago that Lavinia was one of the most reckless women he'd ever met—Parth believed her.

"Lady Knowe, you will be my escort for the evening," Lavinia cried, tucking her arm through the lady's.

"My dear, there is nothing I'd like better," his aunt responded.

Elisa nestled against Parth's side, her eyes sparkling. "Isn't this fun?"

Lavinia was walking directly in front of him. She possessed the sort of curves that a man could never get enough of. Except that now she was too thin. Her mother was—

The moment the thought occurred to him, he could have cursed himself for thoughtlessness. Her mother's illness must be nagging on her spirits, perhaps making it difficult to eat.

He'd never truly known his own mother; he had only a dim memory of a woman in a shimmering sari adorned with gold thread. But if Aunt Knowe—the closest thing he'd had to a mother inasmuch as the duke's marriages during Parth's childhood had been short-lived—were to become addicted to laudanum, he'd be . . . upset.

Very upset.

"Your face is so stern," Elisa said, whispering as if they were in church, rather than ambling down a pathway. "You really must smile more often, Parth."

His smile must not have been very convincing,

because she shook her head at him with a roguish pout. "One might imagine it was you who had been in mourning, instead of me. Not that I am any longer. My dearest conte wouldn't wish me to spend my life grieving for him."

Ahead of them, the first of many tightropes crossed the footpath, and sure enough, his aunt, Diana, North, and Lavinia stopped directly underneath.

"Ah!" Elisa cried, walking faster.

"Why rush?" Parth drawled. He hated the thought of peering up at a man stupid enough to take up rope walking as a profession. Elisa tugged at him in vain until, thwarted, she dropped his arm, and ran ahead to join the ladies.

North had drawn Diana to the side and was, from the sound of it, amusing both of them by making claims about what he would look like in tight pantaloons.

With a shock, Parth realized that he *was* being as sour as Elisa had charged. He had reconciled himself years ago to having a sober countenance—"Sulky Sterling," as Lavinia once called him—yet his face rarely reflected his inner feelings. Many times when she would dash past him, flinging insults, he had had to stifle laughter.

But now?

There was nothing flirtatious in Lavinia's eyes this evening, nothing disappointed or angry. She spoke to him as if he were a mere acquaintance.

Which, he supposed, was precisely what he was.

At that moment, a tightrope walker made his appearance above them. Parth saw instantly why the entertainment had become so notorious among ladies. This fellow was wearing a pair of skin-tight white pantaloons that glowed in the light of the fairy lanterns hanging from the rope on which he balanced.

Parth met North's eyes and had one of those moments of complete accord that happen to men who are brothers in heart, if not in blood.

"Stuffed," North mouthed over Diana's head. His future wife had her head tipped back and was staring with fascination at the man, who was blowing kisses and generally behaving like a fool. He even started dancing on the rope, risking life and limb.

But then, what man wouldn't, given the three beauties who were gazing up at him?

With a surge of outrage, it struck Parth that the rope walker was able to look down the ladies' bodices. That wad of stuffing he had down his pantaloons was probably growing by the moment.

Parth caught the man's eyes. The fellow had an instinct for self-preservation, because he blew a last kiss and nimbly ran on.

Aunt Knowe made a face. "I'm not sure about the authenticity of what we just witnessed, my dears."

"He looked as if he'd put a marrow down his pantaloons," Elisa gasped, starting to giggle uncontrollably.

"That's it!" Lavinia said, giggling as well.

"I believe a stocking filled with sand might be a good explanation," Aunt Knowe said. "If the sand was heavy enough, it might even help him balance. What do you think, gentlemen?"

"I wouldn't want to speculate," North said.

"Did you happen to notice that fabric his pantaloons were made from, Diana?" Lavinia asked.

"No, but they fit *extraordinarily* well!" Diana chortled.

"I'm not considering his front, but his rear," Lavinia

said thoughtfully. "I wonder if the fabric was cut on the bias."

Parth would have scowled, but he had resolved to show a more cheerful countenance.

Elisa clapped. "I'm sure there will be another rope further ahead, ladies! All we have to do is walk there, wait for a performer to appear, and inquire about his pantaloons."

"I'll ask him to leap down," Lavinia said, nodding.

Elisa had linked arms with Aunt Knowe, which left Parth free to take Lavinia's arm. She blinked up at him, startled.

"Why are you so interested in pantaloon fabric?" he asked.

"The type of weave can make a difference in how fabric fits the body," Lavinia said. She went on about biases and selvages, not caring that she was essentially admiring another man's arse. Parth wrestled with that all the way up the path.

The other women were galloping ahead in their excitement to encounter another one of those rope walkers, but Parth kept Lavinia to a decorous stroll. Finally, the group ahead turned a corner, leaving that stretch of path unoccupied. Except for them.

Lavinia didn't notice.

Normally he would feel a swell of disdain at the idea of a woman so excited by tailoring that she didn't notice he'd stopped walking. Just now Lavinia was standing in front of him, holding his sleeve for emphasis, speaking so fast that words were tumbling out of her mouth.

Lavinia had never talked to him this way before.

He didn't know half the terms she was using. If he

understood her right, Mr. Felton had a new loom that created cloth . . .

"Cut on the bias?" he asked.

Her face fell. "You didn't understand?"

"My fault, not yours," he said instantly. "Tell me again. I'm interested in mechanical looms, but I haven't heard of this particular method."

So she did. Parth Sterling stood in the twilight darkness of a meandering footpath in Vauxhall Gardens and listened as Lavinia told him about the new loom that would soon be producing exquisite patterned silks, right here in Britain. Mr. Felton could charge twice as much for it as he might for an ordinary satin. And if the fabric were cut on the bias, she had the feeling that . . .

She lost him again, because she went off into a digression about a new dye made from quercitron, whatever that was.

"Do you see what I mean?" she demanded.

"I agree that offering small bolts in unique colors is an excellent idea."

"That's what I told him," she said, satisfied. Then she tugged on his arm. "I've been talking your ear off, Mr. Sterling. I'm so sorry. Let's catch up with the others."

"Why 'Mr. Sterling'?" he growled.

She blinked at him. "I've already apologized for the childish names I called you. I am truly sorry. I promise never to treat you with such disrespect again."

Parth felt like howling, but he just nodded.

Lavinia started down the path.

"We could call each other by first names," he said, clearing his throat and coming to a halt again. In a moment they would turn the corner. He could hear Aunt Knowe's hooting laugh somewhere ahead of them.

"It's better that we don't," Lavinia said, not looking at him. "We have a history of hurting each other's feelings."

"*What?* When have I hurt your feelings?" The question burst from him with the force of a pistol shot.

She raised her eyes, and even in this dim light he could make out the rueful smile in them. "Oh, you probably never meant to," she said lightly. "We must rejoin the others. Elisa will be wondering where you are."

Parth didn't budge. "I would never wish to hurt your feelings."

"I know. I *do* know," she insisted, apparently recognizing his dismay. "I don't mind in the least. You are . . . You are entitled to your opinion about me, and I completely understand. It's just that I . . ."

"You what?" The feelings crowding his chest were growing violent.

But where most people—bankers and factory owners among them—quavered in fright when he took that tone, Lavinia merely surveyed him and shook her head. "It doesn't matter; it really doesn't."

He caught her hands in his. "It does to me."

Lavinia was as stubborn as Aunt Knowe, which was really saying something. She shook her head again, not unkindly, but with conviction. Many a frustrated businessman had seen a similar certainty on Parth's face, usually when he was pointing out a logical flaw in their manufacturing process.

Parth's gut clenched with frustration. Some part of him knew that it was illogical to be frustrated.

But his logical faculties seemed to have been swept away. He pulled her closer, watching as her eyes grew bigger.

Then Lavinia made a fatal error. "Mr. Sterling?"

He was not Mr. Sterling to her. In fact, he thought savagely, he would *never* be Mr. Sterling to her. He was Parth.

Parth's mouth closed on hers before the last syllable of his name left the air, and Lavinia's mouth opened as if they had been lovers for years. His tongue slid into her mouth and he heard a stifled whimper, before her arms wrapped around his neck. He murmured something and bent his head to kiss her harder.

A proper lady would be shocked and appalled. Lavinia moved closer to him, close enough that he could feel her breasts press against him. Her hands slid into his hair and held him so fiercely that he told himself that she felt as frantic as he did.

One hand came up and cupped the back of her head so he could plunder her mouth. The other stayed at the small of her back. Even though every blinding impulse in his body was urging him to slide his hand over Lavinia's arse, one didn't—

Bloody hell.

One didn't *kiss* ladies like this, rough and possessive. Hell, gentlemen didn't kiss like this. And yet he couldn't stop. She tasted better than anything—anyone. She tasted like honey and spice, like brandy and excitement.

Dimly, he was aware that blood was thundering through his veins . . . from a mere kiss.

He stopped himself just as his treacherous hand was about to slide down her rump and pull her even closer. Lavinia's arse was his weakness, and it always had been. Other men lusted after her breasts, which were magnificent. Her lush mouth, her sweet but naughty eyes, her laughter. God, there were so many things.

Parth only had to visualize the lush curve of her arse and he was hard as rock, breathless, ready to fall at her feet.

The realization shocked him, and he ended the kiss. Lavinia opened her eyes. Annoyed. She was annoyed.

"Kiss me again, Mr. Sterling," she ordered, her voice husky. She tugged at his hair and he dived back into the kiss as if it had never ended.

What shocked him the second time was the sound that came from his own throat. It was something like a groan, but more desperate, deeper. It sounded a bit like the word "honey." Surely he didn't let that word slip . . . even though he thought of it whenever he saw Lavinia's hair unpowdered.

Gold was commonplace.

Honey? Honey lasted for years. It was pure and never spoiled, never changed. It was sweet and good and—

He broke away yet again.

Lavinia looked up at him, her eyes half lidded, her mouth swollen from his kisses. She looked dazed and . . . and desirous.

"I've kissed many men, you know," she said suddenly. "I told you that before."

Parth took a step backward. That was not what he wanted to hear at this exact moment, though honestly, he had no idea what he did want to hear.

She stared at him as if his face was a puzzle she was trying to work out. "You kiss like . . ."

"No comparisons," he barked, and then cleared his

throat. "I don't care who I kiss like. That was a mistake and it won't happen again. I apologize."

Then he watched as the dazed—or was it dreamy?—expression left her face. Her gaze flicked to his mouth, and then to the ground.

"Damn it, you agree with me, don't you?" he said, feeling a bit sick.

"Certainly," she said flatly. "I completely agree. I understand. You don't like me and all this darkness probably went to your head."

"I *like* you," he snarled. "What in the hell are you talking about?" In the back of his mind, he was remembering how he'd described her to North.

Worse: She saw the truth in his eyes.

Her teeth closed down on her plump lower lip for a brief moment. Then she gave him a wry smile. "It's all right, truly it is. It was a very instructive experience."

"What was?" he rasped.

"Hearing that you find me 'shallow as a puddle.' I suspected it, but I . . . I had managed to convince myself that I was exaggerating the distaste I saw in your eyes."

Parth stared at her, unable to find the right words, horrified to his core.

"Are you two bickering again?" Aunt Knowe called, appearing at the turn of the path. "Come along! Elisa has charmed one of the tightrope walkers to the ground, and she's chattering at him in Italian, and I believe he's going to remove his pantaloons and give them to her."

Lavinia turned away with a blinding smile. "Of course we are not bickering, Lady Knowe."

She joined his aunt, and the two of them rounded

the bend while Parth stood in place, feeling like an idiot. Like the stupidest, most idiotic boy in the classroom. Like a man who didn't know the answer to a simple problem.

He had always known precisely who he was—the equal of any man in polite society, even if he didn't choose a courtier's life. But now he was an ass, who'd said a cruel thing about a lady, a cruel, untrue thing, and it had been repeated, and she had heard it—and he could never take back that moment.

He saw in Lavinia's eyes just how much it had hurt her.

Bloody hell.

His cock was aching for a woman whom he'd cut to the bone unfairly. She wasn't shallow.

Not at all. In truth, he suspected she was one of the most intelligent women of his acquaintance. She was a woman who investigated and learned, and was interested in finance and business.

"Bloody hell," he said aloud, the words slipping from his lips unbidden. Naturally she thought he was a pretentious ass. Because he was. Had been.

How many times had Alaric and North—and even Horatius—assaulted someone at school, and he'd discovered later it was on account of a remark a boy had made about him? He'd never forget Horatius holding a boy down and pounding him for saying that Parth wasn't born a Wilde, so he couldn't be a Wilde.

"Parth *was* born to be a Wilde," Horatius had bellowed, defending him.

Better than anyone, he knew that insults eventually found their way to the person described. But he had forgotten it when he said that cruel, untrue remark about Lavinia.

Bent on apologizing, he started toward the sound of women's laughter up ahead.

When he turned the bend, he found a slender performer with a halo of curly hair standing in the middle of the path, wrapped in North's black cloak. Eyes shining, the man was babbling in Italian.

"Parth!" North called. "Will you please come over here and try to make the women in our family behave like ladies?"

Lavinia was turning a pair of white pantaloons over in her hands. As he watched, she gave a sharp pull at one of the legs and nodded, turning to his aunt and showing her the fabric.

A growl rose in his throat before he could stop it. She was handling a pair of breeches that a man had just removed.

Parth was headed straight toward Lavinia when North caught his arm.

"What are you doing?" North hissed.

A muscle jumped in Parth's jaw. "She's handling that garment that was just—"

"She's interested in the fabric. The *fabric*."

It took a moment, but Parth regained control. Lavinia had bundled up the borrowed item and was returning it to its owner.

Elisa turned around with a huge smile. "Parth, *caro*, you must meet Lorenzo. He's from Rome, and he hates walking up and down these ropes all night long."

"*Buona sera*," Parth said, forcing himself to smile and shake hands with the man who'd removed his breeches in front of ladies. He shouldn't blame him. Very few men could resist Elisa and Lavinia when they banded together.

Poor Lorenzo was looking from one woman to the other with the adoring eyes of a stray dog.

"He's been treated despicably," Elisa exclaimed. "My mother was Roman, did you know that, Parth?"

It seemed Lorenzo would be joining Elisa's household as a groom, or a footman, or perhaps a household rope walker.

"I must give a week's notice," he said, which Parth respected. "There are not so many people who can walk a rope." After wriggling into his pantaloons within the shelter of North's cloak, he returned the garment, bowed, jumped to the rope, swung himself up, and walked away backward, waving.

Elisa slipped her hand under Parth's arm. "I love your family," she said, beaming. "I didn't realize, you know. I thought you were merely acquainted with the duke. But the Wildes *are* your family, are they not?"

Elisa was looking at him with a sparkle in her eye. Damn it. Her smile widened. "I believe I might marry you."

Parth flinched, and her laughter rang out.

"You thought I didn't know you were courting me?"

"You showed no signs of it," he said cautiously. "I had the idea you wanted to marry Lord Roland."

"I could never marry a man called North," Elisa said, giggling. "I'd have to call him Roland, which he wouldn't like." She laughed again, and hugged his arm closer to her side. "In any case, the question is theoretical: He is desperately in love with Miss Belgrave."

Parth didn't feel like laughing.

"I shall not be a duchess." Elisa shrugged

"Elisa," Parth said, not knowing how to continue.

"You must continue to woo me," Elisa said. "I am not ready—"

She caught the look on his face, and her sentence broke off. "*Caro*, you don't wish to marry me any longer, do you?"

Parth's jaw tightened. "Indeed I do."

He didn't.

Elisa started chuckling. "I'm glad that I didn't develop a fancy for you! All the same, I will not let you off your promise to take me to Lindow Castle for the wedding, so you are stuck with me for a few months at least. Stuck? Isn't that right?"

Parth found his lips curling into a reluctant smile. Elisa was adorable, and he genuinely liked her. "I am happy to be stuck with you, Contessa."

She came up on her toes and kissed him, not on the cheeks the way she usually did, but right on the mouth. Her lips clung to his for a moment with a sweet regret that suggested she had truly considered marrying him.

He felt nothing.

Except when he looked over her head and caught Lavinia's eye. He felt something then.

"Lady Knowe and I are returning to the table," Lavinia called, smiling as if it were inconsequential to see him kissing another woman no more than ten minutes after he'd kissed her.

"*Andiamo, caro*," Elisa said, turning in the direction of the table. "It's too dark out here."

Feeling hollow was a new sensation, and one Parth found disagreeable. It was an echo of what he'd felt when Lavinia repeated his insult, and he'd seen in her eyes that he'd hurt her.

"What does *'caro'* mean?" Lavinia asked Elisa. "It is such a charming word."

"It means 'dear' in English," Elisa said readily. "One uses it only with people one truly adores."

Lavinia's lips curved up and she said, "What a lovely word." Her twinkling, teasing glance that took in Elisa and Parth was perfect . . . for a betrothed couple.

"Come along, my dear," Aunt Knowe said to Lavinia. Her glance fell on Parth, and she—who was so rarely angry—narrowed her eyes at him.

She disapproved. Perhaps of that kiss.

"Parth, *caro*," Elisa said, as Aunt Knowe and Lavinia strolled ahead of them, "not only are you stuck with me, but I wish you to keep courting me."

"What?"

"It will make everything easier," she said, hugging his arm close to her body. "You and dear Lavinia dislike each other so much. I will keep you close to me, and you will argue less with Lavinia. Diana's wedding should be peace and light, no?"

He swallowed hard. "Yes."

"Now, we should join the others. Unless you wish to kiss me?"

When he didn't respond, she laughed so hard that she was shaking all over.

Chapter Fourteen

$\mathcal{L}$avinia had never known Parth Sterling; that was clear. The Parth she had believed she knew would never kiss first one woman and then another on the same evening. On the same *path*. Within half an hour of each other.

Though—to be precise—the Parth she knew would never have kissed *her*. He had better things to do than splash around in shallow puddles.

Lavinia hadn't allowed herself to remember their first kiss, the one in the rain. It was obviously a mistake. But this one?

This was wrong because he was more attached to Elisa than she had realized. It wasn't just a matter of "*caro*" and umbrellas . . .

It was kisses, in-public kisses.

Lavinia had done a good job that evening trying to be *herself* in front of Parth. She hadn't been flirtatious or insulting. She'd be damned before she let Parth know how it shook her to see that affectionate kiss.

The kiss he'd given her, Lavinia, hadn't been affectionate.

It had been a kiss of an entirely different kind: deep and hard, with no fondness in it. No humor, or teasing, none of the sweetness that she saw in Elisa's face when she called Parth "*caro*."

The truth made her heart ache. He desired her, but he didn't respect her. If he respected her, he wouldn't have kissed her in the dark, in private. And he wouldn't have kissed another woman immediately afterwards, in public.

She had to stay away from Parth; that went without saying. Something about the two of them spurred their worst instincts.

"*Caro*, I would like to dance," Elisa announced, once they were all seated back in their box, champagne in hand.

Parth rose instantly and bowed at her side. "If you would do me the honor?"

Lavinia watched as the two of them walked onto the wooden floor. The dance was the "Hole in the Wall," and Elisa dropped into a curtsy facing Parth. Hands raised, touching, they circled each other. The smile on Elisa's face was utterly charming.

"Diana, North, and I were discussing whether it is time to return to Cheshire," Lady Knowe said, interrupting Lavinia's morose study of the dancers.

"I didn't want to say so in front of Elisa, but the smell of sulfur from the fireworks is making me miserably ill," Diana said. "I want to return to Cheshire, but at the moment I just want to leave *here*."

"I didn't even notice the fireworks," Lavinia exclaimed, as another spray lit up the night sky.

"Not only are they loud, but they smell," Diana said fiercely. Then, when they all looked at her, she shrugged. "I can't help it if your olfactory senses are dulled by the night air. I tell you that the odor is disgusting, and you'll have to trust me."

"If you leave for Cheshire, you would return to London in a few weeks, wouldn't you?" Lavinia asked. "For fittings of your wedding dress and all the other garments?"

"Is there any way around that?" Diana asked. She rose, and North helped her into her pelisse.

Lavinia gaped up at her. "Around fitting your wedding dress? Not that I can think of!"

"I thought perhaps we could bring all the half-made gowns—mine and Ophelia's as well—to Cheshire, along with an extra seamstress or two," Lady Knowe suggested. "Berthe can finish my gowns, but we would need more help for the others, especially the wedding dress."

"We'd need more than one seamstress," Lavinia said slowly. It was a terrible idea—except that it would give her so much control over the finished product. She would know down to the last stitch that Diana's wedding dress was perfect.

"I'm happy to hire as many seamstresses as you wish," North said. "Bribe them if need be. And now, please give our best to Parth and the contessa. I'm going to whisk away my fiancée. I'll send the carriage back."

"I think it would be best for Diana to leave London," Lady Knowe said, as North led Diana away. "She'll likely be ill for another month, if not longer. And North means it about hiring seamstresses, if you could persuade some to travel to the country."

A chance to stay in a residence where the butler was kind and the servants didn't work a hundred hours a week? Lavinia would have her pick of seamstresses, at least those without families.

"I won't have to bribe anyone," she assured Lady Knowe. "It might work."

Truth be told, she loved the idea of overseeing the finishing of each garment herself. They would be *perfect*.

"What are you talking about?" Elisa said, sitting down.

Lady Knowe waved at Parth with her fan. "I should like to dance. Drag me about the floor if you please; Lavinia assures me that you're an excellent dancer."

"He is indeed!" Elisa crowed, clapping her hands.

"It would be my pleasure," Parth said, coming around the table.

Lavinia smiled mechanically, thinking as hard as she could about seamstresses. Could she manage with two, if she and Annie sewed as well?

"Are Diana and North dancing?" Elisa asked, craning her neck to look at the dance floor.

"No, Diana wasn't feeling well, so he took her home," Lavinia said.

"I am happy to have this moment together," Elisa said. "I enjoyed the time we spent together in Felton's tremendously."

Lavinia summoned up a smile.

"If you would ever like a companion at a milliner, for example, I'd be very happy to join you. I am so looking forward to seeing Diana's *trousseau*; Lady Knowe was telling me about it earlier this evening. Thank goodness Parth is bringing me to the wedding, so I shall see her dress!"

For a moment, Lavinia thought that Elisa knew

about her absurd marriage proposal, that Parth had told her.

He wouldn't. And Elisa's eyes were shining with unadulterated friendliness.

"I would enjoy that," Lavinia said, and then cleared her throat and tried for more enthusiasm. "It would be very helpful to have your advice."

Lavinia was bringing gowns to Lindow, and Parth was bringing a contessa. The idea of rounding corners in the castle and coming upon Elisa kissing Parth, or watching them dance together again . . . Everything in Lavinia protested.

"Advice about what?" Lady Knowe said, dropping into a chair and fanning herself vigorously. "Thank you for that dance, Parth. I appreciate the music, but I must admit that I feel a good deal less nimble than I was in my younger years. Lavinia hasn't danced."

He bowed before Lavinia.

"Do you always do what you're told?" she said, as they made their way toward the line of dancers waiting for the music to start.

Parth cocked his head, apparently taking seriously the question that she had rattled out to cover her embarrassment at a man being compelled to dance with her.

"When the order comes from a woman I love," he said.

Lavinia liked that: He loved Lady Knowe and he wasn't ashamed to say so. Without thinking, she gave him a wide smile, a real smile.

And then froze. "You shouldn't look at me like that!"

"Like what?"

No one was better at a placid glance than Parth. Placid Parth. Too bad she hadn't come up with that one, back when she was devoted to baiting him.

"As if you wanted to kiss me again," Lavinia said bluntly. "You don't wish to kiss me, Parth. You have Elisa. I know why you feel this way, though."

He looked startled. "You do?"

She nodded. "I've been Willa's best friend for most of her life. I exist on the edges of the Wilde family, the same as you. We're like two puzzle pieces that don't quite fit on the board."

They went through the movements of the dance in silence after that. When the dance was over, he paused. "I'm not at the edges of the Wilde family, Lavinia."

Oh, damn. There was that mortifying pity in his eyes again.

He wasn't. Of course he wasn't.

She was the one who didn't belong, linked only by a family connection to Diana and friendship with Willa, who was no longer even in England. He'd been with them most of his life, and he was loved by everyone. He was at the heart of the family.

"That was a foolish thing to say."

"It wasn't foolish." Parth paused, clearly searching for words. "I was lucky to have happened into the family after I was orphaned."

"You didn't 'happen' into it," Lavinia pointed out. "Your father chose that family for you when he sent you to England."

Only because she knew him so well—having surreptitiously studied his face any number of times—did she know that he was startled.

"He was a good parent, taking care of you, no matter what happened to him."

She disliked the way her voice became a little wistful. Her father hadn't been quite so thoughtful; he left his estate in the hands of her mother. But who could have predicted that those little drops would have such a dire effect?

Parth looked as if he was considering saying something about Lady Gray's lack of maternal qualities, but couldn't quite find the right words.

"Back to the table," she said briskly, turning about in order to thread her way among the small tables to where Lady Knowe and Elisa sat, heads together, laughing.

His hand caught her elbow. "Lavinia."

She looked up at him. "It's not appropriate to address me by my given name."

"I don't mind being Appalling Parth."

"I am ashamed that I teased you so," she said quietly. "We must stop poking at each other. We aren't schoolchildren, and you have Elisa. She fits with you," Lavinia added, pretty sure her voice didn't sound wistful. Or sad.

"Like a puzzle piece?"

"Exactly." She shook her head. "Why are we discussing this? Excuse me." She turned sideways to make her way between tables as her skirts were too wide to allow her to pass.

"Miss Gray!"

Lavinia jolted to a halt. "Good evening, Lady Blythe! How are you?"

Lady Amaryllis Blythe was a friend of her mother's. She was as thin as a fishing rod, and her tall wig could be a salmon, since it was powdered an unfortunate shade of pink.

"I am marrying again," the lady said, beaming. Her wig quivered in the air above her.

Would that be the third or fourth husband? Lavinia managed a smile. "I offer my most sincere congratulations, and so will my mother."

"Poor dear Lady Gray." Lady Blythe sighed. "If only she weren't such an invalid. I know that she would love to be here, dancing the night away."

Lavinia was less certain about that; in her memory, her mother had always considered that dancing required too much exertion. But perhaps that had been the laudanum, and once she was well again, her mother would bounce around the dance floor.

"Good evening, Mr. Sterling," Lady Blythe said, looking past Lavinia. She kept speaking as Parth bowed and kissed her hand. "I have chosen Madame Cecile to make my gown, and she asked me if I knew you. Can you imagine? I have known you since you were a little girl, and so I told her."

Lavinia's smile thinned.

"May I beg your advice, my dear? I thought perhaps you and I could return to Madame Cecile together. She feels that my wedding gown should be almost puritanically high at the neck, not fashionable in the least. I read in *Beatrix's Babble* about the way you are gathering Miss Belgrave's *trousseau*."

"Yes, I am," Lavinia confirmed.

"There's a print of Miss Belgrave's wedding dress at one of the stationers in St. Paul's churchyard," the lady said. "Those feathers are divine!"

Feathers? There were no feathers on Diana's wedding gown. Moreover, no one outside the shop had seen the design for the gown. Any such print was a sham.

"I told Madame Cecile that I want feathers, all up and down my bodice, exactly the same as the future duchess's." She simpered at Parth. "I'm sure you know, Mr. Sterling, about the betting book at White's as regards Her Grace's lace."

His brows drew together.

"The future duchess," she clarified. "Will the wedding gown feature your lace or Holland lace? Miss Gray surely knows." She gave Lavinia another toothy smile.

"I would be glad to help you with your wedding dress in any way that I am able," Lavinia said. She knew exactly why Madame Cecile had urged Lady Blythe to ask for advice: The *modiste* didn't want this atrocious feathered dress to appear in a print with her name attached.

"Miss Gray will shortly be leaving for the Duke of Lindow's country residence," Parth said. "She has no time to help you at the moment, Lady Blythe."

"I heard that you were offered a title, Mr. Sterling," she replied with a titter. "There are so few gentlemen who would ignore such an honor."

"I didn't ignore it," Parth said. "I refused it."

That was his irritated voice. Controlled, but irritated.

"Forgive me, Lady Blythe," Parth continued, "but I see that Lady Knowe is waiting for us."

"You needn't have been so abrupt," Lavinia whispered as they walked away.

"Why not? Why would you possibly offer her advice about her dress?"

She wasn't ready to tell Parth about the commissions. She might never be ready. As far as she knew, the arrangement hadn't been reported in the gossip columns, even though every *modiste* in London now readily offered her a ten percent commission if she would order their garments for the famous *trousseau*.

"I can see that you are having a wonderful time helping Diana and Aunt Knowe," Parth said. "Elisa is hoping for your advice. But why would you agree to spend time with that ghastly woman? She wants to make use of you."

"I enjoy thinking about fashion," Lavinia said. "Clothing can flatter any figure. A challenge makes the design even more interesting. Do you feel Lady Blythe doesn't deserve a beautiful gown?"

"I don't care what she wears. There was something about that woman's tone . . . almost as if she presumed she could *hire* you to give her advice. If anything, I was restrained in my response."

Lavinia hadn't noticed anything in Lady Blythe's tone, perhaps because she didn't really care what the woman thought.

"Just because you have a brilliant eye for what flatters a woman does not mean that your skills are for sale." His voice grated.

"What if they were?" Lavinia asked.

His eyebrows locked. "No one can buy your advice. You are not for sale."

Stupidly, the gravel in his voice made her pulse quicken. "No one has said *I'm* for sale," she insisted.

"She acted as if you are," he said stubbornly. "The sooner we leave for Lindow, the better."

"What do you mean, *we*?" They were almost at the table.

"I will escort you to Cheshire with the gowns when they are ready to be fitted," he said.

"You certainly will not!"

Parth stopped and glared down at her. "You believe that I would allow you to travel alone to Cheshire? North will escort Diana and my aunt, and I will escort you, whenever you are ready to bring the gowns to Lindow."

She cleared her throat. "May I remind you that I am not a member of your family?"

His jaw tightened. "Don't push me, Lavinia."

Elisa walked around the table and put a hand on Parth's arm. Lavinia bit back the retort she was about to make.

"I am sorry, *caro*," Elisa said. "I can see that the two of you are happily squabbling with each other as a brother and sister might. But I do not feel well."

"What is the matter?"

Parth looked as if he was about to shout for a doctor, but to Lavinia, the contessa looked perfectly well, with a healthy little flush in her cheeks.

"No, no," Elisa said hastily. "It is . . . it is a *female* complaint."

The concern dropped from Parth's face.

Lavinia was nothing but sympathetic. Someday she meant to devise a better way to handle one's monthly. A napkin tied with ribbons had distinct drawbacks, one of which was that it was likely to shift during dancing.

"Lady Knowe will escort me to the entrance and help me procure a hackney carriage," Elisa announced. "Parth, you may remain here with Lavinia; Lady Knowe will return to chaperone."

Parth opened his mouth, but Lady Knowe was on her feet. "Not a word, Parth. A lady's decision is not to be questioned. I shall return in half an hour at the most."

"Certainly," he said.

"We could all return home," Lavinia suggested.

Parth surprised himself by the speed with which he rejected this idea.

"No." Then he added, "It would be rude to leave before Jeremy arrives."

"And before the meal you ordered. I am quite hungry, so they must set a plate for me." Aunt Knowe was putting on her pelisse with the help of a footman. "Lavinia, I saw you talking to Amaryllis Blythe. Did she ask you for advice about her wedding dress?"

"Yes," Lavinia replied, a tone of distinct satisfaction in her voice.

"Splendid!"

Parth frowned. His aunt sounded positively gleeful about Lady Blythe's impertinent request for Lavinia's advice.

"We'll work out the details tomorrow," Aunt Knowe said, waving her hand. "Now I must escort the poor contessa."

Elisa had been gathering up all the bits and pieces that she always dropped around her, like a tree shedding its leaves, Parth thought uncharitably. She took his aunt's arm and leaned on it gracefully. "I am sad to leave, *caro*," she said to Parth. "Lavinia!" She blew a kiss.

"I'll be back in no time!" his aunt caroled.

Chapter Fifteen

"How very awkward," Lavinia said, seating herself again. "Luckily, you and I needn't worry about compromising my reputation."

"No, because I've already done that," Parth said, joining her. He watched with deep satisfaction as her cheeks turned rosy. "I don't mean in my bedchamber or yours, but once in the rain, and again this evening."

Lavinia turned her nose in the air. "No one knows but us, and therefore those kisses do not exist."

"We are ready for our meal," Parth informed the waiter.

"Shouldn't we wait for Lady Knowe?"

"I'm hungry, and my aunt has no sense of time. She'll probably begin chatting with Elisa, and return in an hour." In short order, platters of delicate savories, *petits fours*, and bowls of strawberries were placed before them.

Parth waved away the waiter, loaded a plate with food, and set it in front of Lavinia.

She slowly unbuttoned her gloves. "I'm not very hungry."

"You must eat," Parth said, hearing the clipped tone in his own voice with surprise. "You're too thin."

Lavinia scowled. "Someday, I shall grow tired of your insults and throw something at you. A glass of wine, perhaps."

Parth cut back a laugh that nearly escaped. "Eat," he said instead.

She picked up a ham tartlet and took a bite.

Parth threw one into his mouth. He'd spent the afternoon riding to Hampstead Heath and was ravenous. They ate in silence for a few minutes before he said, "I'd like to hear more about lace."

"Because of Sterling Lace? The truth is"—Lavinia made an apologetic grimace—"handmade lace is more delicate and desirable than anything that can be fashioned by machine."

"It is my understanding that it takes eight hours to create a tiny amount of Holland lace," Parth said. "Of course it's expensive. But why shouldn't everyone wear lace on their collars?"

Lavinia's beautiful eyes focused on him. "You shouldn't attempt to compete with handmade lace."

"Why not?"

Parth listened and ate two more tarts and a slice of ham, while Lavinia laid out the rationale for an excellent plan to increase his business.

"Sterling lace should be fashionable in itself, not as a substitute for Holland lace. That way, everyone from ladies to grocers' wives will be looking specifically for your lace. Luckily, when Diana wears it at her wedding, she will set a precedent."

Parth pushed another sandwich into Lavinia's hand, but she was so interested in her point that she just put it down.

"For example, if I tell Lady Blythe that Diana's gown is edged in Sterling lace, she'll demand the same, from the same bolt, if possible." Lavinia's face was entirely earnest.

"Why?" he asked.

"Lady Blythe wants feathers because she has heard, wrongly, that Diana will have feathers on her bodice." Lavinia rolled her eyes. "As if I would *ever* allow feathers on a wedding dress."

Parth had no idea why feathers were such a bad idea, but he held his tongue. "Is that because Lady Blythe wishes that she were marrying North—or rather, a man who will be a duke someday?"

Lavinia nodded. He handed her a pear tartlet and she bit down on it.

"By wearing the same lace, she feels as if she too were a duchess-to-be?" He could hear the grating disbelief in his own voice. "That's mad."

"Clothing allows a woman to be whomever she wishes to be, however temporarily," Lavinia said. He pushed a tiny meringue with a curl of orange peel on top in front of her.

"That's madness."

"Lady Blythe wouldn't be happy as a duchess. It's tedious and formal."

"Ophelia likes it," Parth said defensively. He'd been living in the castle when the duke fell in love and courted his third duchess.

"Ophelia likes parts of it . . . the duke, for example," Lavinia said. Her dimple showed when she smiled like that.

"The feeling is clearly mutual."

"I know," Lavinia said with a sigh. "They're a model of what to hope for in marriage." She shook her head.

"What am I saying? You hardly need consider models of marital happiness. You've chosen Elisa, and you'll be a wonderful couple."

Parth just managed to keep his jaw shut. Lavinia truly believed he would kiss her—not just once, but twice—while he was courting Elisa? He had been educated to believe that kissing a lady in a secluded alley was . . .

Well, it was practically a marriage proposal.

Lavinia, oddly enough, was feeling quite happy, even though she was having a tête-à-tête with Parth.

They hadn't quarreled again, for one thing. Her new resolve not to care that Parth Sterling was in love with Elisa seemed to be successful.

"Why do you suppose that we rubbed each other the wrong way for so long?" she asked impulsively. She took a spoonful of delicious lemon pudding.

His eyes caught on her mouth. But then they had shared those kisses. It would be disingenuous not to admit that there was desire between them.

"Might it have been because you called me names?" he answered wryly.

"So I did," she said, happily taking another spoonful. "But only you, Mr. Appalling Parth. I've never been rude to another person that I can recall."

He looked at her closely. "I believe you sincerely mean that."

"Of course I'm sincere. I've never seen the point of being rude for the sake of it. Unlike you," she added, grinning at him. "If you and I are to be friends at last, Parth, we must acknowledge the fact that you think—or hopefully thought—me a brainless ninny."

She ate more lemon pudding, and once again Parth's eyes stayed on her lips. For someone practically betrothed to another woman, he seemed terribly attracted to her mouth.

"I thought you a shallow puddle only because you deliberately led me to that conclusion," Parth stated.

That was fair. Almost.

There was also the fact that she'd been smitten with him, and hadn't known what to do with the feeling, because—unlike most other eligible bachelors—he hadn't wooed her.

No, not every bachelor. Alaric and North never looked at her appreciatively either.

"I *am* shallow; I freely admit to it. I love clothing," she said, laying down the truth. "I enjoy studying and playing with fabric, lace, selvages, and feathers." He looked startled, but she just kept going. "Corsets, umbrellas, gussets, spangles—"

He held up a hand. "I understand."

Lavinia smiled at him again, a big smile, the one she gave to Willa and Artie and all those she truly liked. "Whenever I mentioned something that interested me, you acted like a pompous ass. To be honest."

"I apologize," Parth said. "I can be either or both at times."

"I am *always* shallow as a puddle," Lavinia said. "I can't help it. It's simply my nature. Just now some part of my brain is noting the green shade of that lady's bodice to your right. Green was a regrettable choice to pair with orange skirts."

"An appalling lack of taste?" Parth asked, eyebrow crooked.

"Lack of judgment," she said with a sigh. "That green does nothing for her skin."

"She's revealing an extraordinary amount of it," Parth said. He didn't ogle the lady, which Lavinia appreciated. He had never ogled Elisa either, at least when Lavinia was watching, which was most of the time.

Good thing she'd shed her affection for him and no longer cared.

"You're not shallow; you're fascinated by clothing," Parth said.

"Fascinated by puddles," Lavinia pointed out, and shrugged. "Willa is my closest friend, and she has always chosen to read ancient history, if given a chance. Whereas I spent three years deeply besotted with Lord Wilde, and I do mean, *deeply*."

Parth cleared his throat. "I trust your adoration has waned, now that Willa has married the object of your affections?"

"Very disappointing," Lavinia said, staring at her empty pudding bowl and contemplating using her finger, though that would be intolerably ill-bred.

Another bowl of pudding nudged the first to the side. She looked up. "Oh, you mustn't give yours to me! I've had more than enough."

"I don't like lemons. Tell me. Were you disappointed when Alaric fell in love with Willa?"

There was an odd strain in Parth's voice, as if he really cared. Perhaps they could become true friends, even after he married Elisa.

She gave him a lachrymose smile. "My heart was broken. Shattered. Tears every night, weeping into my bath, sobbing over my bacon."

Parth narrowed his eyes.

"It was as if a piece of my heart had been torn away," she added. "Torn on the bias, frayed, and never to be the same, impossible to patch back together."

"It appears you could rival the murderous playwright who was also infatuated with Alaric," he said, digging her spoon into his pudding and bringing it to her lips.

Lavinia obediently opened her mouth, her eyes laughing at his over the spoon. And, after swallowing, "'*Never shall I love another man!*' That's a quote from *Wilde in Love*, in case you'd forgotten it." She took the spoon from him and put it to the side. "I shall be ill if I eat any more, delicious though it is."

"Wasn't the line '*Never shall I love another woman!*'?" Parth asked.

"I altered it for dramatic purposes."

"So Lord Wilde ruined you for other men?"

She rarely saw Parth laughing; it took her breath away and made her feel tipsy.

"You must admit that it's difficult for ordinary men to compete with a man who wrestles giant squid into submission and scales mountains merely for the joy of planting a flag on top."

"Would you accept a stallion rather than an octopus?" he asked, his face alight with amusement.

"I would accept a trip to China. My favorite Lord Wilde book is his first, in which you and he travel together."

"We were young fools," Parth said. "But then most eighteen-year-old men are."

"But the trip to China had an actual objective! You brought home pekoe tea, which happens to be my favorite."

"The objective of Alaric's books is his wanderings," Parth said, pouring her more wine. "They captivate many people."

"Yes, I read them over and over," Lavinia said. She was eyeing the last piece of chicken. It would be very peculiar to eat chicken after pudding.

Parth took the remaining piece and began cutting it up, so that settled that question. "Why?"

"'Why'?" No one had ever asked that question, and she'd never asked it to herself, beyond the obvious answer: She *adored* Lord Wilde, as did most of the women in the kingdom. "I suppose because Wilde—as author of the books, you understand—can do anything and go anywhere. That notion is always implicit: if he's not enjoying himself, he'll simply move on to the next adventure."

"Precisely why the cannibals depicted in the play *Wilde in Love* were absurd," Parth said. He cut the last piece of chicken, removed the empty bowls, and set the plate of chicken in their place. "Alaric has no interest in being cooked in a stewpot, and he'd never bring someone he loved within reach of murderous peoples either."

"I can't eat chicken after sweets," Lavinia said, completely disconcerted. "I thought you were going to eat that slice."

"No, you are."

He held her gaze calmly, unrelenting, until she realized that the chicken smelled very good. Better than anything had smelled in a long time.

"You're very high-handed," she observed, and then ate a bite.

"I do own eight businesses."

"Eight?" Lavinia squinted at him. "Surely you exaggerate."

"I never exaggerate," Parth said, beginning to peel an apple. It had the slightly shriveled look of an apple that had ripened last fall, but it, too, smelled good. "Yes, for you," he said, catching her eye.

"I must finally be entirely well," Lavinia said happily.

"Although it would be terrible to tailor all my gowns again. Impossible, considering how much fabric we cut."

"'We'?"

"My maid and I," Lavinia explained. "Annie and I have been slowly altering my wardrobe."

He gave her a frown. "If you need more servants in your mother's absence, Lavinia, I am happy to help."

"Please understand, I *like* doing it. The truth is, I love it. I've learned so much about how to make women feel beautiful."

"Women are either attractive or they are not," Parth said, demonstrating a typical man's complete ignorance.

She gave him a kind smile. "Nonsense. For example, with proper boning, padding, and seaming, a *modiste* can make every woman's bosom a work of art." Too late she realized this was an invitation to look at her breasts, but characteristically, Parth's eyes didn't waver from her face.

"Your beauty has nothing to do with the size or shape of your breasts," he told her, his eyes as placid as his voice. "Or the fit of your gown, either."

Lavinia managed to snap her mouth shut.

"Men fall in love with the way you smile at them," he said, putting the apple, sliced into perfect white segments, before her. "They can't resist your smile, and the way you flush when you're happy, and the curve of your bottom lip."

Lavinia was having trouble breathing. Joy flickered through her.

"That has nothing to do with your breasts, though I, for one, miss their former glory. Even if men decide—erroneously—that you care for nothing but frivolities, they are likely to be driven mad by you anyway."

Lady Knowe drew out a chair and dropped into it while Lavinia was still staring, silently, at Parth's face.

"My dears!" the lady cried. "You are not quarreling, which I am so happy to see!"

Lavinia pulled herself back together. "I'm glad you returned," she said warmly. "Would you like some . . ." She looked at the table with dismay; somehow she and Parth had managed to eat a great deal of the food.

Parth had already caught a waiter's attention and was ordering more.

"Of course, I returned," Lady Knowe said, looking astonished. "I could scarcely allow you to be compromised by Parth, could I? There's nothing more uncomfortable than those marriages in which husband and wife are constantly at each other's throats."

"I couldn't be compromised," Lavinia said, laughing. "Parth is courting Elisa, remember?" It was a relief to be so open about it. And she was almost certain that her eyes didn't show the least bit of regret.

"Poor Elisa," Lady Knowe said. "Married all those years and without a single child. One has to hope that the problem stemmed from her elderly husband."

Parth said nothing, so Lavinia found herself taking up the cudgels in Elisa's defense. "That is *not* something one should consider when choosing a spouse, Lady Knowe."

"No?" The lady held her right hand out to Parth. "My dear, undo all these buttons, won't you? My gloves are adorable but irksome."

"I have a pair with forty-two buttons," Lavinia said, leaning closer to take a look. "At least yours have pearl buttons and they're slipping free easily. Mine are—"

Lady Knowe coughed. "A time and place, Lavinia, a time and place. This is not button time."

Lavinia felt herself turning pink. "Forgive me. No buttons."

"If not button time, what time is it?" Parth asked, turning to his aunt.

"Well, I believe that Lavinia was about to give me a lecture on the requirements of a spouse before she was distracted by my buttons."

"All I said was that one shouldn't choose a spouse with an eye to offspring," Lavinia said.

"But that's just what one does," Parth said, pouring more wine for Lavinia and refilling his aunt's glass as well. Despite his usual imperturbable expression, Lavinia had the idea that he was enjoying himself.

In fact—who would have thought it?—Parth Sterling had a well-honed, sardonic sense of humor.

No wonder he hadn't considered her as a wife. She was never wry. Or even sarcastic. *You're probably not smart enough for that*, a self-defeating voice inside her suggested, but she shoved it aside.

She wasn't well-read, like Willa, but she *was* smart.

She looked up and found him gazing at her, and there wasn't any humor in his eyes. Instead, they were deep and searching, as if he wondered what she was thinking.

"I meant," he said, "that one may act as if children are irrelevant—though people like North, with the burden of being heir to a dukedom, cannot pretend—but I assume that one considers offspring when making a choice."

"I can imagine your children with Elisa," Lavinia said, throwing more enthusiasm into her voice than was called for.

"Can you?" Lady Knowe said, looking up from her plate. "This is excellent chicken. Did you have some, Lavinia?"

"Too much," she said firmly.

"What would those children look like?" Parth asked, wry humor in his eyes again.

Fine. She was willing to be a source of amusement. It was better than the way he used to look at her.

"Naughty cherubs with loose curls," Lavinia said, picking up a tartlet, even though she wasn't hungry. "Your children will be adorable, *and* they'll speak two languages!"

Perhaps she overdid the enthusiasm on that last sentence.

"I don't see any particular benefit in that," Lady Knowe observed. "Most of the people I know can scarcely manage one language, let alone two." She pushed her plate away. "What happened to Lord Jeremy?"

"I think he is not joining us, since he was supposed to be here well over an hour ago," Parth said.

"I'm too old to be awake this late," Lady Knowe said. "Lord Jeremy will have to fall in love with you another evening, Lavinia. I'm voting for Prince Oskar. I like picturing you with a diadem on your head. Help me up, my dear. It's time to go home."

Parth rose, and Lavinia followed, a feeling of deep gratitude washing down her. She and Lady Knowe had become close in the last weeks and she had the idea that the lady knew just how much Lavinia didn't want to discuss Parth's future children.

This tugging at the heart would go away in time.

Parth escorted them into the townhouse and Lavinia held out her gloved hand for a kiss, pretending that she didn't see that Parth's eyebrows were pulling together. They weren't bushy eyebrows, but thick, like his hair.

"This has been such a pleasure." She turned to Lady Knowe. "Mr. Sterling was kind enough to offer to escort me to Cheshire when I deliver the garments we ordered, but I declined. I'm sure you'll agree with me that two or three seamstresses will be more than adequate companionship for the journey."

"I do agree," Lady Knowe said. "Parth, you'll want to remain in London with Elisa, since you are bringing her to us for the wedding."

"I fail to see what one thing has to do with the other," Parth said. "Miss Gray should not make a five-day journey with no more escort than a pair of young seamstresses."

Lady Knowe fixed him with a peremptory stare. "If you feel the need to escape your work, just come to Lindow. Don't make up excuses; you'll cause Lavinia to feel like a burden, and then she won't wish to visit us any longer."

"Yes," Lavinia chimed in, feeling another surge of affection for Lady Knowe. "I will feel like a burden."

Parth bowed. He had a remarkable ability to show just how much he disagreed, even though his bow was perfect in every respect.

"That boy has a talent for being exasperating," Lady Knowe said, as the door closed behind him.

"He's hardly a boy," Lavinia protested.

Lady Knowe sighed. "To me, he is."

Lavinia held her tongue. To her, Parth was all man: strong, confident, warm, intelligent.

Ugh.

Chapter Sixteen

August 14, 1780

*A*fter the trip to Vauxhall, Diana, North, and Lady
Knowe stepped into a carriage bound for Cheshire.
Lavinia breathed a sigh of relief. She adored them all,
but just at the moment, she felt like a general managing a large-scale military campaign. She didn't have
time for pleasantries.

She spent the ensuing weeks crisscrossing London,
collecting garments from *modistes*, tailors, and
mantua-makers. Back in the duke's townhouse, she
and Annie catalogued everything, along with any
notes Lavinia had taken about the finishing touches
needed. The following morning she would set out
again to visit two cobblers, a milliner, an umbrella
maker . . .

She worked day and night, making certain that she
knew exactly what was needed in terms of alterations,
and compiling long lists detailing the steps required
to finish each garment. Each ornament required for
the finished item of clothing—lace, spangles, ruffles,

plumes—was carefully organized and packed in separate parcels.

Finally, finally, all the items on her list were checked off. The clothing was packed. She had hired two excellent seamstresses. She was ready.

Lavinia set off for Lindow in the first of three carriages. Her carriage held herself, Annie, and two young seamstresses recommended by Madame Prague for their skill, and hired by Lavinia, with the blessings and purse strings of the Duke of Lindow.

The second carriage—one of the duke's sturdiest vehicles—was filled to bursting with gowns in various stages of completion, hanging from numerous hooks specially attached to the ceiling. Diana's wedding gown, swathed in layers of silk, hung from the center hook and was thus entirely cushioned on all sides. Opening the door of that carriage was a bit like opening the door of a dangerously overstuffed cupboard: voluminous, brightly colored silks and satins swelled out as if alive, and made closing the door again an open question.

The curtains of this carriage were firmly tacked closed, and the head groom would be bedding down on the coachman's seat every night—with Lavinia's apologies, and an offer of a superb bonus. No one would be able to gape at the wedding dress under her watch.

The third carriage was loaded with everything else: more gowns, umbrellas, stays, shoes . . . anything and everything that Diana, Lady Knowe, and the duke and duchess had requested, down to a trunk devoted to wedding clothing for the youngest Wilde offspring.

Lavinia relaxed only when her carriage was trundling out of London. For the next five days, work was impossible; she could do nothing but chat with Annie, Tabitha, and Mary.

Some small part of her was surprised that Parth hadn't made an appearance before her departure, or even offered a protest. That he hadn't simply appeared and folded himself into the crowded carriage implied that he had more respect for her opinion than she had believed.

Or perhaps that he didn't really care one way or the other.

On that dispiriting thought, Lavinia banished him from her thoughts.

"I wish we could sew in a moving carriage," Annie said, from the seat across from her.

"Rest," Lavinia advised her.

Tabitha and Mary looked at her uncertainly. They were used to working exhausting days, well into the night if a gown was needed the next day.

"Rest," Lavinia told them as well. She kicked off her slippers, tucking her legs under her and settling into the corner. The duke's traveling carriage, with its padded walls and dark-blue velvet seats, was outrageously comfortable.

The days passed in a soothing haze. Every innkeeper rushed out on seeing the duke's insignia on the carriage door. Baskets of food were offered, foot warmers, blankets, hot toddies.

It was very luxurious.

Before she lost her inheritance, Lavinia probably wouldn't have noticed. She was living more vividly now.

Without the impetus of her mother's thefts, she would never have put herself in charge of Diana's *trousseau*. She wouldn't have gone back and forth with *modistes*, ensuring that every detail of each gown suited the woman who was to wear it. She wouldn't have categorically refused feathered collars—an abominable and sure-to-be-short-lived fashion.

She wouldn't have spent hours choosing just the right plumes to complement each gown, sometimes purchasing them in both short and long lengths, so that ladies' maids would be able to vary the ladies' headdresses.

Yet she loved doing it. While the seamstresses napped, she would pull out the pages of foolscap detailing her sewing schedule and review them again and again, coming up with alternatives in case of disaster.

If Diana were to gain more weight than expected . . . If Lady Knowe's trusted seamstress, Berthe, fell ill, and her gowns had to be fitted as well as completed . . .

Madame Prague had spent two days going over every garment she had created and showing Lavinia, from examples in her showroom, what could go wrong. In the end, Madame gave twenty percent from the cost of each garment—including the wedding gown—to Lavinia. "You will earn it," she had said.

The lady was not merely being kind. Madame was saving herself the tremendous amount of work needed to oversee the final perfection of these garments.

As the girls chattered among themselves, and the countryside rolled past outside the windows, Lavinia steeled herself for the month to come. It was the beginning of September, and Diana would marry on All Hallows' Eve, at the end of October.

She had less than two months, and she would need every day, every stitch, every seamstress.

PARTH PLUNGED INTO work the morning after the trip to Vauxhall and thought nothing of Jeremy Roden other than a fleeting acknowledgment that he would never introduce Lavinia to Jeremy, or, for that matter, any other eligible gentlemen.

He was biding his time, but she was his, and he meant to convince her as soon as he had a chance—after the *trousseau* was finished. Every time he went to Mayfair, the ladies were out.

A week later, he visited his private gentlemen's club and discovered that Jeremy, most uncharacteristically, hadn't been seen there since the night he missed their appointment. That was odd—and concerning.

To have failed to appear at Vauxhall was one thing; to be absent from the club was quite another. He turned about and set out for Jeremy's lodgings, but he found only Jeremy's elderly, distraught valet.

"No, Lord Jeremy wouldn't have gone home," the man said, wringing his hands. "He won't exchange a word with his father, the marquess. My master hasn't slept in his own bed since Tuesday. I fear he's been taken down by ruffians and thrown into the Thames. I went to the constables, but they haven't found a body."

"Perhaps he's decided to visit a friend," Parth suggested.

"Without clothing? Without me to trim his beard? Never!" There was genuine conviction in his voice.

"Have you checked the hospitals?" Parth asked.

"I went to St. Thomas's and Guy's. I meant to try St. Bartholomew's today."

Parth nodded. "I'll go to the London Hospital." He hesitated. "And Bedlam."

"Bedlam! Lord Jeremy isn't insane!" the valet protested, his voice rising. "He might be a trifle twitchy after his experience at war, but that doesn't mean he belongs amongst the madmen. That's not for those of his stature, people of worth and consequence."

"Hopefully not," Parth reassured him. But he had a bad feeling, and over the years he'd learned to trust his instincts.

Those instincts sent him directly to Bedlam, a label that referred to Bethlem, London's lunatic hospital. Parth knew it by reputation to be hellish, squalid, and crowded with benighted souls who heard voices, and others who tried to beat the voices out of those patients.

Jeremy had had a rough go of it since the war, and if by some appalling twist of fate, he'd ended up in Bedlam, he must be found without delay.

Once he arrived, Parth quickly established that no Jeremy Roden had been entered in the ward-book. All the same, he methodically made his way through the men's wards, searching every face, trailed by a keeper who insisted there were no gentlemen anywhere on the premises.

Parth had no idea of the stature of any of the men he was shown; few wore more than tattered garments, and they stared at him with the vacant gaze of men who had lost all hope.

On the second floor, he looked into a chamber that held a narrow cot. A man lay with his back to them, seemingly napping, as he hadn't twitched when the door creaked open.

"This one's a strange case," the keeper reported. "We can scarce get him to wake up, but when he's awake, he's frightful violent."

He began to pull the door shut, but Parth stopped him and entered the chamber. This patient wore silk breeches, filthy though they were.

His instincts proved correct: it was Jeremy. "This is he," he said over his shoulder. He gently shook Jeremy, and his friend's entire body moved. They'd trussed him up like a chicken set for roasting.

"He's wearing a strait waistcoat," the keeper explained. "Keeps him from hurting hisself, or anyone else."

Jeremy showed no sign of rousing at Parth's touch.

"Take this off him," Parth ordered, keeping his voice even. "Why isn't he waking? Has he been drugged?"

"He thought how he was on the battlefield," the man said defensively. "Dangerous, he was. He tried to fight us at first. Finally, they bled him, and he's been like this since."

Parth swallowed a curse. He wouldn't leave a dog, let alone a friend, in this godforsaken hospital. He paid for Jeremy's room and board, hired a stout fellow to help, and between them, they loaded the unconscious man into his carriage.

It was like loading a corpse, for Jeremy was deadweight, his limbs slack, utterly inert. His illness—if that was the correct label—had left dark circles under his eyes, and his forehead was furrowed, as if he were caught in a nightmare from which he couldn't escape.

Parth couldn't send Jeremy back into the care of an elderly valet. Instead he directed the carriage to his own townhouse. A couple of stout footmen helped Parth get Jeremy up the stairs, and then the carriage went off to fetch his valet.

Later that evening, his butler reported that Jeremy

had been given a bath and put to bed, without any signs of wakefulness. "We tried to feed him but he turned his face away without opening his eyes."

"We used to call him 'Sausage' at Eton," Parth said, suddenly remembering. "Tomorrow morning, try sausages."

Sure enough, when an excellent sausage was waved under his nose, Jeremy opened his mouth. The following day, when two footmen put him in the tub and his valet poured water over his head, he suddenly spluttered, opened his eyes, and demanded a brandy.

Parth breathed a silent sigh of relief when his butler told him the news, and headed upstairs.

"What in the bloody hell am I doing here?" Jeremy asked. He was wearing a wrapper, seated by the fire. He looked exhausted.

"You had a turn," Parth said. "What do you remember last?"

Jeremy frowned. "Fireworks. The damned fireworks sounding like cannon fire."

"You might want to avoid fireworks in the future," Parth suggested. "I recommend you stay here for a week or two, and then come with me to Lindow."

"Lindow? The duke's castle? Why in bloody hell would I go there with you?"

Parth shrugged. "Why not? I'm not prying you out of Bedlam again. We're both lucky not to have got fleas."

"Thank you," Jeremy said. "But I don't see where Lindow comes into it."

Parth gave him a faint smile. "North is at Lindow, you know. If anyone understands what you're going through, he's the one."

Jeremy flinched, but Parth could see he accepted the reasoning. "I'll go if you don't tell a soul—including North—where you found me."

"That's your business," Parth said readily.

"When are we going?" Jeremy asked, slumping back into the chair.

"As soon as Miss Lavinia Gray leaves London," Parth said. "She's bound for Lindow, and we will follow her."

"*Follow her*?" Jeremy scowled at him. "Does 'follow' mean that we're sneaking about?"

"She won't allow me to accompany her," Parth explained, "but it's not safe for her to travel so far on her own. I mean to shadow her carriage in order to make certain she's safe."

"Bloody hell," Jeremy said, shaking his head. "Isn't that the woman you were introducing to me? You've stolen my bride-to-be."

"Yes, I have," Parth said.

"She's not quite stolen, if she won't allow you to accompany her," Jeremy said with a bark of laughter.

"It's important to her to feel independent," Parth said. "I don't want to take away her confidence. But I have to make certain she's safe."

Jeremy snorted. "And people think that the title of 'gentleman' means something. You're as much a wolf as any other man—just a patient wolf."

It took five days to reach Lindow, longer than Parth would have taken on his own—but they stopped whenever Lavinia stopped.

On the last morning, Parth woke a cantankerous Jeremy at five in the morning and took off for Lindow. When he walked into the castle four hours later, Aunt Knowe dashed down the stairs to greet Parth, eyes shining. The duke appeared too, his welcome quieter than his twin's, but just as affectionate. Ophelia greeted him with her warm, sweet smile.

Coming home was like sinking into a warm bath after a cold day on the moors.

"Lord Jeremy is sleeping in the carriage?" the duchess said, her brow pleating. "What on earth is the matter with that poor man?"

"He's twitchy and he drinks too much," Parth said bluntly. "North might be able to help. I told my man to let him sleep for another hour or so."

"I shall wake him," the duke said. "I've always liked that young man."

"I'll go with you," said his duchess, and they left, arm in arm.

"I can't believe that you followed Lavinia's carriage all the way from London! Appalling Parth, indeed!" Aunt Knowe said.

"She had only the coachmen and a few grooms, and her three vehicles were obviously carrying valuables. I put one of my grooms outside her room, and another on each of the carriages. Anything could have happened to her."

"But nothing did," Aunt Knowe declared.

"Lavinia doesn't take care of herself," he said, hearing the gruffness in his own voice. "Just look at the way she travels around London with no chaperone."

"Lavinia is not in her first Season."

"What if a ruffian had seen her entering an inn?"

Lavinia was an exceptionally beautiful woman, and he damned well wasn't going to let his future wife be attacked. Or worse.

Parth wrapped his arm around his aunt. "I know I'm a stubborn fellow, but it's paid off, hasn't it?"

"In money," she said, waving her hand dismissively, as if the world's riches meant nothing to her.

They probably didn't. Aunt Knowe was the sort of person who'd be happy anywhere from a castle to a farmhouse.

"Yes, in filthy lucre. And hopefully, in a wife," he said.

"I like her." Aunt Knowe strode over to a window.

Her? She had to mean Elisa. He hadn't said a word about Lavinia.

"You're all falling in love at once," she said in a stifled voice. "My three boys, all leaving the nest, and there's Horatius gone without a chance to fall in love. I don't want to forget him."

Parth wrapped his arms around her from behind. Aunt Knowe was so tall that he easily put a chin on her shoulder. "You, my best of aunts, will never lose us. We'll all be here for All Hallows' Eve, won't we? I wouldn't be surprised if Alaric turned up like a bad penny."

His aunt dabbed her eyes with her handkerchief. "I *want* you all to be happy. I want you to have your own households."

She sounded as if she were trying to persuade herself. Parth rocked her a little. She smelled of warm toast and the face cream she made herself, using honey from estate bees.

"At any rate," she said, freeing herself and turning, "*You* have set yourself a task, Parth."

He hesitated, wondering if it was the moment to mention that he had no intention of marrying Elisa. But she continued.

"Lavinia isn't like those other young ladies of your acquaintance—and I include your adopted sisters in the group. Betsy is independent, but Lavinia is a force of nature."

Parth raised an eyebrow. "You know? Even Lavinia believes I'm courting Elisa."

She put her hand on his cheek for a second. "You're my boy, Parth. It shouldn't surprise you that I noticed how you looked at Lavinia. But, my dear, Lavinia is more serious than most, and I'm not entirely sure you'll make a good pair."

Parth tightened his lips. Naturally, he wanted his beloved aunt to approve of his marriage, but if she didn't, it wouldn't change his mind.

"I'm worried that she might marry you for the wrong reasons," Aunt Knowe continued.

Wrong reasons? He felt his lips easing into a smile. Lavinia would marry him because of their kisses, because of the infatuation that had led her to propose marriage to him.

"I'm aware she has no dowry," he said. "If she had wanted a title, Beck was at her feet. If she chooses to marry me, it won't be for my money."

His aunt made a face. "I don't know why I'm fretting over this, because however much I love you *and* Lavinia, and I do love that dear girl—Wait a minute! What happened with Elisa?"

"I have made no promises to the contessa."

"You brought her to Vauxhall! And invited her to come to the wedding," his aunt cried. "You informed everyone at the tea party, including Lavinia, that you were in love with her."

"I said nothing of the sort. I merely mentioned that I had plans to court her."

"You said you had plans to *marry* her," his aunt retorted.

"I had second thoughts."

"Is Elisa aware of your second thoughts?"

He nodded. "Elisa ordered me to continue to woo her for the moment, because she is looking forward to the wedding."

"Do you honestly mean to woo two women at the same time?" Aunt Knowe broke into a smile. "Not to mention the fact that you brought along Lord Jeremy to court Lavinia! It sounds marvelously entertaining, like one of those comedies in which men hide behind sofas, and kiss all the wrong ladies."

"Jeremy is *not* here to court Lavinia," Parth said. "He's too unstable to make advances to anyone. He's here because I couldn't leave the fellow alone in London."

His aunt leaned forward and poked Parth's waist-coat. "I would advise you to make your case to Lavinia before the contessa arrives. Don't take this the wrong way, my dear, but that strong and silent act you've perfected will not make it easy to court two women at once."

"I won't court them both," Parth said. "Elisa *knows*."

"Well, Lavinia doesn't know—nor that Elisa *does* know," his aunt retorted.

"I'll find the right moment to tell her."

"Hmm, I wish I could hear that conversation." Aunt Knowe headed toward the door. "Do come say hello to Diana. It's going on toward noon, so she's probably thrown up at least thrice and will be looking for diversion."

"What conversation would you like to hear?" Parth said, following her.

"The one in which you explain to Lavinia that you planned to marry Elisa, but now you've changed your mind and you'll marry her, and oh, by the way, you'll still court Elisa in public." She burst into laughter.

Parth said nothing as they went down the corridor. In his estimation, Elisa would be perfectly happy as long as he brought her to Lindow and she could entertain herself with living versions of the Wilde prints she collected.

She would thoroughly enjoy the wedding and ball to follow, surrounded by the very best people in English society, all behaving with the joyful abandon that came along with house parties.

Outside Diana's bedchamber, Aunt Knowe turned, eyes twinkling, and patted his cheek. "Even as a boy, you always kept your promises. Only you would offer suitors to the woman you want for yourself. Of course, one of those suitors sailed immediately for Norway, and the other is so war-damaged that she won't be able to drop a plate in his vicinity."

"But I did follow through on my promise," Parth said, grinning at her.

Chapter Seventeen

Later that morning

The route they took led around the northern edge of Lindow Moss, the vast peat bog that lay to the east of the castle. Lavinia had paid little attention to the bog before, but as she sat at the window and mile after mile rolled by, she understood for the first time how large it was.

It was a chilly cold September, and when they first got in the carriage, frost rimed each blade of grass. By mid-morning, the frost had melted from hillocks, but in lower-lying areas, it stayed, turning into pools colored by fish with flashing silver scales. Or shimmering Indian silk.

"Do you know the story of Lindow Moss?" Annie asked, breaking into her thoughts. "I learned all about it when we visited before."

"No, do tell," Lavinia said.

"It's swallowed up people, hasn't it?" Mary, one of the seamstresses, interjected with a shiver. "I heard as one of the duke's own children was swallowed up there."

"The heir to the dukedom," Annie said, lowering her voice. "Horatius, his name was. He had been drinking in the tavern, more than was good for him. He wagered he could ride across Lindow Moss in the dark and come out safe on the other side."

The other seamstress, Tabitha, leaned across and peered out at the bog. "It doesn't look terrible."

"There are holes that will suck you down," Annie declared, obviously relishing her role as local expert.

Tabitha shuddered and sat back against the seat. "I wouldn't go in there if you paid me ten shillings."

"The poor man never made his way home that night," Annie said. "They managed to save his horse, but the heir was gone, his body swept underground and never recovered."

"Underground?" Lavinia asked.

"Rivers run under there," Annie said, nodding out the window. "The ground looks as if it's solid, but it's not. You can hear the water rushing along under your feet, going to the sea."

Tabitha wrapped her arms around her chest. "That's awful."

"There's them as say Horatius was murdered," Annie whispered. But then she frowned and looked at the two seamstresses. "It's worth your position to say anything like that in front of Mr. Prism. You have to follow the castle's rules or you'll be dismissed without a reference. Might even be thrown out and told to make your way through the bog by yourself!"

"I doubt that very much," Lavinia intervened. "What

are the rules?" Mary and Tabitha were sitting up straight, eyes wide.

"No talking to anyone that asks about the Wildes," Annie said. "Even if they seem like the friendliest person in the world, say, an old woman, just curious about what they ate for dinner the night before. I can promise you that it'll end up in the newspapers and Mr. Prism *always* finds out where the information came from."

Mary pursed her lips. "Who would care about food?"

"The world does, and that's not a joke," Annie said. "Those gossip columns are mad for any sort of information."

"I was offered two pounds if I would describe the wedding dress," Tabitha said. She was the quieter of the two, quite possibly born a lady. Lavinia hadn't pried, because a lady wouldn't want to talk about what had caused her to take up a trade.

"I was only offered ten shillings," Mary said indignantly.

"Accept a bribe, and you'll be gone," Annie stated. "The castle sticks together. Even when the heir died, nobody found out a thing from *them*. Never. That's another rule: I know we were just talking of Horatius, but you mustn't ever mention him to an outsider, nor the way he died, neither."

"Certainly not," Tabitha said.

"Last rule," Annie said, "and it's a big one too. Don't ever, *ever* flirt with one of the Wildes."

"I would never!" Mary cried, indignant.

"You'll think of it," Annie said with a smile. "It's impossible not to. They're that beautiful, all of them, even the boys as are eighteen, nineteen, and only returning home now and then."

"Pshaw," Mary said, tossing her hair. "I'm a London girl, born and bred, and I don't have any interest."

Tabitha was looking down, pleating her dress. "What is on your mind?" Lavinia asked.

She looked up. "It isn't always the maid who flirts with the master."

"True enough, but not in the castle," Annie promised. "The Wildes don't ever do that sort of thing. The rule is there because Mr. Prism got tired of having to let maids go because they'd crept into someone's bed."

"That's absurd," Mary said. "We would *never* do such a thing!"

The conversation changed to something else, but Lavinia stopped listening. Instead she imagined making her way into Parth's chamber and waiting there for him. Tearing off her clothing and hiding in his bed.

Holding her breath as he came into the room. Peeking through the bed curtains at his simple black coat, worn over a plain shirt, even though he owned a lace factory.

Tabitha and Mary were squealing at Annie's tale of a loose-lipped maidservant who had come to a bad end, so Lavinia relaxed into the daydream because . . . why not? She would never do such a thing in real life.

Because it was *her* dream, she dressed him in a plum-colored coat, with deep cuffs of a dull silver. His shirt was superfine linen, so when he took off his coat, she could see the lines of his muscles through the cloth.

His pantaloons were tight, perfectly fitted to his legs so that everyone could see his thighs. In her imaginary hiding place behind the bed curtains, she watched as he kicked off his shoes and wrenched down his pantaloons.

Stretching in the light of the fire, his skin was the color of warm bronze, smooth over taut muscles. She knew what a man's body looked like, because she and Willa had investigated naughty books when they were younger.

But in her imagination, he was better than those illustrations because he was alive, moving . . . *Parth*. He drew back the bed curtains and looked down at her with a start. Her heart pounding, she looked back at him, mute.

Would he . . .

Deep in his eyes, a spark lit, that rare, elusive smile that she'd seen only once or twice. "It must be my birthday," he said, without an ounce of disdain.

Her dream Parth wanted her more than anything else in his life. He bent over her, firelight glinting on his chest, and braced his arms on either side of her head.

"Parth," she murmured, stirring, stretching like a cat, brushing against him.

He bent his head and lapped at her mouth, lazy and wicked. "May I unwrap my present?"

Something touched her knee, and Lavinia opened her eyes.

"We're almost there," Annie said. "I can see it!"

Lavinia turned to look out the window, certain there were red patches in her cheeks. Wisps of her daydream clung to her blissfully. Parth's rod had been heavy, warm. His lips were softer than she thought. His smoldering eyes had not been just admiring: They had been *adoring*.

That was enough to snap her out of her daydream.

She pushed the thought away with disgust. Since when did Lavinia Gray have to create dream men to admire her? Let alone a man who was *bringing another woman* to Diana's wedding?

For some reason she had a weakness for Parth, the way her mother had for laudanum. But enough was enough.

Lindow Castle was a great heap of gray stone against the chilly sky, taking on definition as they came closer, turning into a proper castle, with different-sized turrets and towers and a large stone courtyard.

"It was besieged once," Annie said importantly. "The whole village of Mobberley moved inside, snug as bugs in a rug. The men crept back and forth through the bog, bringing in food and whatever else was needed."

"Without falling into those rivers?" Tabitha asked.

"No, but local story has it that quite a few of the enemy's bodies made their way down to the sea," Annie reported.

"Who were they?" Lavinia asked.

Annie shrugged. "They gave up after a while and moved on, and the castle got stronger and bigger. Queen Elizabeth paid a visit, and, before her, her father, King Henry VIII, too. He practiced archery, and there's an arrow stuck right through a sheep's skull up on one wall, and that's his, or so they say."

"A sheep?" Lavinia asked dubiously. It didn't strike her as particularly heroic. The sheep she'd seen from the carriage just stood around, as if they were waiting to have arrows stuck in them.

The castle was near now, sharp against the silver-gray sky. It looked immense, looming over Lindow Moss, the duke's flag signaling that he was in residence.

Annie bounced on her seat. "You'll like the house-keeper, Mrs. Mousekin," she told the girls. "Mr. Prism, the butler, is a stiff man, and no mistake. But he's fair."

Twenty minutes later, the coaches drew to a halt in the great stone courtyard, whose torches were already lit against the waning light. Lady Knowe emerged to meet them, Prism close behind. Introductions were made, the journey inquired about, and as grooms and footmen surrounded the carriages to attend to the horses and begin the process of unloading, the group made its way into the entrance hall.

After a footman had borne away their cloaks, Tabitha, Annie, and Mary were taken off belowstairs with promises of hot drinks and bedchambers.

"No sewing until tomorrow!" Lady Knowe bellowed after them.

She turned to Lavinia and enveloped her in a hug. "Thank the Lord, you are more yourself! You've lost that peaked look you had, with your cheekbones sticking out like flying buttresses."

"You are exaggerating," Lavinia said, laughing and hugging her back.

"Are the carriages stuffed with delightful garments?"

"Indeed they are," Lavinia promised.

"I cannot wait to see them all!" Lady Knowe cried, taking Lavinia's arm and leading her toward the stairs. "The duchess is waiting for you in Diana's room. Things have gone from bad to worse, and that poor girl can scarcely get out of bed without losing whatever she's eaten."

"Oh, no!"

"Not to worry," Lady Knowe said. "I have her sipping a good bone broth every twenty minutes. She won't have gained much weight by the wedding, which means the guests won't know another Wilde is on the way. At least, not until one appears two or three months after the fact. Or until the bride throws up on her groom's toes, in which case the secret will be out."

"She must be fitted into her wedding dress, if I have to prop her up myself."

"You might have to hold her basin," Lady Knowe laughed.

"We're at a point where the bodice must be tried on," Lavinia said firmly. "Especially because ladies' bosoms change shape under these circumstances. Have you put me in the same bedchamber I had before?"

"No, my dear," Lady Knowe said. "Prism and I have spent hours planning where to put all the wedding guests. I've put you in the North Tower, if you don't mind. It's the family tower, so you'll have young Wildes underfoot."

This time Lavinia's smile was genuine. "That will be my pleasure."

"The chamber directly beside yours was intended by some ancestor for his mother-in-law; it's large enough to accommodate your seamstresses. You'll have Berthe, and the castle seamstress, and I've engaged another girl from the village. If things become desperate, we can always borrow a maid or two as well."

"With luck, we shall keep to my schedule."

"Capital," Lady Knowe said. They had arrived at the top of the stairs. "We'll pop by Diana's chamber to say hello. What I wanted to tell you first, my dear, is not about Diana's troubles."

Lavinia froze. "My mother?"

"Oh, no, Lady Gray is doing well, from what I understand," Lady Knowe said. "It's Parth."

He must have eloped.

Lavinia swayed for a moment, as if taking a blow. It made sense. He would hate the fuss of a wedding. He had declined a title, for goodness' sake. He wouldn't want an audience for his vows.

"I understand," she said between numb lips.

"What do you understand?" Lady Knowe sighed and put her hands on her hips. "I do declare that the two of you are enough to age a body by ten years. He's *here*, Lavinia. I wanted you to know."

"*What?* The *Morning Chronicle* said that he would be speaking to Parliament again this week about banking rules."

"Apparently they had to work out their own rules," Lady Knowe said. "He arrived this morning, bringing Lord Jeremy Roden with him." She paused. "He will stay a fortnight before returning to London to fetch Elisa for the house party. Now, I know that Lord Jeremy was presented to you as a possible suitor, my dear, but the man was badly affected by his experience in war. In short, you can't have him."

"I don't want him," Lavinia said.

"Excellent!" Lady Knowe cried. "I'm just so pleased that Parth will stay with us for a few weeks. I can hardly ever make him stop working for such a length of time."

Lavinia had refused Parth's escort, and he'd arrived in Cheshire virtually the same time as she did? Highhanded wasn't a strong enough adjective for that man. He had chased her here because he didn't believe she could take care of herself. Arrogant. Managing.

But protective . . .

And helpful: He'd brought her another suitor, even if Lady Knowe deemed the fellow unsuitable.

He's going back to London to fetch Elisa.

She slammed an imaginary door on Parth, on Parth's bed, on Parth's . . . everything.

And this time she meant it.

"I shall spend the rest of the day organizing all the work to be done," she said to Lady Knowe. "If you will forgive me, I will have a simple supper in my room and greet the family tomorrow."

"You are *not* here as a member of the household, but as a dear friend of the family," Lady Knowe thundered.

"I have learned a great deal about myself in the last few months," Lavinia confessed, "and it seems I am a stickler for perfection. I promise to join the family tomorrow, but today I desperately wish to organize the garments and trimmings that I brought with me."

"You are an *artiste*," Lady Knowe said, kissing her cheek.

Lavinia laughed. "Clothing isn't a matter of artistry."

"Pish-posh," the lady retorted. "You are a virtuoso, and that's all I have to say about it!"

Chapter Eighteen

September 3, 1780
The next morning

*P*arth emerged from his bath, dressed, and went on a search for North and Jeremy. Instead, he found Betsy in the billiard room, knocking around balls. The oldest of the duke's daughters was enormously fanciable, with all the Wilde beauty, heightened by a mischievous flair.

"Oh, hello," she said, glancing up. "If you imagine I'm dropping a curtsy to you, Parth, you can forget about it. I'm in a rotten mood."

"How about if I take you at billiards instead?"

"Do I look as if I'm still a child? I've thrashed Father the last five games, and North will no longer play me."

"You could tutor me," Parth suggested.

"I suppose," she said moodily. "I've nothing better to do. The girls have taken up paper dolls, which is unendingly tedious, and North has a horse with colic, in case you're wondering where he is. You might as well go first."

"Pearls before swine," Parth said.

She rolled her eyes and set about demolishing his chance of winning before he even got his hands on a cue. He was leaning against the table when she flipped her cue and asked suddenly, "Why did you bring Lord Jeremy here?"

"He's a good friend of mine from school, and he was in the colonies with North." Parth hesitated, but it wasn't as if Jeremy had demanded anything but his stay in Bedlam be kept a secret. "He hasn't been well, and he had nowhere to go. His mother died while he was at war and he's not close to his father."

Betsy went silent while she pocketed a ball a bit more vigorously than Parth thought necessary.

"And?" he asked.

"He's an ass!" she burst out. "He was in here all yesterday afternoon. He has this haggard look, so one might *want* to be sympathetic, but he says utterly withering things."

"To you?"

"To everyone! Last night, before you came to the drawing room, he was even rude to Aunt Knowe."

Parth raised an eyebrow. "North allowed that?"

"Oh, you know Aunt Knowe. She slapped him over the head with a glove and burst into laughter." Scowling, she slammed another ball into a pocket.

"May I take it, then, that you don't like him?"

"No one could like him. He's insulting, sarcastic, and infuriating. North excuses him by saying 'he had a bad war,' but what does that mean, anyway? What excuse is it? At the very least, he could shave!"

"You don't like beards?" Parth grinned at her. "How about mine?"

"You're both absurd," she snapped. "As if you imagine yourself a courtier in Queen Elizabeth's court." The ball missed and caromed across the felt.

"My turn," Parth said. He straightened and grabbed his favorite stick from the rack on the wall.

"You had left for China with Alaric before I was allowed to pick up a cue," Betsy said. "Did you know that Marie Antoinette is a brilliant player?"

Parth didn't play billiards often, but his mathematical bent made the game more interesting than it might otherwise be.

It took a few minutes for Betsy to stop brooding over the grumpy soldier and notice his game. She slapped a hand on the edge of the table. "You've been holding out on me!"

"No, I haven't." He pocketed two balls.

"I wonder if you can beat Father."

Parth gave her a rueful smile. "He refuses to play you? He stopped playing against me when I reached sixteen."

Betsy's ill humor vanished as if it had never existed. Even as a child, she had had a mercurial temperament. "Brilliant!" she cried, clapping her hands. "I'm so glad you're home. Please tell me that you'll stay for a time and not run back to London."

Before he could answer, she answered herself. "But of course you will go away, because you're in love with a contessa! I can't wait to meet her. Diana said that she's absolutely delightful and we shall all love her. Is her name Elisabetta?"

"Elisa," Parth said. He pocketed a few more balls. As his aunt had said, it was a tangled web.

Betsy leaned forward, stabbing a finger in his direction. "You must do something for me, Parth."

"What?" He moved around the table, feeling a reasonable dislike of being cornered by exasperated females.

"Beat him," she said with relish. "Tan his hide. Beat the . . . beat the stuffing out of him. Beat the beard off his face. Beat the—"

"Are we referring to Jeremy?" Parth said, raising his hand. "Why don't you beat him yourself?"

"He won't play me."

"Why not? Afraid of losing?"

She sniffed. "Because he's a misogynistic donkey with about as much finesse as . . . as Hamlet. Remember how Hamlet kept going around and telling women to enter a nunnery?"

"One woman," Parth said mildly.

"One young woman," she corrected. "'Get thee to a nunnery,' et cetera. If Lord Jeremy had his way, we'd all be in nunneries, unable to pick up a billiard cue!"

"In Shakespeare's time, the word 'nunnery' was a euphemism for a house of ill repute," Parth pointed out.

"Don't you dare tell me that in your experience such women play billiards!" his sister squealed.

"I merely meant that those ladies likely have more opportunity to play than the average sister in holy orders," Parth said. "At any rate, Jeremy will remain here until the wedding, so you have time to change his mind."

"The longer he stays, the more opportunity there'll be to . . ."

"What? Trounce him at billiards?"

"I was thinking more in the way of a knee to the balls."

Parth looked up, startled.

He still thought of Betsy as a little sister, albeit one who debuted last Season. But there, across the table, was a glowing, gleeful *grown woman*. A woman who'd just expressed a desire to harm a delicate part of a man's anatomy, and who'd mentioned a crude term for that part without stumbling or blushing.

"Bloody hell," he said. "You grew up."

She rolled her eyes again.

Chapter Nineteen

$\mathcal{L}$avinia tried to pay a visit to Diana, but she entered the room just as a maid was holding a basin for her cousin, so she hurriedly retreated, leaving Lady Knowe in command of the room.

"I'm sorry!" Diana called after her in a hoarse voice. "Please come back later; I'm not contagious!"

"I will," Lavinia told the closed door.

Walking back down the hallway, she heard shouting, and a couple of children rushed by. The duchess appeared at the end of the passage, smiled at her, and shouted, "More slowly!" The sound of thumping signaled their retreat, not at a noticeably reduced speed.

"Good afternoon, my dear," Ophelia said, as Lavinia sank into a curtsy. "It is such a pleasure to have you join us. I'm longing to see the garments you've brought for me."

Behind the duchess, Parth emerged from a room farther down the corridor, one arm around Betsy's shoulder.

Right.

It was time to make it absolutely clear that no matter what those two kisses were, she had no interest in stealing him from the contessa.

"Oh, there you are!" Betsy cried, shrugging off Parth and running toward her. "I can't wait to see my gown!" In lieu of a curtsy, she grabbed Lavinia and hugged her. "Aunt Knowe promised that you are going to make me look as beautiful as Venus. Beautifuler, in fact."

"That won't be hard," Ophelia said, laughing.

Parth bowed. "Miss Gray, it is a pleasure to see you."

"What a surprise, Mr. Sterling," Lavinia said, curtsying. "The last I heard about you, you were bid to speak in Parliament."

"It was a short conversation."

She felt intently aware of every aspect of Parth: his dark-amber skin, his unpowdered hair, the breadth of his shoulders, even the way his blunt fingertips looked useful rather than graceful.

"Their loss is our gain," the duchess said, wrapping her hand around Parth's arm. "Are you aware of how marvelously Lavinia has taken over all the organization of Diana's wedding, Parth?"

"We saw each other in London," Lavinia said, before Parth could reply.

"That's right; Aunt Knowe told me that you went to Vauxhall," Ophelia said. "With the contessa," she added with a twinkling smile. "We'll want to hear more about her before she arrives for the wedding, Parth. Now that she's going to be part of the family."

Lavinia just managed to catch herself before she stepped backward.

"Parth beat me at billiards!" Betsy announced, mercifully interrupting that subject of conversation.

"Astonishing," Ophelia said.

Lavinia had the feeling Her Grace saw more than she let on; she had sweetly wise eyes that had watched ten—no, eleven—children grow up. Lavinia aimed a bright smile at Parth. "I had no idea that you were an excellent billiards player, Mr. Sterling."

He was watching her uncomfortably closely. "When I have time."

"I am desperate to see the wedding gown," Betsy cried. "May we see it? Aunt Knowe brought home the sketch and a swatch of the cloth, and I've been trying to imagine it ever since."

"Of course," Lavinia exclaimed. She and Betsy followed Ophelia and Parth down the corridor.

Betsy chattered on, telling Lavinia about everyone invited to the wedding and masquerade ball to follow. Most of polite society, it seemed, had accepted the duke's invitation.

Why wouldn't they?

The Duke and Duchess of Lindow were charming, powerful, and gracious hosts. Their children were intelligent and amusing—not to mention beautiful and rich.

Lavinia felt a hollow conviction that she no longer belonged at the approaching celebration. Last year, two years ago, she would have looked forward to it with utmost confidence. But now? With her criminally-minded mother addicted to laudanum and her dowry lost?

She belonged in the seamstresses' room, not in the drawing room with all the guests whom Betsy was happily enumerating. With a start, she realized that Betsy wasn't merely listing guests—she was reeling off an account of all the single gentlemen expected to attend the masquerade ball.

She was counting them off on her fingers, rejecting this one or that one because he had proposed either to Lavinia at some point, or to Betsy, this past Season. "You don't want my leavings and I don't want yours," Betsy said with a giggle.

Lavinia somehow managed to smile. She felt a million years from the young girl she had been when she'd first visited Lindow with Willa, more than two years before.

Fatigue was in her bones, perhaps. Or it was part and parcel of the understanding that her life had changed. She didn't want to marry any of the men whom Betsy was so blithely naming. Not to mention the fact that they likely had no interest in her.

Ophelia came to a halt before a door and paused to allow Betsy and Lavinia to catch up.

"Perhaps Lavinia isn't interested in your litany of prospects." Parth's voice was calm, as always, but there was a bit of an edge.

"While you were lucky enough to find this gorgeous contessa of yours without stepping into even one ballroom—and we *all* want to know how that happened!—the rest of us must rely on more time-honored methods," Betsy retorted.

"Mr. Sterling introduced me to a Norwegian prince whom I found quite appealing," Lavinia said to Betsy, averting further discussion of Elisa.

"What did you like about him?" Betsy asked.

"He's very handsome," Lavinia said, trying to remember what Oskar looked like. "Oh, and perhaps because Prince Oskar grew up in a royal court, he has an endless flow of amusing stories to tell."

The way Parth raised his eyebrow made it very clear that he considered this to be a less than manly trait, not worth marrying for. Too bad, because he was the one who'd introduced her to Prince Oskar.

"Not to say anything about the Norwegian prince," Betsy said dubiously, "but look who Parth just foisted on us, apparently telling Aunt Knowe that Lord Jeremy might be a good match for you, Lavinia! Tell me that isn't true, Parth. You wouldn't try to match darling Lavinia with that curmudgeon!"

Lavinia rather enjoyed the taut lines of Parth's face. He looked as if he was in a foul mood. "I'm looking forward to meeting Lord Jeremy. If only I'd had Mr. Sterling as a matchmaker in Paris," she said, "I expect I'd already be married."

"Lavinia, please do us the honor of showing us Diana's wedding dress," the duchess said.

Lavinia pushed open the door, feeling a queer tightness in her chest. She had thrown everything into this dress; she and Madame Prague had discussed each detail, from the precise drape of the pale satin to the placement of every spangle and pearl.

They entered a large chamber to find Lady Knowe chatting with the seamstresses.

There, in the middle of an open space, the wedding dress sat on a dressmaker's form, glowing in the sunshine. It was constructed of a gleaming champagne taffeta that laced tightly up the front, with a low bosom marked with a small lace ruffle that framed the breast and neck. The skirts opened over a petticoat of the same silk, embroidered with blush roses. Pale rose taffeta strips edged in lace formed a wide band down the side of the open skirts, and along the bottom.

"It's exquisite," Ophelia said, her voice awed.

"Oh, what beautiful tucks," Betsy breathed, reaching out.

"Don't touch!" Lady Knowe cried.

"Last April, Marie Antoinette wore a gown that tucked down the front like this," Lavinia explained.

"Oh, my dearest Lavinia," Lady Knowe cried, clasping her hands under her chin. "You are a genius! No one will ever have seen a gown so beautiful!"

"All the lace is Sterling lace," Lavinia said, turning to Parth.

He nodded.

She waited a moment for him to say more, and when he didn't, turned back to the duchess, Lady Knowe, and Betsy. "The overskirt silk was woven on French looms in Lyon. But the embroidered silk comes from looms in London, in Spitalfields."

"I would never know," Lady Knowe said, peering. "They look like the same thread to me!"

"Silk always has variations," Lavinia explained. "The overskirts are a trifle more lilac, but we decided that the roses lend a blush that would offset the shade."

Lady Knowe laughed. "We? We, Lavinia, or *you*?"

"Mr. Felton and I together, with Madame Prague's help," she said. "Here is the headdress." It was a delightful pouf of rosy satin and lace, with ribbons in the back. "Diana requested no plumes."

"Pearls!" Betsy squealed, bending closer to the dress. "I didn't see the pearls at first!"

Lady Knowe squinted. "Why, there are pearls all over it! Lavinia, this is a gown fit for a queen!"

"Those appear to be amethysts," Ophelia said, pointing to the centers of the roses. "Sewn on with silver thread. The gown is *magnificent*, Lavinia!"

Parth was examining the lace. "I don't remember any lace this color coming from my factory."

"I dyed it," Lavinia explained. She picked up one

sleeve, which ended in two generous lace ruffles. "The lace was a bit stiff for what I wanted, so first we boiled it, and then bathed it in black walnut to give it a golden tinge." She smiled at Parth. "I would never have dared be so experimental with hand-made lace."

"This is beautiful," Lady Knowe said with conviction. "Better than handmade."

"The spangles?" Parth asked.

The edge of the lace was sewn with interlocking silver spangles that would catch the light. "It needed something," Lavinia explained. "A touch of luxury."

"It's so beautiful," Betsy crooned. "Please tell me that the gown you made for me is half as gorgeous! Parth, you must leave because I want to try on my gown."

"No telling anyone, Parth, about the wedding gown," Lady Knowe said, leaning over to drop a kiss on his cheek. "I don't trust the stable boys not to pass on a hint in exchange for a shilling."

"I won't," Parth said, bowing. With a glance at Lavinia, he left.

Mary and Tabitha were hovering, so Lavinia summoned them and introduced the seamstresses to Ophelia, and Betsy. Now that Parth was gone, Lavinia felt more like herself. "We have much work to do," she said, smiling at the girls.

"We should leave you to it," Lady Knowe announced. "I can't sew a seam to save my life, and never could."

"I thought we'd be sewing belowstairs," Tabitha said, clearly awed.

"Miss Gray couldn't join us there," Annie said, a bit sharply.

"What Annie means is that I am terribly interfering and I'm likely to pick up a needle myself," Lavinia said. She turned to Betsy. "Your gown isn't unpacked yet, but I'll let you know just as soon as it is pressed and ready to be tried on."

Lavinia spent every day of the next week in the sewing room. When possible, she joined the family for the evening meal, trying to avoid Parth's eye, trying to stay awake, thinking through the progress they'd made.

On the tenth evening, she sent everyone away at twilight before she sat down by the window and examined every stitch of the sewing done during the day. She fixed a ruffle, and sewed in an extra spangle.

Annie came and implored her to come dress for dinner, but Lavinia sent her away so she could finish tightening the thread holding an amethyst to the center of a rose. Standing up, she realized that one rose was slightly off-center, so she sat down again. She was biting off a piece of thread when she heard the door open.

"Annie, I told you—" she began, and looked up.

It wasn't Annie.

Parth was standing in the doorway. As she blinked at him, surprised, he entered the room and closed the door behind him. "Am I likely to find you here at all times of the day and night?"

"Certainly not," she said. But her voice was uncertain.

He reached out and carefully took the length of silk she held, part of the wedding dress's hem, and let it fall. It slid back to the floor with the luscious sound of thick silk.

"Please," she said. "I—"

He drew her to her feet, and the rest of the sentence died on her lips. There was a look in his eyes . . .

"Did you return in order to tell me how beautiful the wedding gown is? Because you unaccountably forgot to mention it the last time you visited this room," she said, babbling.

"It's exquisite," Parth said, his eyes on her, not the gown.

Lavinia chose to be amused by his intent expression, because the other option was to be unnerved. "Let me guess," she said lightly. "Lady Knowe sent you to fetch me for dinner."

"Dinner is well under way. Ophelia is overseeing a rip-roaring discussion of the virtues of something called Syrup of Capillaire, which Aunt Knowe considers a fountain of youth, and the duchess believes to be useless. The younger set is arguing over the relative merits of a play called *The Road to Ruin*. Jeremy is getting drunk. Again."

He turned down the Argand lamp and pinched out the candelabra she'd lit for close work. "We don't want your gorgeous confection to catch fire."

Gorgeous confection?

Their eyes met as he turned back.

"Do you really consider the gown beautiful?" Lavinia asked, her voice rasping as she realized just how much she had longed for his approval.

"You took my pedestrian lace and used it to create a work of art. Those spangles are genius."

Lavinia's smile came from her heart. She had taken two hours to choose spangles with a rosy tinge rather than a silver one.

Parth leaned down and bumped his nose against hers. "That magnificent wedding dress is North's announcement to society. It will inform the world that Diana is not a governess, but a lady."

She leaned back and laughed. "Did you just rub noses with me?"

"It's a family habit." His eyes were so dark that she couldn't see his expression now that most of the candles were extinguished. "When I first arrived at the castle, I was unsettled, and Aunt Knowe taught me how to rub noses."

"How old were you?"

"Five. That afternoon, she taught me, North, Alaric, and Horatius to bump noses and by the end of the first hour, we were brothers."

"I understand that feeling," Lavinia said, quirking a smile. "Willa joined our family at age nine, and I was never happier."

"We are both fortunate." He slipped a hand under her arm and drew her toward the door. "Time to eat."

In that instant, an overwhelming fatigue descended on Lavinia like a heavy woolen blanket. Even her head felt heavy, as if it might fall from her neck. "I fear I am too tired to join the family this evening."

"You haven't joined us the last four nights," Parth observed. He glanced down at her, and walked faster. "I'm taking you to the Solar."

"The Solar? What is that?" Lavinia stopped. "I'm not a substitute for Elisa."

"You are not a substitute for anyone."

"You know what I mean," she said, her protest sounding feeble even to herself.

"No, I do not."

Before she could collect her thoughts, he began moving forward again.

"The Solar is not far. It's at the top of a tower constructed by a Wilde ancestor back in the 1400s. The castle was simply built around it."

Lavinia cleared her throat. "I'd prefer—"

"If I allow you to return to your room, you'll fall onto the bed and not wake until morning."

Lavinia saw nothing wrong with that idea.

"Don't bother," he said, when she opened her mouth. They reached the end of the corridor and he pulled open a heavy oak door, carved so that it rounded outward, matching the curve of the stone wall.

Lavinia walked through and Parth bent his head to follow.

"Watch your feet." A flickering lamp attached to the wall illuminated shallow stone steps that spiraled upward.

Lavinia sighed, looking up. Then, feeling a movement behind her shoulder, "No, Mr. Sterling, you have done enough carrying of me for one lifetime." She began to climb.

Parth was that sort of man. One who rushed around picking ladies up, who summoned doctors and barked about lung infections. "Too protective for his own good"—wasn't that what Lady Knowe had said?

They reached a small landing, with an arched doorway on the left and the steps continuing on the right.

"Keep going," Parth said when Lavinia paused. Her head was starting to throb and her limbs were heavy.

"No," she said, turning around.

He looked at her.

"I want to go to bed. I'm exhausted."

"Lavinia, please allow me to feed you?"

She shook her head. "I appreciate the thought; it is very considerate of you. But I simply cannot climb another spiral of stairs. It's making my head ache."

His mouth curled into one of those reluctant smiles that he offered so infrequently.

"Why don't you smile more often?" she asked impulsively, too weary to guard her tongue. "It suits you."

This time his smile was slow and deliberate, but the gleam in his eyes was anything but amused.

Lavinia shook her head. "Forget I said that. Now I really must go to bed, Parth."

"Appalling Parth," he said.

"No, Kindly Parth." She moved to the side. "You join the others, and I'll just slip away. You will give them my apologies, won't you? I'd love to see the Solar tomorrow."

"I'm feeling appalling tonight," he said. The thoughtfulness in his voice made her narrow her eyes at him, just as he scooped her into his arms.

"Oh, for goodness' sake!" she cried.

He paused and bounced her in his arms, as one might bounce a colicky infant. "You are still too slight. I remember exactly how you felt in my arms two years ago when I first picked you up."

"Oh," she said, disconcerted. "Put me down, please."

"I return to the memory at night, in my bed," he said in a conversational tone, and continued upward. And, without pausing for breath: "Once you've seen the Solar, if you wish to return to your chamber, I'll take you there."

He thought about her *at night*? About her in his arms? Lavinia held her breath, hoping that the shock she felt wasn't reflected in her eyes. Abruptly, she wasn't tired at all. Every sense prickled alive. Parth smelled of fresh rain, and his coat caressed her cheek with its slightly rough texture.

His words hung in the air, punctuated by the sound of his boots striking ancient stone as he climbed. She had to say something. But what? *I thought of you at night too?*

Absolutely not. She wanted to look up at him, but for almost the first time in her life, she found herself in the grip of a paralyzing bout of shyness.

Parth kept climbing, as steadily as if she weighed nothing. She closed her eyes, just for a second, enough to luxuriate in the power of the arms around her. Slowly she let herself relax against his chest. It felt like heaven. Too heavenly. His body was warm and solid.

Her mother's illness left her with a longing for security. That was the only reason she was so drawn to Parth. It wasn't the first time she'd told herself that, and perhaps it wouldn't be the last.

The steps wound around again, and they had reached the top. Soft light poured through an open door.

"Put me down," she whispered. "I don't want anyone to see."

"No one will see," he promised. "My family is still in the dining room."

Now she thought about it, the Wildes could always be heard if they were gathered nearby, like a parliament of squawking ravens, whereas the tower was silent.

Parth carried her through and set her on her feet, then said nothing, giving her time to take in their surroundings. They stood in a circular stone room on whose halls hung eight narrow tapestries, at least ten feet tall. Each glowed a clear celestial blue, and each blue expanse was strewn with snowflakes.

She wrapped her hand around Parth's arm. "It's snowing, but in wool and silk!"

The smile on his lips was reflected in his eyes. "Take a closer look."

Lavinia went to the nearest tapestry and looked more closely.

"These are among Lindow's greatest treasures." Parth's deep voice came from behind her shoulder.

"I thought they depicted falling snowflakes," Lavinia whispered, awed. "But they are *angels*. This is a work of art. The most beautiful tapestry work I've ever seen."

She looked up and around the room. The angels hovered and rose and floated around them. Like snowflakes, they swirled alone, in pairs, in small eddies.

"It's unbelievable," Lavinia breathed.

Parth crossed to the fireplace. "May I introduce you to some particular angels?"

He had moved a lamp to the end of the mantelpiece. When she joined him, he gave her a lopsided smile and gestured toward the tapestry. To the left of the mantelpiece were two angels, hand in hand.

She bent closer. One of the angels had dark eyes instead of blue, and his—her?—skin was golden rather than snow white. "My parents," Parth said softly.

"My mother," he added, a finger gently touching the angel's halo. "I suspect that Aunt Knowe achieved that effect by dabbing her face with tea, though I have never inquired." Then, after a pause, "Though I have a miniature of my parents, I don't truly remember what my mother looked like."

Lavinia's heart turned inside-out at the expression on his face: rueful and loving. She reached out and wrapped her hands around his.

"Aunt Knowe brought me here after the news came that my parents had died, a couple of years after they sent me to England. They had died of a fever."

"I'm sorry," she said, tightening her fingers.

"I was seven. I decided that if I'd been there, I might have been able to save them."

"Oh, dear," Lavinia said, remembering his penchant for doctors.

Parth's mouth twisted with recognition of the thought she hadn't spoken. "It mucked with my head and turned me into a pain in the arse, or so Aunt Knowe says."

Lavinia nodded and decided that if there was a next time, she'd allow Parth's doctor to listen to her chest, even if she was perfectly well.

"She brought me here the following day and told me that two angels had appeared where no angels had been before. These two."

Lavinia felt giggles rising in her chest. "I adore Lady Knowe."

"As do I. It took me years before I questioned why my parents had chosen to predict their angelic fate on a hundred-year-old tapestry."

"Were you an only child?"

He grimaced. "I had a younger brother who died with them. I suppose if he'd made it to five years old, he would have been sent here as well."

"I am so sorry," Lavinia said.

He moved restlessly. "I lost a brother I never knew— and never shed a tear for—and then lost Horatius, an adopted brother. I still have an occasional self-pitying wallow when Horatius comes to mind. He was impossibly arrogant, but he was ours."

Lavinia obeyed impulse and stepped up to him,

leaving whatever happened next up to him. She was offering silent consolation, but given his nearly married state, she couldn't kiss him.

Perhaps "nearly married" was an exaggeration.

Yes, *definitely* an exaggeration, because Parth proved himself to be the sort of man who seized an opportunity.

One arm closed around her back and drew her close. A breath of warm air touched her cheek before their lips came together, as if kissing was something they had practiced with each other.

They kissed as if they had practiced *this* kiss, this silent kiss that had a taste of lost brothers, a note of sorrow and love tangled together. They kissed until sorrow was lost in a slow bubbling of desire. And they didn't stop until her breath was ragged and her body was trembling all over. Still, he didn't let her go.

They took breaths now and then, their eyes meeting, and then, silently deciding not to address it, eyes closing as they dove back into the kiss. This kiss had nothing to do with their kiss in the rain, or the one in Vauxhall.

This one was slower and somehow more *in* the body. Lavinia felt everything, the slide of Parth's tongue, and the way his hand clamped on her back, the faint rasp in his throat, the fact that she wasn't the only one trembling.

When he finally pulled back, she leaned toward him, her brain having dissolved into a hungry fog.

He rubbed his chin, staring at her. At some point in the last thirty . . . forty minutes, his mouth had wandered from her lips and stroked her jaw. Her throat. Her cheekbones. Her ears.

She could feel a faint echo, a prickle, in all those

places. The room was quiet but for the crackling of the fire. He couldn't be marrying Elisa. Surely he would ask Lavinia for her hand—

"Are you hungry?"

"*That's* your question?" Lavinia blurted out. She felt a wash of pink spreading over her cheeks.

Parth's gaze moved over her face, and a gleam of laughter shone in his eyes. "Have I made a faux pas, in that kisses are to be followed by proposals?"

Lavinia twitched. He made it sound as if she'd experienced any number of kisses and proposals. Which she had, but none of them was . . . *that*. That sort of kiss.

No man had ever jested about the proposal either. Typically, they had followed a kiss by looking deeply into her eyes and imploring her to marry them. Parth was breaking that mold. She was being teased, not cruelly, but with a touch of humor.

"I accept proposals only between seven and nine o'clock in the morning," she said. "Kisses affect my judgment. One wouldn't want to make a decision on the basis of something so . . . inconsequential."

Hopefully, she sounded nonchalant, even indifferent. Not as if she'd felt that kiss to the ends of her toes. Before he could react, she moved to the other side of the fireplace and seated herself at a small table set for supper.

She lifted a domed lid and found a tender side of chicken. Under another, carrot pudding. Green beans, a dish of potatoes. How much investigation of their supper could she do without seeming more of a fool than she already did?

Wine was poured into glasses. She watched through her lashes as he seated himself.

"I said that ineptly," Parth said, as Lavinia placed a heavy linen napkin, embroidered with the Lindow insignia, onto her lap. Like a coward, she still hadn't met his eyes.

Parth Sterling, appalling or not, would never kiss her like that if he meant to marry another woman.

Impulsively, in the rain, in the grip of fury, perhaps. Slightly less impulsively, in a dark lane in Vauxhall? Less likely, but . . .

Here? He had compromised her. They weren't in the open now: not in the rain or a pleasure garden. He had kissed her in a private chamber, with no one within earshot.

Whether he proposed now, or at seven in the morning, he would do it. Lavinia's chest tightened, and she curled the fingers of her right hand around the seat of her chair. She'd have to tell him about her mother's thefts—

She couldn't.

"Breathe," a deep voice said, from the other side of the table.

She gulped air, flustered, her thoughts jumbled.

"You look terrified, and yet I didn't propose marriage," Parth said, amusement threading through his words.

Lavinia sipped her wine. "You did so silently."

He laughed. The sound was so unusual that she looked across the table before she stopped herself. He was just so . . .

He was beautiful.

That was the problem. If he hadn't been so *beautiful*, all cheekbones and raw masculinity and that chin, if he hadn't been beautiful, she might have kissed him once or even twice, and gone her way.

A fork bumped her lips, warm chicken. "Stop worrying." A whispered order, but an order nonetheless.

She took a deep breath, and Parth used the opportunity to slip the chicken into her mouth.

"You're hungry, and you need to eat. When I'm deeply involved in a new project, I forget to eat. I become suddenly, tyrannically angry."

She raised an eyebrow, grateful for his light tone. "Something to look out for, then."

His smile was satisfied, almost smug. "Yes, loss of appetite is a warning, like a red sky at night."

They were acting as if . . .

"I haven't accepted the proposal you haven't offered," she stated, needing to assert herself.

"I know that. Eat."

There was nothing conflicted in his eyes, whereas Lavinia felt as if her stomach was a mass of twisting emotions.

"Please."

So she did. She put down her head and avoided his eyes, and ate chicken, carrot pudding, and a small salad of baby leaves, lightly seasoned.

Parth told her stories about his boyhood. He'd been remarkably naughty.

The tension between them evaporated as he described Lady Knowe shaking because she was so angry that she couldn't speak. And about his adoptive father, the duke, so wildly in love with Ophelia, his new wife, that he didn't realize how delinquent his sons had become, until they'd nearly set fire to the smithy, trying to shape their own swords on the blacksmith's forge.

They *had* set fire to the buttery—mercifully, it had been unoccupied at the time.

They had let all the ewes run free, to test whether they had successfully trained an old hound to herd like a sheep dog. Answer: no.

He had her giggling before she finished her first glass of wine, and hiccupping with laughter by the second. By the time he poured her a small glass of elderflower liqueur, she had found her backbone again.

No, she would not marry Parth simply because he'd kissed her. For goodness' sake! The very idea of confessing her mother's crimes made her feel ill.

She put down her fork, finally, and smiled across the table, once more herself. His kisses had temporarily unhinged her but she felt in control again. No longer a shaky, exhausted woman, likely to succumb to the first gentleman who wrapped an arm around her and made her feel safe.

He made her feel other things as well, but she pushed that thought away.

"Ready to return to your room?" His eyes were perfectly friendly.

"Yes. This was a wonderful meal, Parth. I'm so grateful that you brought me here." She placed her napkin on the table.

"Are you certain that you want nothing more to eat?"

"Quite certain, thank you."

He held up a piece of fruit.

"You are going to nag your wife dreadfully," she observed, a smile fluttering around her lips as she rose. "No, there is nothing I want, thank you."

"I want you."

He said it calmly. He stood, of course; Parth's manners were fit for Versailles. Now he skirted the table and stopped. "I want you, Lavinia. And in case there is any doubt in your mind, I want to marry you. *You*, not Elisa."

Lavinia opened her mouth but nothing came out. She just stared at him, her heart squeezing into a little ball. "Why?" she managed.

Parth reached out and took her hands. After a pause, he said, "You're very beautiful, Lavinia. Surely you don't want me to repeat other men's compliments. I am incapable of writing you a poem."

His voice was as calm as ever, but his hands held hers with a kind of forcefulness that carried emotion.

"I don't know," she faltered. She wanted him; she wanted to marry him with every iota of her being. But there was the problem of her mother's thefts. But even more . . . some stubborn part of her didn't want to marry a man who thought she was shallow as a puddle. Or a man who would even say such a thing.

Whether or not she was.

But it was *Parth*. Parth was asking her.

He saw that realization in her face, because his hands tightened and then he pulled her into his arms and kissed her. When she didn't open her lips immediately, settling herself into the feeling of being surrounded by him, he nipped her lip, and then licked the spot, and when she gasped, his tongue slipped into her mouth.

Lavinia leaned into the kiss, and made a decision without even realizing. It wasn't to do with marriage, but with trust.

She trusted him, and whether he knew it or not, he had her heart. She'd stupidly fallen in love with him years ago, and although she'd tried to persuade herself out of that foolishness, it hadn't gone away.

His hands tightened, pulling her closer. The kiss

that followed was like fire, making her shake all over. When it ended—because they both had to breathe— his eyes were glittering at her in the candlelight. He was so solid that she couldn't help sliding her hands down his arms. Solid—and beautiful.

Everything to her.

The realization was terrifying, so terrifying that she heard herself swallow.

"You think too much," Parth said, his voice rumbling.

"I have been under the impression that you believed I didn't think at all." She said it before she could stop herself.

He reached out and cupped her cheek. "I apologize for ever saying that. I was irritated—no, infuriated— that I couldn't get you out of my mind."

That made sense. She believed him, for Parth was not a man who would welcome distraction. She curved one hand around his neck, deciding it was one of her favorite parts of his body. It was strong and muscled. Kissable. Lickable.

"You *are* compromised," he stated.

"I don't know," she protested. "I've kissed other—"

His mouth cut off that sentence. She had never kissed any man the way she kissed Parth. And his hands: His hands owned her. They moved around her body with total assurance, touching her back so gently that she shivered and pressed closer. Curving around one hip and then tightening, which made her mouth open wider, her head falling back with a choked sound. Even through layers of silk she felt the heat of his hand as it slid over her bottom.

"I know you've kissed other men," he growled in her ear.

Lavinia shuddered against him, realizing that she should qualify those kisses. They hadn't been *this*, whatever this was. Yet Parth didn't need her to give an explanation. The truth hung in the air between them as he kissed her again and then, in the middle of heady, silent conversation, he lifted her, took a step, and put her down again.

Not on her feet.

Lavinia's eyes rounded. He had laid her across a divan opposite the fireplace. She hadn't even noticed it.

"Lavinia, may I compromise you?"

The light pooled behind him, and somehow the sight of him standing over her was so erotic that Lavinia could hardly breathe. "Yes," she said faintly.

He knelt, his eyes holding hers. "There is no going back. Men kissed you believing you'd marry them, the poor fools."

Lavinia didn't want to talk about other men. Even mentioning them made her feel unseemly, like a wanton.

He leaned closer. "*Not* like that. There's nothing loose about you, Lavinia. You were testing them, weren't you?"

She nodded. And then froze, because she'd never seen that expression on his face. Eyes smiling, crinkled with laughter. "You're laughing," she said wonderingly.

"Maybe I just need encouragement."

His idea of encouragement took her breath and made her shiver, turning toward him, arms tight around his neck. Her breath broke into a sob, an incoherent command, a plea.

Parth's face was as tranquil as ever, but his eyes . . . his eyes were fierce.

"May I compromise you, Lavinia?" he asked again.

"Whatever happened to Punctilious Parth?" she whispered, tracing his bottom lip with a finger. She was so aroused that she was shaking. "Or to Proper Parth?"

"*Appalling*, if I go forward with this." There was no ruefulness in his voice. Only desire.

Deep, deep desire, which growled through him and came from his chest. She trusted it.

"Yes," she heard herself say. "Yes, I will."

Because he was really asking her to marry him, and compromising was just the cover for that question. But she had to ask, so she blurted out, "What about Elisa?"

He ran his lips over her jaw. She squirmed, the liquid heat between her legs surprisingly unnerving. "Parth!"

"I promised her I'd bring her to Lindow for the wedding."

"Did you promise to court her?" She pulled away.

He grinned again, and Lavinia knew that she would do anything—*anything*—to keep that smile on his face. "I did not. I told her that I wouldn't marry her. She laughed."

"Oh," Lavinia breathed. She raised a hand and ran her fingers down his face, beside his eye, down his cheekbone and strong jaw.

"I planned to announce our betrothal at the masquerade ball," Parth said.

Her fingers froze. "You—you've planned it?"

He looked faintly surprised. "You might as well assume that I plan everything. The duke announced his betrothal to Ophelia at a masquerade ball, the first that we older children were allowed to attend."

"How romantic." She curled her fingers around his neck, promising a kiss there, afterward, to the join of his shoulder. Desire felt agonizingly sharp, like a wound that hadn't healed. She wanted *him*, not a conversation. But she didn't know how to move from conversation to . . .

To that next, forbidden thing.

Kisses didn't offer much guide for what came after.

"Even as a boy, I grasped the romance of it," Parth said, his voice even, but she recognized the desire buried there. She wasn't the only one quivering. "I decided I would do the same one day."

She pushed a thought away, but he caught her chin and pressed a kiss on her lips.

"Tell me."

"Is that why you asked Elisa to come to the wedding with you?"

"Yes," he said calmly.

Lavinia's mouth twitched and the breath caught in her chest. That *hurt*.

"I had made up my mind to woo and wed Elisa," Parth continued. "I always assume that I shall be successful. It's an excellent way to approach business. And life."

He looked amused, which Lavinia found thoroughly irritating. She could not bring herself to say anything. At some point she had replaced Elisa in the masquerade ball scenario. She disliked the chill that crept through her, like a bitter wind.

"Do you know the one situation in which I could not envision success?" he asked.

"I cannot imagine it." A small, shabby part of her wanted to make certain that Elisa had been vanquished from Parth's mind.

Gone, abolished, replaced by Lavinia.

"*You*," he said, lowering his face so that his breath shivered over her lips. "You. You were the one person who would never want me, would never be won over by me, would see through me."

That was disconcerting.

"You want me because I didn't want you? I was the one who proposed to *you*, if you remember."

He had a stubborn look in his eyes, the expression of a male determined not to say embarrassing things. Happiness spread through Lavinia's body. He wasn't ready to say whatever he meant.

She tugged until he started kissing her. Every once in a while they would surface from the kiss and she would tug at him again until finally he shifted and his weight came down on top of her.

"Oh, my God," Lavinia whispered.

"Too heavy?"

"Don't move." She wound her arms around his neck, closed her eyes, and just *felt*. A large, muscled man on top of her. Crushing her dress. She didn't mind. She'd never been happier.

His hips nudged forward, and her eyes flew open. She was staring at his smile, memorizing it, when he rolled on his side again. Lavinia opened her mouth to complain except that his hand was running up her leg. Under her skirts.

A strangled squeak escaped her throat.

Parth leaned over and brushed her lips with his. "I'm inclined to compromise you so thoroughly that you can think only of me for the rest of your life. No more kisses with other men, *ever*. No more testing that involves a man."

"Yes," she said faintly, not really listening. Then: "No?"
"No men."

"None except Parth." His hand wrapped around the soft curve of her upper thigh and her breath caught, waiting.

"Breathe," he said.

She shook her head.

He smiled again, and because he slid his fingers *there* at the same moment, she almost missed it.

Chapter Twenty

*P*arth had fully intended to behave like a gentleman.

The problem was Lavinia. He had always behaved with impeccable restraint. It was something he worked out early; he had felt at home in the middle of the uproarious Wilde family. He *was* a Wilde.

But to the rest of the world, he wasn't. He was merely a ward of the duke, an orphan whose mother was from India and whose father had no inheritance. His behavior never gave the world the chance to question his worthiness, or his right to be called a gentleman and, implicitly, a Wilde.

Lavinia was the only person who bashed through his rules. No: who caused him to break his own rules. He stroked her between the legs with the most delicate caress he could manage, scarcely touching her, but she was plump and soft, and her head fell backward with a moan.

He was about to break another rule. All his rules, for her.

"May I make love to you, Lavinia?" he whispered. He couldn't stop himself from sliding an arm under her neck and pulling her closer, his other hand swirling, making her legs fall open and her breath stutter.

Her eyes opened. "Parth!"

His fingers stopped.

"You already *are*."

He licked her bottom lip. "There's making love and then there's *making love*."

She grabbed his wrist and pressed firmly. Her head toppled against his shoulder and she said something he couldn't hear. He was not an idiot. When he bore down again, adding a twist of his wrist, a note of desperation broke from her throat and she shuddered.

"I'll take that as a yes," Parth said, kissing her hard. Moving to her jaw, nipping her neck, and all the time his fingers making her tremble. Her whole body was taut and her hand still gripped his wrist, holding him in place.

In case he tried to leave her, presumably.

As if he ever would.

One finger went deep, owning her, and she made a desperate sound, rubbing her head against his shoulder. A curse came from his chest and he added another finger, listening to her sobbing breath, treasuring the way her back arched toward him, her hands clutching him, her face buried in his coat.

He coaxed her into kissing him again, showing her a rhythm that matched above and below, tongue matching his fingers, buried inside her. She gasped, cried, said unintelligible things—and then shook hard, waves going through her body. He treasured every one.

He kissed her ear and thought about what might come next.

No gentleman—

The sentence evaporated from his mind, because Lavinia opened her eyes and fixed him with a gaze that saw to the bottom of his soul.

"You can't . . ." Her voice was ragged, hoarse. "We're not done, are we?"

"We ought to stop," he said, reluctant, pushing the words out.

Lavinia's face crumpled. "It's not enough." The words were like a sob, and she arched up again, her mouth on his, *her* tongue caressing, demanding entrance.

Not enough.

His lady wanted—more.

Parth tore himself away and stood up. Lavinia lay on the divan, skirts billowing around her waist, the most beautiful woman he'd ever seen. He hadn't even touched her breasts.

She looked up with no shame. None. There was delight in her eyes, and desire, and hunger. For him, for Parth.

He kicked off his boots, stockings, wrenched down his breeches. Her eyes widened.

"I'm not small," he said, glancing down.

"No, you're not," she said.

A movement in her legs caught his eyes. She wasn't squeezing them together, refusing him, as she'd have every right to do. Instead, her sweet thighs fell open.

Parth came down on his elbows over her, kissing her ruthlessly. Even in the white heat of the kiss, he was ticking over facts in the back of his mind. She had said yes. She had said yes several times. She was marrying him. He would announce it at the masquerade. Hell, maybe he would marry her that night. Forget a betrothal.

Wedding dresses floated through his mind and he dismissed the thought. Lavinia rubbed herself against his cock and he groaned, an agony of lust washing over him. He'd never felt like this.

He'd bedded women—but he'd never *made love* before.

He'd never held any woman like Lavinia, kissed a woman like her. She was soft and fragrant, and so fucking alive that he wanted to bite her all over. Caress her so hard that he left marks, *his* marks.

His cock slid through sleek warmth and he almost—
Stopped himself.

Virgin. Pain. No. The idea of causing pain to Lavinia, any pain to Lavinia, was anathema.

"Wait," he commanded, the word rasping in his throat. He backed up, pushed her skirts even higher, and dipped his tongue into sweet honey. He had the vague sense that ladies didn't like this sort of intimate attention, but Lavinia fell backward, and there was a moment of silence before she shrieked. "Yes!"

Good thing he'd banned the servants from the tower, he thought dimly. He brought his hand into play and soon she was shaking and pleading for more.

Laughter was trapped in his throat because he was licking her too hard to laugh, his fingers moving in concert. She bucked against him, crying out desperately. When her inner muscles began to tighten on him, he pulled free.

"No!" she ordered.

But he straightened, pulling up her hips, sliding through sleek warmth, then pushing inside. For a moment he froze, *Never hurt Lavinia* clashing with *Take Lavinia.*

She opened her eyes, pleasure-drenched. Demanding.

"Parth! That's not enough," she said, reaching for him, her voice high but fierce. "Not—"

The word was lost in a gasp because he thrust forward, past her virginity, past sanity, past everything but pleasure.

A desperate groan broke from his lips and he was deep, as deep as possible. His eyes narrowed, searching her face. She was glistening with sweat, pink-cheeked, and when he didn't move, her eyes opened again.

"Bloody hell," she whispered.

"Pain?" he managed.

"No . . . *Yes* . . . Just keep going."

He kept it slow and gentle, stroke after stroke, his patience immense. For once, he had control of himself around her. Lavinia was his, all his, and he was responsible for giving her pleasure, more pleasure. The thought kept his balls tight. He pushed his need to the side. He eased her bodice down and palmed one breast, his palm caressing the taut bud, watching as her breath shuddered.

She pulled him down, closer to her. He could feel her body softening. Still, he managed to keep his slow, deep glide.

Until she opened her eyes and he caught just a hint of disappointment. His hips jolted to a stop.

"No, please keep going," she gasped. "It's probably just because . . . it's the first time. I've heard that women—maybe I'm one of those women. It's very pleasant."

Her words went through Parth's chest like fire. "No," he gritted out. "Tell me what you need, Lavinia." He came down on his elbows and despite himself, his shaft thrust forward hard.

She grunted, surprised, her body jolting. "I don't—"

"Sorry," he said, gritting it out, his voice deeper than normal. "Won't do that again." He eased into a slow glide again.

But Lavinia had always surprised him, and she always would. With a purring laugh, she bent her knees and arched up, toward him. "Anything I need?"

"Anything."

"I need *that*."

"What?"

"Like that." Her voice had a trace of frustration and Parth frowned, not sure what she meant. She tightened on him and lifted up fast, slamming into him.

The pleasure was so acute that he lost vision for a moment.

His response was instinctive. One hand wrenched her right knee higher and he thrust into her with a heavy grunt, hard and possessive.

In a white heat, he heard her cry out, but not in pain. It set something free in him and he let his head drop, licking her face like a crazed man, biting her bottom lip, thrusting his tongue into her mouth as ferociously as his cock.

She was gasping now, groaning, eyes shining with dazed pleasure.

And then she was coming, and her throat had to be raw because, damn it, Lavinia was as wild in bed as she was in life. As she shuddered in his arms, Parth closed his eyes and let himself go.

Three, four thrusts home and he felt himself empty out, cock deep inside her, shaking, sweat dropping onto her, groans torn from his chest.

A man is never more vulnerable than in the moment he gives everything to a woman.

It was the first time he'd experienced anything that felt as if he'd given his heart away.

It was her first time.

But also his.

Chapter Twenty-one

September 11, 1780

*L*avinia woke the next morning with a gasp.

It had really happened.

All of it, including a giggling, breathless return to her room through the back corridors and even a secret passage. Inside her room, the door shut, one of those kisses again.

Watching Parth, her future husband, reluctantly leave.

It seemed she was to be married. Staring up at the bed curtains, Lavinia made one decision, an important one.

She would marry Parth, obviously. Her virginity was gone. But she would not marry him until she had repaid the emeralds her mother had stolen.

Perhaps she would earn her own dowry.

Parth was rich, yet she wanted to bring him the inheritance she was supposed to have. Or at least a small dowry, enough to keep her pride.

She rang for a bath, and spent half an hour calculating when she could afford to marry Parth. Probably in a year or two, depending on how things went. As soon as her mother was well enough, they could open the townhouse.

She had a feeling she could afford a string of emeralds from the commissions related to Diana's wedding, and perhaps even repay the money owed to Willa's estate. Lady Blythe's *trousseau* would give her a small dowry.

She took a deep breath.

A year's betrothal was by no means uncommon; some people waited two. Her mother had to recover.

And . . .

It was foolish, but she needed time to woo Parth.

He was in the grip of lust, that was clear. But she needed time to show him that her love for clothing wasn't shallow. An inappropriately dressed man was unlikely to succeed. A superbly dressed woman could marry far above her station.

She was imagining that conversation when Annie entered. "The girls are at work, miss. That French-woman, Berthe, has already finished the embroidery on the right sleeve!" She stood back and ushered in three footmen carrying cans of water, which they poured into the bath in its alcove.

When they had withdrawn, Lavinia slid from the bed and discovered that she must have been drugged with passion not to feel pain last night. She felt it now. She hobbled over to the bath and sank in with a sigh.

No more of that.

What had she been thinking? A liquid warmth

stirred in her legs, in the back of her knees, in other places, and she remembered exactly what she had been thinking.

She'd had that huge, beautiful man literally at her feet. His body had glowed in the candlelight as if he were made of gold, some sort of ancient god come down to earth to worship her.

Parth might not think much of her intellect, but he was wild about her body, and she felt the same way about his. He had looked at her ravenously, as if she was the only woman on earth for him.

"Well, you're in a good mood and no mistake," Annie said, pouring out soft soap so she could wash Lavinia's hair. "The castle is so pleasant, isn't it? Everybody's loud and a bit mad."

She talked on while Lavinia thought about the rough caress of Parth's tongue. The possessive curl of his fingers. The way he lost control at the end, caught up by the demands of his body.

She'd done that.

She'd driven the man with the greatest control she'd ever known into a storm of desire so potent that he succumbed.

"Would you like me to bring tea or will you go to the breakfast room?" Annie asked, when Lavinia was seated by the fireplace, her hair drying.

"I'll go to breakfast," Lavinia said.

Not to see Parth.

He probably wasn't there.

She might turn red if she saw him. Married women ordinarily ate breakfast in their bedchambers, and now she had a good idea why.

"No, I'll go see what progress is being made on

the dress," she decided. "If you could have some tea brought to the sewing room, I'm sure everyone will appreciate it."

"It's not many mistresses who drink tea with maids and seamstresses," Annie said, straightening out Lavinia's ribbons. There were many ribbons, because . . . ribbons! Who could resist them?

"I sew with you as well," Lavinia said. "I'm not like the other ladies, Annie."

"No, you're not that," her maid said, rolling a last ribbon and tucking it carefully back into the ribbon box. "Would you like powder this morning?"

"No," Lavinia said, remembering the way Parth thrust his fingers into her hair. She'd heard hairpins falling to the stone floor. "No powder."

"Lip salve?"

The salve tasted slightly fishy, though it had never mattered to her before. But just in case . . .

"No. I wouldn't want to accidentally stain the dress." That was a good reason.

Not the only reason, but a good one.

Chapter Twenty-two

$\mathcal{P}$arth sat at the breakfast table and sparred with Betsy until it was clear that Lavinia would not make an appearance.

Then he extricated himself from a lively discussion among the younger Wildes about whether women should be allowed to sit in the House of Lords alongside men. Parth thought it depended on the woman, just as it ought to depend on the man. And he was damned certain that he wasn't capable of judging either sex.

A year ago, he would have categorically said that Lavinia was not such a woman. He would have been very wrong.

He made his way up to the chamber devoted to the wedding dress and walked in on a scene of organized chaos. No one noticed his entrance, likely because Aunt Knowe was laughing so uproariously. He watched Lavinia dart from one seamstress to the next, answering a question about the placement of spangles.

"We need a cluster of them just here," she said,

pointing. "The light should reflect from all angles. If you bunch them up like this, they'll reflect on three or four sides."

"Come over here, Parth!" his aunt roared from the side of the room. "Just look at what this impossible girl is trying to get me to wear to the wedding!"

Lavinia looked up and their eyes met. Parth didn't smile often. It was a habit of mind, born from being— along with the entire Wilde clan—constantly and closely observed. But now his smile was unguarded. Lavinia's hair shone gold in the sunlight streaming in the window. She was outrageously beautiful. Unfair-to-other-women beautiful.

His.

After last night: *his.*

As he watched, a delicate wash of pink appeared in her cheeks.

He made no effort to approach her, because if he did, he would take her in his arms, and that wasn't in the plan. At the moment he couldn't remember the reasons for the plan.

But her eyes held a warning: No one should know about them.

Right.

He crossed the room to Aunt Knowe instead.

"It's checked!" she cried gesturing at the gown on a dress form.

The fabric was indeed checked. "They are small checks," he said, unsure what the problem was.

"Just look at the back!"

His aunt tended toward the dramatic, but even so, Parth saw nothing out of the ordinary.

"The collar is huge *in the back* and it comes to a point," she cried.

"Double points, actually," Lavinia said, joining them.

"You must conceive me a paragon of fashion," Aunt Knowe moaned. "I can't wear this! Look at those enormous buttons all the way down the skirt in the rear!"

"Perfect for you," Lavinia said, unperturbed. "The gown will flatter your figure, and at the same time, it is *à la mode*."

"I like it," Parth put in.

"You would like a blue sun if this young lady selected it," Aunt Knowe muttered. "At least my chest won't be exposed to all and sundry; I'll give you that. But checks! Checks are for men's garments!"

Lavinia frowned. "Fabrics shouldn't be designated for one sex or the other. If I had my way, I would dress Parth in lavender silk."

Parth glanced down at his black coat and breeches, feeling a strong surge of gratitude that Lavinia was not dressing him for the festivities.

"I trust you have new garments for the wedding?" Aunt Knowe asked him. "Or a new coat?"

"No," he said.

"The owner of Sterling Lace ought to wear his own products," Lavinia said. Her eyes were dancing with laughter. "We could add lace to one of your cravats."

"Parth is smiling!" Aunt Knowe exclaimed. She turned to Lavinia. "One year all the boys came home from Eton looking as if they'd been carved from granite. It was a terrible shock."

"No self-respecting man smiles and smiles," Parth said. "Just look at what happened to that character in Shakespeare's *Twelfth Night* who was tricked into smiling: He was thrown into a dungeon, for the crime of smiling too much."

"No, his imprisonment was due to garish cross-garters," Lavinia said. "They tricked him into wearing yellow garters and since he was a Puritan, his mistress decided he must have lost his mind."

"Cross-gartering? What's that?" Aunt Knowe asked.

"Yellow bands that cross over the calves and make a man look like a chicken," Parth said.

"A perfect example of the significance of clothing," Lavinia said.

"My question, Lavinia, is whether people will mock *me* for wearing checks and large buttons down my derrière."

"No, they will not," she answered. "They will be in awe of your elegance and run out to buy checked fabric immediately. Mr. Felton and I agreed that he should order at least three more bolts, because *you* will spur a fashion."

"I have no aspirations for that," Aunt Knowe said dubiously. "I don't even go into London society."

"Society will come to you," Lavinia announced.

Parth caught himself on the verge of smiling again.

One of the seamstresses touched Lavinia's elbow, and she moved away, closer to the window in order to examine a lace ruffle.

"She's refashioning your lace to resemble the handmade variety," Aunt Knowe observed.

Parth nodded.

"Lavinia hasn't eaten a scrap of breakfast, and as long as she's here, she won't."

He waited until the young seamstress sat down before he caught Lavinia's elbow and guided her out of the room. "Breakfast," he said in her ear.

Whatever protest she was about to make subsided when their eyes met. "How are you feeling?" he asked in the corridor, trying to ignore the impulse to back her against a wall and kiss her senseless.

"Perfectly well," she said, her cheeks reddening.

"Tell me why I can't tell the world that we are betrothed?"

"Because you are courting another woman who will arrive here in just over a month."

"Elisa knows, so why not everyone else?"

Lavinia shook her head. "My mother is not here."

"I apologize," Parth said, annoyed at himself for not remembering. "I should never have assumed— Damn it to hell, Lavinia, I *am* sorry."

Her smile was a tight-lipped version of her usual merriment. "Asking my mother for my hand is a mere formality. But she might be wounded to find that I took care of the matter entirely by myself."

"I understand," Parth said.

"You can't, not really," Lavinia replied.

She was keeping something from him about Lady Gray. He already knew she had no dowry, so it must be something else.

As they made their way down the corridor, Parth decided that Lavinia would tell him whatever it was in her own time. He had never really pictured marriage—or rather, a marriage in which he was a participant. It seemed to be more complicated than he might have presumed.

Just as Lavinia was more complicated than he had thought.

"So the only scene you remember from *Twelfth Night* is the cross-gartering?" he asked, guiding her into the breakfast room. Thankfully, his excitable siblings were gone, and the table was freshly laid.

She flashed a look at him. "Willa used to tease me

that the only reason I attended church services was so that I could examine the vestments."

Parth shook his head. "You have a unique way of looking at the world, Miss Lavinia Gray."

"I know," she said, allowing a footman to give her a spoonful of coddled eggs and some toast.

Parth narrowed his eyes, and the man ladled some more eggs on her plate.

"I prefer to manage my own meals and choose the quantity that I eat," Lavinia said to him.

Parth nodded and changed the subject. "If I were to choose a profession by its garments, I would choose to be an old-fashioned knight. I used to love crashing about in the old suit of armor down in the entrance hall."

"The one with the rusted helmet?"

Parth nodded. "An early Wilde planned to battle a neighboring lord but he drank too much, and when he woke up he was on a boat. Apparently his wife felt fighting was a rotten idea, so they traveled to Paris together and bought casks of French wine instead."

"Good decision," Lavinia said, finishing her eggs. "Men are proud of heroically laughing in the face of death, but we women find it vastly preferable to put off extinction until old age."

Parth watched her in silence. Then he found himself asking, without conscious volition, "Do you suppose that we shall live together until we are old, Lavinia?"

"Hush!" she whispered, blushing yet again.

"I should like to grow old with you," he said thoughtfully. "Your hair will turn silver and you'll be as managing as Aunt Knowe."

"You are the managing one!" she retorted.

"Only at times," he said, letting innuendo slide into his voice.

"All the time," she stated. "Even two years ago when we had scarcely met, you liked to tell me what to do. '*Ride more carefully, Miss Gray. Eat your apple, Miss Gray. Put on a coat, Miss Gray, you'll . . .*'" Her voice faltered and she met his eyes.

"Infatuated without knowing it, and therefore behaving like an ass." He gave her a lopsided smile. "Even two years ago, I'm afraid."

"But you were always criticizing me," she whispered.

"At least I didn't call you rude names."

"As much as," she retorted. "I know I called you 'Appalling Parth,' but that was only because you—because you scorned me so much."

He put down his toast, pushed back his chair, and moved unhurriedly around the table and drew her upright. "I'm used to winning, Lavinia."

"You never tried to win me."

He paused. "I was ill-tempered because I don't go in for impossibilities."

Lavinia blinked at him, and her lashes were so extravagantly long and she so extravagantly beautiful that he felt it like a jolt. "You are you." That was hopelessly inadequate, but most women heard accounts of his wealth and threw themselves at him. "You didn't need my money."

She visibly flinched.

He was a fool. He should be praising her eyes or her intellect. "I apologize," he said. "That is irrelevant, obviously."

"It is hardly a reason that a lady wishes to hear regarding a gentleman's decision to court her," Lavinia said. "She doesn't need my money, therefore I will scorn her. Now she does need my money, so I will woo her?"

There was just a hint that she might need reassurance, which was absurd coming from the woman who had been besieged by proposals on both sides of the Channel.

Parth's hands closed around her shoulders and never mind his silent vow not to touch her again until Lady Gray had left the sanitarium. "You're impossibly beautiful, to be blunt, and what's more, you're funny. You make everyone laugh. That's not to mention the fact that a man no sooner sees you than he desires you. I was not unusual in that respect."

Parth was through with talking; he pulled her into his arms and kissed her. They kissed differently, now that they had made love. Everything in him was alive to her every whisper and movement. He'd seen her at her most vulnerable, and the shiny, fashionable Lavinia would never dominate his understanding of her again.

Lavinia *was* shiny and fashionable.

But his Lavinia was shy one moment and bold the next. Gasping with desire, and then laughing. Her breath hitched when his fingers closed around her hip, and she made a bewitching little pleading sound in the back of her throat. She held him as if she'd never let go, and he knew in his bones that she was stopping herself from running her hands over his chest.

Last night her eyes had taken on a feverish look after he stripped off his shirt. Who would have thought that it would be so damned satisfying to have one's future wife dazed by one's body?

Aunt Knowe adored Lavinia, as did Ophelia. But his realization that he would have married her even had the Wildes disliked her?

Too sobering to examine.

"I must return to London tomorrow morning," he said abruptly.

She nodded. "You plan to escort Elisa here for the wedding."

"I have work to do in London. And I'm captivated by you, not Elisa." The words came from his lips as flatly as he might say, *The interest rate is acceptable.* Or: *Sheep farming is rarely a profitable venture.*

Her mouth curled into a generous smile.

"I don't suppose you wish to accompany me to London?"

"Absolutely not. We are not wed," she pointed out. "And I will be very busy."

That was true. He'd rarely seen anyone work so hard. It reminded him of the men whose ideas he'd backed, the ones who had helped him make a fortune.

He escorted her to the door of the sewing room in silence.

"When will you return?" she asked.

"For the wedding," he said, because part of him wanted to tell her that he would turn around directly. He'd be damned if he found himself at a woman's beck and call.

Not that Lavinia had beckoned or called.

He had spent the previous night after they parted thinking about her breasts, when he wasn't thinking about other, more delicate parts of her. Though sometimes he varied that by thinking about her voice. The way she pleaded for more, for example.

Quietly. Almost under her breath, as if she didn't

want to hear her own words. Lavinia was not a woman who would ever beg.

Was she disappointed by the fact she wouldn't see him for weeks? There wasn't any sign of it. Lavinia's features wore their usual cheerful expression.

"Do you become melancholy once a month?" he asked.

Her eyes rounded. "What are you implying?"

In for a penny, in for a pound.

"A husbandly question," he said. "When you have your monthly courses, do you find yourself weeping?"

"No!" she snapped.

"Angry? Ready to throw things?"

"Are you really asking me this?"

Parth shrugged. "We shall be married. It's to my advantage to understand your temperament."

Lavinia glowered at him. "Men and women do not *ever* discuss that sort of thing between themselves, and I'll thank you never to bring it up again."

"Why not?" Parth was genuinely confounded. He had never discussed it with any other woman, obviously, but he had dimly envisioned marriage as a relationship in which one *did* discuss the unmentionable.

"It's private." Her mouth closed mulishly, and Parth felt that errant tremor of laughter again. Lavinia was always merry; it was absurd to find that he liked making her prickly.

He edged closer, enough so he could smell her honeysuckle scent, and took a slow, deep breath. "I thought marriage was about private matters. Sharing them, that is."

Lavinia narrowed her eyes. "Do you mean to share personal things as well?"

He couldn't help it; he put his arms around her. "Is it shameful to want to kiss you as much as I do?"

Lavinia's body relaxed and humor threaded through her voice. "No." She turned her face up, and when he didn't immediately put his mouth on hers, she rose on her toes and brushed her lips against his.

A kiss. A kiss from her.

Parth brought her toward him and their bodies met with a barely audible kiss of worsted against silk. Lavinia relaxed against him and made a little humming sound in the back of her throat. He didn't stop kissing her until it occurred to him that he had to pull away or he would pull up her skirts.

"Is it shameful to need to bed you day and night— and not always in bed?"

She didn't seem to mind that so much. In fact, a smile was hovering on her lips. Beautiful, raspberry-colored lips.

"I could take you on the breakfast table, for example. Push the oatmeal to the side, lay you on your back, and paint your breasts with hot chocolate. Not too hot."

Her eyes rounded and she finally managed to splutter, "It's time to go to work."

Lavinia said goodbye to Parth at the door to the sewing room and went inside feeling disconcerted. He wasn't precisely who she had thought he was. He had a wicked streak, if that was the right word. She always thought he was solemn, but he wasn't. He was protective, and domineering—

But also naughty. She had a strong feeling he meant it about the breakfast table. She caught herself smiling into the distance.

Late in the day, Parth entered the sewing room and strode over toward her with no more than a nod for the assembled women. Before Lavinia could say a word, he picked her up and carried her from the room with a brisk "Good evening!"

The door closed on a storm of giggles.

"What happened to the idea of telling no one?" Lavinia inquired. Her arms were wrapped around his neck.

"You're mine and I want everyone to know it."

"I'm perfectly capable of walking."

He dropped a kiss on her lips. "I like to hold you."

"Huh," Lavinia said. Not exactly articulate, but she was tired. Whenever she closed her eyes, lines of stitches reeled in front of her. Everything hurt, especially her fingers. She leaned one cheek against him with a sigh. "What did you do today?"

"What gentlemen do," Parth said, an edge in his voice. "Visited the stables and decided a mare was in foal."

"Goodness," Lavinia said, stifling a yawn.

"Then we migrated to the billiard room where Jeremy bet recklessly and won two games. When he sat down so North could take his place, he slid under the table and we discovered he'd drunk an entire bottle of brandy."

"He's very handsome," Lavinia said, covering her mouth as she yawned again.

"Hideous," Parth corrected. "Weak chin. Terrible hair. Habit of sleeping under tables. Damned good at billiards, though."

"You don't know anything about his chin," Lavinia said, an undignified giggle escaping.

"I know that you called him handsome."

Lavinia thought about that and a hazy idea made its way through her exhausted mind. "Are you *jealous*?"

"Of a man who sleeps under the billiard table?"

"That jaw," she said, dropping her voice. "Like an Adonis. Well, perhaps not an Adonis," she said, remembering who they were talking about. Jeremy's good looks were matched only by his foul temper. "A fallen angel!"

Parth snorted. "Devilish, all right."

"Lucifer," Lavinia said, feeling more awake every moment. "That smoldering look is so romantic."

"I can smolder," Parth said, looking down at her.

Lavinia felt the shock of his gaze all the way down her legs.

"Here, you," he said, his voice dropping. "No looking at me like that. Damn, I wonder if other men realize how effective this smoldering business is."

Lavinia squirmed. "Put me down, won't you?"

They were in one of the interminable corridors that wound around and seemed to go nowhere other than rooms that no one frequented.

In short, they were alone.

He instantly complied, and then leaned one shoulder against the wall, looking down at her with a lopsided grin. "Please tell me you're done with manual labor for the day."

"It would seem you gave me no choice."

Lavinia came up on her toes and tugged at his cravat, pulling it free of its simple knot. His eyes darkened but he said nothing. When she began to unbutton his waistcoat he silently moved her a few steps to the right, opened a door, and backed in.

"No lace," she said, surveying his plain shirt, ladling mock sorrow into her voice.

He shook his head.

Lavinia wound her arms around him. He was warm

and strong, and he smelled wonderful. Like home, she thought dimly. Like . . .

Like the man she would marry.

"My mother isn't coming to Diana's wedding," she told him, nestling closer. "Lady Knowe had a letter saying that there'd been an 'incident,' whatever that means."

His arms tightened around her, and she felt his cheek on the top of her head. "I'm sorry, Lavinia. I know you miss her. I look forward to coming to know her better."

Even two years ago, when they first met at Diana's betrothal party, Lady Gray had spent much of her time in bed. Shame was a corrosive emotion. "I wish you didn't have to leave tomorrow morning," Lavinia whispered.

"I can stay," he said, pulling her more tightly against him.

"No, you must go. I shall be sewing morning, noon, and night."

Parth backed up a few steps, and then dropped onto a bed, bringing her with him. The next instant she was lying on top of him, her body tingling. She'd be a fool to take the risk . . . look what had happened to Diana.

But it had been such a long day.

"This must be what marriage is like," she whispered, turning her head just enough that she could press a kiss on his chest. Or rather, on his shirt, so she pulled until she was able to kiss a broad swath of golden chest.

"A good husband must minister to his exhausted wife," Parth said, his voice a lazy invitation. His hand on her back began a slow journey downward. "This particular husband—or husband-to-be—is very grateful that you have left off those outlandish panniers. They hide your hips. And your hips are marvelous."

Lavinia wriggled, enjoying the unusual mattress beneath her.

"We mustn't be intimate again until I can ask your mother for your hand in marriage." His hand stopped its caress.

That would not do.

Lavinia engaged in a somewhat prolonged wriggle that managed to make her opinion clear without words. Then she raised her upper body—which pushed her lower half directly against Parth's—and began kissing wherever she could reach.

"I suppose I could be persuaded," Parth said, after her lips grazed his left nipple.

It was copper-colored and flat, not at all like hers. Lavinia stole a glance at him and then, holding his gaze, licked it. The expression on his face was entirely satisfying, as was the hoarse sound from his throat.

An unplanned sound.

She liked that.

And she liked the unmistakable evidence of desire throbbing against her belly. Almost as much as the desperate look in his eyes. Parth was never *desperate*.

She had the feeling that he didn't allow himself to care enough to be desperate. If a business transaction wasn't successfully negotiated, why, there were others to be had.

But every time she wriggled against him, and every time her tongue caressed that flat nipple, the look in his eyes deepened. His hands were hovering now as if he was afraid to touch her, afraid he'd lose control.

"Lavinia." It was a groan. And a plea. That was another thing Parth never did, she thought with deep happiness. He never pleaded.

"May I break our agreement?"

That was a *plea*.

She gave one last wriggle and then sat up. In such a way that the softest part of her was in direct contact with the hardest part of him.

Yes, he was desperate. She grinned, running her fingertips down his powerful neck, hesitating at his nipples, and then—because unladylike wickedness seemed to come naturally—she gave him a pinch, to see what happened.

What happened was wondrous. His eyelids fell to half-mast; he surged up to kiss her and did that so thoroughly that she didn't even notice the moment when he rolled her onto her back.

She *did* notice when he managed to pull down her apron and wrench her bodice down enough to free her breasts. "My nipples are so different from yours," she said, gasping, because his hands were shaping her breasts, and the expression in his eyes . . .

"Very," he agreed, bending his head and leaving searing kisses on the slope of one breast. "Yours are so deliciously red." His rough caress made them swell and then when he sucked them into his mouth, Lavinia found herself writhing against him, and pleading.

Who was desperate now?

"More," she whispered, her voice rasping. It was embarrassing, but before she could dwell on that thought, he took one of her nipples between his teeth and gave it a small bite.

That was no ladylike moan; it more closely resembled a shriek. And her hands wound into his hair to hold him in place at the same time her legs wound around his hips. She put the erotic demand that was fueling her body into a kiss, her tongue winding around his, her breath sobbing into his mouth.

Parth's hands settled on her hips and he pulled her sharply against him. "I want you."

"Yes," Lavinia sobbed.

"You're sure?"

Lavinia's eyes opened and she made a face. "Stop being so . . ."

"So *appalling*?" She could feel his laughter like a caress all down her front.

"Yes!" Lavinia said, a smile breaking out against her wishes. She reached down and tugged up her skirts but they were tangled in his legs.

He took over the task, and a moment later she was surrounded by mounds of petticoats, underskirts, a silk overskirt. "Bloody hell," he growled. "Do you suppose that women will ever wear sensible clothing?"

Lavinia was beating down the heaps of cloth to her left and right so she wouldn't be swallowed in crushed fabrics. "You mean like Egyptian queens?" Since he had wrenched open his placket and pulled down his breeches, she wrapped her legs around his hips and tried to pull him down toward her.

He laughed as his hand stroked up her leg, making her gasp. Her eyes glazed over, but even so, she could see the possession in his eyes as he came forward over her on his knees, braced on one hand, the other hand stroking her. "Cleopatra was a demanding woman. Caesar couldn't satisfy her, so she turned to Mark Antony. Or maybe it was the other way around."

Lavinia slipped her hands down the tight muscles of his waist. The smile fell from his face and his jaw tightened. "Cleopatra was a woman who knew what she wanted," she retorted, smiling. "She was an excellent dresser as well."

"Not the time to discuss clothing," Parth growled. "Are you sure, Lavinia?"

She nodded.

His hands settled on either side of her, and he stroked inside with one smooth movement of his hips.

Lavinia's gasp turned into a deep moan. It felt wonderful, a fierce intrusion of the best kind.

But it was the look in Parth's eyes that made her light-headed. Her breath shuddered as he slowly lowered his head and his lips met hers. Below the waist was raw erotic passion as their bodies slammed together in a shameless rhythm. But that kiss? It was tender and . . . and *respectful*.

She knew that Parth wanted her. He liked to laugh with her.

But this kiss felt like the kind a man gave a woman whom he really admired. For the right reasons. Lavinia could only breathe in shallow pants, and yet she couldn't stop her heart from blissfully adding up the tender look in his eyes, and the sweet way he was stroking her forehead with his thumbs.

Men had lusted after her since her first Season. They had supposedly fallen in love with her, and then wasted paper describing her eyes and her skin. They had danced with her and walked with her.

But they hadn't ever really come to know her. Probably that was her fault. She didn't reveal much of her character to others, because she was certain she was shallow.

The way Parth was looking at her, the way he was kissing her . . .

It felt as if he was looking deep into her soul and seeing all her fear of being unlovable. Not unloved, but undeserving of love.

Her breathing was growing more shallow, and she was starting to snap her hips up to meet his, chasing a sensation in her legs, that burning, crawling, utterly pleasurable storm.

She couldn't have remembered it right. It couldn't have been—

It was.

She stiffened and screamed. Parth threw back his head with a muffled oath and urged her on, making one explosion of pleasure lead into another until the tide of it swept him under as well.

Afterward, he lay on his back, gusty breaths shaking him. Lavinia tucked her head against his shoulder and ran a hand down his sweaty body, feeling shy and loving, both at once.

But she held her tongue. She couldn't say, "I love you."

Even if it was true.

Once they were truly betrothed . . . when he knew everything about her mother. But meanwhile, she loved his tattered breath, and the salty gleam on his chest, the greedy way he had lost control at the end, the way joyous pleasure shot down her legs.

It was all mixed up in her head, but mostly she thought about the look in his eyes when he kissed her. She propped herself up on one elbow. "You've traveled to China; have you thought about visiting India?"

"England is my home."

"Yes, but India was your home as well. Perhaps you still have family there."

He stared up at the ceiling and didn't answer. Lavinia sat up, so she could see his face. Finally, she asked, "What do you remember of your parents?"

"I was terrified that I'd forget them," Parth said, just when she thought he wouldn't answer that either. "Aunt Knowe knew I wasn't sleeping, and on the third night after the news of their death she strolled into the nursery well after midnight."

"She did?"

"Wearing a magnificent wrapper and smoking a cheroot. She quit smoking only a few years ago."

Lavinia's mouth tucked into a smile. "I can imagine that."

"She dragged a rocking chair up to my bedside and made me tell her everything I remembered of my family, no matter how insignificant it might seem. She came in night after night, after all the other children had fallen asleep, until finally I had nothing left. Some weeks later, she presented me with a commonplace book with every one of my stories in it, arranged more or less chronologically."

"That's beautiful," Lavinia said, her smile wobbling. "She is an exceptional person."

"I would have forgotten my parents," Parth said. "I was too young and it was easier to push the pain away. But for years I read that book over and over, until the stories became part of me. At the same time, the Wildes became my new family."

"That easily?" She could hear the wistfulness in her own voice.

"Yes and no." Parth was silent a moment. "I sometimes think that if my father had returned, I might have turned into a far more proper Englishman, spending my time in ballrooms and the like. Sterling Lace and the Sterling Bank wouldn't exist. Their deaths gave me a ferocious wish to succeed. To prove myself, I suppose."

"Tell me one of the stories that Lady Knowe wrote down."

"Most of them aren't about my parents. My nanny liked stories about emperors and I told Aunt Knowe all that I remembered. My favorite emperor, Shahab-ud-din Muhammad Khurram, was a warrior and a poet."

"What did you remember of your mother?"

He smiled wryly. "I had clear memories of a time when she came into the nursery, burst out laughing, and then summoned my father."

"What happened?"

"I had painted a beard on my face with an ink made from tar and pitch, the better to look like an emperor."

"Just look at you now," she teased, running her fingers over his silky, close-cropped beard. It was a caress that had all her love in it, had he but known.

He looked startled. "I suppose I might have grown this beard in honor of the emperor."

"Perhaps in honor of your mother's laughter," Lavinia suggested.

He surged up, pulled her down into a hungry kiss. A growl in the back of his throat made her sink against him, desire running like a deep river through her body. His hand ran up her leg and rounded her bottom; the river overflowed into pure carnal lust.

After that, they didn't speak for long minutes, apart from moans, sighs, a command here or there.

"Do you know what Shakespeare would have called

our recent activities?" Lavinia said sometime later, rolling onto her side, luxuriating in the erotic burn between her legs and the way muscles that had been tense and desperate were now completely relaxed.

Parth's chest was still rising and falling in a very attractive manner but he turned his head. "Bedding? Shagging?"

"'Ferking,'" Lavinia said. "Isn't that interesting?"

"There is a clear similarity to a word now in use," Parth allowed. But she could see crinkles at the corners of his eyes. "Is that the sort of bawdy joke you tell your friends?"

Lavinia ran a hand over his stomach, loving the corded muscles there. "I am a very proper young lady, Mr. Sterling. What would I possibly know of bawdy humor?"

He gave her a kiss. "I watched you making people laugh for years. And I always wished that you were telling *me* the joke."

Her hand stilled. "I always thought you were . . ." She didn't finish that sentence because it was all too uncomfortable. "Very well, here's a joke that goes all the way back to the ninth century before Christ."

"How do you know it's that ancient?"

She blinked at him. "I read it in a book! You haven't even heard the joke yet."

"My mistake," he murmured. He rolled on his side as well and leaned forward and kissed her eyebrow. "I'm ready to be amused."

"What hangs at a man's thigh, under his coat, and wants to poke a hole that it's often poked before?"

Parth let out a bark of laughter and leaned closer, rubbing against her thigh. "This?"

Lavinia shook her head. "Incorrect. Guess again."

"A key," Parth said.

"You knew already!"

"Very few jokes involving poking exist that schoolboys haven't memorized by the age of twelve," Parth admitted.

"Schoolgirls are just as intrigued," Lavinia said, letting her fingers wander over Parth's "key." He felt so good: silky and warm and firm.

He let out a deep breath. "I don't know much about women. I always told myself that I wouldn't marry."

Her fingers curled around him possessively. "Until you met Elisa?"

"I met you first."

"You didn't think much of me, so it must have been Elisa who convinced you that marriage was a possibility." She pulled her hand away and sat up. "I was there, on the terrace at teatime, remember? I know you planned to marry her."

Parth smiled. "It's true. I *had* decided to marry her. It was a rational, pragmatic decision, but an exasperating woman kept disrupting my logical plans."

Lavinia tried to scowl at him, but a smile emerged instead.

"She intruded on my heart," he said, his voice dropping. "I couldn't keep her out, and I realized that Elisa had never had a place there."

Lavinia opened her mouth but no words emerged.

"I discovered that I could imagine her—*you*—at my breakfast table, and in my bed, and next to me my whole life. My life would be barren without you."

Lavinia blinked away tears. "Oh, Parth." She leaned forward and put her hands on his shoulders. "Are you certain?"

"I fought the way I felt about you for years, telling

myself that you weren't enough. If I had told myself the truth, I felt you were deserving of a duke, if not a prince."

Lavinia choked on a watery laugh. "That's absurd."

Parth ran his knuckles gently down her cheek. "No. It's absurd that you'll have anything to do with me, Lavinia. You don't need my money; Prince Oskar will be devastated when he finds I've snatched you for myself."

"You must stop talking about money," Lavinia ordered. "You say it as if it were some sort of magic sentence, as if it made a difference. You are *you*, Parth. You have no idea what it's like to survey a ballroom and realize that every available man is tedious in his conversation and, even worse, never asks what I think."

"Huh."

She looked down at his chest again, running her palm slowly over the lovely ridges of muscle. Had he said he loved her? Not exactly. But he had said she had a place in his heart. Was that the same thing? He used to believe she "wasn't enough," but now she was. She was foolish to feel a trickle of unease.

"I would never want to be a princess, or duchess." Her voice, even to her own ears, was heartfelt. "I just want to be with you, Parth."

His arms pulled her closer to him and his lips brushed hers. "I'm yours, Lavinia."

"Oh." The tiny, involuntary sigh was surprising. *Hers?* No person had ever put her first. Her mother was affectionate, if fretful. Willa was loving, but married. Her friends were . . . friends. "Mine?"

His lips nuzzled her cheek and slid down to nip her mouth. "Only you. Yours."

She turned, just enough so that his tongue slipped between her lips. The word echoed in her bones. She wound her arm around his neck and fell into a kiss that was as sensual as it was profound.

Her heart was singing and she could feel tears on her cheeks. Parth Sterling wanted her. Loved her, maybe.

Treasured her, definitely.

Chapter Twenty-three

$\mathcal{P}$arth departed the next morning at dawn, and Lavinia settled into a rhythm bounded by the walls of the sewing chamber. She had six weeks to complete every garment. In the next few weeks, she and the seamstresses faced an occasional hitch, but to her enormous pride and pleasure, the garments were being completed on schedule.

When Lady Knowe's daring gown for the wedding was finished, the lady tried it on, looking extraordinarily dashing. Lavinia found herself grinning helplessly at the look in Lady Knowe's eyes as she stood before the mirror.

Lady Knowe turned around, examining the oversized collar and the distinctive buttons running down her back. "I would never have imagined," she said, her voice softer than it was usually. "Why, Lavinia, you've given me a waist and hips. I look . . ."

"You look marvelous," Ophelia said, giving her a hug.

That evening, while dressing for dinner, Lavinia found an emerald tiara on her pillow. Confounded, she brought it to the dining room and waved the piece before the assembled Wildes, but no one claimed responsibility for it.

Lady Knowe laughed and said that she believed that Diana had had a tiara like that a few years ago. Diana promptly took it from Lavinia's hand, placed it on her head, and declared that indeed it *was* her lost piece, and perhaps the matching necklace would be found in some corner.

His Grace said, gravely, that stray jewelry was regularly being found in the castle's nooks and crannies, adding, "One of my ancestors was very fond of emeralds."

"Your Grace—" Lavinia began. With exquisite kindness, the duke had just doubled the commissions she had made from merchants. He had given her the emerald tiara that she meant to buy with that money.

He raised his hand, and she closed her mouth.

She could hardly believe it, but perhaps . . . perhaps her skills *were* worth that much. As much as a set of emeralds. Every single Wilde would attend Diana's wedding in finery such as was rarely seen outside the royal court. Diana's *trousseau* rivaled anything Lavinia had seen in two years of attendance at the French court.

That wasn't even counting the wedding dress itself.

During the last days of October, Lavinia scarcely emerged from the sewing room, taken up with questions of buttonholes, ruffles, and too-delicate lace. She stopped joining the family for meals and ate with the seamstresses while they talked over the day's sewing. They had to finish not only each family member's attire for the wedding, but the myriad garments for the masquerade ball that would follow.

The ball at which Parth would announce their betrothal, if her mother agreed, and she would.

Members of the family trooped in and out of the chamber as they were fitted and refitted for various garments. Diana, in particular, tried on parts of her wedding dress a total of five times.

Lady Knowe often stopped to "cheer on the troops," as she said, and the duchess came by to encourage them, in her gentle way, to rest. Even Mrs. Mousekin, the housekeeper, took to sewing for a few hours every morning.

Then . . . they had completed their work.

On the morning of October 28, a day before planned. Not inconsequentially, the day that Parth was due to return to the castle.

Every dress, every cloak, every bonnet, every headdress was finished and dispatched to the bedchamber of its owner, including the wedding gown. When Annie bustled out of the room holding the last of Diana's *trousseau*—a revealing chemise trimmed with scarlet love knots—Lavinia collapsed in a chair. A deep satisfaction hummed through her.

She'd always known that she wasn't as intellectual as Willa. Willa read the Greek philosophers, while Lavinia kissed her prints of Lord Wilde before sallying forth to fail yet another French examination.

Willa adored visiting the British Museum, and was fascinated by Egyptian hieroglyphs. Lavinia returned from those excursions with a precise image of Cleopatra's pleated costumes in her head, but no memory of hieroglyphs whatsoever.

Sitting in the empty room, after the only triumph of

her life that mattered, she finally understood that she had succumbed to the idea that Parth had disdained her because she'd welcomed that disdain. She had been furious at him for reflecting her own opinions of herself. She saw herself as shallow, and so she acted that part for him.

No longer.

She, Lavinia Gray, had given her cousin the most beautiful *trousseau* that any future duchess had ever had. Whether Diana became that duchess or not— for North still seemed determined to relinquish the title—no one in all England would doubt that Diana would be worthy of that rank.

A great many members of the aristocracy would be descending on Lindow for the wedding. Those not invited would see Lady Roland presented at court—in her splendid wedding dress, as was the custom.

Diana stuck her head around the door. "Sweetheart!" she cried. "May I entice you downstairs for luncheon for the first time in *days* and *days*?"

"Has Parth arrived yet?" Lavinia asked, not even caring how transparent her question was.

"Not yet," Diana said. "More importantly, when will you and Parth announce your betrothal?"

"We could not possibly be betrothed, because no one has asked my mother for my hand in marriage," Lavinia said, unable to stop herself from smiling.

"Pooh, what a trifling excuse," Diana said. "It's not as if *my* mother has given permission for my marriage. Though I did receive a letter from her this morning."

Lavinia straightened. "What does she write? Does she regret disowning you, now that you're to be a duchess?"

"Not quite. The gist of the letter insists that the

value of my emerald parure is equal to a dowry. Which reminds me . . ." Diana's face took on an impish joy. "I have some tremendous news!"

"Do tell!"

"Just look what His Grace found under a small table in the drawing room." She added with a mischievous giggle, "I do remember wearing it in that room during the betrothal party."

Lavinia shook her head at the magnificent string of emeralds that Diana was waving in the air. She blinked away a burning sensation in her eyes. Diana had emeralds again—probably superior to those she had lost two years ago. The duke had been far too generous in this second, surreptitious gift.

The Wildes were so *dear*, so honest, openhearted, and true. All of them: from the youngest children all the way up to the duke and Ophelia. Parth was part of them. She would be part of their family, which was almost too much to imagine.

"No one has told Parth about my mother's theft of the emeralds, have they?"

"Tell him what?" Diana asked, fastening the emeralds around her neck. "I lost some jewels two years ago, and now they have been found. What luck for me, since my mother regards the set as my dowry."

"I don't want him to know."

"Not ever?"

"I'll tell him when my mother comes out of the sanitarium. I will need help keeping her from stealing again."

"Why not simply tell him now?"

Lavinia fiddled with a button. How could she explain

how fragile his respect for her felt? And yet it was everything to her. To have him look at her with admiration was like a drug, as powerful as Dr. Robert's drops.

Just imagining the conversation in which she confessed her mother's crimes made Lavinia's skin chill. She was bringing nothing to the marriage, other than a mother tucked away in a sanitarium. No dowry, just debt. Of course she had to tell him, but perhaps not right away?

"Don't you agree that my mother should have the chance to confess?" she said, equivocating. "He'll be her son-in-law."

Diana dropped into a chair and frowned at her. "He already knows the worst, Lavinia. He knows she squandered the inheritance your father left you, and he knows she's addicted to laudanum. Parth would never respect anyone who spent her daughter's dowry, so you might as well tell him now."

Was it so awful to want a little more time, just enough to make him truly appreciate that she had good things that outweighed the bad? Make love a few more times?

If she closed her eyes, she could see his cold expression, the one that had assessed her and found her lacking. Even imagining it made her heart pound with sick dread.

"I can't allow him to know that my mother is a thief, when he already knows she is addicted. Not yet." The words came from the deepest part of Lavinia's heart. "She's my mother, Diana, and the only relative I bring to this marriage, other than you. He brings all the Wildes." She held back more tears.

She was allowing fear to govern her actions. Instead,

she should remember the moment when she saw respect, genuine respect, and admiration in Parth's eyes.

"Parth doesn't need a family," Diana stated. "He has one. He needs *you*. You must promise to confess once you're betrothed."

"I promise," Lavinia said quickly. "I shall need his help to determine whether my mother was involved in other thefts, and to keep her from going to prison in the future."

Diana snorted. "Not usual son-in-law duties." She brightened. "But if anyone can do it, Parth is the man."

"I know," Lavinia said. "Prince Oskar and Lord Jeremy are rich, but that's not good enough. Parth was the only one who could really help me."

"I *told* you Parth was the man to marry, Lavinia, back when I sent you in to propose marriage." Diana's voice was deliberately cheery.

"He refused me," Lavinia pointed out.

"But you didn't give up," Diana said, grinning widely as she grabbed Lavinia's knee and squeezed it. "My cousin *never gives up*!" She narrowed her eyes. "Now I am hoping that you don't end up with a three-month baby because you traded your virginity for that victory."

"It wasn't like that!" Lavinia protested.

Diana hopped up and adjusted her emeralds in the glass. "May I wear these with my wedding dress?"

Lavinia gaped at her. "Are you jesting?"

"It would be fitting to wear them. Perhaps the tiara as well. Though you made that beautiful flowery pouf. Maybe we could fit the tiara over the pouf."

"You will not wear green stones with a silver and white dress with rose accents," Lavinia said, her voice rising. "You will wear the set of diamonds that Her Grace inherited from her mother."

Diana blinked at her.

"I'm sorry," Lavinia said abruptly, climbing to her feet. "I'm just tired. I don't mean to be such a dragon."

"I know you miss your mother," Diana said, and hugged her. "Your birthday is tomorrow, isn't it? The first birthday after my sister died, when my mother had banished me, I missed them both dreadfully."

"Actually, I might pay my mother a visit tomorrow," Lavinia said. "Lady Knowe says that she is not well enough to come here, but the sanitarium is only an hour's drive."

"Parth can escort you," Diana said. "He can ask your mother for your hand at the same time. What a lovely birthday present!"

Lavinia had so many blasted emotions swirling inside her that she felt positively ill. What happened to the days when Willa mocked her for being endlessly cheerful? When she thought that any difficult situation could be eased with a smile?

She pictured confessing Lady Gray's thievery to Parth, and no smile appeared. She thought about her mother, alone in a sanitarium, and couldn't curl up even one corner of her mouth.

Chapter Twenty-four

Meanwhile

*I*t had been six weeks since Parth had last seen Lavinia, though he was secretly embarrassed by his precision. He helped Elisa from the carriage with barely concealed impatience, after which he had to introduce her to Prism, who summoned Aunt Knowe, who summoned the duchess.

Then all three ladies chattered about the journey, about Italy, about Parth's luxurious carriage.

Finally, finally, they bore Elisa away to her chamber to bathe and ready herself for luncheon. Elisa's eyes were shining as she bid him goodbye. She was ecstatic to find herself in the bosom of the Wildes.

Parth bowed, and took off for the north tower. He bounded up the steps two at a time. He paused outside the sewing room, and just as he was about to enter, Lavinia's voice floated into the open corridor.

"Prince Oskar and Lord Jeremy are rich, but that's not good enough. Parth was the only one who could really help me."

A grin spread over his face. Damned right, Oskar and Jeremy weren't good enough.

"I *told* you Parth was the man to marry, Lavinia, back when I sent you in to propose marriage," Diana crowed. Lavinia murmured something he couldn't hear.

"But you didn't give up," Diana cried. He could hear the triumph in her voice. "My cousin *never gives up!*"

The air in his lungs felt queerly hot, and it occurred to him that he was eavesdropping, like a housemaid hovering in the corridor.

Parth's stomach knotted. He felt like a prize awarded after a horse race.

"Now I am hoping that you don't end up with a three-month baby because you traded your virginity for that victory," Diana said.

God, he did too. He turned and headed for his chamber before he could hear Lavinia's answer. He felt pity for her, he decided. That was why he felt sick. He felt an edge of contempt as well, and that was dangerous.

Whatever the emotion, it was bitter on his tongue. Lavinia had needed a rich husband, and she and Diana had chosen him. Focused on him. He *knew* that. Bloody hell, she'd told him everything, and he'd offered to find her a husband who was rich enough.

Why, in that case, did he feel so angry?

Air sawed through his chest and images, unbidden, started coming to him. What had Lavinia been doing outside Felton's in the pouring rain, her soaked clothing pasted against her admittedly magnificent chest? No lady went out the back door of an establishment and stood in the alley. She must have known that his carriage had pulled out of Oxford Street.

It had been a deliberate seduction.

Coming to his bedchamber hadn't worked, but the wet gown certainly had. From that moment he abandoned serious thoughts of Elisa. Lavinia had scooped him up as neatly as she had those other men who had offered her a ring.

A cold bleakness descended over him.

Lavinia had maintained that she didn't want to announce their betrothal until he asked her mother for her hand in marriage—but she had slept with him. Lady Gray had no choice in the matter; neither did he. No gentleman breaks off an engagement after taking a lady's chastity.

His jaw tightened so much that he could feel his back teeth clenching.

It was . . .

Nothing.

Not important.

He *was* a rich man and he would not have backed out, whether Lavinia had bedded him or not. She had given him something priceless in return for his money: her virginity. Her . . . her pleasure. Her future.

That was enough.

This was nothing more than a shock. Lavinia had needed a rich, powerful husband, and he happened to be the rich man who was lucky enough to be chosen.

He rubbed his chest as he entered his bedchamber, as if something thornlike pricked him there. He found his new valet, Bell, waiting to help him change from his traveling garments.

"Belowstairs, sir," Bell said abruptly, "they seem to be under the impression that you are courting a young lady here in the castle."

Parth merely nodded. Bell brushed an invisible speck of dust from the coat he held, adding, "Rather than the contessa."

If Bell imagined that he and Parth would share a warm intimacy in which they discussed Parth's love life, he was mistaken. Parth gave him a steady look.

"As your valet, sir, I frowned on such impertinent speculation, but I thought you should know about the erroneous impression."

"I intend to marry Miss Lavinia Gray, not the contessa. I was very good friends with the contessa's late husband."

At that, Bell demonstrated the intelligence that Parth required in a valet, and held his tongue while Parth changed clothing, after which Parth headed down to the drawing room to wait for luncheon. His mood lifted when he found North there, a glass in hand.

North came to his feet and they met in a rough hug that two gentlemen would never exchange in public. "Thank God you're here," North said.

"Missing Alaric?" Parth asked.

"And Horatius." North raised his glass. "In honor of whom . . ." He took a healthy swallow.

"What's that you're drinking? And how's Diana?" Parth crossed to the sideboard and considered a glass of whisky. "When last I saw her, she was unable to keep anything down."

Diana had certainly sounded well when he'd eavesdropped on her celebrating Lavinia's "victory."

"She's not my wife yet," North said. "I keep remembering that Godfrey's father died before he could marry, before he even saw his own son."

Something hot and angry was still beating in Parth's chest, but he made himself listen to North. "Is Aunt Knowe worried about her or the baby?"

"No. Diana keeps down food now, though nothing before noon. She looks better." His voice trailed off. "I'll go see how she's feeling." He set down his glass with a sharp click, and bounded from the room without looking back.

Parth sank into a chair, enjoying the abrupt silence in the room. Lavinia was . . . what she was. He knew who she was. Hell, he could afford a hundred bonnets.

For God's sake, he'd already *known* that she'd decided to woo him. Could a woman be more candid than Lavinia? She'd come to his room and proposed marriage. She had told him that she needed to marry a rich man.

That's what made the air in his lungs feel painful. He had wanted to do the pursuing. The idea he'd been stalked—as one of the richest men in England—and then scooped into a net by a drenched bodice and a pair of wide blue eyes didn't sit well with him. Especially given Diana's smug claim that they'd bested him.

He wasn't surprised when Lavinia entered the room before anyone else; it was that sort of day.

Her dress was made of a peachy fabric that looked silky, as soft as her hair, and she'd piled all her ringlets on her head. She ran through the door and looked about, freezing when she saw him.

"Parth!" Her voice was so lovely, throaty, and full of affection—and she ran straight toward him.

He was damned lucky to have her—no matter how he got her, or why. He forced a smile and strode over to her, bowing and kissing her hand.

"My hand?" Lavinia asked, her voice dropping to a near whisper. "But we're alone."

Parth looked down into her eyes and knew it was a watershed moment. "I want you to know that there's nothing to confess," he said, his voice as soft as he could make it.

"Confess?" Her eyes filled with apprehension.

He stepped back. Perhaps they should conduct this conversation somewhere else. But, damn it, he hated the distance that lay between them. He could tell her it didn't matter, and then . . .

Well, she would have to promise not to lie to him again.

"It's not important now," he said.

"Parth?" She was utterly still, like a nocturnal animal caught in the glow of a lantern. "What isn't important?"

When he didn't answer immediately, she asked again, "What isn't important, Parth? What are you trying to say?"

"That you made up your mind to marry a rich man. That you—that you chose me."

"You already know that," she said. Her eyes glittered, and for a moment he thought she was tearful. But no, because oddly enough, the corners of her mouth tipped up. She was smiling. A bit.

"It's not as bad as you think. I *will* bring you a dowry. The money my father left is gone, but if we wait to marry, just a year or so, I can supply my own dowry."

He frowned. "What do you mean?"

"Well, that I am making commissions from planning *trousseaux*," Lavinia said.

He noticed that her hands were shaking. "You can provide your own dowry." The words dropped into the silence like pennies onto flagstones.

"It won't be as large as it might have been, but I won't come to you empty-handed."

No one had ever surprised Parth as much as Lavinia Gray did. Probably no one ever would. "I don't need your dowry, no matter where it came from," he said flatly.

"I know you don't need it. But I would rather have it."

His mind was slowly catching up to what she was revealing. "In essence, the odious *Lady Blythe* is supplying your dowry?"

Lavinia nodded, her eyes wary.

"That's hogwash," he said, the words rasping from his mouth.

She flinched.

"I want to bring a dowry," she said haltingly.

"No!"

"No?"

"You will *not* work for a wretched woman like Lady Blythe. No wife of mine will be beholden to a woman like that. Ever."

"But what I do for her is important," Lavinia said.

He was too angry to listen. "I don't care that you schemed to catch my attention. I can pay for all your bonnets and frivolities, all the things you squandered your dowry on. I'll give you an allowance, Lavinia. You can spend it any damned way you please."

The moment the words left his mouth he knew he'd made a mistake.

Chapter Twenty-five

$\mathcal{L}$avinia sucked in a breath of air in a futile attempt to stop her chest from tightening. Parth's eyes were so cold. She opened her mouth to defend herself—to explain everything to him about her mother's thefts—but then she saw it would make no difference.

What mattered was the look in his eyes and the tone in his voice. She knew that look, that tone. He was back there again, or maybe he'd never really left there. Perhaps he'd never stopped believing she was shallow as a puddle.

They were back to those cursed bonnets.

"You believe that I recklessly wasted my dowry, don't you?"

He raked a hand through his hair. "I don't know, Lavinia. You love clothing. You likely had no idea what kind of money you were running through. Did you?"

Lavinia couldn't lie; she had had no idea. He thought of her as a frivolous butterfly, who had bought every color that struck her fancy. And yet . . . hadn't she been precisely that?

The scorn in his voice fed directly to the chilly whisper in the back of her head that had told her the same. She was no good at anything.

No. She stopped herself. Only now was she cobbling together a sense of pride in herself, and she could not allow that precious part of her heart to be trampled.

If Parth didn't know what she was like *now*, then there was no point to this marriage.

Despair wrapped around her heart and twisted hard. "Is this because of Elisa?" she asked impulsively. "Would you prefer to marry her? Have you changed your mind while you were in London?"

His eyes narrowed. "Is that what you think of me? That I would leave for a few weeks and change my mind? After *sleeping with you*?"

"That needn't stop you," Lavinia said, keeping her voice steady. "I am not carrying a child."

"I am a man of honor!" The words roared from his mouth.

"I know," Lavinia said, scrambling. Parth's eyes burned with anger. In that moment, she envisioned a marriage in which her husband would roar at her for being frivolous. Day after day of facing the sort of censure she was being subjected to now. Asking her scathingly if she'd overspent her allowance. Or asking her kindly.

It hardly mattered.

The truth was that he thought nothing of the commissions she'd earned. He scorned them.

Why not spend her days shopping? He wouldn't expect anything else.

"I'm sorry, Parth, but I cannot marry you." Anguish caught at her throat but she made herself continue. "I have changed my mind."

Because, she said silently, *deep down, you believe I'm an idiot. Because you believe I have a head stuffed with feathers. Because you believe that I . . .*

Because you agree with all the worst things I think about myself.

"You refuse to marry me *because I don't want your dowry?*"

She shook her head, unable to speak.

"That is the only piece of new information between us," he said, his voice so chilly that she felt the fine hairs on her arms stand on end. "Well, that and the fact you ventured into the rain to lure me with a wet bodice. Entirely successfully, by the way."

"What are you talking about?" Lavinia asked incredulously. And then, shaking her head, "It doesn't matter. My dowry has nothing to do with my refusal to marry you."

He crossed his arms over his chest. "Then?"

"It's the way you look at me," she said raggedly. "The way you see me."

"I look at you with desire. And possession. You will be my wife. You are *mine.*" His voice growled from some place deep inside him.

"You look at me as if I'm shallow and extravagant," she said, choking back a little sob. "It's because you see me that way, Parth."

He started to say something and she held up her hand. "I know you've said otherwise, but the truth is that whenever you're annoyed with me, the truth comes out, as it just did."

"What do you mean?"

"The way you looked at me when you said I didn't know how much clothing cost. When you implied that I had squandered my dowry." Her voice trembled, and she had to stop for a moment to recover herself. "You were right. I did not know the cost of the things I bought."

His face softened. "But I have seen how much you've learned."

"Yet you neither respect nor sanction my occupation," she said dully. "I cannot marry you, Parth." Despite herself, tears spilled down her cheeks. "I consider myself to be so much more dull-witted than Willa."

"What are you talking about?"

"I *am* the one who bought eight bonnets. I'm also the one who never reads ancient Greek history, who failed at French, and who adored Lord Wilde. I'm the one who's shallow as a puddle."

She saw him flinch, and a muscle ticked in his jaw. "You are not shallow and you can buy fifty bonnets if you like!" His eyes were dark with . . . something. It could be torment. Guilt, perhaps. He wouldn't want to hurt her feelings. He was a gentleman.

"I know." She turned away, heartsick. "But it hurts, Parth, and if you cannot see why, then I cannot explain it."

"Please try, Lavinia. Help me to understand."

She dashed tears away from her cheeks, cursing her inability to keep her emotions under control. Then she forced herself to meet his eyes. He deserved that. It wasn't his fault, after all.

"You're a good man, and you deserve a woman who is as—as splendid as you are." For a moment she almost lost composure again, and caught herself. "I will always disappoint you, Parth, and I can't bear that. I am . . . I *am* all those things you believe of me. But despite that, I still deserve—I still deserve—"

Sobs overtook her, and words became impossible.

His arms closed around her like steel. "Please don't cry, Lavinia. Please. I'll do anything to make you feel better."

"Then let me go," she said, her voice shaking. She pulled away, and summoned what inner strength she had. "I no longer wish to marry you, Parth. I hope you can forgive me."

With that, she turned and slipped from the room, closing her ears and her heart to the low, hoarse shout that followed her down the corridor.

"Lavinia!"

No.

She walked faster, but he didn't follow. Once in her room, she sank onto the bed. Parth's infatuation with her had been a glimmer that skimmed the surface of what he really thought about her. Her shallow puddle had been disguised by a thin layer of glittering ice for a while that readily cracked.

Perhaps even more readily, she thought dully, because she had played the loose woman. She had gone to bed with him, and she hadn't been ladylike about it. She had let herself be seduced in a tower, where anyone might have entered. She had virtually torn off his clothing in a corridor. Behaviors that confirmed his opinion of her that she was manipulative, and would do anything for money.

The pretty, deceptive ice was shattered. Feeling as if her heart, too, was shattered, Lavinia got up. If she stayed here, in her bedchamber, he would find her.

She knew Parth. His conscience would not allow him to accept her decision without protest, even if what he felt was relief. His instinct to protect would be aroused if she refused to marry him.

Unless she married one of the men he had obligingly introduced to her, with that express purpose in mind.

All of a sudden, a sob ripped through her chest and she doubled over as if she'd been struck. Parth's protectiveness had felt so reassuring. So safe. During his absence, knowing they would be married, she had felt as if she could do anything. She had made her way through endless lists, setbacks, and difficulties with a glad heart, because Parth would be returning from London. Because he made her feel safe.

That was the problem, right there.

He had made her feel safe.

She was a pathetic, useless excuse for a human being, and the fact that Parth Sterling recognized the truth was just—just the way it was. Parth was right. She *was* shallow. Finding that her hands had tightened into fists, Lavinia took a painful breath.

She pulled herself upright, went to the basin, and washed her face. Then she applied a thick mask of white powder, as if she were disguising scars instead of the ravages of weeping.

Countless women had no idea how much their dowry was worth, or the cost of a gown. That she had been among them wasn't her fault as much as it was an accident of birth. Of the way things were for women like her. She felt hollow, like a tree that had been carved out from the inside.

She didn't belong here, at Lindow. Willa was long gone, and Diana was to be married soon. Only one thought was pounding behind her swollen eyes: *I want to go home.* Her lips trembled again at the thought. Her family's country estate was closed long ago, the furniture draped in holland covers, the servants let go.

With another aching swallow, she pushed the desire away. Returning home was an impossibility, but she *could* go see her mother. Five minutes later, she stood at the door of Lady Knowe's private drawing room.

Chapter Twenty-six

$\mathcal{N}$orth came striding out of the stable yard just as Parth came through the gate. He took a quick look at Parth's face and clearly had second thoughts about whatever he was about to say.

"Have you been out on the bog this fall?" North pulled a silver flask from his pocket. "Remember when we used to sneak into the bog and drink ourselves into a stupor?"

"I have no impulse to repeat the experience," Parth stated. He felt too bitterly miserable to stay inside but that didn't mean he wanted to get drunk.

"We've grown into such behemoths that we'd need a barrel of whisky," North pointed out, but he started in the direction of the Moss, and Parth, for want of a better plan, went along.

Out of the shelter of the woods they cut across the front of the castle, skirting the courtyard, and headed toward Lindow Moss, the bog that stretched for miles to the east. On the other side of the gate they followed an ancient path marking solid ground.

"Snow's coming," North said, after they'd tramped a good twenty minutes.

"Can you really smell it over the peat?" Parth asked.

The peat's distinctive odor rose from the bog with an acrid force.

"Smells like home," North said.

"You're damned cheerful." Parth knocked a clump of muddy sphagnum moss from one boot.

North elbowed him and they silently watched as a pale gray bird drifted over the moorland, a moving wisp of fog but for the black tips on its wings.

"Horatius would have known what bird that is," Parth said.

"It's a hen harrier," North said. "Male. The females are dark brown and keep to the ground." He met Parth's raised eyebrows with a shrug. "I've had trouble sleeping since returning from war. The Moss is a good place to be, and Horatius left his birding books behind."

"She's changed her mind," Parth said, apropos of nothing, and started down the path again.

"I assume you're talking about Lavinia, not the contessa? Why on earth?"

"She thinks I don't respect her."

"Well, you are the one who called her—"

"Shallow as a puddle," Parth growled. "She overheard you repeat it—not your fault; I'm the idiot who insulted her in the first place."

"Your opinion of her has altered?"

The words hung in the air. It was growing thick with snow; Parth could feel the air gathering itself, preparing to split into tiny floating drops of white.

"*Yes*, damn it."

"We should turn back at the birch," North said. "Lavinia used to poke at you quite mercilessly."

Parth shrugged. "I was always looking for her, even when she lived in Paris, wondering if she'd fallen in love."

North said nothing, so Parth found more words. "She was always at the center of everyone's attention. Laughing, darting here and there, collecting men as if they were hairpins. I didn't want to be attracted to her."

"We can't choose who we'd like to be attracted to," North said. "Life would be easier if I hadn't fallen in love with a governess who happened to be the fiancée who jilted me and supposedly bore my purported child."

They reached a silver birch surrounded by a rudimentary screen for hunters. North threw himself down on the wooden bench at the tree's base with the familiarity of someone who had made a second home in the bog. He carried no visible wounds from his time at war in the colonies, but obviously they existed.

"On the other hand, life without Diana isn't worth living," North said. He uncorked his flask, took a long swallow, and passed it to Parth. "It's peaceful out here. I miss Horatius, and I feel closer to him here."

Parth frowned, and North added, "Not because he died here, but because he loved it so much. He spent whole days looking for birds, remember?"

"I've spent whole days looking for Lavinia," Parth said, as the drink burned a welcome path to his stomach. "I could say whatever I liked about her, but she drew me like a flame draws a moth whenever I was in her vicinity. She teased me, and called me names, and I just kept finding her, following her, so she could do it again."

North grunted. "Tell her that."

"If I stop looking for Lavinia, if I stop waiting for Lavinia, what is the use of it all?" Parth asked.

"Did you tell her?"

"Tell her what?"

"That you're hopelessly in love," North said, taking another swallow. "You're sitting around with tears streaming down your cheeks at the thought of not seeing her again."

Parth looked at him incredulously.

"Metaphorically," North said, handing him the flask.

Parth took a gulp, looking over the bog. North wasn't so far off, in truth. He wasn't given to crying, but something ragged and hot in his chest cut more sharply than the wind. His longing for Lavinia was raw and dirty—and at the same time, it was tender and profound. "I can't," he said, finally.

"I disagree. You can."

"She says I don't respect her. I can't . . . what can I say? I did say that thing. And when I heard she used those commissions she earned to put together a dowry, I . . ."

"You said something even worse?" North snatched the flask back. "Women never forget that sort of thing."

"Diana congratulated her on *winning* me."

"So?"

He refused to describe what had happened when Lavinia came to his bedchamber. That was private.

"She could definitely have done better than you," North said. "Did you hear what Beck told the king?"

Parth braced himself. "No."

"He told His Majesty that he'd fallen in love with Miss Lavinia Gray, and that he was coming back for her. And His Majesty offered St. George's chapel at Windsor Castle for their wedding, with a celebration to follow."

Parth watched his breath puff out in a ragged white cloud. "How do you know that?"

"I'm not even in London, and I heard about it. Aunt Knowe had a letter detailing the whole conversation— which apparently took place in the throne room, surrounded by courtiers. What the hell have you been doing?"

"Working, when I wasn't on the road, and frequently when I was on it. Not listening to gossip."

"More the fool you," North said unsympathetically. He handed over the flask again. "You might as well drink the rest. She's 'won' better than you, damn it. The problem is that you didn't win *her*. She worked like a mad person to earn those commissions, and she loved every minute. If you stripped away her pride in what she's doing, then she'd be right not to marry you."

"I had no intention of doing so."

"Tell me you didn't imply the commissions weren't important because of your fortune."

"In so many words." Parth's voice rasped in his chest. "I told her that none of her work mattered. In my defense, she had never told me that she was working to make money, and I was off my guard."

Parth leaned his head back against the tree bark and stared up through its branches. The sorrow in his heart was a clawing pain now. It seemed that despair had a sour taste that even canceled out the smell of peat.

"Why didn't she tell you?" North asked, getting to his feet. "Come on, my balls feel like lumps of ice."

They started back, heads down, into a biting wind.

"We act as if we're invincible," North continued, his shoulder bumping Parth's. "We were taught to live our lives as if we were right at every moment. You'll have to discard that attitude in order to win her back."

Parth grunted.

"Beg," North said flatly. "You must tell her the truth. How much do you love her?"

"What in the hell do you want me to say?" Parth demanded, suddenly livid, his heart burning with it. "That I love her more than the moon and the stars?"

"Hackneyed," North said. "Try again."

Parth cursed. "I can't do this. She doesn't care how much I love her. She says I don't *respect* her."

"Where's the difference?" North's strides lengthened and he moved in front. "It's freezing out here." The wind whipped away his words.

"She's better than me," Parth said, letting the words go on the wind, not sure North could hear them, not caring. "She's kinder, smarter. If I had never loved her . . . If I had never loved her, I would have no goals that matter."

North turned to face Parth. "Tell her that." He walked backward, risking falling from the path into the bog. "Tell her that."

"Turn around, damn it," Parth snarled. "Diana will kill me if you disappear before the wedding."

North grinned at him, but he stopped. "That would certainly solve your problem. Who would have thought that you, Parth Sterling, would love a woman that much?"

Parth shook his head.

"Follow me," North shouted, turning about.

So Parth did.

Chapter Twenty-seven

*L*avinia caught the exact instant when Lady Knowe gave in, when her eyes sharpened and she saw that Lavinia had been crying. "Oh, my dear. You miss your mother," she said, surging upright. "I'll send a groom ahead by horseback with word that you're on the way."

After that, it was easy. Annie packed a small portmanteau, and an hour later, Lavinia descended the stairs into the entry, wearing her traveling costume and a fur-lined cloak because snowflakes were swirling in the afternoon sunshine.

"Why are you taking clothing?" Lady Knowe cried, looking alarmed. "Do you intend to stay the night? You haven't said goodbye to anyone."

"I know that you will explain everything to His Grace and the family," Lavinia said. "It's my birthday tomorrow, and I know my mother will want to spend the day with me." In truth, she wasn't sure her mother would even remember.

"What about Parth!" Lady Knowe hissed, waving

Prism back into the drawing room. "You mustn't leave without saying farewell, Lavinia."

"You will give my farewell to Parth and the contessa along with everyone else, won't you?"

Lady Knowe tilted her head to the side and examined Lavinia as carefully as if she were a recalcitrant nephew. "Something has happened," she deduced.

"No, nothing has happened," Lavinia said wearily. "I miss my mother, Lady Knowe." Then, in case the lady kept protesting, she went in for the *coup de grâce*: "I am grateful for all you did for her when I was ill. But I never said goodbye to her, and I had no say as to her care. Diana's *trousseau* is finished; I have fulfilled my responsibilities."

Lady Knowe clasped her hands together. "You are offended! My dearest Lavinia, I never meant to be obstructive, or keep you away from your mother."

Lavinia felt a pang of guilt—but she was so desperate to leave that she squashed the impulse to apologize. "I must see how my mother is faring," she said instead. "I'm sure you can understand."

"Certainly I can!" With that, Lady Knowe practically threw Lavinia into the carriage. "I feel so thoughtless. Here you were, working endless hours on the wedding clothing, and I never once asked if you might wish to pay a visit to your mother. Naturally, you want to spend the night there. Luckily, the sanitarium can easily accommodate visitors."

"I shall make arrangements to stay nearby," Lavinia said, climbing into the carriage. "I shall send for my clothing when I am situated; Annie packed sufficient for a few days."

"*What?*"

Lavinia leaned forward and kissed the shocked lady on the cheek. "I cannot leave my mother alone any longer. Thank you so much," she said sincerely. "I am so grateful and . . . I truly adore you."

"Lavinia! Don't you dare stay away from the wedding!" Lady Knowe bellowed.

Lavinia smiled, pulled the door closed and rapped on the ceiling, and the carriage lurched forward. She glanced out the window and saw Lady Knowe standing in the courtyard, looking thoroughly puzzled.

It hurt to see her turn and go back toward the door, but at the same time, Lavinia was convinced that she had made the right choice.

The carriage trundled off with Lavinia tucked in one corner and Annie in another. Perhaps half an hour into the journey, Annie asked, "Miss, I wonder if you might like to look out the window?"

Lavinia drew back the curtain on her side and looked out. Not far from the road was a graceful manor with a collection of outbuildings neatly arranged behind it. The manor, which appeared to be quite new, was built of cream-colored stone and seemed to float slightly above the dark ground.

"That's Mr. Sterling's estate," Annie said. "I don't know that you've seen it."

Lavinia let the curtain fall. She took a deep breath and met her maid's worried eyes.

"Is everything all right, miss?" Annie asked.

"Yes," Lavinia said. "I'm sorry to take you away from the castle."

"I agree that you ought to be with your mother," Annie said stoutly. "Everyone belowstairs agrees." She stopped and then added, fiercely, "And I just want to say, Miss Lavinia, that there isn't a soul in the castle who doesn't frown on Mr. Sterling for bringing that woman with him!"

"Oh!" Lavinia said, startled.

"It's nothing against the contessa, or however she calls herself," Annie continued. "It's just that he shouldn't have led you on. Everyone knows how hard you worked on Miss Belgrave's gown and then to have to leave like this, chased away just before the wedding! It isn't right!"

Lavinia was touched to see Annie's eyes glistening with tears. She reached out and caught her maid's hand. "Oh, Annie, you don't understand. Parth—Mr. Sterling—has no intention of marrying the contessa."

"That's what you believe," Annie said. "Because you're too good to see the darkness in men's hearts."

"That is most generous of you, Annie, but you are wrong. I refused to marry him."

"Beg pardon, miss?"

"I refused him," Lavinia said flatly.

"As well you might," Annie said, recovering quickly. "With that contessa in the way!"

Lavinia sighed. "Only time will tell what will happen with Elisa, whom I sincerely like, as a matter of fact. I can tell you that Mr. Sterling offered to marry me and I refused him. We wouldn't suit."

"I don't care for a man who has a lady on the side, waiting for his nod. No matter how rich he is," Annie said, nodding.

It didn't matter why Lavinia wouldn't accept Parth's hand in marriage. With every revolution of the wheels, her conviction grew that she was doing the right thing. She was even considering not returning for the wedding. Lady Knowe, Betsy, or even Ophelia could act as a witness; they all adored Diana, and the feeling was returned.

Diana would understand why Lavinia desperately needed to get away from Lindow. As soon as she reached the sanitarium, she would write a letter to her, explaining everything.

"I may marry Prince Oskar," she said aloud.

Annie's eyes rounded. "Really, miss? Will you be a Norwegian queen someday?"

"No, a princess, attached to a royal court."

"Better than the contessa!" Annie clapped her hands, chortling with triumphant laughter. "Yes, you must do that!"

"*Not* for that reason."

"No indeed," Annie said, sobering. But her smile broke through again. "We will all be happy for you."

We? The Lindow Castle *we*? The kindly group of people who worked under Prism, attending to the duke and everyone else in the family?

Lavinia smiled at Annie. "Lady Knowe told me three or four times that she would love to have a maid like you to take care of the girls. I would entirely understand if you wish to take up a position at Lindow rather than travel with me. Tabitha has agreed to stay on in the nursery, and Mary will stay as a ladies' maid to one of the younger girls."

Annie stared at her for a moment, and then leaned forward earnestly. "Miss, you have no idea who you are, do you?"

Lavinia blinked at her.

"You worked alongside us," Annie said. "Remember that conversation we had with Tabitha about the buttons on the back of Lady Knowe's gown—whether they should be brass or cloth-covered?"

Lavinia nodded. "It took most of the day," she said wryly. "It's a miracle we finished that gown at all."

"You listened to her. I didn't think it right to tell you before, but that night Tabitha burst into tears at the supper table downstairs. She's been sewing for four years, and no one has ever listened to her. No one ever made her stop sewing when the light was gone. No one ever asked her what she thought."

"Oh . . ." was all Lavinia could manage; she had no idea how to respond.

"It's not just that," Annie said. "You thought they should be brass buttons, remember, and it was Tabitha who thought they should be cloth, and they are cloth. You had the idea of a violet feather in Lady Betsy's headdress."

"Mary didn't agree."

"And you took Mary's idea and now the pouf has two blue feathers, rather than one violet."

"I saw that her idea was better than mine," Lavinia explained.

Annie nodded. "You're brilliant, and we all know it. If you hadn't been born a lady, you could be the best *modiste* in the whole of Britain."

"That is very great praise, although unwarranted," Lavinia said, a smile stretching over her face, "but I am so grateful for it. Thank you."

"It's not just me," Annie said. "That's a fact, miss. Everyone knows it. You worked for weeks without once losing your temper. You didn't dismiss Mary when she accidentally cut that ruffle. We couldn't scarcely believe that."

"Goodness," Lavinia said. "I would never dismiss her for something so trivial."

"Trivial? It took seven hours to redo," Annie reminded her. "Believe me, there are those as would have docked her pay for the entire week to make up. You didn't even chide her."

Lavinia smiled again, not knowing what to say. She'd been so happy in the last few weeks, the secret knowledge of her betrothal to Parth humming along under her joy at working with fabric and lace and gowns.

"My point is that I would never leave you, miss, unless you sent me away," Annie concluded.

Lavinia's smile wobbled, and Annie quickly added, "We'll be old ladies someday, doubtless arguing over the placement of fichus, and I don't care if we're doing it in Norway or England."

"You'll want me to expose my wrinkly bosom," Lavinia said, reaching out and squeezing her hand.

"That's right!" Annie beamed. "Gentlemen of that age are just as lustful as the young ones, at least my grandfather was. He got to be a handful in his eighties, snatching at any woman who entered his bedchamber—even the vicar's wife."

She launched into a story about her grandfather. And Lavinia let Annie ease her sense of humiliation and pain . . . because that was what friends did for each other.

Chapter Twenty-eight

$\mathcal{L}$avinia hadn't known quite what to expect of her mother's private hospital, but when she alighted from the carriage upon arrival, she was surprised to find that they had drawn up before a fine country manor, one that could easily have belonged to a squire. It was mellowed brick, with wings on either side and lawns bordered by lilac bushes. She could see a lake in the distance.

"I shouldn't mind suffering a nervous complaint here," Annie said, looking around.

The front door opened and a stout woman came toward them with a smile. "Miss Gray," she said. "A groom from Lindow rode here and informed us of your visit. I am Mrs. Aline, the matron of Gooseberry Manor. May I show you to a chamber where you might refresh yourself?"

"It has been less than an hour's drive," Lavinia said, feeling unexpectedly nervous. "Would it be acceptable if I spent the night? Lady Knowe seemed to believe—"

"I expected it!" Mrs. Aline motioned to a footman, who leapt to take the portmanteau from Annie. "Gooseberry Manor is designed so that families can stay for indefinite periods with their loved ones."

Lavinia followed her through the doorway, feeling apprehensive. What would her mother say to her? Lady Gray had been so angry the last time they spoke, alternately screaming at her and sobbing. A cowardly part of Lavinia wanted to turn around and run back to the carriage.

"How is my mother?" she asked.

"Lady Gray is doing as well as might be expected," Mrs. Aline replied. "I did not know her in her previous life, of course, but it is quite normal for family to find a patient nervous and jumpy at this stage in the recovery."

"Are there many patients here now?" Lavinia asked.

"Generally, we have four patients, but your mother is the only person here this week; I have one open bed, and two patients are visiting their families. Now, your mother has spent most of the fall in the gardens," Mrs. Aline continued, ushering Lavinia toward the door that led to the back of the house. "On chilly days she can be found in the orangerie."

Lavinia couldn't remember an occasion when her mother had enjoyed being outside, even declining to attend the fashionable Parisian picnics held in the Tuileries Gardens.

"Lady Gray tires easily," Mrs. Aline said. "Perhaps a short visit, and then if she feels well enough, you might share a light meal later?"

Lavinia nodded, and followed the matron into a spacious glass conservatory attached to the back of the manor. Five tall, arched windows admitted whatever sun there was to be had; although the sky had grown overcast, the room still managed to be bright. A row of potted trees stood along the windows among great baskets of fragrant apples and a profusion of potted herbs and other growing things.

Lavinia saw her mother across the room, her back turned as she bent over a large flowerpot.

"She's probably pinching back the withered blossoms," Mrs. Aline said. "I jest with Her Ladyship that I shall have to let one of my gardeners go because she has made him redundant."

Despite herself, Lavinia gave the matron an incredulous look.

"Come," Mrs. Aline said, smiling.

As they crossed toward her, Lady Gray straightened and dropped a handful of wilted flowers into a wicker basket at her side. Lavinia put a hand on her nervous stomach, conscious of an absurd wish that Parth was with her.

"Lady Gray," Mrs. Aline called, "I have a surprise for you!"

Lavinia's mother turned at the salutation. For a long moment they just stared at each other, and then Lady Gray's face crinkled into a smile and she held out her hand. Lavinia ran to her and kissed her cheek. Her first impression was that her mother's face was hollow, but her eyes were bright.

Her second was that Lady Gray was *grimy*. She wore no gloves, and her fingernails were dirty. This, when her mother had always been quick to retire to her room with a nervous spasm if a servant even brushed against her.

There had been other reasons to retire to her chamber, of course. Those soothing drops.

With a gentle jingle of keys, Mrs. Aline withdrew, and they were alone.

"I'm so glad you have come. Do come sit with me, dear," Lady Gray said, leading Lavinia toward a wooden bench. The windows faced the gardens. Beyond them, great chestnut trees reared against the afternoon sky.

"How are you, Mother?" Lavinia asked.

"As well as could be expected," Lady Gray replied.

After that, they sat in silence for some moments.

At length, Lady Gray said, "We have both become unnaturally slim. Have you been ill, dear?"

Now that Lavinia was finally here, sitting with her mother, she found to her horror that she was in the grip of fast-rising, involuntary anger that caught at the back of her throat. "Merely an influenza," she replied.

They lapsed into another silence. Her mother's smile had fallen away, but Lavinia could think of nothing charming or light to coax it back. Nothing came to mind but incoherent, bitter words.

"I'm sorry," Lady Gray said, finally. "I have thought of you often. I fear I made a poor job of being a mother."

Lavinia decided it was best not to agree.

"I intend to sell the country house," Lady Gray said. "It will replace your dowry."

Lavinia cleared her throat. "Isn't it more important to repay Willa and Diana?"

"As I understand it, *you* have done that already," her mother said. "Lady Knowe has written to me weekly since I entered Gooseberry Manor. I received your letters as well, and was grateful for them." Her smile was still beautiful, even on her wan face. "Lavinia, I beg you to forgive me for not answering your letters. I have not been myself."

"I know," Lavinia said.

"I wrote one letter, a short one to the duke, enclosing a diamond ring that your father gave me. It was the only ring I never sold. I asked His Grace to use it to pay for my room and board here."

"I'm glad," Lavinia managed. "I thought . . ."

"Laudanum is the sort of drug that leaches away all moral resolve," her mother said. "You are right. I would have accepted charity from the duke, as easily as I stole the set of emeralds belonging to my own relative."

"After which Diana was obliged to work as a governess."

Her mother took a deep breath. "Yes."

A shaft of sunlight broke through the clouds and slanted into the room near where they sat.

"It will take time for you to forgive me," Lady Gray said. "You may never forgive me. But you shall have your dowry again, Lavinia. You will be able to go to London and buy as many beautiful gowns as you wish."

Lavinia winced. Her mother's opinion of her was in precise agreement with Parth's.

"Unless you have already found someone to marry," her mother added.

"I have declined every proposal I received."

"Lady Knowe seemed to believe that Mr. Sterling had caught your fancy. A man who owns a bank, by her account."

"I refused him as well."

"Because of me?"

"No, not at all."

"Lady Knowe thinks the world of the man."

"He believes I am frivolous and spend too much on clothing," Lavinia said wearily.

"He's right," her mother said. "We ladies are all frivolous. One could argue, I suppose, that we *do* spend too much money, inasmuch as we earn none at all. But society does not permit us to do anything of substance other than adorn ourselves."

Lavinia's mouth fell open. "I agree!"

"I used to tell your father as much." Lady Gray smiled into the distance. "He was of the opinion that ladies could run the House of Lords better than the lords did. You must find a man who is more like your father," she said firmly. "All this . . . this *nothingness* is bearable with the right man at your side."

"I have been introduced to a Norwegian prince," Lavinia said. "He may well become a king one day, of Norway or Denmark."

"'Princess' is a very agreeable title," her mother said, betraying no sorrow at the proposition that Lavinia would have to live in another country.

Faced with the likelihood that she might ask her mother for something Lady Gray could not give—or worse, that she would start crying—Lavinia stood. "Mrs. Aline cautioned me that we should have only a short visit, Mother. I don't want to weary you. I promise to seriously consider accepting Prince Oskar's hand."

"Oskar? Oh, dear," Lady Gray said. "Well, I suppose the man can't be blamed for the idiocy of his parents, any more than you can. 'Oskar' is a better name than 'Parth.'" She came slowly to her feet, pushing herself up with obvious effort.

"Shall I fetch your basket?" Lavinia asked. And then, unable to stop herself, "What's the matter with the name 'Parth'?"

"No gentleman should sound like a hearth," her mother stated. "No, don't bother with the basket, dear. Someone will throw away the vegetation. There's any number of servants wandering around the place, most of them tasked with keeping the patients from fleeing."

"I see," Lavinia said, although she didn't.

"Yes, indeed," Lady Gray said serenely as she went toward the door. "Polite society is a prison as well, isn't it? You'll do well to get away, Lavinia. You might be a trifle chilly in Norway, but you can wear extra layers. It would be worth any number of woolies never to be caught in a snarl of carriages around Blackfriars."

"Will I see you at supper?" Lavinia asked.

"I'm afraid not. I am exhausted by this fond reunion," her mother said, drifting into the corridor and disappearing without another word.

Lavinia stood, stock-still, listening to her mother's soft footsteps receding.

She had never felt more alone in her life.

Chapter Twenty-nine

October 29, 1780

avinia woke the next morning after a restless night. Through sheer force of will, she banished the memory of her dream about Parth from her mind. She was going to marry a Norwegian prince and live with him in his country.

After dressing, she went looking for her mother, whom she found in her chamber, sitting up and drinking tea. "Good morning," Lavinia said, bending to kiss her cheek. "How are you feeling today?"

Her mother cocked her head. "Imagine you were a very ripe bilberry and you ruptured . . . it feels like that."

"Willa always made fun of me for imaginative descriptions. I have a suspicion that I inherited that from you."

"I am not exaggerating about the bilberry. I always covered up the feeling with my drops." The last word sounded like a caress.

"I wish I'd known they were dangerous," Lavinia said.

Her mother started fiddling with a hairpin. "I don't know if you're expecting me to accompany you to London for the upcoming Season."

"I am not," Lavinia said gently.

Lady Gray's thin hands twisted the hairpin this way and that. "I took the drops to cover up the nervous spasms. I still feel it would be better to take laudanum than to endure this agony."

Lavinia took one of her restless hands in hers. "If you take too many drops, you might never wake up."

"I know it." Lady Gray nodded. "I do know it." Her eyes were the faded blue of skimmed milk. "Sometimes I don't care."

"I see," Lavinia said. The desperately sad, sinking feeling that gripped her was no surprise. It was familiar. She'd felt it in her bones for years, but she hadn't known why.

"It doesn't mean I don't love you. I don't believe I can leave this place yet." Her hand escaped Lavinia's clasp in order to retrieve her dropped hairpin.

"Mrs. Aline seems an excellent woman. Why would you want to live elsewhere?"

"I should take you to London. I should make sure you marry properly. I should go to balls." She dropped the hairpin over the side of the bed; Lavinia glanced down and saw a small pile of mangled pins on the floor. "I meant to love you better."

Lavinia flinched, not sure how to answer that.

"Christmas, for example, was always such an exhausting day," her mother said fretfully. "I used to mean to have you down from the nursery to sing a carol or whatever it is one is supposed to do with children, but it was so much more pleasant to take some drops and relax. Your father never understood how hard holidays were on my nerves."

Lavinia had spent all her holidays in the nursery, but without understanding that she could have been loved *better*.

"*Humpty Dumpty sat on a wall,*" her mother sang in a thin soprano. "*Humpy Dumpty had a great fall.*" She looked up at Lavinia. "I don't mean to suggest that it would take royal assistance to put me back together again. Did I ever tell you that His Majesty complimented my nose?"

Lavinia shook her head.

"It was back when he was a stripling and I a mere girl," her mother said, pleating the sheet. "My mother always said that beauty was skin deep, but it isn't as if a man falls in love with a woman because she has a stout liver. Which I do have. Mrs. Aline says that for all the years I've been taking drops, I should have a liver like a piece of lace, but mine seems to be functioning well."

Lady Gray settled back on her pillows. "I would like drops now." Her voice roughened. "It's the only thing I can think about just at this moment. It is most shameful."

"Oh, dear." Lavinia searched for the bellpull. "Would you like me to summon Mrs. Aline?"

"I would like to be alone." Lady Gray reached out and picked up another hairpin from the bedside table.

"I wish there was something I could do for you," Lavinia said.

"You paid back those emeralds," her mother said, twisting the hairpin. "I fretted about them in the middle of the night, and what a relief it was to think no one will know." She dropped the hairpin and reached for Lavinia's hand. "Did I say thank you?"

"Yes," Lavinia lied. "Yes, you did."

"I just can't take you to London for the Season," her mother said, returning to that topic. "I don't—"

Lavinia interrupted. "I have decided to marry Prince Oskar Beck, Mother."

"Have you?" Her mother's faded eyes brightened. "Have you truly?"

Lavinia nodded.

"You must tell this prince that the proceeds from the country house will be entirely his."

"I will."

Outside the window, snowflakes were drifting through morning sunshine, though the sky had a frosty sheen to it.

"I'm so glad you will be a princess, Lavinia. 'Mrs. Sterling' is not a desirable title." She picked up another hairpin. "Lady Knowe seems to consider Mr. Sterling akin to the Second Coming, but no one knows his parents. You will be *much* happier as a princess. Princess Lavinia. It has a nice ring."

"I agree."

"I suppose you refused Mr. Sterling quite firmly?"

"Yes," Lavinia said, wondering what she meant.

Lady Gray nodded toward the open door.

Lavinia turned her head. Parth stood in the doorway. Of course. If he had followed her all the way from London, why had she not imagined he would follow her now? The man was protective to an extreme.

Lavinia straightened her spine and rose. "Good morning, Mr. Sterling," she said.

"May I come in?" Parth asked.

"You may," Lady Gray said, as indifferently as if she had welcomed him into a sitting room rather than her bedchamber.

"You remember my mother?" Lavinia asked him.

"Good morning, Lady Gray," Parth said, bowing over her mother's hand.

Lavinia nodded. "Now that you have ascertained that I have arrived at Gooseberry Manor safe and sound, Mr. Sterling, may I request that you return to Lindow and spend the day with your family, as I shall do with mine?"

He did not answer her, but turned to her mother instead. "Lady Gray, may I request the honor of your daughter's hand in marriage?"

Lavinia's heart felt naked. She felt like a childish fool. *You don't really like me. You will never forgive me for being . . . myself.*

"You may not," her mother said without hesitation, startling Lavinia so much that she almost gaped. Lady Gray was smiling faintly, but her voice was firm.

Parth turned to Lavinia, and the look in his eyes affected her so deeply that her heart skipped a beat. He was so *good* at looking as if he adored her. Maybe, in some queer way, he did adore her.

It's just that he felt she was . . . well, all those things he didn't admire at the same time.

"We wouldn't be happy, Parth," she said, her heart pounding. "Please, accept my refusal."

"I will not," he said stubbornly. "I don't care that you have no dowry. You never gave me a chance to say it, but I am *proud* that you earned commissions."

"My daughter does have a dowry," her mother intervened. She dropped another pin over the side of the bed with a distinct pinging sound. "I shall be selling my country estate and deeding the proceeds to her; her dowry will be one of the largest in all the British Isles. Other than royalty," she tacked on.

Parth's eyes didn't shift. *"Lavinia."*

"You may not want the dowry, but you cared about how mine was spent," Lavinia said quietly. "The scorn on your face—"

Her mother interrupted. "The dowry was lost through my misfortune, and you, Mr. Sterling, are not welcome to air your opinion on the matter."

Lavinia's heart was beating quickly. She had to head off this conversation or her mother would tell Parth the truth. She still didn't want . . . she didn't want him to know. "I choose not to marry you, and that is the end of it."

"That is not the end of it," Parth said. He turned to Lady Gray. "I took your daughter's virtue."

Silence.

Parth had the scalp-tingling feeling he had only experienced in moments that would make or break a fortune.

But this was his entire life.

Lady Gray regarded him thoughtfully, her eyes resting on his hair, taking in the color of his skin, drifting down his face, down his coat, breeches, riding boots, wet from snow.

"I am sorry to point out an obvious fact: My daughter must not have found you acceptable in the deed," she said, in the haughty tones of an aristocrat born and bred. "I trust she will choose better the second time."

Lavinia made a choked sound, almost a laugh.

"She is mine," Parth said bluntly. "I will not give her up."

She was angry at him; he accepted that. He'd hurt

her feelings. He could have killed himself for wounding her.

"I love you, Lavinia," he said hoarsely. "I love you."

Lavinia's eyes were bright with tears, and one slipped down the curve of her cheekbone.

"Please don't cry, love."

"My daughter can do better than you," Lady Gray said. "She deserves a better husband, and a better mother as well. When I became addicted to laudanum, I spent thousands of pounds on nothing."

Lavinia groaned.

Parth dragged his eyes from Lavinia's face. "You did?"

"The dowry that my husband carefully laid out for Lavinia's future marriage was squandered in a series of opium-induced wagers."

"Please don't," Lavinia whispered, her voice pained.

"Once, when I had taken a great many drops, I gave an opera singer forty guineas for a kiss," Lady Gray said, holding Parth's gaze. "So if you have been blaming my daughter for rashly spending money, you were far from the truth of it."

"Oh, Mother," Lavinia whispered.

"What is more, I stole jewelry and money from young people under my care. My daughter, by her own diligence, has earned the money to pay back my thefts."

Parth made a hoarse sound.

"I swore for years that I would stop taking drops, and I was unable to do so." Lady Gray turned to her daughter. "Make no mistake, Lavinia, if the doors of Gooseberry Manor were not locked, I would walk down the front drive and buy what I need. No matter what I had to do to get it."

Parth was aching to take Lavinia in his arms and absorb the pain he saw in her eyes.

"It's all right," Lavinia said, taking her mother's hand.

"I can't get overly excited," Lady Gray said, her voice trembling.

Lavinia patted her hand. "I'll ring for Mrs. Aline." Without turning, she said, "Parth, please leave. Go back to Lindow, and close the door behind you."

Parth bowed to Lady Gray and walked down the stairs feeling dazed. He had lost Lavinia.

He'd had her, and now he'd lost her. Desolation hit him like a tidal wave. He had hurt her. He had made her feel as if she was soiled. He felt as if that word plunged a knife into his heart to prove what a shallow, despicable man *he* was.

In the entry, a liveried butler handed him his greatcoat.

The matron of the house advanced toward him. "Lady Gray is still recovering," she said, without preamble.

"I understand that."

The chatelaine at her waist jingled like small bells. "If you wish to stay for dinner, Mr. Sterling, your presence might make a more pleasant day for Miss Gray. We welcome friends and family. We sometimes have large families pay a visit to a patient, at Christmas, for example. In time, Lady Gray may leave for short occasions."

"Do you mean to tell me that she has to remain here for the rest of her life?"

"Laudanum addiction is not easy to overcome, Mr. Sterling. The cure can take years."

Parth nodded. "I'm happy to hear that you invite large families to visit, Mrs. Aline."

HALF AN HOUR LATER, Lavinia left her mother's room, closed the door behind her, and leaned against it.

Nothing in the world would make her happier than to be married to Parth. To have his conversation, and his embrace, the erotic delight in his eyes, and his rare smile.

But she would be content without him. She would *will* herself to be content. By next Christmas, she'd be married. She would have a masquerade ball to go to, and it wouldn't be in Cheshire.

Lost in thought, she slowly descended the stairs, hoping to find Mrs. Aline. At the landing, she felt a draft and saw the front door was open. A light swirl of snow was covering the parquet floor, but there was no sign of the butler or the two footmen who had been there the night before.

Shivering, she hurried down the steps in order to close it, but when she reached the opening she came to an abrupt halt, mouth open.

A large bulbous traveling coach had drawn up in front of the house, with another behind it, and a third bowling up the drive. She recognized those carriages. She knew the insignia, the gilded embellishment, the coachmen.

A liveried groom pulled open the door of the lead carriage and Wildes poured out. Lady Knowe, the duke, the duchess, Diana . . .

More Wildes exploded from the second carriage, laughing and shouting. Lady Knowe trotted back toward the third carriage, and the duke took the duchess's arm so they could walk to the manor.

Lavinia didn't move. Her eyes were fixed on Parth, who stood beside the first carriage, his face guarded, looking at her.

Waiting for her to move. Waiting for her to do something, say something.

Lavinia felt as if her heart had frozen. More than anything, she wanted to throw herself down the steps and into his arms. But—

She couldn't.

She couldn't do it again. Giving herself to Parth would confirm all her own worst fears about herself. It would be like embracing the pain of never being good enough.

In that moment, she was certain of one thing: Her mother loved her, but not unconditionally. When she married someone, he had to love her more than she loved herself.

It wasn't too much to ask.

With that thought, she looked away from Parth. The duke and duchess were almost at the door, so she dropped into a deep curtsy. "Your Graces. This is a wonderful surprise."

Before they could reply, Diana ran up the steps and wrapped her in an embrace. "I didn't want you to be lonely on your birthday, so Aunt Knowe had the idea of paying you and Lady Gray a visit. Isn't this fun, Lavinia? We've brought the cook and there's a carriage following with a feast!"

Parth was not behind this visit.

Lavinia had foolishly thought this turn of events was his attempt at a grand gesture. Bringing the whole family to her as a way of saying, *Please marry me. Please be a Wilde. You may not be born a Wilde, but you can be a Wilde, just as I am.*

But no.

Lady Knowe bounded up the stairs and gave Mrs. Aline an embrace. "We've been friends since the time we were too young to know better!" she cried. Then she looked at Lavinia and laughed. "We look silly together, I suppose?"

Indeed, Lady Knowe looked like a stork with her wings around a cabbage, though Lavinia would never say as much.

A footman staggered past them, weighed down by a platter containing a roast goose. "We brought half the castle," Lady Knowe explained to Mrs. Aline. "Far too many guests will arrive tomorrow for the wedding, and I decided that we will all be better for a day away."

Artie ran by. Diana's nephew Godfrey was holding one end of the open belt on her pelisse and appeared to be steering her.

"It's wonderful to hear children laughing," Mrs. Aline said. "The house is so quiet."

"We'll leave you to your peace tonight," Lady Knowe promised. "But first I plan to beat you soundly at Snapdragon. I've promised the children we'll play games with them. And then we'll have a feast to end all feasts."

A fourth carriage had drawn up, and servants were emerging carrying boxes, platters, and baskets of fruit.

"We couldn't do without music, so my butler found a few musicians who were at loose ends and brought them along as well."

"Guess who hasn't thrown up in six hours?" Diana murmured in Lavinia's ear.

"You?" Lavinia hazarded.

"I *am* the only one who's made a daily habit of it," Diana agreed. "Let's go to your bedchamber before Elisa catches us. She's in the last carriage with North, and I told him to delay her."

For a pregnant woman who appeared to have lost rather than gained weight, Diana had a great deal of energy; she ran straight up the stairs.

"Why?" Lavinia gasped.

"I need to know what your intentions are," Diana said, following Lavinia into her bedchamber. "Oh, by the way, Lady Knowe says Gooseberry Manor used to be a house of ill repute. Isn't that fascinating? I'm going to lie on your bed, if you don't mind. I'm less prone to nausea if I'm flat on my back. Now, tell me what your intentions are for Parth. He is madly unhappy and I overheard him tell Aunt Knowe last night that he'd ruined everything."

"He didn't ruin everything," Lavinia said. "We're simply not meant to be together."

"Don't tell me you believe in fate, because I don't."

"I can't be with him," Lavinia said, ignoring that. "I just can't."

"Why not?"

"It's embarrassing."

"You think it wasn't embarrassing to face North when he came back from war and found out I had told everyone he had a son—when he knew perfectly well that he'd never done more than kiss me?"

"Your humiliation doesn't make mine any the less," Lavinia pointed out.

"Is Parth terrible in bed? He doesn't look as if he would be, but I did hear that—"

"No!" And then, because her cousin would not give up, Lavinia said, "He told North that I was as shallow as a puddle, if you must know."

Diana frowned. "That's horrid. Obviously he changed his mind."

"I don't like 'horrid,'" Lavinia said. "It sounds like

something children say to each other. He meant it. Though there are other parts of me that he likes, obviously."

"I don't know a man in the kingdom who doesn't like those 'other parts' of you, Lavinia."

"Yes, well, I don't really care. My mother is selling the country house and I shall have a dowry again," Lavinia said dully. "I doubt I'll have trouble finding a husband. I'll take Prince Oskar."

"But you want Parth."

"He grew angry two days ago and suddenly, we were back where we started: I am shallow, and the only thing I care about is bonnets. The important thing is that he's not *wrong*, Diana. I do love bonnets. I just . . . I just can't be scorned for it by the man I'm marrying. I *can't*."

"Come here," Diana said firmly.

Lavinia plucked out a handkerchief and wiped her eyes. "No, thank you."

"Lavinia Rose Gray, come here now."

"It sounds as if you're taking lessons from Lady Knowe," Lavinia said. But she went over and sat on the bed.

"You told me when you first came back from France that you had fallen in love with a bad-tempered man. It was Parth, wasn't it?"

"Yes," Lavinia said. "My feelings aren't the issue, Diana. I don't think he's truly bad-tempered. It's his opinion of me that I can't abide."

Her cousin was silent for a moment, and then her hand tightened on Lavinia's. "You deserve better than that."

Lavinia gave her a wobbly smile.

"You are brilliant and creative. In fact, other than Parth himself, you're probably the most exacting and brilliant person whom I've ever met," Diana said.

"Don't be absurd."

"I'm not. Plenty of people think badly of Parth because he's soiled his hands with trade. How is your work with clothing any different?"

Lavinia shrugged.

At that moment, Betsy poked her head in the door, saw they were both decent, and invited herself in. "Come along, you two! We're about to play charades. Aunt Knowe is writing out the parts."

Lavinia considered saying "Please, no," but instead she powdered her nose.

Betsy snatched up the puff by its wooden handle, thrust it toward the ceiling, and cried, "Is this a dagger that I see before me?"

"You could try stabbing yourself and see what happens," came a wry voice from the door.

Lavinia looked sideways, under her lashes. Two gentlemen stood in the open doorway: Lord Jeremy and Parth.

"I've heard all the Shakespeare I want to in this life," Lord Jeremy drawled. "Stab *me* if you intend to spout any more of it."

Betsy threw the puff at him and it hit his wig, causing a tiny explosion of powder. "You need this more than any of us. Did you even powder that wig?"

"No," Lord Jeremy said flatly.

Under cover of the ensuing clatter, Parth went to Lavinia. "May I talk to you?"

"I think not," she said brightly. "I can see no reason for that."

From below, Lady Knowe shouted up the stairs. "Time for charades! Hip hop, skip skop, hockey pockey!"

"Is it just me or does that woman make no sense?" Lord Jeremy asked Parth.

"It's generally understood that Aunt Knowe is the most sensible of us," Parth said.

"Shall we bring Lady Gray downstairs for charades?" Diana asked, sitting up. "At the very least, I would like to say hello."

"My mother mentioned that she'd like to be quiet today," Lavinia said.

"Alas," Diana said, "the house is anything but quiet at the moment."

"I sympathize with Lady Gray," Lord Jeremy said. "I'm going outside because I would rather freeze than play charades."

A moment later Lavinia and Diana knocked on Lady Gray's door, but there was no answer. They waited a few minutes while Diana told Lavinia all about the clever things that Godfrey and Artie had said in the last twenty-four hours, but even after Lavinia knocked again, there was no sound from the bedchamber.

Finally she pushed open the door of Lady Gray's bedchamber.

Her mother wasn't there.

And the nightdress she had been wearing lay on the floor, atop a scattering of hair pins.

Chapter Thirty

The front door was standing open when Lavinia ran down the stairs. Footmen were still unloading bundles from the carriages, and in the interim, still another carriage had pulled up behind the first arrivals. Mrs. Aline was nowhere in view.

Lavinia ran to the conservatory but returned immediately as it was empty. She grabbed the arm of Mrs. Aline's butler. "My mother!" she gasped. "She's not in her room! Has she left?"

"Certainly not," he said, freeing his arm from her grasp and brushing his woolen coat. "My men and I have been guarding the door ever since His Grace and his family arrived." The way his voice dropped told its own story.

Lavinia would bet her nonexistent dowry that Mrs. Aline's butler had a sizable collection of Wilde prints in his pantry. Or hidden under his bed. In the present circumstances, he wouldn't have noticed if Lady Gray had walked straight out under his nose.

Not when his house was full of the infamous Wildes.

Lavinia ran outside into the chilly air, looking around for Parth. A dark head jerked up, as if he knew instinctively that she needed him. The instant he caught the expression on her face, Parth began running toward her.

"My mother," Lavinia cried. "She's not in her room, and I can't find her anywhere in the house!"

Parth nodded, wheeled about, and strode first to the men clustered by one carriage, then to the next. At the third, a servant pointed . . .

In the direction of the road.

Lavinia's heart sank.

"She told one of the grooms that she wanted a ride to the village in order to buy you a birthday present," Parth explained after he came back to her. "He's not to blame; he knew only that she had been ill. She told him she was feeling better."

Lavinia was rather stunned to know that her mother knew it was her birthday, although she very much doubted that Lady Gray intended to buy her a present. "How long ago?"

"Ten minutes, he estimated. We can catch her. We'll take the coach at the end of the drive, as the horses are still in harness," Parth said. He barked at Mrs. Aline's butler. "Give me the lady's pelisse and my greatcoat. *Now!*"

A minute later they reached the small coach. Parth opened the door and boosted Lavinia inside with an "I'll drive," then slammed the door behind her.

"Oof!" Lavinia cried, as she landed not on the carriage seat, but on top of a man who answered her ungraceful arrival with a curse. A pair of strong hands picked her up and deposited her on the other seat. The carriage was already in motion and now swung sharply as Parth turned it onto the road.

"What in the bloody hell is going on?"

Lavinia squinted through the bluish smoke that filled the carriage, discovering Lord Jeremy Roden on the other seat. She coughed and pushed open the small window beside her. "What are you doing in here?" she gasped.

"Avoiding the circus," he said, drawing on his cheroot and blowing out a perfect smoke circle. "More to the point, why are you interrupting my peace, and where, pray tell, are we going as if Beelzebub himself were behind us?"

"My mother has escaped, and we are going to look for her," she said, flapping the curtain at the smoke. "Would you please throw that out the window?"

"Absolutely not! These are imported from Madras and likely worth more than that circlet of artificial pearls you're wearing."

Lavinia shook her head, incredulous. "You're choosing this moment to insult my attire?"

Lord Jeremy was lounging on the seat opposite, his wig askew, dark tendrils sticking out on one side. He looked as if he'd been up all night. No: He looked as if he'd been up since last *week*.

He leaned forward. "Since this is the first time we've been alone together, Miss Gray, I want to make it very, very clear that we aren't suited. I could never take a wife who wears paste jewelry. What's more, while I'm aware that mannish attire is fashionable this year, I fear your coat is a step too far for me."

"Don't be a fool," Lavinia cried. "This is a *footman's* coat! My pelisse wasn't readily at hand."

"Nothing would get me into a crimson coat with those buttons," Lord Jeremy remarked. He blew another smoke ring and Lavinia flapped the curtain at it.

"I have no interest in marrying you," she said sharply.

"Oh, good," he said amiably. "Life is so much easier if we get these little truths out of the way, don't you think?"

"Why on earth did you come to Cheshire?"

"Why not?" He shrugged. "I knew *I* wasn't going to marry you, but any fool could see that Parth believed *he* was—so I assumed you wouldn't bother to compromise me."

His words were careless, but Lavinia saw something raw in his eyes.

"Why?" she asked.

"What do you mean, 'why'?"

The man had ridiculously long lashes, but his face fell into naturally sarcastic lines. "I mean," Lavinia said, "what gave you the idea that Parth wanted to marry me?"

"Surely you are aware that he and I arrived at the castle following an absurd five-day journey in which we shadowed your bloody coach, are you not? Every night our vehicle would draw up behind yours, and Parth would jump out and throw coins in every direction, stationing his grooms on your carriages and outside your bedchamber. Then he'd berate the innkeeper to make certain that no sick people were in your vicinity, and that you had only the best food. It was marvelous."

He blew another smoke ring, but this time Lavinia let it float across the carriage.

"He *did*?"

"The pleasure was matched by the long stretches in which he informed me of your fascination with looms, fabric, and the pantaloons of rope-dancing Italians. The last hinted at intriguing possibilities, except it was so clear that he intended to occupy your bed before any exceptionally nimble Roman had a chance at it."

Lavinia sank back on the bench, staring at the man. "I don't believe it."

"I confess I too found it amazing. Especially now that I have a close look at you and those pearls. You have a certain *je ne sais quoi*, I suppose. Mostly in the bosom area. But are you worth a five-day journey of that nature? I am not persuaded."

After that, they sat in silence while the carriage tore down the road.

"Do you suppose you could give me a hint about your mother's plans?" Lord Jeremy said, after a while. He pushed open his window and seemed about to throw out the lit cheroot, but stubbed it out on the windowsill and tossed it to the floor.

He slid farther down the seat, stretched his legs, and crossed his boots on the seat next to her. "Where are we going, Livvy?" His lids drooped closed as if he were going to sleep, despite the carriage's constant rattle and jostle.

"We are not friends, Lord Jeremy," Lavinia replied.

"Mmm. Life is so full of disappointments." His eyes flew open. "Where in the hell are we going, *Miss Gray*?"

"We believe she's gone to the nearest village to buy laudanum."

"How many drops a day was she taking before you stowed her away?"

Lavinia looked down at her lap and found her hands twisting together. An image of all those hair pins came into her mind. "I've been wondering about that. I don't know, but I suspect she may have taken as many as twenty."

"Means she was around forty," Lord Jeremy said, an unmistakable ring of indifference in his voice.

"Perhaps there won't be an apothecary in the village," Lavinia said. "Or perhaps he won't sell Dr. Robert's Robust Formula. That's her preference."

"They'll have something; she'll not be in the least selective." He reached up and pushed open the hatch through which riders could communicate with the coachman. A gust of snow blew into the carriage and Lavinia shrank back, pulling the footman's coat around her.

As she watched, he hoisted himself up and through the hatch. For several moments, she could hear nothing but the howl of the wind, then a pair of boots appeared, and then legs, and Parth dropped through the opening.

He pulled the hatch closed and sat on the seat opposite. His hair was iced with snow.

"You look so cold," Lavinia exclaimed. She removed the borrowed coat and awkwardly threw it over his head, rubbing his hair.

From under the coat, she heard deep laughter, and something eased in her heart. Parth would . . .

Parth would make it all right.

He pushed off the coat and smiled at her. "I'm dry." He wrapped the coat around her again. "It reeks in here."

"Lord Jeremy smokes cheroots—imported at great expense, he emphasized." She narrowed her eyes. "I can't believe you thought I might marry a man like that. At any rate, will we catch up with my mother soon?"

"In the next five minutes," Parth said. "She's in the duke's town coach, being drawn by four horses instead of the usual six. They cannot have made very good time."

"What will we do when we overtake her?" Lavinia asked, peering out the window.

"Jeremy will pull our coach in front and wave at the coachman, who will pull over, recognizing our rig. Then we'll take Lady Gray back to Gooseberry Manor. She may not be very happy."

Parth watched Lavinia flinch at that understatement, feeling deep sympathy for the anxiety in her eyes. He and Jeremy had been in agreement about just how unhappy Lady Gray would be.

"She won't be dignified," Lavinia said, swallowing, "in my experience."

Parth would do anything to protect her from the unpleasant scene ahead—but there was nothing he *could* do, except offer a distraction.

"I would have preferred to marry Elisa," he said. "We would have had a genial marriage. She wouldn't have provoked me or challenged me or lectured me about bonnets."

Lavinia's blue eyes flashed at him and she straightened in her seat. "Marvelous. The option is still available to you, although I think you might find Elisa more challenging than you seem to believe."

"I *want* to be lectured about bonnets."

"I doubt that very much."

"Our conversations in Vauxhall and over dinner intrigued me. You know they did." He caught her eyes and held them.

"Perhaps," she admitted.

"Please give me the benefit of the doubt. Allow me to convince you."

Lavinia opened her mouth to reply, but at that moment the carriage swerved and she was thrown against the side. She righted herself, drew back the curtain, and saw that they were neck and neck alongside the duke's town coach. She caught a glimpse of her mother's strained, wan face in the window, and then they pulled past the coach and came to a halt on the verge.

"Could I convince you to stay in the carriage?" Parth asked her.

Lavinia shook her head. She knew how unpleasant this would be. All the scenes her mother had thrown when she misplaced the valise carrying her drops, or ran out of her special tincture, racketed about in her brain. How could she not have guessed that her mother was suffering from an addiction?

Parth pushed open the door and leapt out. He turned around, held out his arms to Lavinia, and lifted her to the ground, after which he buttoned the footman's coat and pulled the collar as high as it would go.

She heard a shout from the other side of the coach. "This will pass," he said to her quietly, "and then we'll talk."

She nodded.

"God, you're so beautiful," he muttered. His kiss was so fleeting that it landed on her lips like a snowflake and was gone.

He disappeared around the back of the carriage.

Lavinia ran after him, dreading the confrontation.

She was surprised that she couldn't already hear her mother shrieking.

When she rounded the carriage, all was silent but for the sound of the wind. She froze, trying to make sense of the tableau.

Her mother was standing beside the carriage she had appropriated, a pistol clutched in her gloved hands. She was aiming it at Lord Jeremy, who was standing a short distance away. The duke's coachman was gaping, dumbfounded. And Parth, meanwhile, was stealthily moving toward the rear of the carriage.

"Mother!" Lavinia shouted. "What are you doing? Where did you get that weapon?"

"It was in the carriage," Lady Gray said, not glancing at her. "I've informed this miscreant that if he doesn't back away and allow me to take the carriage to the village, I'll shoot him."

"I refused," Lord Jeremy stated. Characteristically, he seemed to be enjoying himself.

Lavinia recognized her mother's expression. She was maddened and hysterical—in the sort of mood in which she threw china at the servants.

Or fired a pistol at a lord.

The report, like a sharp clap of thunder, was followed instantly by a great jangling as the horses screamed and reared. Simultaneously, Lord Jeremy clapped a hand to the side of his head and fell to the ground, and Parth threw himself at Lady Gray and pinned her against the carriage.

Lavinia could hear only the rough sob of her own breath, because the shot was still reverberating in her ears. To her horror, she saw blood pooling under Lord Jeremy's head.

Her mother wasn't just a thief; she was a *murderer*.

Lavinia dashed across the snowy road and fell on her knees beside Lord Jeremy, clapping her hands to his head, trying to stop the blood. To her immense relief, his skull felt intact and his eyes flew open.

He responded with a flood of language so exotic that she understood almost none of it.

"You're not dead," she cried. Blood oozed between the fingers of her right hand.

"I've lost my bloody ear!" he shouted. He was shaking violently, almost as if he were having a seizure.

"Your ear is untouched," Lavinia said quickly. "You are missing hair above your ear." Grabbing his hand, she brought it to the shallow track of the bullet. "You could have died. You could so easily have died."

His eyes were glassy and blank and he didn't seem to be listening to her.

"Get up, Lieutenant," Parth said sharply, from behind her.

Lord Jeremy took a gasping breath and got to his feet. In an instant, she saw him transform from a shaking man to the insolent aristocrat who had shared her carriage.

"Bloody hell," he spat, probing his head wound.

"M-Mother?" Lavinia asked Parth, clambering to her feet.

"She's feeling the effects of excitement, so I tied my coat around her and put her in the carriage. Bartleby is turning the vehicle around and will return directly to Gooseberry Manor."

"I must go with her," Lavinia cried.

But he caught her arm. "No. You're not going anywhere near her."

"She might free herself and open the carriage door,"

Lord Jeremy said. "I'll travel with her." The large town coach was turning so slowly that he was able to open the door and leap inside without bothering to wait for it to stop.

Lavinia huddled against Parth's chest, shaking uncontrollably, as he and the coachman exchanged a few shouted directions and reassurances. Mollified, Bartleby set off in the direction of Gooseberry Manor.

Without a word, Parth lifted Lavinia onto the coachman's seat of the small carriage and then leapt up beside her.

She clutched the seat and looked around her, unable to find words. With a snap of the reins, Parth drove the vehicle down the road, and then, just when Lavinia was gathering herself to inquire why they weren't returning to Gooseberry Manor as well, he turned off the road.

The closest village must have been in the direction of the castle, because Parth's house, the house Annie had pointed out, was just before them.

"One minute," Parth said. They drove around the gracious circular drive, and he jumped down and held up his arms. The country manor's cream stone stood out against the blue sky. Curls of snow eddied and fell.

A startled butler threw open the door, a circle of warm light behind him.

"My house," Parth said, carrying her toward the entrance.

"Parth," she whispered, holding up her gloved right hand, which was covered with sticky blood. "There's blood on the seat too."

"Buckler," he called, striding up the steps, "pull this

wretched glove off my lady's hand, won't you? No, she's perfectly all right."

After that, he carried her upstairs into a gracious bedchamber, and left her with the housekeeper, who helped Lavinia out of the bloodstained coat. It turned out her dress had blood on the hem, so Mrs. Buckler took it away and bundled her in a thick, warm, and voluminous dressing gown that must have been Parth's.

Twenty minutes later, holding up the hem of the wrapper, her hair brushed out and tied at her neck, and her face scrubbed to a youthful pink, Lavinia followed the housekeeper down the stairs and to the door of the library.

Mrs. Buckler melted away with a promise of hot tea, and Lavinia went in.

Chapter Thirty-one

I must return to Gooseberry Manor," Lavinia said quietly. Her eyes were swollen, and she'd obviously cried in her bath.

Parth drew her over to the fire. "Not yet."

"My mother . . ."

"Lady Gray is safest in the hands of Mrs. Aline. I doubt you would be allowed to see her until she is calmer."

Parth relaxed as he saw Lavinia accept that truth. "I'll take you there within the hour. You have had a scare and a shock, and you must recover. I've called for tea."

He caught up both her hands and brought them to his lips. "I pride myself on not making rash assumptions, and yet that is exactly what I did to you. I apologize, Lavinia, with all my heart. You must have been so afraid when you realized the result of your mother's addiction. I would have given anything to spare you that."

"I appreciate your kindness," Lavinia said, gently pulling her hands away.

"I do respect you, Lavinia. As much as I love you."

She flinched, but Parth continued.

"You are afraid to trust yourself to my safekeeping," he said, putting the ugly truth into the air. "I've been an ass." His heart was beating a sluggish, unhappy rhythm. "I'm a bad bargain, and I know it. I suspect most men would be on their knees, imploring you at this point."

She sighed. "No." Then, with a flash of humor, "Most men would have implored much earlier in the proceedings."

"I implored once, a great many years ago." The words poured from him. "It was the night after the letter arrived saying that my family had died of a fever. I stayed awake that night and the next, begging for another letter that would say that it had all been a mistake."

"Oh, Parth." Lavinia's voice trembled. She sat down and with a gentle tug, brought him next to her on the settee.

Parth watched Lavinia discreetly, intoxicated by the curve of her cheek and the way her lashes edged her eyes with black fringes. "I found myself begging last night with just as much fervor," he said flatly.

Her eyes flew to his.

"I couldn't sleep, believing you were lost to me. North suggested I drink myself into oblivion, but I couldn't manage that. I—"

He stopped and cleared his throat.

"Please give me one last chance, Lavinia. I love you.

I truly love you. I vow here and now that I will never treat you with such disrespect again."

She was looking at him, but he couldn't read her expression. His chest tightened as she remained silent.

"If you won't have me," he added, "I will respect your decision. But you must eat more. Please, don't ever go out in the rain again. Or the snow. You might fall ill."

"Not even to seduce a man?"

He winced. "That was an absurd accusation, wasn't it?"

"I don't want to boast, Parth, but if I wanted to catch a man using my bosom, I need not wait for a rain shower." A smile trembled on Lavinia's lips. "I will divulge a trade secret: It's all a matter of corsets and boning."

"It was the most erotic moment of my life. Until we went to the tower together. And until the following day."

Lavinia took one of his hands and turned it over. "I was unhappy to meet Elisa. Unhappier still to find how much I liked her. That's what sent me into the rain."

He held his breath.

"Why on earth would I know that your carriage was drawn up in an alley, anyway?" she added, throwing him a frown. "You left Felton's by way of the front door."

"I was looking for an explanation for why you wanted to be with me," Parth said, keeping his voice even. "I overheard you and Diana talking, and I lashed out."

"You already knew I had no dowry," Lavinia said. "*You* presented me with eligible bachelors—although I would beg to differ, as far as Lord Jeremy is concerned. What could you have overheard that angered you so?"

"That you 'won' me on Diana's orders."

"Diana had very little to do with it. I believe that you love me. But I'm afraid that you will never respect me." Lavinia hesitated. "The things that interest me, and for which I have a talent, will never benefit mankind, or—or make a million pounds."

"May I show you something?" Parth asked.

She nodded. He stood and lifted her up in his arms again.

"Really?" she demanded. But she rubbed her cheek against his shoulder.

He carried her from the room and up the stairs, stopping before a closed door. He shouldered it open and placed her on her feet.

"This is for you, if you'll have it," he said at length, when she didn't speak.

He'd created the room by knocking down a wall between two smaller bedchambers, forming a long, sunlit room with windows that looked east and south. Along one wall were rows of pigeonholes, filled with bolts of fabric.

Like gossiping villagers, three dress forms stood before a window, just as they had in the Lindow sewing room, next to chairs angled so that seamstresses would have the best light. To the other side, boxes held buttons and spangles.

And lace—all of it from his factory, naturally.

"Where did you get the fabric?" Lavinia asked, sounding dazed.

"Mr. Felton. He had it shipped here. To be honest, I have no idea what he sent, but he knows your taste better than anyone."

"You were so certain that I'd marry you?" Lavinia asked faintly, looking up at him.

He put his arms around her and nuzzled her ear. "You made love to me, Lavinia. You loved me. And I loved you. I put in the orders the morning I left Lindow, and I've had men working on it ever since."

Chapter Thirty-two

*L*avinia wrapped her arms around Parth, and pressed her cheek against the wool of his coat. Though he had changed clothing, he still smelled of snow.

Like snow and love. Because it turned out that love had a scent. It smelled of fresh wood, of bolts of silk and wool, of boxes of buttons.

She swallowed hard, and a few tears escaped.

"Lavinia?"

Parth never sounded uncertain; it wasn't his nature. But his deep voice was a bit unsteady.

He rubbed his thumb over her wet cheek, and his large frame curved over her, as if to protect her from the world's ills. "Sweetheart, please don't cry. This was probably an idiotic idea."

"It wasn't," she said, her voice as unsteady as his.

"No?"

She pulled back her head, tilted it so she could look into his serious eyes. *Love* his serious eyes. "My mother wouldn't have thought it appropriate. She—she doesn't know me, and she's not interested. Perhaps because of the laudanum. She is very ill, for lack of a better word."

Parth nodded. "I understand."

"She may live at Gooseberry Manor for the rest of her life, or she may be able to live with me someday, but I don't think she can ever be alone."

He nodded. "I agree."

Lavinia swallowed hard. "You bring the Wildes, and I . . ." She faltered. "I don't have money, or a family, and it's hard to believe that I'm worth—"

He cut into her sentence. "I respect you, Lavinia." His voice was raw with passion, his eyes intent on hers. "You are a brilliant woman, who sees the world as an artist does: in color, light, and shape. And like any other artist, you want to spend your days creating beauty. My only excuse for what I said is that I wanted you too much for sanity. My sanity."

"I love you," she said. The words hung in the air like dust motes in the sunshine. She clung tighter, feeling her heart as if it were a lamp that could light her entire body. "I truly love you."

She smiled up at him. "From the moment I met you, I wanted you so much that I couldn't be civil, which made no sense at all," she said, the calmness in her voice masking a dizzy happiness in her heart. "You have to understand that I am civil to *everyone*."

"I assumed the worst," Parth admitted.

"Appalling Parth," she said ruefully, "Proper Parth." She came up on her toes and pressed her lips to his. "I couldn't say what I really meant: *Ravishing* Parth. *Seductive* Sterling. Fascinating man. Love of my life."

"You couldn't?" He sounded dumbfounded.

"Most men smile at me. They bow and kiss my hand and sometimes propose marriage. You scowled at me, and yet you were the only one who seemed to be doing anything interesting. I wanted to talk to you—but I stumbled every time I tried. I felt like a fraud, as if I were trying to sound intelligent."

"But you *are* intelligent, Lavinia."

She shrugged a little. "The things that interest me are considered frivolous. I do love bonnets, Parth. I always will."

"I love your bonnets. I love every bonnet. I will listen to you talk about bonnets all the days of my life and count myself the luckiest man on earth."

He pulled her closer. Lavinia tilted her head again. "I've given you several opportunities to kiss me, but you haven't."

"I want to be sure."

"Of me?"

"Of us. I love you too much for peace of mind."

"Parth Sterling, are you saying that you're afraid to kiss me?"

"Only if you're going to break my heart."

His dark eyes searched hers and he must have found his answer in the glimmer of happy tears, because he caught her in the strong circle of his arms and his mouth captured hers.

They kissed in the quiet room, next to the dress forms, and the bolts of silk, and the bundles of Sterling lace. Outside the window, snow swirled down and began to fall more heavily. They were still kissing when Parth's housekeeper came to find them.

After hot tea, Lavinia put on her freshly pressed gown, though she left the footman's coat to be properly laundered. They climbed into the coach, and without words, Lavinia collapsed onto the broad seat and opened her arms.

Parth laughed, a belly laugh, a joyful sound that

she'd never before heard him make. They kissed until Lavinia felt weakness take her limbs.

"We don't have time," Parth growled.

"Mmm," Lavinia murmured, nipping his lower lip.

"I told North that I looked for you everywhere."

Lavinia tried to focus on what he was saying, but desire had splintered her mind and sent it in every direction. "You looked for me . . . in London?"

"Everywhere."

"You never came to Paris."

"By then I had told myself that I had to stop looking for you. I had to stop waiting for you. I felt like such a fool, falling in love with a woman whose laugh I coveted." He buried his face in the curve of her shoulder. "This hunger to have you all to myself, Lavinia. It's unnerving."

She was silent. Then, very softly, "No one has ever said anything so beautiful to me, Parth."

"The day I stop looking for you, the day I stop waiting for you, will be the day that I die," he said, meeting her eyes. "And then I'll just wait for you to join me again."

Tears welled in Lavinia's eyes. "Every man I met just strengthened this irksome, embarrassing love I have for you."

"You must be mad." He kissed her.

"No," she gasped later. "Not mad. But in love."

"I'm bewildered by that," Parth whispered. "But I'll take it. Damn it. I'll take it, Lavinia, and give you all my love in return. A bad bargain for you, but it's everything I have."

"It's everything I want."

Chapter Thirty-three

The wedding of Miss Diana Belgrave
* to Lord Roland Northbridge Wilde*
The Wilde Family Chapel
October 31, 1780

The wedding was held in the morning, and the cream of high society had begun pouring into Lindow Castle the day before.

Every member of the immediate Wilde family except for Alaric and his wife, Willa—who were voyaging abroad—was home for the event. Betsy, Joan, and Viola had given up their bedchambers and were sleeping in the nursery with Artie and Godfrey. Leonidas, Alexander, Spartacus, and Erik were bedding down in the governess's bedchamber, where Diana had slept not so terribly long before.

By All Hallows' morning, the castle throbbed with activity, as if it had finally been invaded by a conquering force.

"You look pretty but so modest." Annie sighed, examining Lavinia's pale gold gown, which had been designed to complement the bride's attire but certainly not outshine it. Then she laughed. "Anyone who finds you demure this morning will be shocked to see you tonight at the ball!"

The door burst open and Elisa stuck her head in. "Lavinia, you must come! Lady Knowe has decided that purple feathers would look better—"

"Oh, no, she hasn't!" Lavinia cried, and flew past her into the corridor.

The duchess's bedchamber was enormous, but filled as it was now with the female half of the Wilde family, the contessa, and a number of maids, it was as busy and crowded as a beehive. The bride was standing before a large glass as her maid carefully adjusted the jeweled flowers in her hair.

Ignoring the purple-feather crisis for the time being, Lavinia headed for Diana. "You look so beautiful!" she cried. "How do you feel?"

Diana kissed her cheek. "How do I feel?" She gave a giddy smile and turned back to the mirror. "Look at me, Lavinia! When I debuted, the gowns my mother chose made me feel gaudy and unattractive."

"You were *never* that," Lavinia said. Behind her, the room quieted, as others stopped to listen.

"It's part of the reason that I ran away from my betrothal party," Diana said, her eyes glinting with tears. "I didn't believe that North could possibly be attracted to me because I looked like a scarecrow set up to frighten children. My wigs and skirts were always the largest and the most garish in the room."

"Not today!" Betsy cried.

Diana's gown framed the bride, rather than claiming all the attention. She wore no wig; her hair was caught up in ringlets and lightly powdered. On her face, she wore lip paint, a little more powder, and a single patch, high on her right cheekbone.

And she was radiant.

"*You* are wearing this dress, not the other way around," Ophelia said softly, coming forward and tucking a handkerchief into Diana's hand. "I am so proud of my lovely daughter-in-law."

Diana gave her a watery smile. "I *know* that North loves me. I do. But today everyone else in that chapel will believe it as well." She turned to Lavinia and embraced her. "I will be confident walking into that chapel, sweetheart, because *you* made me feel beautiful. This is the best gift that anyone has ever given me."

After that, Lavinia borrowed Her Grace's handkerchief, and both she and Diana had to be powdered again, after which Lavinia wrested the purple feathers away from Lady Knowe. But it wasn't until Elisa modeled the chic pouf especially designed for Lady Knowe's gown that the plumes were banished.

Two hours flew by, and before Lavinia knew it, she was standing at one side of the altar, with Parth and North waiting opposite. The chapel ceiling was decorated with an elaborate design of rosettes, which Lavinia stared at in order to distract her attention from Parth.

If she met his eyes, she would blush. So she kept her eyes resolutely on the rosettes, first counting them, then naming them, until—out of ideas—she finally settled on watching the door.

Lavinia had pictured Diana in her wedding gown countless times. She had considered the way the morning sunshine would enter the chapel's high windows and be reflected and multiplied by the gown's pearls and spangles. She had imagined Diana's slow procession, giving the assembled guests time to absorb her magnificence.

But Lavinia had never imagined that when a bride appeared at the back of a chapel—perhaps especially a bride who had once taken flight—her groom might be overcome by joy. *So* overcome, in fact, that he might desert the altar and stride down the aisle toward the woman of his heart.

In that case, the bride might stop and smile. No one present would scrutinize her dress; they would be too busy applauding, laughing, and wiping away tears.

Even Lavinia neglected the wedding gown until Diana and North finally stood at the altar. And then she saw it through a haze of tears. The bride and groom had been through so much pain before this moment, and now at last were surrounded by adoring family and any number of guests sighing with envy.

Joy and gratitude filled Lavinia's heart, so much so that she had to close her eyes for a moment and compose herself.

When she opened them, she instinctively looked at Parth, opposite her. His eyes were hungry and respectful.

He looked like a king.

Like a happy man.

Like a man in love.

He nodded at her and mouthed two words. "Nice dress."

No one is supposed to laugh during a wedding service. But Lavinia couldn't stop herself, and then Diana started giggling, and in the end the vicar began again.

"Dearly beloved friends, we are gathered together here in the sight of God, and in the face of his congregation, to join together this man and this woman in holy matrimony, which is an honorable state, and therefore is not to be enterprised, nor taken in hand unadvisedly, lightly, or wantonly, to satisfy man's carnal lusts and appetites."

The giggles that broke out at that point came not from Lavinia, but from the raucous group of young Wildes in the first pew.

No one laughed when North took Diana's hands and looked down at her with all the joy he felt.

"I, Lord Roland Northbridge Wilde, take thee, Miss Diana Belgrave, to have and to hold from this day forward, for better, for worse, for richer, for poorer, in sickness, and in health, to love and to cherish, till death us do part . . ."

Chapter Thirty-four

$\mathcal{A}$ ball at Lindow was an event people would remember for their entire lives. The castle was tailor-made for frolicsome evenings when the flourish of violins filled the ballroom, guests chattering behind painted fans filled the drawing room, and whispering couples filled the alcoves. People invariably fell in love or in lust, with all the attendant consequences: happy marriages, lost reputations, broken hearts.

But a masquerade ball was even more exciting. Young ladies prepared their *toilette* in shivering anti-cipation. In particular, those who had no diamond brooches to flaunt on their bosoms or pearls to wind around their arms were elated.

Wealth and hierarchy would be hidden by costume. If a lady dropped her fan, anyone might pick it up . . . a viscount, for example. Or a duke's son. Even one of the famous Wildes!

Chaperones were less enthusiastic, especially those mothers who generally lined ballroom walls, watching their daughters with forbidding expressions. No matter how often they had recourse to smelling salts—or laudanum drops—their precious charges might well take the hand of a dissolute rake or a penniless third son.

Thus the reckless, the prudent, and the hopeful saw the Duke of Lindow's masquerade as an evening in which hierarchy would be flaunted. They dressed in a quiver of excitement, intoxicated by the idea of freedom.

Lavinia knew better.

At a masquerade, hierarchy shifted from one's ancestry to one's costume. A few tiresome men would come with a simple strip of black over their eyes. But most guests would have put months into planning their costumes.

And she—whose betrothal to one of the richest men in England was being announced that very evening?

Her costume had to be intoxicating and delightful, not an easy combination. In the end, she turned to Shakespeare. She wouldn't be the only Queen of Fairies at the ball, but she would be the most enchanting.

Lindow's ballroom had been added to the castle by an early Wilde; the architect had taken advantage of a slope that necessitated it be lower than the ground floor by creating a huge sweep of shallow stairs that led into the room.

Lavinia waited in the entry, hearing the hum of voices that rose when Prism announced, "Poseidon, God of the Sea, and the sea goddess, Amphitrite."

In other words, the Duke and Duchess of Lindow. Voices rose again when Prism bellowed "Diana and Actaeon," and the newlyweds descended the steps.

Not having a mother or a spouse to accompany her, Lavinia had chosen to come with a troupe of fairies, all of whom were attired in elegant rose velvet that harmonized with her fanciful gown. She wore a confection of exquisite gold lace layered over pink silk. The lace was made in the Sterling factory, but the daring idea of using the newest dye, quercitron, to color an entire bolt gold, was entirely hers. In a nod to fairyland, she wore strings of pink silk flowers that gathered into rosettes around the hem, and formed a small train. The effect was extravagant, daring, and altogether delicious.

"Time to go inside!" one of her attendant fairies yelped.

"Are we ready?" Lavinia said, smiling down at the cluster of children.

Artie held up her arms. "I can't see!"

"Miss Gray can't carry you," Erik hissed. "You'll ruin the line of her gown!"

"But I can't see!" Artie's eyes filled with tears. "You're all bigger than I am, even Godfrey. And Fitzy's feathers are tall." The fairies were wearing turbans with peacock feathers donated by the castle peacocks, Fitzy and Floyd.

Lavinia leaned down, scooped up the little girl, and put her on her hip. "Does everyone have a mask on? Wands in hand?"

A scuffle ensued because Godfrey hit Erik with his wand for being mean to Artie. But finally they were ready, poised behind the door. Prism gave Godfrey a stern glance and nodded to the footmen to open the doors. "Titania, Queen of Fairies," he bellowed. "Accompanied by Peaseblossom, Moth, and Mustard-seed!"

Parth had been standing with Ophelia and the duke; he turned at the announcement and felt his heart actually stop. Lavinia was poised at the top of the steps, surrounded by his family.

There was an audible gasp in the ballroom as the guests registered the effect of the gold lace, the train, the flowers, the three adorable children around her.

But all Parth saw as he walked forward was Lavinia: saucy, sweet, complicated, brilliant Lavinia. The woman of his heart. Her eyes met his, and a smile broke over her face.

He stopped at the bottom of the steps and held out his hand. He had planned to make a formal announcement of their betrothal. He had planned to stop the music, and then begin with a waltz. He had planned exactly what to say.

But instead Parth lost his head and kissed his lady in front of all polite society—passionately, tenderly, and without a speck of shame.

And that's how polite society learned that Mr. Parth Sterling had stolen the heart of Miss Lavinia Gray, the most beautiful—and fashionable—heiress in England.

Chapter Thirty-five

Later that evening

$\mathcal{L}$ady Betsy Wilde was lonely.

It was absurd to feel lonely, because the castle was filled to the brim with Wildes and their guests. If flesh and blood didn't suit, two of her brothers had managed to snare clever, charming women, with whom she would be glad to chat.

But it was almost dawn, the merrymaking had subsided into a pleasant languor, and Lavinia and Diana were now cuddled up with those brothers. Betsy had no illusions about the levels of morality in the castle; copulating couples abounded, married and unmarried.

That was rather clever, not that she had anyone to share it with.

She picked up the red billiard ball and placed it in the center of the table again. "Remind me, if you please, why you won't play me?"

Silence.

A low voice drawled, "I'm already bored."

"You're a brute," she tossed over her shoulder. She bent, eased the cue onto the felt, and lined up a shot that might—just might—go from the left to the right to the center pocket. It was all a matter of angles. Sometimes she fancied she could see the degree of the angle she needed, though that wasn't the same as making the ball strike the cushion and rebound *at* that angle.

No answer from behind her; Lord Jeremy had probably fallen into a stupor again. His sole contribution to wedding cheer had been to sit by the aisle and mutter insults.

Even nearly escaping death hadn't softened his mood. From the corner of her eye, she kept catching sight of the white bandage wound around his head.

"You're holding your right elbow too high," he growled.

She adjusted her elbow because, damn it, he was often right. Then she replaced the ball and tried the shot again. It worked.

"Do it again but bend lower over the table."

She reached over to retrieve the ball and put it into place—and narrowed her eyes. Turning around, she crossed her arms over her chest. "Why?"

"So I have a better look at your arse, it should go without saying."

"I should whack you over the head and put you out of your misery—and mine," Betsy muttered, moving around the table.

"This angle isn't bad either," he said a few minutes later, after she'd managed to get the shot twice, but only—damn him!—if she kept her elbow down.

Betsy glanced down and realized her breasts were on full view. She straightened, turned her back to him, and adjusted her bodice. She and Jeremy had spent so much time together in the billiard room in the last few weeks that she'd started treating him the way she treated her brothers.

Not that she really felt that way. But it was safer. Less awkward. She couldn't imagine a worse fate than having an acid-tongued aristocrat with a dark soul and a weakness for drink believing she was infatuated with him.

She'd never hear the end of it.

"You must be desperate," she said.

"I am," he agreed, upending his glass. "These old stone walls are crowded with Wilde women, each more luscious than the last. I meant the Wildes, obviously, not the walls."

"You're desperate *and* blind," Betsy said, setting up the table again. "I'm not luscious. I could put on boys' clothing and no one would know the difference."

"Not you." He put the glass down on the floor with a click. "The others."

Wonderful.

"All the same, you couldn't pass for a boy," he scoffed.

That was better. True, her breasts were small, but—

"You're flat enough on top, but you wiggle when you walk," he said, his voice hoarse with whisky and exhaustion. "Makes a man want to watch your arse." After a moment's silence, he presumably remembered that she was a lady, because he said, "Sorry."

"You've hurt my feelings," Betsy said.

"No I haven't. I can tell."

"You must play me a game or I'll tell the duchess that you praised my arse—and guess who'll be asked to leave?"

God only knew why he lurked in the billiard room, since he wouldn't play. She suspected it was because the room was relatively tranquil. North, her oldest brother, used to haunt the room, but now he was in love and newly wed, and that drew him to other games.

Ha.

Jeremy rose without a stagger, which was amazing, considering how much whisky he'd put away. "I don't play without wagering."

Betsy shrugged. She intended to win, and didn't give a damn. "What will you wager?"

"What do you want?"

At least he recognized she was going to prevail.

"An adventure," she said, propping her hip against the table and staring at him. He was a broad-shouldered, brooding type of man, the sort she would never go for. Darkness in his soul and his hair, for that matter. She preferred cheerful men with blond eyelashes.

"Adventure," he said, trying the word out.

"Three syllables shouldn't be too hard even for a drunkard like yourself."

Jeremy had washed up on their doorstep like jetsam thrown from a ship. But North had decreed that no one could question the man about his time at war. Betsy suspected something terrible had happened.

"What sort?"

"The sort boys can have," Betsy said promptly. "I

want to put on boys' clothing. I want you to take me to London and show me things that only men can see. No, *not* a brothel," she added, when he scowled. "A gentlemen's club, like White's or Brook's, where I can play billiards."

"That's it? That's your adventure? Going to London and playing billiards? You'll likely beat most every-one."

"You're not as drunk as I thought, if you've reached that conclusion."

"Much to my dismay, I never am."

"I should also like to go to an auction at Christie's and bid on something. I *loathe* that women aren't allowed to bid in auctions."

Lord Jeremy muttered something that sounded like "Ferk me." Or worse. Betsy let it pass because she wasn't supposed to know the word.

She grinned at him. "Well, then, are you ready to take me on an adventure?"

The look of horror on his face was almost comical. "Impossible. You might be compromised."

"Nonsense," she said. "A woman can't be compro-mised unless a man wants to sleep with her."

He took a step closer. She kept forgetting how large he was because he was always sitting in the shadows.

Lounging in the shadows. His black hair had a touch of silver in it, even though he couldn't be older than North, since they'd been schoolmates at Eton.

"What?" she demanded, pushing away a feeling of unease. "My father wouldn't permit the two of us to spend so much time together if you were a man who felt—" She broke off.

His brows drew together. "Desire?"

Betsy frowned at him. "Do you mean to be missish with me? Yes, *desire*."

"I feel desire." The words growled from deep in his chest.

"Oh, for goodness' sake," Betsy cried. "For me, you cretin! I don't mean you ogling my bottom. I mean proper desire, the sort that makes people behave like fools."

"I could be that sort of fool."

His eyes were burning at her, and Betsy caught herself before she shifted her weight. Likely this was one of those odd male things. She'd insulted him somehow.

"I've no doubt," she said, carefully.

"If I win, I want a night with you," Jeremy said, staring down at her. "One night and no ring to follow."

Betsy's mouth fell open. "What in the bloody hell—"

The look in his eyes was diabolical. Betsy had obviously trod on his precious male dignity. She sighed. "You don't want me, and even if you did, you're a gentleman. If you won, you could never claim your wager."

His lips stretched into something that was nowhere near a smile. "War burns the gentle out of a man."

"I don't believe that."

"Believe it."

She tossed her head. "You've had most of a bottle of whisky and you've never beaten me, even once." A reckless, heady pleasure filled her.

He just looked at her.

"Ladies play first," she pointed out. That way she could shut him out of the game, as she had the other three times they'd "played." He'd never even gotten to his feet those times, just lounged in the corner calling out insults.

He nodded.

Now the idea was in the air, she was desperate to escape and go to London. "Would you truly bring me to the city? You'd have to show me how to walk like a man."

He nodded, his shadowed gaze burning at her. He really was a beautiful man. It was a pity he was so damaged by whatever had happened in that war.

But no one else would even consider taking her to London in boys' clothing. Her brothers reserved their adventures for themselves.

Ladies weren't allowed to have any.

Righteous indignation and rebellion stirred in her, not for the first time. "Right," she said, turning away and reaching for the ball.

He touched her elbow, and a prickle went down her arm. "Is the wager on?"

"It is, and you are about to lose," she snapped. She'd been running games with herself all evening, and had allowed her invisible opposition a chance at the cue only twice.

He moved to the opposite side of the table and stood there, arms crossed, watching with an intensity she hadn't seen before. Halfway through the game, she saw his jaw twitch, and she hastily lowered her elbow. "Better?"

"Better."

"You're hardly helping your own cause by correcting my stance," she said, glancing up and catching him looking at her bosom again.

He cocked an eyebrow.

"Last shot," she said calmly. If she made this, he was shut out.

She kept her elbow down, planned a simple shot: left wall to the right pocket. She took a breath, steadied herself. The cue struck the ball, the ball spun . . .

She couldn't even hear his breathing.

Slowly she straightened and met his eyes.

Epilogue

*T*hey had been married exactly three years, eleven months, and twenty-two days. An excellent anniversary to celebrate.

"I have a surprise for you," Lavinia said, entering her husband's study although she knew he was working. Parth always looked up with a smile, even when he had estate managers and clerks with him.

Today he was alone, and instantly pushed back his chair in a manner that suggested she was welcome to sit on his lap. Or on his desk, though that often resulted in crumpled contracts.

She maintained some distance, because experience had taught her that she might not leave the room for an hour, and she was too excited to accept a delay.

"Please reassure me it isn't another oddly colored cravat," Parth said. He rose and went toward her. Her husband's face wasn't nearly as somber as it used to be. She caught the humor in his eyes—but these days, other people sometimes saw it too. Joy, it seemed, was hard to disguise.

"But the violet cravat you're wearing today is splendid," Lavinia teased. "Perhaps only better if we had edged it in silver lace."

In the years since their marriage, Sterling Lace had, under Lavinia's guidance, originated and pioneered techniques of dyeing lace. Now it would be hard to find a lady in the land who didn't own at least one garment trimmed in rose or blue or even crimson lace, made, naturally, by Sterling Lace.

After their trip to India—during which they not only visited Parth's family's graves, but met his maternal grandmother—Lavinia brought home ideas about irregularly dyeing the warp or the weft before weaving threads together. After that, Sterling Lace branched out into silk, and Felton's became the most fashionable shop in all London, offering fabrics that—since they were the product of Lavinia's imagination—could be bought nowhere else.

"Come along," she said now, drawing Parth from the study and toward the staircase.

"Upstairs?" Parth said happily. "In our bedchamber, I hope?"

She shook her head.

"Afterwards?"

"Perhaps." She couldn't stop smiling as she pulled him down the corridor.

"Ah, the nursery." Parth brought her to a halt and kissed her, one large hand cupping the swell of her belly. "Your best surprise isn't quite ready to join the world."

"Today I'm giving you my *second-best* surprise," Lavinia whispered, kissing him back. And then, because she couldn't wait a minute longer, she pushed open the door to the nursery.

Her husband stopped in the doorway with a sharp inhalation of breath.

The room's east-facing windows looked out over the apple orchard; on clear days, the towers of Lindow Castle could be made out in the distance. But the view was not what she had brought him to see. Her surprise filled the south wall, now hung from ceiling to floor by an exquisite, sumptuous, outrageously costly tapestry.

Of angels.

Some were in pairs and groups, and others with harps or lutes, a few just floating.

If one squinted or didn't look closely, one might not see them at all; one might believe the tapestry depicted snowflakes swirling in a celestial sky.

Parth turned and drew Lavinia abruptly into his arms, burying his face in her hair. "How?" His voice was harsh with emotion.

Lavinia wound her arms around her husband's powerful body. "Not long after we married, Mr. Felton made a buying trip to France. Because His Grace had a record of the original weavers, Mr. Felton was able to locate the firm, happily still operating. They found the cartoon, the design, in the attic. Felton commissioned it on my behalf. They needed two years to complete it, but here it is, at last."

Parth kissed her, and then gently bumped her nose with his, the cherished family habit first taught by Lady Knowe. "I don't know what I did to deserve you," he whispered, his voice gruff with emotion.

"You love me," Lavinia said, looking up at him. She didn't add anything. He wasn't the only person in the world to love her. Her friend Willa, her cousin Diana, Artie, Lady Knowe, the duchess . . . her mother, as far as she was able, from her comfortable refuge, Gooseberry Manor, where she still lived.

But Parth loved the inner Lavinia. Parth wouldn't change a single thing about her, and that was the greatest gift in the world.

"I have one more surprise to show you," she said, because his kiss changed, and she knew that in a minute or two she was going to find herself carried down the corridor and into bed. A few months ago, she might have been pressed up against a wall, but more recently Parth had grown absurdly protective of the baby she was carrying.

"You may have one minute," Parth commanded. His voice was hungry and left no doubt about his intentions.

With a grin, Lavinia guided him to the center of the tapestry, and pointed to a particular group of angels.

"My mother," Parth said with wonder, tracing the delicate contour of a smiling angel's face. "How on earth?"

"I had a copy made of the miniature of your parents and gave it to Mr. Felton to carry to France," Lavinia said happily.

Even so small, he could recognize his parents' faces. Between them, holding their hands, was a very small cherub, surely less than five years old. And above that little family a pompous-looking angel hovered, with a cocky tilt to his head and a ducal air.

"Horatius," he said with delight, one finger touching the small figure.

"You don't mind that they're together, do you?"

"God, no. It's perfect."

"I wanted them in the nursery, all of them, watching over the baby." She pointed. "The fifth angel is my father."

"Lord Gray had a mustache?"

"They were quite fashionable when he was young. My mother says he cut a dashing figure."

Parth's kiss said everything he couldn't put into words, and when he raised his head, Lavinia's eyes were brimming with happy tears.

So he lifted her up, because no matter how much Lavinia teased him for it, he loved carrying his wife. Down the hall and into their bedchamber.

"Have you any plans for the rest of the day, Mrs. Sterling?"

Lavinia giggled. "None at all."

He pushed open the door and, once inside, kicked it shut behind them. "You have plans now."

He dropped her on the bed and bent over, cupping her face in his hands. "I love you." The words were so deep and true that they must have been engraved on his heart.

"You're my Perfect Parth," his wife whispered. "I love you."

A Note about Addiction, Seamstresses, and Anglo-Indian Children

J came up with the plight of Lady Gray, Lavinia's mother, having been struck by the similarities between the opiate crisis of the late 1700s and the crisis that America is going through today. Sadly, it would have been all too easy for Lady Gray to obtain drops specially calibrated for ladies, containing powerful tinctures of opium. Before 1868, when these drugs were finally regulated, nearly every "patent medicine" contained some form of opium.

Lavinia's work as a personal shopper—or *trousseau* consultant—also sprang from the present. *Modistes* in the Georgian era wielded tremendous power, and I thought it was fascinating to consider how an enterprising and talented lady might have thwarted the less honorable of them by choosing her own fabric and trimmings. As you may know, the position of seamstress was difficult and ill-paid. I couldn't save Lady Gray from the consequences of her addiction, but I was happy to give Mary and Tabitha quite a different future.

And I wanted to say something about Parth's parents. We now regard the history of Anglo-Indian marriages through a Victorian lens, when such cross-cultural unions were disdainfully regarded. That was not the case in the late 1700s. To quote a fascinating article in the *Guardian*, written by William Dalrymple, English culture was "far more hybrid, and had far less clearly defined ethnic, national and religious borders, than we have all been conditioned to expect." In the 1780s, more than one-third of British men in India left their possessions to their Indian wives and Anglo-Indian children. Like Parth, a great many such children grew up in England; for example, Lord Liverpool, the prime minister from 1812–1827, was of Anglo-Indian descent.

In writing this novel, I benefited from the expertise of academic colleagues knowledgeable in Anglo-Indian relations, and learned a great deal from history books such as those written by Mr. Dalrymple. I would especially recommend his *White Mughals: Love and Betrayal in Eighteenth-Century India* for those readers interested in learning about the true story of a love affair that took place in Hyderabad between James Achilles Kirkpatrick and Khair-un-Nissa Begum.

The marvelous author Sonali Dev suggested a historically appropriate name—Uma—for Parth's mother; I learned a great deal from her explanation of the religious connotations of various Indian names.

Finally, an expert reader gave many thoughtful hours to this manuscript, paying particular attention to Parth and his childhood. Her critique pointed to lines in which I unwittingly used negatively charged descriptions, and I am deeply grateful for her expertise.

Do you love historical fiction?

Want the chance to hear news about your favourite authors (and the chance to win free books)?

Mary Balogh
Lenora Bell
Charlotte Betts
Jessica Blair
Frances Brody
Grace Burrowes
Gaelen Foley
Pamela Hart
Elizabeth Hoyt
Eloisa James
Lisa Kleypas
Stephanie Laurens
Sarah MacLean
Amanda Quick
Julia Quinn

Then visit the Piatkus website
www.piatkusentice.co.uk

And follow us on Facebook and Twitter
www.facebook.com/piatkusfiction | @piatkusentice

piatkus